In the Devil's Name

D. A. Watson

Ringwood Publishing
Glasgow

First published in Great Britain in 2016 by

Ringwood Publishing

24 Duncan Avenue, Glasgow G14 9HN

www.ringwoodpublishing.com

ISBN 978-1-901514-37-7

British Library Cataloguing-in Publication Data

A catalogue record for this book is available from the
British Library

Cover design by Eilidh Muldoon

Typeset in Times New Roman 11

Printed and bound in the UK
by
Lonsdale Direct Solutions

PART I

Every moving thing that liveth shall be meat for you, even as the green herb have I given you all things.

Genesis 9:3

King James Bible

1

Dean Griffiths, or Griff as he was better known, wasn't what you'd call a weird kind of guy, but there he sat in a room full of people, and he was the only one who was enjoying himself.

Simon Galbraith, head of the school history department and notorious shagger of Ms Fabiani, the middle aged, yet disturbingly good-looking school nurse, waffled on in his barely interested monotone.

> 'We eat this meat in the Devil's name,
> With much sorrow and muckle shame,
> We shall destroy both house and hold,
> Both sheep and cattle in the fold,
> Little good shall come to the fore,
> Of all the rest of the little store.'

Galbraith abruptly slammed shut the thick red book from which he'd been reading with a sharp report that woke up a few pupils with heavy eyelids and rubber necks, and removed his glasses.

'That,' he said 'is part of what supposed witches would intone before the feasting part of their unholy sabbaths. A sort of graceless grace, if you like.'

He chuckled at his own lame attempt at humour, the kind that only teachers can pull off without sounding sarcastic. Unimpressed by his comic stylings, the class looked on, skin crawling on their backs with the desire to be free of this boring arsehole, and counting each agonising second to the sound of the school bell that signalled the end of class, the end of term and the end of high school. Time not only dragged, but actually slowed down, stopped and started going backwards for many of the pupils.

Outside was beautiful. A full on, in your face, roast the

bollocks off you summer's day. You could even see the nearby beach through the classroom window, a mere half a mile west of the school, tantalisingly close, and here they were trapped in a hot sticky classroom with possibly the most boring man on Earth.

'In the year of our Lord sixteen sixty two,' Galbraith continued, (someone sitting in the back row actually whimpered aloud in abject misery) 'one of Scotland's most famous witch trials was held in Auldearn. Isobel Goudie confessed, so the story goes, of her pact with Satan, her prowess in witchcraft and even of her ability to turn herself into a cat ...'

That made Griff smile. He liked cats. He also thought that there was a good chance you'd confess to a lot of crazy shit when you were tightly bound to a cartwheel and brutally flayed to within an inch of your life. Not because the pain inflicted upon your heretical, witchcraft conducting ass by the devout men of God known as the Inquisitors made you confess in hope of divine redemption. You'd confess just to get them to stop torturing you. That was how the Inquisitors got you to say what they wanted to hear. That was how they rolled. Griff was well versed in the standards and practices of the witch finders.

Likewise, he already knew the story of Isobel Goudie and her trial having spent what was once thought to be an obsessive amount of time reading as a child and into his teenage years. He was universally regarded by the faculty as the best pupil in the school, had in fact been regarded as such when he was only in third year, just halfway through the Scottish high school education system. He'd refused point blank to skip a year when teachers had encouraged him to do so, not wanting to draw attention to himself. That had always been his way. Coming from a line of nobilty, and being heir to the title Earl of Ayrshire would have been the envy of most teenage boys. For Griff though, this birthright was nothing but a fluke of chance. The way he saw it, it was only blind luck that he'd been born into a noble family that was centuries old. He could just as easily

2

have been living under the bread line in a one bedroom flat somewhere. Fate could have given him a random throw of the dice that saw him born into a family fighting starvation in Somalia, but as it happened, he'd ended up the son of an earl, living a privileged existence in what some called an extended mansion, but what was really a modest castle. He wasn't ashamed of his family's wealth and position, but he wasn't so arrogant as to take it for granted, and he was well grounded and humble enough to be slightly embarrassed by it.

As flippant as he was towards the title and money that had fallen into his lap just by being born, he took great pleasure in one thing he had inherited, and that was his intelligence. From an early age, it had seemed there was nothing he couldn't pick up and just naturally understand. His mother would often tell him how he'd been forming whole sentences at seven months old, but he suspected this was an embellishment of the truth. By the time he turned thirteen, he'd been fluent in French and German, having learned them in his own time outside of school. His incredible ability in mental arithmetic had even led to him being sometimes nicknamed 'Rain Man' by his friends. His real academic passion, however, lay in myths and legends from countries all over the world. Ancient civilisations and beliefs enthralled him like nothing else, and he could quite happily shut himself in his room for hours at a time, devouring texts on folklore. Griff's main reason for being in the class he was in at the moment was that it contained a module entitled Scottish Folklore. Fair enough, he'd had to sit through other modules on the English Civil War, the Depression, early French government and all sorts of other tedious pish just so he could do the module dealing with the myths and legends of his homeland, but it'd been worth it.

He wasn't arrogant about his intelligence, far from it in fact, but he'd half expected to already know everything that Galbraith was going to teach them that year. He'd been pleasantly surprised when the folklore module had turned out to consist of several stories he hadn't known about or previously studied on his own. These particular tales came from the thick red book Galbraith read from during the lessons, and the course module only lasted for two weeks. Griff estimated with three history lessons a week in the timetable, with say, two or three short chapters from the book studied per session, that made about eighteen chapters covered in total. The prodigious size of the book Galbraith held told Griff that it contained a lot more chapters than that.

He had an almost photographic memory for books he'd read, and the library at home had an impressive collection of volumes dealing with the subject which he had already devoured, but he didn't recognise the title of Galbraith's teaching aid: *A Study in Scottish Folklore*.

It was a damn shame, he thought, having to sit through all that dull nonsense that came with higher history for the sake of two weeks of cool stories about witches, ghosts, bogles and the Baobhan Sith, *then* finding that there was a lot more good stuff in the book he'd miss out on.

A *damn* shame.

2

At approximately the same time that Griff was plotting to appropriate a piece of school equipment, a fine tome of literature from the history department, two of his friends were sitting on a hillside overlooking the school a mile away.

Joshua Cairns, or Cairnsey, as he was better known, took a deep drag on the joint he held. The exotic flavour and smooth texture of pungent Moroccan hashish filled his mouth, throat and lungs. He smiled to himself in appreciation of the superior quality of the contraband, and blew some smoke rings which rose slowly and lazily in the warm summer air.

'This is some nice gear, Sammy,' he said. 'Barnsey brought the good stuff this time and no mistake.'

'Barnsey's a dodgy cunt, Cairnsey,' Samuel Jethro Anderson said, matter of fact. 'He'd bump you off with fuckin' oxo cubes if he thought he could get away with it.'

'Barnsey *is* dodgy as fuck,' Cairnsey agreed, 'but he's got good contacts up in Glasgow. This soft black's excellent and you don't get it all that often down this way. Can't look a gift horse in the gub and walk away, even if it is a knob like Barnsey selling it.'

He passed the joint to Sam.

'I'll smoke to that,' his companion said.

They sat there and watched the school in silence for a while, passing the joint back and forth, each lost in their own thoughts. The only sound was Jimi Hendrix playing on Cairnsey's stereo. Summer's heat enveloped them.

This is what it's all about, Cairnsey thought. *Good tunes, a wee smoke, nice weather and no more school. Minted.*

He almost felt guilty, thinking about Griff and Phil still sitting in class, sweating their balls off and probably bored as fuck, while Sam and himself, who had already ended their time at the school earlier in the day, sat and got good and stoned, looking with glazed eyes at the grey slate prison which held their unfortunate mates.

'No luck for Griff and Phil, eh Sam?'

Sam chuckled.

'Has to be nasty in there on a day like this. It's fuckin' roasting.' Sam considered just how nasty it must be for Griff and Phil, and chuckled again at his mates' misfortune.

'Mind you,' Cairnsey said, 'Griff's in History the now. He said this morning he had that folklore class so he'll be lovin' it.'

'Right enough,' Sam agreed. 'That's definitely his bag.'

'What time did they say they'd be here anyway?'

'Phil said about four. He's meeting Griff at the gates then they're heading up here after they pick up some beers from the shop.'

'Sweet.'

This, Cairnsey thought, *is a fine day.*

3

Let me the fuck out of here, thought Phillip Densmore.

This was the worst day of his life. Actually, his mother's funeral had *really* been the worst day of his life, but at that moment, this felt pretty bad.

Double Maths, last ever class of high school, it's fuckin' boiling, my pen's just run out and there's still an hour to go. Pure pish.

He could just imagine Sam and Cairnsey, sitting up on the hill watching the school, probably mangled by now and laughing at him. As he had the thought, his mobile vibrated in his pocket, silently informing him that he'd received a text. He took a quick glance around to make sure Mayfair's eyes were elsewhere, then surreptitiously withdrew the phone, holding it out of sight below his desk. He opened the inbox and saw the text was from Sam.

Hows maths goin? Ha! it read.

Bastards! Phil raged internally. *Jammy fuckin' bastards! Okay, here we go, put your hand up and ask Mayfair for another pen. Probably get a bollocking just because he's a prick and would love to dish out one last earful of shite my way before I finish with this place.*

Phil put his hand up.

'What is it, Densmore?' Sean Mayfair growled.

'Can I have another pen please? This one's…'

'How many times have I told you to bring your own pen to class, Densmore?' the maths teacher interrupted.

'Twice, sir. I do …'

'Do what, Densmore? Do not have the necessary intellect

to bring a pen to a class where writing is an integral part of procedure?'

The class giggled. Mayfair was one of the most feared teachers in the school, but no one could deny his patter could be pretty good when he was tearing some wayward pupil to shreds.

You old wanker, thought Phil.

'Sir …'

'See me after class, Densmore,' Mayfair cut in.

'But, Sir …'

'SILENCE!' Mayfair screamed, making the whole class flinch.

Phil stared at the teacher, mouth agape.

This can't be happening, he thought, *what'd I do to deserve this shit?*

But he knew exactly what he'd done. He'd gone to the same school as his older brother.

4

The bell finally rang.

'Okay everybody,' Galbraith raised his voice above the sound of chair legs scraping on the floor as the class immediately got up to leave as quickly as possible. 'Good luck with the exams. You've all worked very hard this year and I know you'll all do me proud. Just remember to relax and take your time with the paper, and you'll be fine ...'

No one was listening to the teacher as they hurriedly left, bursting to leave the suffocating classroom and Galbraith's cheesy pep talk behind. School was over. Summer had begun, except for the minor inconvenience of the exams in a few weeks, and most of the pupils' minds were concerned with the more important issues of parties, holidays, booze, recreational drugs ...

Griff purposely lingered behind, taking his time to put his books and folders into his bag and letting the other pupils leave the room ahead of him. He casually walked over to the teacher who was cleaning the blackboard, and positioned himself beside Galbraith's desk upon which the thick red book he'd been reading from lay. He took a folded piece of paper from his shirt pocket.

'Excuse me, Mr Galbraith,' he said.

'Ah, Dean,' Galbraith said, turning from the blackboard. 'Good luck with the exams, not that *you* need it. I expect great things from you. Off to uni after summer is it?'

'Yes, Sir,' he lied, not having the inclination to get into his future plans with the man.

Griff had bagged five highers in fifth year; English, maths, physics, computing and German, all A grades, and he had no worries about getting another couple this year in history and French, plus advanced highers in physics, maths and computing. He'd already received unconditional offers of acceptance from a host of universities who were eager to have the child prodigy heir to the Earl of Ayrshire as part of their student body, but he wasn't sure he even wanted to go to university after the summer. If ever.

He'd intentionally taken on every subject he could in high school, and had even sought special permission from officials at the Scottish Qualifications Authority to take extra subjects above the normal curriculum. Even with the extra workload, he'd barely been intellectually challenged, and he suspected that university would be no different. The way he figured it, if there was anything he wanted to learn, he could do it from a book in his own time and without the cost of tuition fees. Plus, despite his young age, Griff appreciated that some things, maybe the most important things, can't be learned from a book and must be experienced. As such, he'd recently been thinking an extended period of travel might be an idea. That'd be a laugh! He couldn't wait to see his dad's face when he dropped that one on him. *Sorry dad, I know you were expecting me to go to St Andrews, or Cambridge, next year, but I'm thinking getting stoned in Thailand, or maybe India, for a few months, shit, maybe even a few years, might be a better plan ...* Ha! The old cunt would shit a brick!

'Ms Fabiani asked me to give you this note, Sir,' he now said to his history teacher, holding out the piece of paper. 'I meant to give it to you when class started but I was looking forward to the lesson so much, it just slipped my mind.'

Griff saw Galbraith's eyes light up at the mention of his not so secret lover's name.

Sucker, he thought.

'A note, eh? Let's see it then.'

Griff held out the piece of paper and fumbled it just as Galbraith went to grab it. It fell from his hand and landed on the floor behind the teacher's desk. Just where he wanted it.

'Oops! Sorry, Sir,' he said most convincingly.

Galbraith stooped down to get the note. When his head had gone below the level of the desk, Griff, smooth as silk, slid the red folklore book off the desk and into his ready opened bag. He'd already padded the inside with his jumper, and the heavy tome slid into the backpack without the slightest whisper of sound.

Galbraith straightened up.

'Ha! For the brightest pupil in the school, your motor skills are somewhat lacking, Dean!' He laughed at this as if he'd just cracked the funniest joke in the history of comedy.

'Yes I guess so, Sir,' said Griff and managed a weak chuckle in return. 'I also wanted to give you a big thank you for all you've taught me this year, Mr Galbraith.'

'Thank *you*, Dean, for being such a good pupil,' Galbraith beamed.

'And give Ms Fabiani one from me.'

Galbraith's face fell.

'What was that, Griffiths?' he asked, a tremble in his voice.

'Give Ms Fabiani a big thank you from me. She's been a real inspiration this year. I was thinking of maybe doing medicine myself when I leave school.'

Galbraith stared at Griff for a full three seconds, trying to figure out if the boy was being genuine or taking the piss. He eventually replied,

'Yes … I'll, ah, do that, erm … Dean. Thank you.'

'Have a nice summer, Sir. Thanks again.'

Griff sauntered out of the classroom, leaving Galbraith looking after him with a befuddled expression.

He met Phil outside the school gates. His friend didn't look happy.

'That old fuckin' wanker Mayfair just gave me a right ear bashing for fuck all. Can't believe that prick. Last day of classes, man ... what're you grinning about?'

Griff told him about Galbraith.

This brought a huge smile to Phil's face.

'Fuckin' topper, mate! What'd the note say?'

'Pick up some baby oil, a cucumber, some rope and be at mine at nine.'

Phil doubled up.

'Tremendous! Will Galbraith not recognise your writing though?'

'Na,' Griff replied, 'I copied Fabby Fanny's writing from a reference she wrote me this morning.' Forgery was another of Griff's talents.

'Clever cunt, aren't you, Rain Man?'

'You fuckin' knows it.'

'Okay; we're going to go buy the beers now. Say each can theoretically costs fifty nine pence when bought singly. We need to buy a case of twenty four. If the case costs, say ... sixteen pound fifty pence, how much do we save per can?' He took his calculator from his backpack and entered the numbers. Phil enjoyed testing his friend's mental gymnastics at random intervals, and knew Griff also enjoyed the challenge.

'Ten pence a can,' Griff said almost immediately, 'if you're rounding up.'

'Impressive as ever, my friend. Let's go get the Mick Jaggers in.'

Griff looked at him blankly.

'That's *lagers*, mate,' Phil informed him.

'Oh, right.'

Phil chuckled. 'A clever cunt you may be, dude,' he said, 'but your rhyming slang abilities are pish.'

5

'Bout' time you bufties got here,' Sam informed them as Griff and Phil staggered to the top of the hillside, sweat running down their faces and gasping for breath.

'Fuck ... off ... ya bastard ...' Phil managed, and collapsed onto the grass.

'This weather's unreal, man. Way too hot for hiking up a hill with a slab of beer,' Griff wheezed, setting down the twenty-four cans of lager.

'This is true, bud. Drinking weather if ever I saw it,' Cairnsey said. 'Give us a beer over.'

Griff passed cans over to Sam, Cairnsey and Phil, getting one for himself.

'School's finished, amigos,' he said. 'Cheers.'

The four boys toasted the end of their cruel enslavement, drinking long and deep.

'So sweet ...' moaned Phil.

'And it gets sweeter still,' Cairnsey said, passing him a joint. 'This stuff's fuckin' magic, mate. Me n' Sam's been sitting here for a few hours now, getting smoked up, sun-tanned up ...'

'Aye, alright, ya dick,' said Griff, still short for breath after the torturous walk up the hill. Phil drew delicately on the joint Cairnsey had passed him. He savoured the warm feeling in his chest and blew the fragrant smoke gently out through his nose after holding it for a few seconds. He took a sip of beer and lay back on the grass.

'Oh, yes indeed,' he murmured as pleasant rush of the tobacco and hash hit him, making his head swim deliciously.

'So how was school this afternoon, son?' Sam asked, not prepared to stop tormenting Phil just yet.

'That old prick Mayfair gave me a right dressing down after class. My pen ran out, and the bastard just went nuts. Wouldn't let me speak or fuck all. Just made a right dick of me in front of the whole class, then decided some further abusive shite was in order before I could go.'

'Ah, fuck him in the ear, Phil,' Cairnsey advised sagely. 'School's finished now, so you'll not have to hear his pish ever again. And anyway, you know fine well he's just a sad old prick that can't handle the fact you didn't turn out like James.'

Phil had been dismayed when he'd found out that Sean Mayfair was to be his teacher for higher maths. His older brother James had been a pupil at the school, and Mayfair had been *his* maths teacher on the rare occasion James attended classes. He'd been what some referred to as a problem child, but what others less concerned with political correctness simply referred to as a *bad wee cunt*. Mayfair had one day caught him smoking heroin in the school toilets and James had tried to stab him with a craft knife stolen from the art department. Sean Mayfair, who had spent ten years in the army and was a large and muscular man, had easily overpowered the skinny fifteen year old and 'subdued' him until the police came. James, who already had a school disciplinary file several pages thick, had been arrested and expelled.

Phil's elder brother had almost destroyed his family because of what child psychologists had called his learning difficulties. Phil knew though, that James had never had any difficulties learning how to steal, bully, hot wire a car, cook up a shot of junk or generally cause misery to all those around him. Although five years his junior, Phil had learned through long painful experience that his elder brother was just a *bad wee cunt*, and lived in constant fear of him.

A few weeks after he had tried to stab Sean Mayfair in the school toilets, James had walked casually into Phil's room one morning, held him down on the floor and crushed a lit cigarette out on his neck. His reasoning for this was that he'd had a hangover, and Phil, who'd been only ten years old at the time, had been playing his stereo too loudly. Phil had screamed and begged him to stop. Such was his distress that he had wet his jeans with fear and pain. This had enraged his big brother further, and he had proceeded to lay into Phil with a golf club. Had in fact come close to killing him, and probably would have if their father hadn't heard his younger son's screams and violently intervened.

That was the last time Phil had seen his brother. Standing over him, face twisted with a grotesque expression somewhere between blind rage and wild excitement, flailing away with that nine iron.

When he'd got out of the hospital some time later, his brother was gone. He hadn't asked his parents what had happened, and they hadn't volunteered an explanation. His father had just simply told him that his brother had left home, and that they probably wouldn't be seeing him around anymore. That was just fine and dandy with Phil. Best day of his life, and he'd been in traction.

Unfortunately for Phil, when they looked at him, Sean Mayfair and quite a few other people in the town saw only Jim Densmore's wee brother, who'll turn out just like him, just you wait and see. No matter how well Phil did, to some people he'd be tainted forever; doomed to walk in his brother's *bad wee cunt* shadow.

Phil was no boy scout though. He smoked weed and drank beer, popped an acid on occasion, same as the rest of his friends, but there was a difference between him and his elder sibling. He was careful, and never let his standard teenage revelry get out of control, because he knew that if he did, then that would be it for him. There would be no second chance for Jim Densmore's wee brother.

For all these reasons, Phil wouldn't *piss* on his long lost sibling were he to come across him ablaze in the street.

'Well, Phil,' Sam said, 'me and Cairnsey's come up with a bit of an idea that'll cheer you up.'

'Oh, aye? What's on your mind?' asked Phil.

'Trip night.'

Phil sat up, interested.

'Do tell.'

'Got a phone call last night from some guy asking if we wanted any trips,' Cairnsey said. 'Said he knew Barnsey.'

'You know him?' asked Griff.

'Naw, man. Said his name was Ozay. All he said was that Barnsey'd told him he knew some boys down the coast who were into good trips and had given him my number.'

'Sounds a bit shady, Cairnsey,' Phil said. 'Some stranger just calls you up and wants to sort some tabs for you?'

'Not exactly a stranger. He asked if the Moroccan hash Barnsey was punting was any good. Said he thought Barnsey was full of shit sometimes.'

'He got that right,' Griff said.

'That's what I said,' Sam concurred.

'Anyway, he seemed sound,' Cairnsey continued, 'Ended up we were talking away for a good while about the fitba, tunes, Barnsey, gear and everything. Guy was well cool.'

'So what's the story with the trips then?' Phil asked. 'Did he give you a price?'

'Three bucks a tab,' Cairnsey said and grinned.

'Three bucks? What kind of acid do you get for three quid a pop?'

'Dude said they're fuckin' mental. Said he'd do them for three this time but he knows we'll be back for more, then he'll charge the normal rate of ten.'

'Doesn't sound too bad,' Phil agreed.

'I'm up for that, man,' said Griff.

'Excellent. He said I was to give him a phone later and we'll meet him up at Bennane Head tomorrow night. You boys doing anything?'

'Not me, mate,' said Phil.

'Cool with that,' agreed Griff

'Excellent,' confirmed Sam. 'Should be a good night, lads. One last fry up before the exams.'

'How come we're meeting at Bennane?' asked Griff. The cliffs were a ten minute drive outside of town.

'He said he's dropping off some other gear in Colmonell and he's not got the time to come away down here,' Cairnsey informed him.

'Fair do's. He's the man selling acid for three quid a go.'

'So we're agreed then? Trip night?'

'Fine by me,' said Phil

'No bother,' from Sam.

'Oh, aye,' Griff finished.

'Minted. I'll drive us up there. Me n' Sam were talking about taking the tents up with some munchies, the stereo and a few beers. Get a fire going, make a night of it you know?'

'Sounds brilliant. A fine plan,' Griff complimented.

'What did you say this guy's name was, Cairnsey?' asked Phil.

'Ozay,' he said. 'Guess he's Turkish or something.'

6

Samuel Jethro Anderson arrived home a few hours later.

After struggling to get his key in the lock for a few miutes, he eventually managed to open the front door and unsteadily navigate his way through the hall and into the kitchen where he found his mum preparing tacos for dinner.

'That's what AH'M talkin' about!' he announced.

His mother looked up.

'Alright, son. Good last day of school was it?'

'Yes indeed, mother dearest. T'was filled with splendour at every turn, and now I've come home to you, and you're making tacos, which is splendouresserer still.'

'Have you been drinking, Samuel?' his mother asked, one eyebrow arched in suspicion.

'Oh, mother. You shame me with these allegations,' he exclaimed in outrage. When he'd had a few drinks, Sam tended to speak like a high-born English gentleman from the eighteenth century.

Maria Anderson came around the kitchen table and embraced her son.

'I'm proud of you, Sam,' she said, 'You've done your six years at high school and you've done them well. And that's a lot better than some of the boys your age have done. You deserve a drink.'

Sam hugged his mum back, and was embarrassingly close to letting a drunken tear spill from his eye.

What a woman, he thought.

'Cheers, maw,' he said, reverting back to his native accent.

'Now sit yourself down and have your tea. Thought you might like a few tacos to celebrate.'

'A few? I could eat a scabby horse in a folded over mattress right now. Luckily, there's at least eight tacos with my name on them.'

Sam eagerly sat down at the table and nearly fell off his seat.

'Woah! Steady as she goes, cap'n!' he laughed.

His mum put down in front of him the three ceramic bowls Sam always used when eating tacos. One full of finely diced onions, one with grated mature cheddar, and one with shredded lettuce. She then placed a plate with four heated corn shells on the table, and handed Sam the saucepan of seasoned minced beef, hot from the stove. Sam used a soup spoon to fill the bottom of the shells with a generous portion of the aromatic, sizzling beef, then topped the mince with onions, cheese and lettuce in that order. *Always* in that order. It would be the height of madness to do it otherwise.

He sat there swaying slightly, just happily looking down at the meal for a few seconds, savouring the moment with his mouth watering in anticipation. Finally, he could wait no more and picked up a shell, careful not to let too much filling spill from the side (tacos being virtually impossible to eat without making a mess, especially when the one consuming them is less than sober) and took a huge crunching bite from the side. Of course, some of the hot mince dripped down his shirt leaving a reddish brown trail when he took the taco away from his mouth, but he was past caring. He had a plateful of fine Mexican scran and that was all that mattered in the universe to him at that moment.

'Good Lord! Such flavour! Such cuisine! Mother, I'd get down on my knee right now and propose to you for making this heavenly spread if I didn't think dad might not like the idea much,' he said between chews.

'Just how many drinks have you had, ya wee steamer?'

Maria Anderson asked her son with a smile as she sat down opposite him and began assembling her own tacos. 'You're talking a lot of pish.'

'Just a few aperitifs with my associates after classes, mother dear. We retired to the men's club for a brandy and a good cigar over some light banter about the ghastly business with Densmore and Mayfair.'

'Phil still getting bother from that old fart?' his mother asked. She knew Phil well as he had been Sam's closest friend since primary school.

'Quite so, mater. Jolly bad show indeed, what.'

'And how's Joshua? Staying out of trouble is he?'

'Oh, mother. That business last week was nothing but a trifle. Ol' Cairnsey merely gave that bounder Jannets a cuff on the ear and sent him on his way, the cad.'

'Really?' asked Maria doubtfully. 'Your dad told me he was speaking to Cairnsey's brother Grant at work, and the way he heard it, ol' Cairnsey kicked the cad about like an empty shell suit.'

'Really, mother. T'was a trifle I say,' Sam said with a dismissive wave of the hand, and continued to devour the tacos with gusto.

*

(One week earlier)

Cairnsey kissed his girlfriend Alice goodnight at her front door for a while, then turned into the rain to walk home.

'I'll see you tomorrow, stud,' she called after him saucily.

'Minted, my little minx. See you in registration.'

Cairnsey set off at a leisurely pace with his hood down and his head held high. The rain came down in a windless, steady mist that was almost warm and no heavier than a haze, but which would still penetrate all but the most heavy duty waterproof clothing. Cairnsey loved to walk in these soft showers that always seemed to come to the south west coast of Scotland just before a rare spell of hot weather engulfed the area, almost as if nature was preparing the town for the dry times to come. It'd happened every year they'd had a good summer since Cairnsey could remember, and he'd refused Alice's offer of an umbrella. She'd thought he was mental, and had told him so with a smile.

'True,' he'd replied with a wistful nod. 'I don't know why I like it and I know I'll probably get pleurisy, but this weather's the business.'

Because he'd brought a bottle of wine to Alice's place, he'd left his car at home and was now pleased to be walking home in the rain, enjoying the whispery sound of it on the air.

He ambled along now, taking his time and enjoying the moment. Smiling slightly even. He'd been going out with Alice for a few weeks now and was pleased with their progress. Tonight they'd gone physically further than before; the musky scent on his fingers and the pleasant, chaffed feeling in his loins was a big part of his good mood. Afterwards they'd just lain at peace with the world and everything in it, feeling a warm, tingling contentment, sharing a cigarette.

Cairnsey stopped to light another smoke, shielding the lighter's flame from the rain with a cupped hand, then walked on.

Yes, it's a fine thing to have a fine woman, he thought to himself and grinned foolishly.

There was someone walking up the street on the other side of the road. The figure, dressed in a white tracksuit and baseball cap, looked quite tall and walked with a swaying, shoulder-driven swagger.

Cairnsey saw the figure look his way then start across the road towards him, striding forward more purposely. He kept walking.

'Here, mate. Got any smokes on ye?'

Cairnsey turned at the sound of the nasal voice and recognised the figure at once.

It was Eddie Jannets, an old associate of Phil's brother James. Jannets was known in the village as a 'bad one', having been in trouble with the police several times for various misdemeanours. It was also common knowledge that the twenty one year old was a hopeless junkie.

'Sorry bud, last one,' Cairnsey said, indicating his cigarette.

Cairnsey knew what was going to happen next. He'd been through it a few times before and experience had taught him to show no signs of fear to people like Jannets. Fear was what they fed on.

The older youth took a step towards Cairnsey, trying to intimidate him with his superior height. He had a good four inches on him.

'Don't geez yer shite, wee man,' he sneered. 'Let's check yer pockets then if that's yer last wan.' He moved forward another step, hands reaching for Cairnsey's jacket.

Cairnsey took a step forward himself so he was right in Jannets' pale, haggard face, their noses nearly touching.

'*Fuck* off, Jannets, ya junky bastard. There's no smokes for the likes of you, and you're sure as shit no goin' in ma pockets, so just do one.'

Eddie Jannets wasn't used to this kind of reaction. His skag-ravaged brain was confused for a second, and he inadvertently took a step back.

'Don't get fuckin' wide wi' *me* ya wee knob, or ah'll cut ye up,' he snarled. His glazed eyes took on a hint of recognition as he stared at Cairnsey. 'Ah know you. You're that poofy Grant Cairns' wee brother int' ye?'

'Call my brother poofy again and I'll shove yer cookin' spoon up yer arse sideways, ya no mark *wank*,' Cairnsey said calmly.

Jannets was again momentarily taken aback by the smoothly delivered affront, and then decided he could under no circumstances let this little cunt rip the piss out of him in such a way. He swung a sloppy right hook at Cairnsey's face.

Cairnsey was expecting the attack and ducked under the punch, simultaneously driving the heel of his palm hard into Jannets' solar plexus, knowing that a well placed blow here was usually much more effective than going for the face of an assailant. His kickboxing instructor had shown him just how to deliver this and many other strikes, and as a result of five years hard training in martial arts, Cairnsey, who wasn't the biggest of guys, was known by most people in the village as an individual not to be trifled with.

Unfortunately for Eddie Jannets, he had missed this information.

Jannets' breath exploded out of him as Cairnsey's precise blow connected at the bundle of nerves just beneath his breastbone where the ribs met. He doubled over and staggered back, wheezing and trying to recover his breath as Cairnsey readied himself for another attack. He knew Jannets didn't have the sense to leave it at that, and knew there was a good possibility he had a weapon on him. He was proved correct in this estimation, for when he straightened up again, Jannets held a Stanley knife in his right hand and pointed it at him.

'You're gettin' chibbed, cunt,' he snarled and started foward.

Jannets swung the blade in a high wide arc from the right, aiming at Cairnsey's face. Cairnsey simply put up his left hand, grabbed Jannets wrist, shifted his feet slightly, and delivered a low, stomping kick to the inside of Jannets right knee which bent outwards, just slightly, but grotesquely.

Jannets bellowed in pain and went down like a sack of spuds. He dropped the Stanley knife and lay on his side holding the damaged knee with both hands

Cairnsey stood over his inert body and flicked his smoke at Jannets' face, seeing with satisfaction that it hit his cheek glowing end first, sending up a shower of sparks and causing his attacker to flinch and yelp.

'There's yer smoke, arsehole,' he said and turned to walk away.

He'd gone about thirty metres when he heard a sound behind him and turned.

Jannets was rushing him, Stanley blade in hand and glinting in the rain. The loping berserker charge was almost comical due to the heavy limp caused by the blow to his knee. He must have taken a hit of smack fairly recently or the pain would have made him unable to use his right leg at all, Cairnsey assumed.

He held his ground until Jannets was about two metres away, lunging with the chib again, then he ducked, side-stepped and turned in a single movement every bit as fluid as the rain that drifted down around them, sending Jannets rushing past without even touching him. Jannets hit the brakes and turned, and was met with Cairnsey's elbow which smashed into his face, breaking his nose with an clearly audible crunch. Jannets let out a surprised 'Ugh!' and blood immediately flooded the lower half of his face as if a dam had been breached in his nostrils. He dropped the knife again and held both hands to his nose. Cairnsey kicked at the knee again, sending Jannets down for the second time. He didn't expect the junkie would want to continue in his efforts, but amazingly, on his hands and knees, Jannets groped for his blade once more, not yet giving up the fight, although surely he must know he was facing a far superior opponent.

Cairnsey kicked the weapon away from his searching fingers and knew he had to put an end to it.

He grabbed Jannets greasy hair with his left hand, pulling him onto his knees, and screamed into his face, punctuating each syllable with a hard right fist into his now impossibly angled nose.

'DON'T, (punch) YOU, (punch) PULL, (punch) A, (punch) FU- (punch) -CKIN', (punch) BLADE, (punch) ON, (punch) ME, (punch) EVER, (punch) EVER, (punch) EVER, (punch) *EVER*, (punch) A- (punch) -GAIN! (punch)'

He let Jannets go and watched coldly as he collapsed to the side and sprawled in a puddle of rainwater, his face a bloody misshapen mess.

'Now you've gone and fucked up ma good mood, ya dick,' Cairnsey told him, shaking with anger and the rush of adrenaline. Another thing Jannets was ignorant of was Cairnsey's temper, which when aroused could spell dire consequences, as he had just found out.

Jannets lay there wheezing as blood and small pieces of cartilage flowed freely from his pulped nose.

'Ah told you to leave it, Jannets, but you had to come ahead, didn't you? Now look at you, lyin' in a puddle with yer coupon all burst tae fuck.'

Cairnsey was feeling a strange mix of emotions vying for dominance in his body. There was the satisfaction of the victor, relief that he had come through unscathed, but also there was a part of him that was appalled at the damage he had wrought on Jannets, even if he had pulled a knife. He was just glad that he'd had enough control to pull his punches, or he may well have killed him.

'You'll … get … yours …' Jannets somehow managed to say, although it was barely recognisable as speech. There was a wet rattle and rasp to his words.

More bits of nose in his throat, Cairnsey thought, and

his pity faded and died. He drew back a leg to deliver the coup de grace … and stopped. He gritted his teeth and had to make a conscious effort to stop himself from letting his boot slam into his attacker's bloody head.

Fuck him, part of him said. *Just let that kick go and cave this junky prick's fuckin' face in. No more than he deserves. He'd do it to you if it was* you *on the deck. It's so easy. Just let that foot go, catch him sweet on the temple and watch that ugly fuckin' mug crumple. Do it.*

He took a deep breath, counted to five and relaxed his leg again. *Not worth it*, the rational part of his brain said.

'Come after me again and you'll end up where you are now, or worse,' Cairnsey said, trying to keep the tremble from his voice. He walked away wiping blood from his knuckles, leaving Jannets lying on the pavement behind him, gasping for breath.

*

'Seriously, mum,' Sam said, 'That dick was trying to chib Cairnsey. Got what he deserved if you ask me.'

'Well, maybe so, but did he have to pulp the boy's face?' Maria asked.

Her son shrugged. 'Cairnsey's got a temper, and Jannets should have known better anyway,' he replied simply.

Sam continued to demolish the plate of tacos before him, secretly wishing he'd been there when it had happened. Jannets had bullied Sam mercilessly on a regular basis in the few years they'd both attended the high school, and he would have paid handsomely to have witnessed Cairnsey's demolition of the guy who'd laughingly slapped him around and humiliated him for no other reason than that he *could*.

There'd been no police involvement after the incident.

Cairnsey considered the matter hopefully settled, and the thought of Jannets going to the police was almost laughable. He had a police record which included arrests for robbery, assault, drugs, drunk and disorderly, car theft and even public exposure and lewd behaviour, which had come about in an incident legendary in the local folklore.

Jannets had been found by the police frantically masturbating in some bushes, not far away from where one Leanne McPherson (a girl Jannets had fancied), had had some underwear stolen from the washing line in her garden about half an hour beforehand. The two officers had found him there, beating away happily with the black lacy g-string on his head. Better yet, one of the officers had arrested Jannets only a week before for punching an eight year old boy, so had no qualms about throwing him in the back of the panda, once he'd managed to stop laughing, that is. A lot of people would wonder, some time after, if Jannets' name and address would have been included in the story, which was on the front page of the local evening paper, had the editor of the paper not been Peter McPherson, Leanne's father. The whole episode had earned Jannets the nickname Jannets Jostlin'. He'd left school a week later and never returned.

Now remembering the episode, Sam laughed out loud, spraying a decent mouthful of semi-chewed-up Mexican cuisine across the kitchen table.

His mother frowned at him disapprovingly. The airborne, half-masticated food had barely missed her.

'For God's sake, Sam,' she scolded. 'Clean that up will you? What's so funny that you have to spray your tacos around my nice clean kitchen anyway?'

'Aw, nothing, mum. Sorry,' he said still chuckling. 'By the way, can I borrow your Janis Joplin CD tonight? Something just reminded me of it there.'

'Sure you can. As long as you clean up that mess.'

'No bother,' he promised, still chortling to himself as he

picked up another taco.

Maria gave her son a puzzled look.

7

Griff lay on the bed in his room, trying to read the book he's swiped from Mr Galbraith's history class earlier on that day.

He'd attempted to get into it when he'd come stumbling home after his afternoon spent with Sam, Cairnsey and Phil, but the lager and hash he'd ingested had sent him to sleep halfway down the first page. He'd awoken a few hours later with a thumping headache and a hellish thirst.

He checked his digital bedside clock. Two a.m.

Griffiths Hall, the seat of his family for centuries, was deathly quiet. Not so much as the normal groans and creaks an old house normally makes as it settles and cools in the night could be heard. The only other people currently in the huge property were the two live-in housekeepers. His father was away on business (as usual) and his mother was staying at their second home in Glasgow for the weekend, enjoying yet another of her frequent shopping trips.

Griff put the book aside and got up from his bed. He walked across the bedroom, which was cluttered with piles of books on every subject from history and physics to philosophy and chaos theory, and stood gazing out over the expansive moonlit grounds of the house, the town of Ballantrae below and the darkling water beyond.

During the day, the large bay window gave an excellent viewpoint out onto the Firth of Clyde, and on a clear night he could see scattered lights glimmering faintly on the isle of Arran, miles across the cold water. On other nights when the sky was cloudless, Griff would sometimes spend hours with one eye glued obsessively to the powerful telescope he now stood beside, studying the far off stars and planets and reluctantly stopping only when the coming of dawn caused the awesome light show of the cosmos to fade. Astronomy was another of his many fascinations.

Tonight though, Griff gazed less skyward and more inland in the direction of Bennane Head, the series of tall cliffs a few miles north up the coastal road, and thought about the camping trip there that he, Sam, Cairnsey and Phil had planned for tomorrow to celebrate the end of classes.

Everyone who lived in the area knew the local legend of Sawney Beane, the seventeenth-century mass murderer and cannibal, who along with his inbred family, had supposedly inhabited the caves below Bennane Head and preyed on late night travellers. Some people said that over a thousand souls had perished at the hands of Beane and his diabolical brood.

Cairnsey's elder brother Grant used to scare the crap out of them when they were kids with stories of him and mates of his encountering ghosts on the road at Bennane Head and in the haunted caves themselves, where some local youths would go for a drink or a smoke from time to time, and Grant wasn't the only one who had stories to tell.

Griff's descendants, the Earls of Ayrshire, had lived in the area for several generations, and were locally recognised as the authority on the Sawney Beane myth. His great grandfather had published a book on the subject, and the family did little to quell rumours and whispers that the Griffiths family had even been involved in the eventual capture of the monstrous Beane and his clan. They would just smile and wink if you ever asked them.

His grandfather was especially legendary in the village for his storytelling. His most famous fable, and Griff's favourite, involved the man himself.

Griff could still remember with clarity the first time his grandfather had told him the tale. Sitting on his lap in the library of Griffiths Hall one stormy night when he was five years old, the wind had been blowing a gale outside, and the big library had been lit only by the blazing logs in the large open fireplace in front of which they sat. His grandfather's intense blue eyes, unfaded by age, regarding him piercingly through a haze of pleasant smelling pipe smoke, and his papery, rasping voice shutting out all other distractions lest

31

the story be taken lightly or without dire warning.

Returning home from an evening of debauchery in Girvan one cold winter's eve in the year nineteen-forty-two, the story went, Alexander Griffiths, accompanied by a friend of his by the name of Joe Crawford, had stopped to rest in the Bennane Head area …

*

So there we were, Dean; me and auld Joe sitting on a boulder just above the cliffs at Bennane Head. It was late, way past midnight, dark and bitter cold. The snow'd been coming down in a howling blizzard earlier, and the ground was buried under a foot of powder all around us. We were having a woodbine, and to be honest with you, feeling the effects of a few drams.

I turn to pass my hipflask to Joe, and there's this young lassie coming towards us along the road maybe thirty yards away. She was walking in the same direction we'd just come before stopping.

'Look at that lassie,' I said to Joe. 'She shouldn't be wanderin' about this time o' night,' and I start walking over to her, meaning to ask what she thought she was up to, going for a stroll in weather like that at one in the morning. I mean, the lassie looked like she couldn't have been more than fifteen.

Once I start walking over though, I realise there'd been nobody on the road behind me and auld Joe when we last stopped for a smoke. See, in those days it was a straight path between Girvan and Ballantrae, and there were no other roads joining on between the two towns, so she couldn't have joined the road me and Joe were on from another one. There were no other villages between the two towns either; just the big forest on one side of the road, and the sea on the other.

I turns to mention this to Joe, but I saw from the look on his face that he might have been thinking the same thing. So I just stands there, watching as the girl gets closer to us.

I could see that she looked scared. She kept glancing over to the side of the road at the cliff tops, as if she could hear or see something there, and then she starts to walk a bit faster, starts running towards us, and as she got closer, I could see she was dressed old fashioned like, with a heavy scarf over her head, a thick woollen shawl and a long sackcloth dress.

By now, the young lassie was only about ten yards away, still hurrying towards us, but she hasn't so much as looked at me or Joe, as if she couldn't see us. And she's looking more scared than ever, as if the Devil himself were after her.

I catch sight of something moving at the edge of the forest on the other side of the road just ahead of the lassie, and I look a bit closer there. At first I couldn't see much, just shadows and trees, but then I make out the shape of something coming out of the darkness there, heading straight for the girl.

Like a flash, three men come screaming out onto the road and are on her before I can so much as shout out to the lassie. I turns to auld Joe and see him looking at the cliff top, his face as pale as the snow and his mouth hanging open. There were another two men crawling over the ledge.

They were all naked as they day they were born, skinny and filthy, covered in streaks of dirt and filth. They had long hair all the way down their backs, and tangled beards that covered their chests. The worst thing though, was the daggers they had. It was a clear night, and the moon was full and reflecting off the snow, so we could see that the daggers weren't made of steel, but were white, as if they were made from bone.

The two that came over the cliff joined the three from the trees and fell on the poor lassie like a pack of wolves. She didn't even get a chance to scream.

I'll not tell you what they done to her then, Dean, 'cause you'd have nightmares, and your mother'd have my guts for garters. I wish I'd never seen it myself, because I still have bad dreams now and then.

I'll never forget the one scream that lassie managed to get out before they dragged her over the edge of the cliff. It wasn't the scream of a woman who's had a mouse run over her toes, and not even the scream of a woman giving birth to a bairn. It was a scream like she'd caught a glimpse of hell and knew her very soul was lost. It was the scream you might make when you know you're about to be eaten by a monster.

Then she was gone.

The men that grabbed that poor girl hadn't even looked at me or Joe, just like the lassie, it was as if they didn't even see we were there.

After a wee minute or so standing there shaking, I got my legs working again.

I walks over to the spot where they'd fell on her, and there was nothing on the road there. No blood or bits of the lassie's dress, nothing. And besides, the snow on the ground hadn't been disturbed.

Save for the footprints me and auld Joe had made leading back the way we'd come, the foot of fresh snow on the ground was untouched.

'Are we at Bennane Head, Alex?' Joe asks me.

'I think so, Joe,' I said back.

Well, that was all it took, Dean. We ran like hares the rest of the way back to town without stopping, or even looking back over our shoulders for the fear of God of what we might see behind us.

I've never walked past Bennane Head at night again, Dean, and heaven help you if you do.

*

Alexander Griffiths had been well known locally for that and many other fables, many of which were collected over his long and colourful life. Despite being heir to an earl and therefore exempt from national service, he'd volunteered at the age of nineteen and fought in the war, seeing action in France and Holland and winning citations for valour. After the war was over, he'd travelled extensively through India and Africa as a travel writer before returning to Ballantrae to take his ailing father's place as Earl of Ayrshire and to run the many family businesses. He'd often hold court down in the Douglas Arms tavern, relating tales of his many adventures to a roomful of captivated locals while he sat there at his spot (which no one ever dared invade) next to the huge open fire, smoking his pipe of aromatic shag and drinking Talisker malt whisky.

Griff missed the old guy sorely. Alexander Griffiths' remarkable journey through life had come to an ironically unremarkable end when he'd suddenly been taken by a devastating stroke last winter, and Griff had been bereft. As long as he could remember, his grandfather had been there and had been the main father figure in his life. His *actual* father was a cold, rarely seen presence with whom Griff shared little in either character or interests.

As he stood in his dimly lit bedroom looking out over the moonlit coastline, Griff decided that as long as he was awake, he might as well start getting his stuff together for the camping trip tomorrow.

Almost as he had the thought, a slight draft from somewhere stirred the hair at the back of his neck and his grandfather's words whispered in his mind again.

I've never walked past Bennane Head at night again, Dean, and heaven help you if you do.

Griff felt a shiver run the length of his spine, and couldn't help but turn to look around his bedroom, half expecting to see his dead grandfather standing in the corner.

8

BANG, BANG, BANG, BANG …

Phil was standing naked in the middle of his bedroom. Something was terribly wrong.

BANG, BANG, BANG, BANG …

He couldn't move. His entire body was gripped in a cold steel paralysis. Fear squeezed him in a marrow freezing embrace. His breath was fast and shallow. He stared at nothing.

BANG, BANG, BANG, BANG …

That terrible sound. Every few seconds it came. Blasting through his head like canon fire, though his expression remained as blank as a mannequin's. He smelled smoke, and could hear other sounds between the awful banging. Whispers, mutterings, screams that sounded very far away yet pierced him like slivers of ice.

BANG, BANG, BANG, BANG …

He abruptly found himself gliding like a wraith down the stairs to the living room. The wall at the side of the staircase crawled and bulged with vague shapes, as if something sought to claw its way through the brick and plaster and drag him screaming into the house's very fabric.

BANG, BANG, BANG, BANG …

He could hear a soft weeping now, and the crackle of flames. The stench of smoke in the air grew stronger. Still the whispers and agonised cries filled his head. Half heard warnings, curses, chewing, the crack of bone.

BANG, BANG, BANG, BANG …

Something was very, very wrong.

He stood now at the bottom of the stairs, looking into his living room. It was engulfed in flames. Fire covered the walls like surreal wallpaper and the ceiling was a vertically inverted river Styx. The curtains were aflame and billowing in the intense heat, as if they were dancing to an unheard beat in the firestorm. Phil could feel the hairs on his arms shrivel and his skin tighten before the blaze's fury.

The centre of the room however, was untouched by the inferno. The couch and two armchairs were in their usual position but they were no longer composed of soft upholstery and cushions. The living room furniture was made of stone, as if someone had clumsily carved out a three piece suite with a chisel and hammer.

BANG, BANG, BANG, BANG ...

He now found himself sitting on one of the chair boulders. On the stone armchair across from him, Griff sat, chewing something that he held with both hands. It looked like a table leg or ... something. Sam and Cairnsey were perched on the couch-boulder to his left, drinking from and passing a white, hard-looking chalice between them.

Phil knew it was made of bone.

All four of them were naked and covered in blood.

All around them, the living room burned and the air was thick with heat and the sickening aroma of blood, shit, smoke and roasting flesh.

BANG, BANG, BANG, BANG ...

It was a severed human leg that Griff was chewing on. Phil could hear his friend's teeth scrape on the femur as he sank his teeth into the meaty thigh, and listened, rapt, to the hellish wet music of flesh tearing away from bone with a moist ripping sound.

Sam and Cairnsey sat on the couch-boulder with blank eyes, now cutting each other with long curved daggers that were white as death shrouds, filling the bone chalice with the claret that flowed from each other's rent flesh and drinking, drinking …

Griff started to laugh.

On the floor in front of Phil, Mr Galbraith and Ms Fabiani writhed naked. She was straddling him, riding him with frantic urgency and screaming obscenities. He stabbed her in the breasts with another of the long, bone daggers, stabbing her in time with her frenzied sexual rhythm till both were drenched in blood, and still they rutted, howling in ecstatic, perverted agony.

BANG, BANG, BANG, BANG …

Cairnsey grabbed Sam by the hair, pulled his head back and sank abnormally large teeth into his friend's throat, sending a huge gout of blood spraying into the air.

Griff discarded the leg he was eating and got off his chair. He walked over to Mr Galbraith and Ms Fabiani, took the dagger from his history teacher's hand, and drove it into his own face with a powerful two fisted thrust. He started to caper around the living room, laughing insanely.

The living room burned on, the inferno now more intense. The picture window exploded outwards as did the television screen, sending out a deadly hail of glass slivers which embedded themselves in the flesh of the room's blood drenched occupants.

Sam and Cairnsey were on the floor now, tearing away at Galbraith's torso with their teeth. He smiled fondly and stroked their hair as they devoured him.

The sound of madness raged still in Phil's head as he saw all this, and he knew his sanity was about to snap. But the screams went on, the blood, *Jesus Christ, so much blood* flowed, ran, *gushed* from a thousand wounds, the sound of tearing flesh, meat being chewed, weeping, the smell of smoke and the fire all around …

BANG, BANG, BANG, BANG, BANG …

Phil screamed out loud and found himself crouched in a corner of his bedroom, naked and soaked with sweat.

Early afternoon sunlight filtered through a gap in his curtains, throwing a shaft of brightness upon his glistening, shaking body. Dust motes floated gently in the ray of light, seeming to mock his distress with their gentle motion.

Phil managed to stand up. He tried and failed to control his breathing. He wiped tears from his face.

Fucking hell. What was that *all about?*

BANG, BANG, BANG, BANG ...

Phil shrieked in panic and threw himself back into the corner of the room, curling up in a foetal position; his nerves totally shot and fear the only thing he knew.

Stop it, stop it, stop it, please God, make it go away ...

'Phil? Phil, answer me!'

His father's voice, from the other side of the bedroom door. His father banging on the bedroom door.

'Dad?' Phil called, his voice cracking.

'Phil! Phil, open this fucking door right now!'

There was panic in his father's voice.

Phil quickly pulled on a pair of jeans and walked shakily over to the bedroom door, having to make a conscious effort to keep his hands from trembling long enough to turn the key and unlock it.

His frantic father pushed into the room and took hold of his son by the shoulders, his anxiety apparent in his face.

'What's up, son? What's all the shouting about?'

'Nightmare. Real bad one. Sorry, I didn't mean to scare you, dad. I'm okay.' He gave his father a weak smile and a shake of the head.

His dad let out a long, stuttering sigh. After everything that had befallen the family, Kyle Densmore was very protective of Phil and constantly worried about his son.

'Christ Almighty. I thought someone was bloody murdering you the way you were screaming. Are you sure you're okay?'

'Aye dad, no bother.'

Kyle gave a slight smile and knuckled his son on the shoulder.

'Come downstairs and get your lunch, alright?'

'Cheers, dad.'

His father left the room.

Phil sat down on his bed and put his head in his hands, still shaking.

He'd never had a nightmare like that in his life, at least not one that had freaked him out so badly. Already the memory of it was starting to dissolve, the way memories of dreams often do. But before it was gone, just for a second, he heard in his head the hideous sound of Griff tearing a hunk of flesh from a severed human leg with his teeth, and he shuddered.

Then that too was gone, and he found himself wondering why he'd woken up naked when he'd gone to bed wearing a t-shirt and boxer shorts, and more so, he wondered with no small amount of disquiet what had scared him so badly that he'd got out of bed and locked his bedroom door while still asleep.

9

'Is there really any need for these lights to be so bright?' Sam complained grumpily, squinting his eyes as he and Phil made their way round the local general store's aisles collecting supplies for the night's trip to Bennane Head.

'Actually, I reckon they heard you had a hangover and turned the lights up just to piss you off,' Phil answered.

'The bastards.'

They were currently in the aisle displaying crisps and soft drinks, the bright, garish colours making Sam wince and screw his eyes up further.

'What do you reckon then, man?' asked Phil.

Sam scanned the shelves of crisps, savoury snacks and drinks. A large green bag caught his attention.

'Now there's a thing ...' he mused, wandering over.

He held up the big lime green and yellow bag.

'Twenty-four bags of scampi and lemon Nik Naks,' he proclaimed.

Phil pulled a face.

'They're not bad, but I don't fancy smelling of fish for the next few weeks. Twenty-four bags is a bit overkill.'

Sam was outraged.

'What? You can *never* have too many bags of scampi Nik Naks. And anyway, I didn't think smelling like fish would be a problem for you.'

'Shut yer ass.'

Phil spotted a huge white and blue bag.

'Now we're talkin',' he said. 'Thirty-six bags of Salt n' Shake.'

'Oh yeah, Phil,' Sam said sarcastically. 'Tremendous idea. I can't wait to try and get my nut 'round a bag of crisps that you need to self flavour when I'm tripping out my skull.'

Phil gave him a deadpan look.

'You're not funny, Sam.'

'Fuckin' Salt and Sake! Get a grip, Phil. They're the most boring crisps ever made. How about we just buy a big sack of tatties and we can eat them raw with a pinch of salt?'

'Alright, alright, smart arse. How's about a big variety bag?'

'Now you're speaking my language. Here's one here. Four ready salted, four salt n' vinegar, four cheese n' onion, four smoky bacon and four prawn cocktail.'

'Sweet,' Phil said. 'Throw the fuckers in the trolley.'

In they went.

'You alright, man?' Sam asked as they moved along the aisle. 'You've been pretty quiet this morning.'

'No big deal,' replied Phil. 'Didn't sleep too well. Had a fucked up nightmare. Dad said I was screaming like fuck. Found myself lying in the buff on the bedroom floor when I woke up.'

Sam snorted laughter at this. 'Buftie. Imagine squealing like a bitch 'cause of a nightmare.'

'Tell me about it. Never had one like it before,' Phil said with an embarrassed shake of the head.

'So what happened in it?' asked Sam.

'Beats me, mate. It was all messed up. Y'know that way when you wake up and you can remember what you've just dreamed about, but after a few seconds, it's gone?'

'Aye,' Sam said.

'It was one of those things, except it hasn't completely gone away. I've still got these ...' he searched in vain for someway to express the curious anxiety he felt.

'Images?' Sam offered helpfully.

'Sort of, but more like ... feelings with pictures.'

Sam gave him a puzzled look.

'It's hard to explain,' Phil went on, shaking his head. 'I'm pretty sure fire was involved somehow, and you boys were in it.'

'The dream or the fire?' asked Sam.

'Both ... I think. It's not like I can remember any certain part with fire or you, Cairnsey or Griff. It's just like, I know that stuff was involved somehow, but still ...' he finished falteringly, looking confused.

'There's something else,' Sam said. Not a question, and Phil thought, not for the first time since he'd known Sam, just how perceptive his friend was beneath the flippant, wise-ass facade.

He met his friend's even gaze and again looked embarrassed.

'I'm still scared, Sammy.'

Sam looked in Phil's eyes and saw that he was being serious. He also checked the automatic impulse to give him a roasting for being such a poof.

Instead he said, 'Scared of what?'

'Fucked if I know. Feels like I'm waiting for something bad to happen.'

Sam thought about this for a moment.

'Wouldn't worry too much about it, mate,' he said. 'I

44

knew something bad was going to happen when I went to my pit last night, and I woke up this morning with the worst hangover in recorded history. Everything seems a bit off kilter, a feeling like you've done something shady and are just waiting for a phone call asking *what the fuck were you all about last night*? It's just *The Fear*, mate.' Phil smiled at his mate's attempt to cheer him up and was grateful for the distraction. He knew *The Fear* though; the ugly cousin of the hangover, and this wasn't it.

'Guess we did put away a few beers yesterday.'

'Fuckin' right we did, amigo. That's probably what caused your night terrors. Plus we smoked roughly a quarter in about three hours. Think about it; how fucked up do things seem when your blootered and you've smoked a power of gear?'

'Pretty fucked up,' Phil conceded, remembering a conversation they'd had the previous evening about making a pornographic episode of the Flintstones.

'Damn skippy,' Sam continued, 'and dreams aren't the most coherent things in the world at the best of times either, correct?'

'Correct,' said Phil.

'So add these two factors together, taking into consideration that the dream *you* had happened to be a nightmare, and it's only logical that you're feeling weird.'

'Your powers of deduction astound me, Holmes,' Phil said dryly.

'I know. Nobel prize for logical deduction and stud-muffinliness next year, I reckon.'

'Let's get some beer,' Phil said.

'Doesn't really explain why you were naked when you woke up, right enough,' Sam mused. 'Guess you're just a superfreak, ya shady bastard.'

*

Just as they were leaving the store, Eddie Jannets was painfully making his way up the street on the opposite side of the road, hobbling along ungainly and intent on swiping a pain relieving bottle of booze from the shop when he recognised Sam and Phil, and stopped dead. His eyes narrowed.

He was still limping pretty badly from his encounter with Cairnsey. His nose was in plaster and both eyes were underscored with dark purple half moons, but the biggest bruise he had was to his ego. The wee prick was five years younger than him, and he had to all intents and purposes, kicked his cunt in. This was of course, unacceptable and he fully intended on evening the score, one way or another.

He reached into the inside pocket of his tracksuit for his Stanley blade, ready to run across the street and chib Cairnsey's poofy wee mates right there and then. If the wee prick himself wasn't about, he'd make do with his friends for now.

He had the advantage. They had their backs to him and hadn't seen him as they exited the shop. He would come up behind them, get one across the back of the neck then rip the other one on the face as he turned round. Easy.

It was always a good laugh slashing some cunt in daylight, he thought. You could see the blood better and their reaction was *always* funny. People usually expected that kind of shit to happen at night.

He started across the road, one hand inside his jacket, gripping the metal handle of the knife.

Just at that moment a police van turned the corner at the end of the road and Jannets hesitated.

46

He was on a good behaviour bond. If the police caught him in the act of an assault with a deadly weapon he was getting put away. No doubts about it. Also there was a street full of witnesses and he wasn't exactly inconspicuous with the cast on his nose and two black eyes.

He quickly withdrew his hand from inside his jacket and turned his face away from the oncoming meat wagon, watching Phil and Sam as they made their way up the street. He thought about the problem, then got out his mobile phone, which had become his after he'd stolen it at knife point from some wee cunt a few weeks ago, and made a couple of calls.

Griff stood in Cairnsey's bedroom, studying the impressive CD collection which spanned almost the length of an entire wall in two neatly ordered rows.

'Okay … trip music …' he mused.

'Most of the sixties stuff's over there, Griff,' Cairnsey was pointing to the CDs to the left end of the rack. 'Top row.'

He went back to rolling the joint he was working on. He'd already prepared six for the evening ahead, so they wouldn't have to build while they were tripping.

'Here we go,' Griff said, having found the section he was looking for in the vast collection. 'Hendrix, The Doors, The Stones, Cream, Jefferson Airplane …'

'How much smokeables d'you think we should take the night, Griff?' Cairnsey asked him.

'Quarter of solid?' Griff suggested.

'How 'bout just a half quarter solid and a bit extra green? It brings the trip on better.'

'Sweet.'

Cairnsey went back to his task, singing the theme from *Rawhide* under his breath.

'Rollin' rollin' rollin'…'

Griff continued his examination of the music.

'Think we should bring the Jefferson Airplane CD? Remember last time we were tripping with that on? Sam was convinced he could see white rabbits all over the shop?'

Cairnsey burst out laughing at the memory. Sam's confused/worried/amused expression and the way he'd whipped his head from side to side, seeing rabbits everywhere, had reduced them to tears of hilarity.

'That was funny as fuck,' Cairnsey giggled. '*Definitely* take that one.'

'Cool, how about The Doors?'

'Mr Morrison and co? Couldn't have a trip night without them. It'd be plain rude. Take that red and white greatest hits one. It's got the version of *The End* from *Apocalypse Now* on it, with the helicopter sounds and the insects.'

'How about …' Griff considered, then: 'Oh, shit! Have you got *Magical Mystery tour*?'

'Think so,' Cairnsey said. 'Check the Beatles section, to your right a bit.'

Griff scanned through the CD'S going to the right and found it between *Abbey Road* and *Sergeant Pepper's*.

'Ya fuckin' dancer!' he exclaimed with a huge smile, as though discovering lost Inca gold. Then he frowned.

'You're a thievin' rat, Cairns. This is mine!'

'I know. Think you gave me a loan of it a few years back.'

'Ya bastard! I thought I'd lost it for good.'

'You would've done if you hadn't found it just now,' Cairnsey replied with a smirk.

'Thievin' rat,' Griff said again, shaking his head. 'Just you keep rolling those joints and I'll see what else of mine you've got here. Tramp.'

'You can take your maw's knickers back,' Cairnsey said without looking up, 'she left them here the other night.'

11

As Cairnsey's car made its way north up the coast a few hours later, carrying its cargo of four eighteen year old boys, a crate of beer, a pencil case jammed with joints and other supplies, the atmosphere in the vehicle was good.

Cairnsey was driving with Phil next to him in the passenger seat. Griff and Sam sat in the back playing a game of switch. Sam was down to two cards while Griff sat with six and a frustrated expression on his face.

Sam was a jammy bastard at switch.

The Stones played on the car stereo. Time was definitely on Mick Jagger's side.

The sun rode high in the vast late afternoon sky the same shade of blue as Phil's Rangers top, and the sea rolled on by on their left as Cairnsey's dad's Peugeot followed the coastal road that would lead them to Bennane Head where they'd arranged to meet the dealer Ozay at seven pm. There was a bench on the cliff top there where some wit had carved *Sawney woz ere* on the left armrest then filled in the raggedly engraved letters with blood red paint, and this was the arranged meeting point.

Cairnsey had been surprised to find out when talking to the guy on the phone that afternoon that the dealer knew of the bench, seeing as he'd said he was from Barrhead near Glasgow, which was a good sixty miles away, and the bench was generally unknown to anyone who didn't live locally. It was also close to their intended campsite; a small clearing in the woods a few hundred metres back from the road, and the convenience of it all seemed like a good omen it was going to be a good night.

Phil took a deep pull on the joint he held and proffered it towards the back seat where Sam relieved him of it.

'Cheers, mate,' he said and threw down the ace of hearts on top of Griff's four of clubs, changing the suit.

'Spades, last card,' he said holding up his one remaining card and smiling.

Griff inspected his six cards.

Not a single spade or an ace with which he could change the suit to something more useful and prevent Sam from winning the hand yet again.

'Fucker!' he moaned, and picked up a seventh card, knowing the game was already over unless Sam was bluffing.

'Out!' Sam proclaimed in triumph, and threw down the King of spades. 'Pick up five just for being so shite at this game!'

Griff tossed down his cards face up.

'That's four games in a row you've just beat me, ya spawny bastard,' he said.

'You're no kidding its four games in a row, mate. Sheer skill and instinct though. Spawny fuck all.'

'Shite.'

'Your deal, loser,' Sam said and chuckled. 'The Rain Man in the film was fuckin' brilliant at cards as well. What happened to you?'

Griff picked up the cards and grumpily shuffled before dealing them out, eager for another chance to break Sam's stranglehold on the game. His impressive mental abilities, as varied as they were potent, did not include card counting it seemed. No matter how much he concentrated on the cards used in the game, trying to apply logic and win the game by mentally calculating odds, Sam won the vast majority of their contests.

'You're goin' down this time, chump,' he promised.

'Bring it on ya wee bitch,' Sam retorted with a grin.

In the front seat, Cairnsey grinned at his mate's patter.

'We'll need to get a few games going once the trips kick in later,' he said. 'Always a good laugh.'

'Like poppers chess,' Sam said from the back seat, referring to their version of the game where the players had to take a whiff of amyl nitrate after each move. It wasn't uncommon for the games to be abandoned after five or six moves, both players falling about, giggling and red faced, not even knowing whose turn it was.

Cairnsey laughed at the image. 'Do we actually have any poppers?' he asked.

'Well, it just so happens,' Sam said with a sly smile and reached into his jacket pocket, withdrawing a small brown glass bottle with a white cap. 'We're fuckin' jammin'.'

Jammin' by Bob Marley started playing on the stereo and they all laughed.

No one paid any particular attention to the beat-up black Ford Fiesta that followed them along the coastal road like a shadow in the early evening sun.

12

There was no one at the bench at Bennane Head at seven. Only a note pinned to the backrest written in elegantly flowing cursive.

Cairnsey and co.

Sorry I couldn't be here. Had some things to attend to at the last minute. Your goods are in the paper. B will explain.

Eat, drink and make merry,

O

'What the fuck?' said Sam with a scowl.

'Our goods are in the paper? What's that supposed to mean?' asked Phil.

'Let's see it,' said Griff.

He held the sheet of A4 up to the light and scrutinised it closely. After a few seconds he nodded and chuckled.

'Old Ozay's a smart bastard. Check this shit out.' He pointed to the bottom left hand corner of the sheet of paper. There was an inch long horizontal line of tiny holes punched into the paper a few millimetres up from the bottom, with four smaller lines of holes running down off it at right angles to the edge of the sheet, creating four small tear off squares of different texture to the rest of the page.

'No way,' said Cairnsey, unbelieving.

'Our goods are in the paper,' Griff said with a shrug. 'I've no idea how he's done it but it looks like these are the trips.'

'How the fuck did he do that?' wondered Phil.

'Maybe cut out the shape of the four trips and attached them along the edges with PVA or something,' suggested Sam.

'Seems like a lot of bother, and risky as fuck too. Anyone could have found this,' Griff pointed out. 'Right enough, if anyone else did find it they probably wouldn't understand the message.'

'True,' Phil said. 'Weird though. You'd expect to just get bumped if your man can't make it. 'Specially seeing as we don't even know the guy.'

'Well, it looks like we've got our trips regardless,' Cairnsey said. 'You boys still up for it?'

Phil hesitated. 'I'm not sure, man. Seems too easy, know what I mean?' he said uncertainly.

'Relax, mate,' said Sam, remembering Phil's earlier anxiety in the shop, 'either they're good trips or nothing happens. The guy hasn't shown so we haven't parted with any cash and I doubt anyone's trying to poison us.'

'It's not that,' Phil persisted. 'It's just a fucked up deal. It's shady enough getting trips from people you know cause you're never a hundred percent sure if they're going to be any good, but we've never even met this guy Ozay.'

Cairnsey laughed. 'Mate, you're supposed to get paranoid *after* you take your trip, not before. Tell you what, I'll buzz Barnsey and see what the score is. He's got to be 'B' on the note.'

He took out his mobile phone and made the call. It was answered on the second ring.

'Yeah?'

'Barnsey? Cairnsey here.'

'Awrite, mucker? Havin' a good time yet?' Barnsey said

with his annoying guffawing laugh that Cairnsey always thought sounded like Goofy.

'Not yet. We're at the Head but your man isn't here. D'you know what the score is?'

'Has he left a note?' Barnsey asked.

Cairnsey frowned.

'Aye. How'd you know?'

Again came that annoying idiot snort of laughter from the other end of the line. 'Don't worry about it, man. Daft cunt does it sometimes. Busy man y' know? It's sound though. You understand the note?'

'Aye.'

'Cool. Like a says, don't worry about it. It's all good,' Barnsey reassured him.

'You know this guy well then? Never heard you mention him before,' Cairnsey asked.

'Well enough', said Barnsey, and laughed again, for too long this time, as if he'd said something hilarious.

Cairnsey shook his head, wanting now to be off the phone. 'Aye alright, whatever. Just seemed a bit weird y'know. Catch you later.'

And again Barnsey's ridiculous sounding guffaws came blaring over the line, way too loud this time, as if he was actually *trying* to irritate. It was so loud that Sam, Griff and Phil could hear it.

'Later on, pal,' he said, and hung up, still laughing.

Cairnsey turned to the others.

'Don't know what that cunt's on, but if it's these trips then we're in for a good night. He says it's cool. Knew about the note and everything.'

'Ah, well then …' Griff said, sold.

'Still paranoid, Phil?' Sam asked him.

I do feel paranoid, Phil thought, and as he did, his scalp prickled and he had to repress a shudder. Half remembered images from his dream the night before flashed across his mind; fire, flesh, blood, but were gone again, dancing away elusively before he could grasp them. All he knew for sure was that something felt wrong, and the more he thought it, the harder it became to shake off the strange consternation. His mind was made up. This was no mood to be tripping in.

'Sorry to be a buftie, lads, but I think I'll sit this one out. No feeling the best for it.'

'Ah, c'mon, man. Relax. We've had weird deals before,' Cairnsey said.

'Aye, mate,' Sam said, 'It'll be sweet. Don't worry about it.' But he already knew that Phil wouldn't be tripping that night.

Smiling wanly, Phil shook his head.

'You're not changing your mind here are you?' asked Griff, knowing how stubborn Phil could be when he'd made a decision.

'Nope. You three split mine between you.'

'Fair do's then,' Sam said.

'Your call, mate,' said Cairnsey, ending the discussion, and Phil was glad they hadn't made a big deal about it.

'Don't know what the script was with Barnsey there though,' Cairnsey said. 'Laughing his fuckin' ass off.'

'Dodgy cunt,' said Sam.

13

They pitched the two tents in the clearing in the woods, far back enough from the road so as not to be noticed by cars travelling the coast. *Behind the Wall of Sleep* played on the portable stereo they'd brought. Its laid back blues groove washed over the setting, heavy then soft by turns. Cairnsey was just hammering in the last ground peg when Griff said, 'I have a cunning plan.'

'How cunning?' enquired Phil, who was feeling more relaxed after having a blast of Thai stick from Sam's bong. He was smoking it himself for now. The others would wait till after they'd taken their trips then start on the water pipe to help bring on the effect.

'So cunning you could pin a tail on it and call it a weasel.' Griff was a huge *Blackadder* fan.

'Do tell,' Sam prompted him.

'How's about we take a wander down to the caves once the trips kick in? Get some ghost stories on the go.'

This was typical of Griff, and the others chuckled. Any night they camped out, his impressive repertoire of urban legends and ghost stories would keep them riveted. This was a talent he'd obviously inherited from his family of storytellers and the others lapped it up.

'Capital idea, old Beane,' Sam said, lighting up one of the many pre-rolled joints.

Phil, who was in the process of filling up the bowl of the bong again with a goodly spread of grass, paused and frowned as a strong feeling of déjà vu hit him. A shiver rippled in his gut, and his throat, still hot from the first blast of Asian contraband, tightened.

'Aye, good call,' Sam was saying as he passed out beers

from the large cooler they'd brought. His voice had taken on a compressed sound to Phil's ears as his first hit from the bong started to take real effect. He'd always thought that after a few blasts on a pipe or bucket, sound, and particularly music, 'felt like aural 3-D' as he sometimes put it. And now his mind wandered, his déjà vu forgotten …

'Hello! Earth to Phil!'

He shook his head and looked up, a big dumb grin on his face. Sam was looking at him with some amusement. Phil realised his friend had been speaking to him, but he'd been intensely involved in an in depth mental evaluation of the benefits and drawbacks of 3D technology, and hadn't been listening to him.

'Are you stoking that bong or what?' he asked him.

Phil laughed.

'Was in a wee world of my own there. Good grass,' he said, and went back to crumbling the sticky green shredded leaves into the small metal gauze-bottomed bowl.

'Okay, gentleman,' Cairnsey said, holding out the trips to Sam and Griff. 'Good to go?'

'Damn right,' affirmed Sam, raising his can of lager.

Griff, for no reason he could think of, abruptly recalled the witch's grace Galbraith had read from *A Study in Scottish Folklore* the day before in history class, and he heard it coming from his lips before he even knew he was going to say it.

> 'We eat this meat in the Devil's name,
> With much sorrow and muckle shame,
> We shall destroy both house and hold,
> Both sheep and cattle in the fold,
> Little good shall come to the fore,
> Of all the rest of the little store.'

They all looked at him, puzzled. Especially Phil, who felt the hair stand up on the back of his neck as Griff intoned the sinister sounding verse. Even Griff himself wondered where it had come from. He looked around at the bemused faces of his friends and shrugged.

'Heard it in history yesterday. Guess it's sort of appropriate, listening to Sabbath and all.'

'You scare me sometimes, Griff,' Sam said, mock seriousness in his tone. They had a laugh and the weird moment passed.

'Cheers, boys,' Cairnsey said and raised his own can of beer.

They toasted the trip, as was their tradition, then threw the small pieces of unmarked paper into their mouths and washed them down with lager to avoid the foul chemical taste.

Phil joined in the toast. 'Have a good one, lads,' he said, and lit up the bowl of the bong again.

*

Fifty metres back in the trees, out of sight of the campsite, three figures crouched behind a massive fallen pine tree and watched over the top of it as the boys set up the tents.

'D'ye want to get the cunt now, Eddie?' one asked.

Eddie Jannets shook his head and said nothing. He didn't take his eyes off the campsite.

'C'mon tae fuck, Eddie,' the second one whined. 'Let's just do the bastard and get tae fuck. Ah cannae be arsed hangin' about in these fuckin' trees aw night.'

'Shut the fuck up you,' Jannets hissed, shooting John

McCabe an acid look. His companion fell silent.

The first figure, Warren Kerr, or Bunny as he was more widely known, was nervous.

'There *is* four of them, Eddie,' he said uncertainly.

'Fuckin' shitebag you, so ye are,' Jannets replied and gestured in the direction of the tents. 'Cairns is the only cunt that can fight. Ah used tae boot that wee poof Anderson along the corridors in school, and Jim Densmore used to slap his wee fag brother about aw the time. An' that other wee cunt Griff's fuck all but a smart arse. They'll probably shite it n' bolt.'

Bunny fell silent, brooding and thoroughly unconvinced. Jannets was out of control sometimes. He regretted answering his phone that afternoon.

'We'll wait till it gets dark and they've had a smoke and a drink,' Jannets continued. 'It'll be easier once they're wasted.'

McCabe was aghast.

'You want to sit aboot in the fuckin' bushes for what? Another three hours? Well, fuck that,' and he made to stand up and leave. It was his car that had brought them here, and he had no intention of waiting around for ages in the cold forest till Jannets decided to go and do this wee fanny.

Jannets grabbed him by the throat as he was trying to rise and slammed him back to the forest floor. With his free hand, he reached inside his tracksuit jacket and pulled out a foot long machete. He put it to McCabe's throat.

'You're fuckin' stayin' here till ah tell you to leave,' Jannets spat. He moved the machete up McCabe's face and drew the edge down his cheek. Jannets had spent two hours straight that afternoon sharpening the weapon. Blood ran.

McCabe drew in a breath to shriek, but Jannets clamped a hand over his mouth and held the point of the huge blade over his left eye. His scream died before it reached his lips.

McCabe seemed to be trying to melt into the moist forest floor in a futile attempt to get away from this lunatic and his machete. He squirmed there, prone and whimpering.

Jannets turned to look at Bunny, who just sat there, pale in the face and mouth hanging open, a look of disbelief in his eyes. He pointed the giant blade of cold steel at him.

'Goin' anywhere, Bunny?' he asked, almost casually.

'Naw, Eddie. Cool, man. Just chill, eh?'

'Ah'm chilled as you like.'

'Cool, mate. Whatever you say, big man. Ah'm no goin' anywhere,' Bunny assured him, palms outward in a placating gesture. *This cunt's fuckin' lost it big time,* he thought to himself.

Jannets turned back to McCabe; still prostate on the ground, looking like he was deciding what music he'd like played at his funeral and blood running in a thin trickle from his cut cheek into his ear. Jannets took his hand away from his mouth slowly but pointed the machete back at him.

Oh, Jesus. The crazy bastard's gonnae kill me ...

'Car keys,' he ordered.

McCabe slowly reached into his jacket pocket and withdrew the plastic tab with his keys attached. He wasn't about to argue. Jannets snatched them from him with his free hand and deposited them in his own pocket.

'We're stayin' for a while. Right?'

'Nae bother, Eddie. Just cool out, man, ok?'

14

'Anyone getting anything yet?' Griff asked.

Sam blinked, looked around, seemed to listen to the forest for a second, examined his palms briefly, then shook his head.

'All systems normal so far,' he said.

'Nothing yet,' agreed Cairnsey 'but it's only been fifteen minutes. Remember the trips we had at Glastonbury last year? Took an hour for those ones to kick in.'

'Got them from Barnsey, didn't we?' asked Griff.

'Dodgy cunt,' confirmed Sam, nodding.

Cairnsey looked over at Phil.

'And how you feeling mate?' he asked.

Phil had been sitting for the last five minutes sipping slowly from a can of Tennent's and not speaking, just staring off into space immersed in his own thoughts. Occasionally his head would start nodding to the music coming from the portable stereo. He looked up at Cairnsey's question.

'Feeling good, my man,' he said with a bleary eyed smile.

'Ya fuckin' stoner!' crowed Sam as he lit up a joint.

'Damn straight. Don't need no steenkin' acid.' He patted the bong which lay against his thigh like a lapdog. 'Got me all the fun I need right here,' and he arched his back and stretched luxuriously. He was sitting on the forest floor with his legs stretched out towards the as yet unlit fire they had built, his back propped against a tree stump, which was surprisingly comfortable, although that might have been something to do with the three hits from the bong he'd taken so far.

'Don't get *too* comfy there, Phil,' Cairnsey said. 'We've still got to walk down to the caves. You'll be too stoned to move soon.'

'Don't you worry about me, young Joshua,' Phil replied. 'I'll worry for all of us. Especially the carrots.'

The others looked at him as if he'd just said he wanted to shag his pet hamster, such was the absurdity of the statement.

Griff gave a weird, uncertain chuckle.

'What are you talking about, man?' he asked with a giggle.

Phil looked confused. He frowned and almost smiled, then blinked a few times. Shook his head.

'Erm … ha … emmm ...'

Sam started to giggle as well.

'Er … I mean … ehhh …' Phil was saying.

Cairnsey now started to chuckle, way down in his belly, and for the first time noticed a slight feeling of nausea.

'What were we … who ... what the fuck …' Phil continued his baffled, fractured sentence.

'What the fuck were we just talking about, man?' he asked, having completely forgotten. Then he stated to laugh as well.

In a split second it happened, and in that tiny splinter of time, Sam, Cairnsey and Griff, unknown to each other, felt a glorious shining moment of pure euphoria. Every nerve ending in their bodies lit up ecstatically and they shuddered inside with a blissful rush. For a fraction of their lives, they were superhuman. Then it passed, leaving the unmistakable feeling of a strong trip, broken through at last.

And the laughter took them; crashed down and obliterated them.

Cairnsey fell forward onto his face, laughing a very loud, donkey-like, braying laugh and pounding the ground with his fists.

Griff had fallen backwards off the log he had been sitting on, and lay there on his back, helpless, with his legs drawn up and hugging his ribs, laughing in a shrieking girlish manner.

'Carrots!' wailed Sam. 'What've carrots got to do with anything?!' He somehow forced the words out through lungs and a throat blissfully contracted with mirth, struggling to breathe.

Phil was just sitting there, chortling away and shaking his head, still wearing that hilarious baffled look on his face.

'Why would I say anything about carrots?' he asked, completely clueless.

The other three laughed even harder.

'Ahhhh! Stop it, man! I'm gonnae pish myself!' pleaded Cairnsey between his donkey brays.

Sam was now rolling about on the ground, kicking his legs and holding his face, which was going purple and felt like it would explode if he laughed anymore. An agony of pure happiness.

Griff was trying to stand up, but fell over again, his legs with all the consistency of sponge.

'I think the trips have kicked in,' he managed to gasp, then gave up and just lay there, his body shaking with great racking spasms and close to losing control of his bladder.

It went on for some time.

Finally, the fit passed and they could speak again.

'Ohhh, Jesus, Phil you crack me up,' said Griff in a strangled voice, rubbing his stomach.

Sam was wiping his eyes with his sleeve.

'Never hit the giggles like that before, man,' he said.

Cairnsey stood up, still chuckling a little, and went over to put right the stereo which had been knocked over during the laughing fit. He stretched his legs and flexed his fingers. A pleasant buzzing sensation seemed to flow through his body and he gritted his teeth and flicked his tongue, enjoying the simple tactile pleasure of just *feeling*.

'Well, my trip's definitely kicked in,' he said. 'How 'bout you bums?'

'It's all good,' Sam said and lifted his beer. Griff agreed.

'All feelin' fine my friends?' Phil asked with a wistful smile, for a second regretting not taking the trip and despite himself, feeling a little left out.

'These are good, mate' said Sam. 'Damn shame you passed it up.' He grinned at him, winding him up a little.

'Screw you, punk,' Phil came back.

'You want to start heading down the cave while it's still light, and before we start tripping too much?' Cairnsey asked.

Phil tensed at his words. Again a flash of apprehension shot through him, but again it was gone before he could grab hold of it properly. The peculiar feeling was even more so now that he was stoned. When he tried to analyse it, the inside of his head felt like cotton wool and he couldn't focus on anything at all.

Forget it, he told himself. *Just enjoy the night. Start thinking about it too much and you'll be stuck in a downer all night.*

'Caves it is,' Griff announced, clapping his hands together with a report like a pistol shot, making Phil jump.

15

After a brief and unsteady walk down the steep rugged path that traversed the cliffs and led to the beach, they arrived at the mouth of Sawney Beane's cave.

The opening in the rock had at one point been sealed off, as the cave led into a labyrinth of tunnels that some said went back into the cliffs for a mile or more. The Sawney Beane legend was known among those interested in folklore and those simply of a macabre slant all over the world, and tourists would sometimes visit the grisly attraction. Before the entrance had been sealed, a local who had been walking his dog on the beach outside one day had noticed a ghastly smell emitting from the dark opening in the rock, and being a concerned citizen had contacted the authorities fearing that maybe a gas or sewage pipe had been ruptured underground. What they had instead found, deep inside the twisting labyrinthine cave system, was the half rotted corpse of an American tourist, a camera still round his neck and wearing a t-shirt emblazoned with a grinning Nessie and the slogan 'I Love Scotland'. As it turned out, the unfortunate individual had been reported missing a few months previously. The local council had had the entrance to the caves sealed up as a precaution against the same thing happening again, but the safety measure hadn't lasted long. A few months later, the entrance was breached again, presumably by some over enthusiastic sightseer with a tool kit, a morbid sense of curiosity and too much time on their hands. The authorities had never got around to resealing it again.

Griff took a torch from his backpack and shone it into the dark opening. The initial passage led back into the cliff face for about fifteen feet then twisted away to the left. The rocky corridor was empty but for a few discarded drinks cans, old cigarette butts and joint roaches, and a used condom. Graffiti decorated the walls in a riotous clash of spray painted and marker drawn tags and mentions: people's names, dates, crudely rendered pornographic illustrations and declarations of adolescent love and footballing allegiances covered the stone surfaces of the cave walls and ceiling in a variety of colours, lending a strangely chaotic urban feel to the natural cavity in the earth. The cave had been used as a hang-out spot for decades by generations of local teenagers, and some of the dates inscribed on the walls went as far back as the sixties.

'Helloooooo,' Griff called into the darkness in a wavering singsong voice. 'Any insane cannibals home?'

Not a sound came from within but a steady drip, drip, drip of water leaking from the tunnel roof and echoing around the stone walls. They filed inside, Griff taking point with the torch.

They rounded the corner at the end and it opened out into a large, roughly oval chamber with the roof seven feet overhead. As with the entrance tunnel, the walls here were covered with graffiti and there were odd bits of litter strewn around on the ground plus the charred remains of an old campfire. There were two narrow, inky black openings in the rock walls of the chamber which led deeper into the cave system. The boys had explored these two passages on a previous trip to the caves some years before, and had found that each of them had several more ever narrower, but still passable tunnels branching from them. They hadn't explored much further, such was the danger inherent in the disorienting and claustrophobic nature of the underground maze. It was also very dark, narrow and generally unsettling as fuck.

'Let's get some candles set up here,' Sam suggested. 'Not freaking out or anything, but a little light wouldn't go amiss. Don't fancy breaking my ankle down here.' Griff handed him the torch and from his backpack produced a box of long red dinner candles and a couple of ornate, silver-plated three pronged candle holders. He'd taken them from the dining room at Griffiths Hall and knew they were antique items, each worth thousands of pounds if sold at auction. Cairnsey grinned in appreciation of Griff's forward thinking and refined aesthetic taste.

'Nice touch, dude,' he said.

'Be prepared,' Griff replied seriously, giving the Boy Scout salute, 'and when possible, be classy.'

He handed out the candles and holders to the others and soon the cavern was lit in an ambient flickering glow, which caused shadows on the rough graffitied stone walls to change shape and position in a fascinatingly eerie way.

Beers were opened, a joint was sparked. A CD was played on the portable stereo; a slow bluesy ballad with a lone singer, his haunting voice accompanied by a softy plucked acoustic guitar.

Phil recognised the melody. He'd heard it in a film they'd all watched at Sam's place a few weeks before, but he'd be fucked if he could remember the name of it now. It was hard to recall details like that when you were cataclysmically stoned.

'Sam,' he said. 'What's that tune called?'

'*Hard Time Killing Floor Blues*,' Sam answered absently, looking around the walls and ceilings.

Griff looked up from studying his palms.

'Really? I'll be damned. That's mighty interesting,' he said.

'What is it?' Phil asked. The name of the song had for some reason sent a jolt of ice into his gut.

The others smiled. Whenever Griff said something was 'mighty interesting', you could bet your ass that he would proceed to go off on a lengthy, yet entertaining and often educational monologue. It was Griff's story time, as they liked to call it.

'Do tell,' Cairnsey invited him.

Griff accepted the invitation, and sat forward.

'Well, the Beane family had their shit organised. As we all know, these caves go back into the cliff and underground for a good distance, and the family had separate chambers for different purposes. They had chambers for storage of loot, and another for keeping the pickle jars they kept their victims' body parts preserved in, one for cooking, chambers for sleeping in, and of course, the killing chamber.' Griff paused for effect to let his words sink in. He saw that his friends were looking at him expectantly and he went on, subtly dropping his voice to a near whisper.

'When they grabbed someone on the road above the cliffs, some of their victims would have been killed on the spot or dragged into the woods. In fact, the remains of the Beane's last victim were found in the woods not far back from the road, probably close to where the tents are. But most of the time when they snatched someone, the actual slaughter would take place in the killing chamber.'

Griff paused again, looking at his friends' expressions. He could see they were into the story now. He was even feeling a little spooked himself. Damn, these trips were good.

'They were eventually caught when someone got away,' he continued. The boys all knew the story, but Griff was just so damned good at telling it.

'This guy and his wife on horseback were on their way home from a fair when they were attacked on the road. The guy was tooled up with a sword and pistol, and managed to fight his way free, but not before his lady had fallen from the horse in the struggle and got killed in front of him. He later told how the cannibals had slashed the woman's throat with their bone daggers and lapped up her blood like it was a fine wine, then they gutted her right there on the road.'

'At that point, the story goes, the guy bolted and rode furiously back to town. He returned later that same night with a group of thirty or so people and discovered what was left of the woman's body in the woods. There wasn't a trace of any attackers.'

'A couple of days later, King James heard about it and sent a platoon of his soldiers with bloodhounds to try and find the killers, and that's when they discovered the caves. They say that the hounds wouldn't go inside at first and had to be beaten by their masters, and that when they did get inside they found severed limbs hanging from the cave ceiling on hooks, big barrels of vinegar with more preserved body parts inside, piles of clothing, weapons and valuables taken from their victims. They say that the cannibals attacked them, and there was a brutal fight which left four of the soldiers and a bunch of the Beane family dead. When it was over, they rounded up Sawney, his wife Black Agnes and the forty or so surviving inbred relatives, and they were all carted off in chains and burned at the stake in Edinburgh.'

It was taking all of Griff's concentration to keep his mind on the narrative. He could feel the chemicals from the acid coursing through his veins like a sweet lava, and found it increasingly difficult to keep his train of thought on track. He glanced at one of the candles and saw how the slight draft coming in from the beach was pushing the flame back and forth, making the tiny tongue of fire resemble a small, swaying dancer. He sat there silently rapt, oblivious to his friend's expectant expressions, mesmerised by the subtle hallucination and having completely forgotten he was in the middle of telling a story.

'And?' Sam prompted him.

Griff jumped a little and looked at Sam as if he'd never seen him before.

'And what?' he asked, having no idea what his friend was talking about.

'The story. Finish the story,' Sam said, laughing.

'Was I telling a story? What about?'

Sam considered this for a few seconds, chuckling in his chest.

'Shit, man, I've no idea. These trips are awesome! Cairnsey, what was Griff's story about?'

Cairnsey wasn't listening. He sat there facing the wall and running his fingers along the rough surface, a fascinated look on his face. 'Man, this rock feels like ... like skin or something,' he was saying, apparently to himself. 'Scaly, rough skin ...'

Sam and Griff doubled up with hilarity again, the all consuming mirth of strong LSD. Their hoots of laughter echoed and reverberated loudly around the stony chamber. Cairnsey joined in the laughter, though he wasn't sure why.

Phil wasn't tripping though, and had been paying devout attention to Griff's tale. It seemed very important somehow that he finish it.

'You were telling us about Sawney, Griff. Something about the killing chamber,' he reminded his friend.

Griff managed to get control of himself again.

'Oh yeah, that was it. Sorry, got distracted by the flame on the candle there. Look! It's like a wee dancer shakin' its ass there!'

'Hey, you're right!' Sam exclaimed in childlike joy, noticing the usually unremarkable spectacle which now so entranced his mate and leaning in close to the candle flame himself, completely fascinated. 'Check this out, Cairnsey. We've got a fire dancer in the cave!'

Cairnsey looked round.

'Cool!' he said. 'That's brilliant! You should check out the walls, man. They feel really weird!'

Sam and Griff suddenly found the bare rock as intriguing as Cairnsey had, and forgot all about the dancing candle flame, immersed in running their fingertips across the chamber wall.

Phil was becoming more agitated by the second, frustrated

by his mate's inability to focus on one thing for more than a few seconds. He leaned forward and shook Griff by the shoulder.

'The story, Griff,' he said with urgency in his voice.

'What story?'

'For fuck sake, something about the killing floor!'

'*This* is the killing floor,' Griff said, as if Phil was arguing with him.

'What?' Phil asked, suddenly cold.

'*This* chamber is the killing floor,' Griff repeated distractedly, not looking at Phil and stroking the wall. 'They used this room because it's closest to the beach. Back then, the tide used to come up higher than it does now, and when it did, this chamber would have been underwater. The sea would come in and wash it clean, take out all the bones and shit, which is why people would find them washed up on other beaches for miles around. Through there,' he gestured in the direction of one of the dark passages, 'was the storage cave where they used to keep body parts on the hooks and in the barrels. Check out the wall, man! It's awesome!'

The cold feeling in Phil's bones radiated out through his body till it consumed every inch of his flesh. He could hear his friend's laughter in the background, but it seemed more like a compressed recording of the sound. He had the feeling of being a half step out of the real world, where everything around him seemed slightly different, as though what he was seeing and hearing was a split second delayed somehow. On top of this, the creeping apprehension he'd been feeling all day following his forgotten dream the previous night returned, but it came back with a vengeance; stronger and colder. A layer of chilled sweat had seeped out from his pores and now covered his shoulders. It began running in trickles down his sides making him shiver.

This was not good. Something definitely felt wrong.

He'd passed up the trip thinking that some quality time with the bong would calm him down, and for a while it had worked, but now the subtle, unsettling feeling of something being off kilter heightened in a sudden spike. His shivers became shakes.

Phil ran his fingers through his hair and they came away wet with perspiration. Cold sweat beaded the goose-bumped skin of his forehead and ran down into his knotted brows. He hunched forward, screwing his eyes shut and trying to take deep breaths.

Get it together, for fuck's sake.

The cold sweat on his shoulders and forehead now covered his entire body, and he trembled so hard that he imagined he could hear his bones rattling loosely in their sockets. He could sense his friends talking around him and recognised the words, but couldn't make sense of the conversation.

Sam, who was sitting next to Phil, went to pass him a joint and noticed his friend's haunted demeanour.

'Shit, Phil, you ok?' he asked, with genuine concern in his voice.

Phil's head snapped up at the mention of his name.

'What?'

'You all right? Look like you're whiteying,' Sam said.

'I'm … I don't know, man. Something's wrong.'

Griff and Cairnsey caught the sudden tension in the atmosphere.

'What's up?' Cairnsey asked.

'Phil's not doing too good,' Sam informed him.

'Fuckin' hell, Phil,' Griff said. 'You look awful.'

'This isnae good, lads,' Phil said in a quivering, cracked voice. *This is fear,* he thought. *Pure fear.*

'Jesus, man, look at him. He's shaking,' someone said. Phil couldn't tell who. His vision had started to go grey at the edges. The voice and the music from the stereo took on a weird echoing quality, as if he was hearing it all from inside a vast tin can.

'Chill out, mate,' a voice said. 'We're the ones that are tripping here. You're not supposed to be freaking out. We are.' Phil felt an arm go around his shoulders. There were more voices, trying to talk him down and relax him. They weren't working.

'You're alright, man.'

'Just relax, Phil.'

'Take deep breaths.'

They sat that way for a few minutes, vainly trying to chill him out with soothing words and gestures. Phil's mind, however, was a whirlwind of dislocated images and thoughts. He was bent over at the waist, facing the ground and hugging his knees. His eyes were shut so tight that his face ached, and he shook uncontrollably. He tried to tell himself it was just the grass, just the grass, but it did no good. Thoughts ricocheted around his consciousness, bouncing around frantically like stray bullets. Parts of Griff's story intertwined with single frame flashes of images from his dream, painting a nightmarish spectral landscape inside his head from which he could not escape.

... killing floor ... bones for miles around ... the blood ... fine wine ... fire ... gutted her in front of him ... bone daggers ... the slaughter ...

'C'mon Phil, calm down,' someone said from the end of a tunnel a long, long way away. Phil could recognise anxiety creeping into that voice now as well. A high pitched whine built in his head, blocking out all other sensory perception. He could neither feel, hear, taste nor see. The whining internal feedback grew and grew, reaching an all consuming volume. It was too much, too much ...

He slid bonelessly off the rock he'd been sitting on like a puppet whose strings had been severed, flopping to the ground in a dead faint.

*

They put Phil in the recovery position at Griff's prompting. He'd done a first aid course as part of his scout training and knew this would prevent Phil from choking on his own vomit if he threw up.

'We'd better get him back up to the tent,' Sam said, concern in his voice. 'Probably wasn't the hottest idea coming down here. He's been acting weird since he had a nightmare last night. He was pretty freaked out.'

Griff was kneeling over Phil's prostrate body and checking him over, his first aid knowledge coming back to him despite the trip.

'He feels like he's got a bit of a temperature, but his heart's slowing down again. Was way too fast a minute ago. He's breathing okay as well. He should come round in a minute or so, then we can get him back up to the tents and get a fire going. Get some food and water in him. He'll be fine.'

'Good call,' Sam said. 'Bit hungry myself.'

'Must be the trips. I'm fuckin' starving,' Cairnsey agreed.

'Tell me about it,' Griff said nodding, then turned back to Phil, giving him a light slap on the cheek to try and rouse him. Phil moaned softly. 'Good, he's waking up.'

Sam stooped over him.

'You quite finished freaking us out now, mate?' he asked.

'Tents … need to get back …' Phil murmured.

'That's the plan, bud. Just need to give yourself a second to get your legs working and we'll help you up,' Cairnsey said.

'Got to go … the tents …' Phil moaned with more urgency. 'Not ... safe … something's … coming …'

'It's alright, Phil,' Sam was saying. 'Just relax.'

Griff pulled back one of Phil's eyelids, checking the pupil.

'He's still not conscious. Must be dreaming.'

Suddenly, Phil began to thrash around on the ground, shaking his head wildly and lashing out with his fists and feet at assailants only he could see.

'Help me hold him, Sam,' Griff ordered. Sam and Cairnsey immediately knelt on either side of Phil, restraining him so he wouldn't injure himself on the stone floor with his violent movements. 'Grab his feet, Cairnsey.'

'What's happening, Griff?' Cairnsey asked.

'He's havin' another *fuckin'* nightmare obviously,' Griff snapped at him, glaring daggers. Cairnsey was taken aback by the harsh way he'd spoken and the dangerous gleam in his eyes.

'Cool yer fuckin' beans, man,' Cairnsey retorted, suddenly angry himself.

'I'm sorry all right,' Griff muttered, 'but I'm a bit freaked out here myself, y'know?'

One of Phil's arms got away from Sam and his fist cracked against Griff's cheek, snapping his head to the side.

'For fuck's sake, Sam, *hold him*!' he yelled at his friend angrily.

'Calm down, Griff,' Sam shouted back. 'We're tripping here as well you know.'

Sam could also feel a slow anger building in his blood and found himself grinding his teeth together till they creaked in the gums. He was very hungry.

Phil's struggles became even more frantic, and small sounds of distress escaped him.

Cairnsey tried to grab hold of his flailing legs, but one of Phil's feet caught him in the groin. Cairnsey let out a strangled cry and doubled up, cupping his crotch with his hands.

'*Phil, fuckin' stop it!*' Griff screamed in his face, then pulled back a hand and cracked him across the cheek with his knuckles once, twice, three times. A thin trickle of blood emerged, and ran from the corner of Phil's mouth.

Sam was looking at Griff's face, and what he saw there scared him badly. Griff's face was contorted into a mask of pure hateful fury, and yet he was smiling. It was not a pleasant smile.

Cairnsey had recovered enough from the blow to his testicles to straighten up, and there too on his face, Sam saw the same raging excitement that had seemingly taken hold of Griff.

'Fuckin' bastard,' Cairnsey hissed and swung a vicious kick at Phil's writhing body. The force of the blow turned Phil over on to his side.

What the fuck's happening? Sam wondered in a near panic. He could feel his own control slipping, and the urge to lash out at someone, something, *anything* became almost unbearable.

He got to his feet and grabbed a hold of Cairnsey who was lining up another kick at Phil, still thrashing around on the floor.

'*Cairnsey stop it!*' he screamed in his face. 'It's the fuckin' trips, man!'

Cairnsey's face cleared for a second and he blinked and shook his head. 'What the fuck's going on here?' he asked with real fear in his voice. He stumbled back, stunned at his own actions.

Sam turned back to Griff who was still holding Phil's head as he writhed around like a landed fish on the floor. Griff's normally calm expression was still distorted into that horrible grin, and an insane excitement etched his features. He was visibly panting, and looking at the thin trickle of blood that seeped from Phil's mouth with unmistakable naked hunger.

Sam watched in stupefied horror as Griff leaned forward slowly, tongue extended to lick the blood from Phil's face.

He shouted out and leapt at Griff at the last possible second, only just managing to push him away before his tongue could make contact with Phil's blood. Sam clambered on top of his friend and grabbed Griff's face in his hands, forcing him to look into his eyes.

'Get a grip, mate. These trips are fucking with our heads big time. We need to get Phil up and get out of here, alright?'

Griff's eyes cleared, and he nodded a dumb acknowledgement.

A sudden, savage cramp gripped Sam's belly in fiery claws and he cried out; falling to his side with his face a desperate rictus of pain and need. The scent of Phil's blood, impossibly strong for such a small wound, seemed to fill the stone chamber, infecting the three boys with a ravening hunger that tore at their guts and minds like a scythe.

Sam could hear Griff and Cairnsey screaming, and he felt his mind tilting and slipping. He was spiralling down into a dark place where unspeakable things crept and sniggered.

He forced open his eyes to try and banish the mental darkness that threatened to overwhelm him, and saw that somehow there were suddenly three more people in the cave.

One of them had a machete.

At that moment, something very bad found a crack in the thin membrane between worlds, and slithered through it.

They flew at each other.

16

Phil woke up alone.

For the few seconds before full consciousness came, he expected to find himself in bed, the nightmare past, and he would get up and go for a shower then have some breakfast with his dad. He fancied bacon rolls.

Then the terrible reality of his situation became apparent.

He realised he wasn't in bed, but lying on cold stone, and there was a taste of blood in his mouth.

Phil sat up quickly, wincing as pain lanced through his ribs, and then he saw the blood.

The floor and walls of the stone cavern were marred by sporadic streaks, splashes and pools of it that glistened blackly in the candlelight. The air was rank with the sickening stench of iron. As Phil frantically looked around, trying to make some sort of sense of the situation and fighting off panic, the nightmare experienced the night before came crashing back to him in violent clarity like déjà vu to the nth power. Every deranged scene and image collapsed like a burning building into place in his memory, and the mental force of the recollection caused his breath to explode out of him like he'd been punched square in the gut.

He began to hyperventilate, bald terror building in a slow, squirming crescendo. Phil closed his eyes tightly and tried to control his breathing, repeating to himself desperately, hopelessly, *just a dream, not happening, just a dream, not happening.* The pain in his ribs and face, and the thick taste of blood in his mouth were all too real however, and made a convincing case that this *was* in fact actually happening. He dared not open his eyes again though, lest they be greeted with the sight of his friends; naked, crimson-skinned and smiling soulless smiles, displaying oversize teeth and clutching those white daggers ...

The fear of what might be seen was trumped by the fear of what he might *not* be seeing though, and Phil opened his eyes again and staggered to his feet, spitting blood in horrified disgust. The sharp pain that flared in his mouth indicated that it was his own blood and not ... He didn't want to consider other possibilities.

His back to the wall, still struggling to control his breathing, Phil tried desperately to arrange his thoughts and assess the situation.

The guys. He'd been with Sam, Cairnsey and Griff in the cave and he'd started to feel shady after Griff had been talking about the killing floor. Then, it seemed like hours later, and he was still in the cave, but the guys were gone and there was a serious amount of blood splattered all over the walls and floor. He tried to quell the rising panic in his tightening chest. His breath began to accelerate again and his heart pounded like a double kick drum.

Get a grip Phil. Don't lose it. Find the guys. Get out.

He suddenly became aware of a soft voice coming from somewhere beyond the chamber he was in, but the sound echoed and bounced around the stone walls, making it difficult to pinpoint the point of origin. Phil noticed for the first time that one of the pools of blood that lay close to a dark opening in the rock featured a wide ragged drag mark that led away into the inky blackness beyond. He looked around the cave floor again and saw another three drag marks all going in the same direction, all starting from glistening concentrations of blood of varying sizes, and leading into the narrow, gloomy passage.

Griff's backpack was still lying on the floor. With shaking hands, Phil retrieved the torch from inside and shone it into the dark opening, seeing that the bloody trail continued along the small tunnel for about twenty metres and then disappeared out of sight round a bend in the passage. Phil stepped closer to the entrance of the tunnel, his breath coming in short rapid gasps. It was from here that the voice came. Although he couldn't make out the words, he recognised the tone. It was a voice he'd grown to know well since he was a small boy in primary school.

It was Sam.

As he listened closer, he became aware of a second voice, again familiar. Griff.

'Lads?' he called out, 'Are you in there?'

The voices abruptly stopped.

Phil stood there holding his breath and shining the torch down the length of the claret-stained passage, his heart beating so hard and fast it was almost painful.

'Griff? Sam?'

He gasped in surprise as something came sailing though the air out of the darkness and landed at his feet with a quiet thud.

He pointed the torch down at the object, and for a split second was confused. It seemed to be a hair covered football. Frowning, Phil squatted down and took hold of it, turned the ball over, and found himself staring into Cairnsey's face.

For what seemed like an eternity, Phil couldn't move. He was rooted to the spot in abject terror, his mind a complete blank. He just could not comprehend or process what lay in from of him. Cairnsey's head stared back at him, grinning a grin that displayed too-big teeth.

Then the jaw creaked open and it spoke.

'We eat this meat … in the Devil's name,' Cairnsey's head rasped in a voice like rusty razor blades on a blackboard. The dead eyes rolled upwards and to the right, as if indicating something behind.

Phil fell backwards and tried to scramble away, a scream lodged in his throat. All the noise he could make was a strange choking whistle. As he retreated in dumb terror, shaking his head in futile denial of what he was seeing, the hand holding the torch came up and illuminated the blood stained tunnel.

There stood Sam and Griff; naked, red skinned and grinning.

They exploded towards him.

17

Phil found himself running through the forest.

He had no recollection of leaving the cave or ascending the rough path up the cliffs from the beach, only becoming aware of himself as he bolted in a sightless panic through the dark woods making small, childlike whimpering noises in his throat. Branches from the trees lashed at his face as he blundered on, stumbling over roots and stones, crashing heedlessly though bushes and underbrush.

What the fuck just happened? What the fuck just happened? Oh, Jesus ...

He tried not to think about what he'd seen, but it was like trying to appeal to the wind not to blow on a stormy day.

We eat this meat ... in the Devil's name.

Phil tried to block out the memory of Cairnsey's dripping, impossibly loquacious severed head, but his traitorous mind kept replaying the image in hideously detailed clarity, scaring him more and more until he became aware that he was screaming as he ran.

He could hear them behind him as they raced through the trees in pursuit. Sam and Griff. Hunting him. Calling his name and laughing. They didn't sound like they were very far back.

Phil looked back over his shoulder as he hurtled blindly through the thickly wooded forest.

These are my best mates. What the fuck is going on here?

Sudden blinding pain crashed through his head.

Don't pass out! Stay on your feet! Move!

Phil crumpled to the forest floor in black oblivion.

He awoke suddenly and sat bolt upright, expecting to see Sam and Griff standing over him wearing red grins, but he was alone again, lying prone in front of the large pine he'd run into at full speed.

His head hurt like nothing he'd ever felt. Phil raised a hand to his throbbing temple and winced at the sudden bright flare of pain as his fingers touched the split skin. He could feel blood on his fingertips and more drying on his face. He started to get to his feet again but staggered; his legs unsteady and soft at the knees, and his pounding head swimming sickeningly. Leaning against a tree, Phil desperately tried to will strength to his legs. He had to keep moving. With every second he stood still, Sam and Griff could be closing on him. The panic that had fuelled his blind charge through the woods began to build again, and Phil pushed away from the tree, ready to continue his mad dash through the dark woods, weak kneed or not.

A noise stopped him.

Off to his left there was a soft rustle of leaves, then silence again.

Phil froze; his heart pounding and his scalp crawling.

Another crack of dry branches, a twig snapped underfoot. Closer.

Phil was frozen for a moment, torn between the urge to bolt away into the trees and the simultaneous urge to hide. His legs still felt like soft jelly, and he realised that weak as he was with a probable concussion, he wouldn't get far if he tried to run.

The tree he'd run into was partially uprooted, and there was a narrow dark opening in the earth beneath the torn up base. Phil quickly dropped onto his stomach and squirmed forward till he was concealed in the dark muddy space beneath the half-toppled pine. He tried to slow his breathing.

Something was moving towards him outside, and Phil shuffled backwards till his back was pressed against the moist earthen wall of his hiding place. He tried not to think about the multitude of bugs that were doubtless crawling all over him and finding gaps in his clothes. Even as he had the thought, some many-legged beastie scuttled coldly across the back of his neck. He shook in revulsion and covered his mouth with both hands to stop himself from giving voice to the whimpers of terror that he felt build within him.

Moonlight filtered down between the treetops, and outside his shelter, Phil saw a shadow move stealthily among the trees, silent as a hunting animal.

He became aware again of the throbbing of his head which pulsed painfully in time with his pounding heart, and he felt fresh blood running down his cheek. He remembered Griff after a first aid class once, talking about how even shallow head injuries bled like a bitch.

The shadow outside his foxhole moved closer, and Phil could now hear a sound that accompanied it. Sniffing. Long drawn out inhalations like a wine taster would perhaps make when trying to distinguish a Burgundy from a Bordeaux while blindfolded.

'Are you here, Phil?' a voice asked from the shadows. It was Griff.

Sniff sniff sniff.

The shadow stepped out of the darkness into a small clearing. Griff stood ten metres away, holding a machete and sniffing the air. His entire body was coated in blood, as if he'd been rolling in it. His eyes seemed to glow, but that must be a trick of the moonlight Phil reasoned. Surely.

'You're here somewhere, mate. I can *smeeell* you,' Griff crooned in a hideous singsong tone.

Without really thinking about it, Phil silently scooped up some wet mud from the ground of the hollow in which he cowered and coated his face, smearing it painfully over the wound in his temple and trying to cover the smell of his leaking blood.

That's Griff out there. I've known him for ten years.

'It's nothing personal, Phil,' Griff said out in the woods, 'You're food now. That's all. Meat. You didn't take the trip. I'm still me, but now …' he tailed off with a strange almost regretful little chuckle.

Sniff, sniff.

Phil saw Griff suddenly snap his head in his direction and his blood froze. Griff sprinted forward at an impossible pace and Phil almost screamed out loud.

Just as he expected Griff to come scuttling into his dark recess under the tree, he suddenly stopped and stood directly outside the hollow, his bloodstained knees a mere foot away from Phil's face.

Sniff. Sniff.

Directly overhead.

There was a sudden frustrated bellow, a chilling animal-like noise that was not even close to human, and then a frantic chopping as Griff began frenziedly hacking at the tree. Phil could see a storm of woodchips falling around his friend's ankles.

After a full minute, the hacking stopped, and Phil heard Griff panting raggedly, then Sam's voice was calling out somewhere further back in the dark forest.

'Did you find him?'

'No, just blood on a tree,' Griff called back.

They sound so normal. Like they're looking for a lost Frisbee or something.

Phil heard Griff move away. His muscles, wound tense as a coiled spring, relaxed and he let out a long shuddering breath. He wanted to sleep. His mind and body felt stretched beyond their means, and all he wanted to do was curl up and seek shelter in oblivion. Cairnsey was dead, but not so dead that his disembodied head hadn't been able to speak to him. Sam and Griff had lost it and were now hunting him, apparently for food. It was all too much. He closed his eyes, and felt himself starting to drift away …

No, he told himself and forced his eyes open. If he stayed he would die. He knew that for sure. He had to get out of the woods. It was only a matter of time before his friends found him.

Phil wearily crawled forward, hesitating before he emerged from under the lopsided pine tree, and listened. The only sound was the wind blowing through the treetops and the creak of branches.

Phil crawled out from the dark recess like a nocturnal animal from its burrow and stood in a shaft of moonlight.

He tried to get his bearings. Looking around, all he could see was dark forest in every direction. He didn't even know from what direction he had come, nor could he tell how long he'd ran through the woods after escaping the caves before his senses had returned. He couldn't hear the sound of the water on the beach, so he assumed he must have run for some distance away from the coast. Other than that, he was completely disorientated.

There was the sudden sharp crack of foliage from somewhere back in the forest to his left. It didn't sound close, but there was definitely something there, and it was approaching.

This time Phil decided to run.

He looked at the maimed bark on the tree trunk where Griff had hacked in frustrated fury at the bloodstain left over from his collision. Using this as his only point of reference,

Phil ran into the woods with his back to this marker, hoping beyond hope that he was going back in the direction he'd come.

18

As he fled from the uprooted pine, the panic that had gripped Phil subsided enough for him to think practically. He made a conscious effort to slow his pace and began moving quickly but quietly, every once in a while pausing and listening for signs of his pursuers.

He needed help, and cursed under his breath as he realised that his mobile phone was in his jacket pocket. He remembered removing the jacket when they'd been back in the caves, aeons ago. With this realisation, Phil became aware for the first time that there was a chill in the night air, but he'd been too afraid and pumped full of adrenaline to feel it until then. He'd been thinking only of evading and escaping from his pursuers, and had not even noticed that he was without his jacket; wearing only jeans, his beloved Rangers football shirt and trainers. Shivering now, he continued forward, praying that he would soon find his way back to the road.

After what seemed like hours, he caught the faint briny scent of salt water and seaweed on the air, and hope bloomed in his chest. Phil recklessly abandoned the furtive manner in which he had been moving and started running again, heedless of the noise his passage made.

As he hastened forward, Phil became aware of a new scent in the air; that of wood smoke, and seconds later he stumbled out of the underbrush into the clearing where they had set up the tents earlier that evening.

Phil could hardly believe his fortune. Falling to his knees, he could have wept in relief, but again the natural instinct for survival kicked in, and he forced himself to his feet once more, exhausted though he was.

The fire they had lit had died, but a thin tendril of smoke still rose from the charred wood and ashes. The tents seemed untouched. No one had been here since they'd left to go down to the caves.

Phil forced himself to think.

Okay. Car keys. Find Cairnsey's car keys.

He prayed Cairnsey had not had them with him down in the caves. He would not go back down there.

We eat this meat in the Devil's name ...

Phil forced himself to concentrate on his current situation. If he let that fearful memory get a hold of him again, the little calm he'd forced upon himself would be lost, and he felt he would just sit down and gibber till someone found him, dead or alive.

With trembling fingers, he unzipped the flap of the tent Cairnsey was sharing with Griff and located Cairnsey's backpack. A quick search through the pockets proved fruitless. He briefly looked through the rest of the tent. No car keys. Phil did however find a torch and Cairnsey's mobile phone.

He switched the flashlight on and doing his best to stop his hands from shaking, began flicking through the phonebook on the mobile till he found his home number and pressed the call button.

Please let him be in, he prayed.

'Hello?' His dad's voice, groggy with sleep. Phil almost broke down in tears of relief.

'Dad, it's me. Something's happened ... the lads ... Cairnsey's dead ... they're chasing me ... trying to kill me ...'

'What? Who's chasing you? Where are you?' There was real fear in his father's voice.

'Bennane Head ... they took his fuckin' head off, dad ... please help me ... please ...'

91

There was a sound. The rustling of leaves from the direction of the woods at the edge of the clearing.

Shaking, Phil peered cautiously out of the tent opening.

Griff came hurtling out of darkness beyond the tree line as if fired from a cannon, machete raised high and howling in an inhuman, blood-freezing shriek. His eyes were locked on Phil.

He knew he was too tired to run anymore. His only hope was to fight.

Phil burst out of the tent and grabbed the first thing that came to hand that he could use as a weapon; a piece of firewood from the pile Sam had collected earlier that evening, thick as his wrist and a foot in length. How much good it would do him against his insane, machete wielding friend, Phil didn't know, but he didn't think it would be all that much.

Griff ran at him, screaming like a banshee, and swung the machete at Phil's head. More out of paralysing fear than as an evasive manoeuvre, Phil fell backwards, feeling the blood-stained blade part the air inches above his head. He landed on his rump and instinctively swung the short log at Griff's knees. The thick piece of wood connected, and Griff staggered to the side with a grunt. Phil scrambled to his feet and backed off, holding the cord of wood before him like a short sword, staying out of the reach of Griff's far more formidable weapon which he swung back and forth casually.

Griff advanced on him as he chopped at the air with the machete, grinning and shaking his head.

'What you thinking, Phil? You going to kill me with that wee log? Bash my head in? Thought we were mates, you and me? Come one, buddy, give me some random maths question.'

'What the fuck's going on, Griff?' Phil asked in desperation, hoping he could talk to his friend and make him snap out of this madness.

'You wouldn't understand it if I told you, mate. You didn't take the trip.'

'Griff your head's fried, man! Cairnsey's dead. You get that? He's dead,' Phil shouted.

Griff just laughed.

'Of course he is. I took his fuckin' head off with this,' he held up the machete, still advancing towards Phil. 'Don't look so upset though, mate. He was already dead by that time. I didn't actually *kill* him. He was already ... *hungry* when he died. After that he was just food, like you are now. Me and Sam, we ate a good bit of his leg before we heard you in the cave. You know how good it tastes, Phil? Raw, hot flesh? This is no bad trip, mate. This is *real*.'

Phil kept backing off, shaking his head in denial, tears streamed down his face and he was sobbing like a frightened child.

Griff laughed again.

'How'd you like it when he spoke to you, Phil? Eh? Cairnsey's bloody, smiling head? Bet you've been trying not to think about that, eh? Could drive you mad, a thing like that. Thinking about it, and *thinking* about it, and *thinking* about it. Your mate's severed head. *Talking*. In the Devil's name, Phil.'

With impossible speed, Griff suddenly sprang forward again with a guttural growl and slashed at Phil with the machete. This time Phil couldn't evade the blow, and a terrible pain flared as the blade sliced into his upper left arm, biting deep and breaking the bone beneath. Griff's head snapped forward like a striking snake, his mouth fastened on the wound and Phil felt teeth madly gnawing at his flesh. He screamed, and finding strength in his pain and terror, somehow managed to bring the short log around in a short arc with his right hand, striking Griff on the side of the head. The impact was enough to dislodge Griff's teeth from his arm, and Phil's flesh tore as his friend's jaws were ripped free, blood leaping from the deep, mangled wound. Snarling like a beast, Griff raised the machete high over his head, about to bring it sweeping down on Phil's scalp. Still screaming, Phil brought the short log up in a quick movement, catching his friend square on the chin. Griff stumbled backward, tripped on a tent rope and went down, losing his grip on the machete. Like an animal, he was instantly on his feet again and groping for the weapon, but Phil closed in and swung the cord of wood with all the strength he could muster, this time crashing it hard into Griff's temple and sending him sprawling senseless in the grass.

Phil dropped the log and in a daze walked over to the machete lying on the ground. His left arm was numb now, and blood poured in a steady stream from the deep, ragged gash just above his elbow. His vision was starting to go grey at the edges and he was aware he would lose consciousness soon. He bent down and grasped the handle of the machete with his right hand.

As he straightened up, he heard running footsteps and an animalistic snarl close behind him. Without conscious thought, with the very last reserves of his fading strength, half mad and howling himself, Phil spun towards the sound, blindly bringing the machete round in a backhanded swipe.

There was a sudden impact that Phil felt all the way up to his shoulder as the foot long blade bit deep into something, and the snarling and footsteps abruptly ceased.

Phil turned round and saw Sam, naked and caked with dried blood, drop to his knees then keel over in the grass, the blade of the machete half buried in the side of his head just above his right ear. He was grinning.

There is only so much a mind can take, and as Phil watched his best friend's body slump to the ground and lay still as stone, something in his brain shut down. His eyes glazed over and an unnatural calm seemed to wash over him. He was partly aware then of a cold feeling creeping through his bones, and his dislocated mind recognised this was an effect of shock mingled with blood loss. On autopilot, his vision coming from the end of a long grey tunnel, he walked on brittle legs back over to the tent, crawled wearily inside and found Cairnsey's mobile lying on the groundsheet.

'Hello? Hello? Phil? Phil, can you hear me?'

His dad. Hysterical.

'Hi dad,' he said in a faraway tone. 'How you doing?'

'Phil, thank God! Are you okay? What the fuck's happening there? I heard shouting. Are you okay?'

'I've killed Sam dad he was my best friend and he was going to eat me, and I killed him with a machete I think maybe I've killed Griff as well they turned into cannibals dad and they killed Cairnsey and cut his head off and ate his leg and they threw it at me and then he spoke to me and then they chased me and now I'm cut in the arm and there's lots of blood and I think maybe I'm going to die here dad and I'm scared ...'

'Calm down, Phil, you're okay. I'm on my way and I've phoned the police and an ambulance. Now listen to me, are you badly hurt?'

'I'm cut in the arm dad, Griff tried to eat me and I can't see very well and there's lots of blood and I'm cold and I'm scared ...'

'Phil, Phil, Listen to me. You need to find something to put on the cut, a jumper, anything and press hard on it. Take your belt off and fasten it tight above the wound. Lie down and raise your legs above your body...'

'... I love you dad ...'

'Phil, *PHIL!* Stay on the line, please son, don't go. Listen to me. I'm coming for you. Just lie down and ...'

'They ate him dad ... in the devil's name ... and I'm sleepy now ...'

'No, stay with me, son, please try and stay awake, it's

okay ...'

'He spoke to me ... afta they cut his head off ... how'd tha' happn'...'

The tunnel in his eyes was getting longer every second and now he couldn't speak anymore. So tired.

Just before he faded away he could hear sirens in the distance and his father crying on the phone.

The mobile slipped from Phil's lifeless fingers.

PART II

And I will cause them to eat the flesh of their sons and the flesh of their daughters, and they shall eat every one the flesh of his friend in the siege and straitness, wherewith their enemies, and they that seek their lives, shall straiten them.

Jeremiah 19:9

King James Bible

1

When Phil woke up, he was in a hospital bed.

As before, he hoped upon waking that it had all been a nightmare. Then again, the terrible reality of the situation became apparent.

His dad was sitting at the bedside. The drugs they'd given him made Phil's mind feel like a damp sponge, but not so much that he couldn't remember what had happened. If it hadn't been for the sluggish way in which his brain was working, he might have started screaming at the memory. As it was though, all he could only close his eyes and moan a bit.

'Phil?' his dad was saying. 'It's okay, you're safe now. It's over.'

Phil cried for a bit then. Two of his best friends were dead, and for all he knew, so was Griff. He'd really hit him hard with that log. He'd killed Sam. His closest friend since they were five years old.

His dad didn't say anything for a while. He just sat there holding Phil's hand and letting him cry. After a while, Phil stopped.

'Is Griff alive?' he asked, and noticed the strange look that passed over his father's face.

'Yeah, he's ... alive.' His dad replied, although in a hesitant way that hinted that he wasn't actually sure of the answer himself.

'What is it?' Phil asked.

'Don't worry about it right now, son. Just relax and enjoy all these free drugs they're pumping into you.'

'I need to know, dad. Please, tell me. Where's Griff?'

His dad's weak smile slipped off his face and he sighed.

'They've arrested him. Phil, you need to rest, son.'

It was obvious he was holding something back. Something important. 'I need to know, dad,' Phil repeated.

Kyle Densmore sighed heavily, shaking his head. 'When we found you,' he said falteringly, 'Griff was there. He was … at Sam.'

Phil was confused for a second, his heavily sedated mind struggling to comprehend his father's meaning.

'*At* Sam?'

Then Phil saw the horror in his father's haunted eyes. A look he could identify with, and he understood.

'He was eating him, wasn't he?'

His dad just turned his head away.

'Get some sleep, son,' he said after a moment, stroking Phil's brow. 'You're going to need your strength.'

Phil drifted away again.

*

When he next awoke, surfacing slowly from a strange dream where dark things clawed and bit far below the earth, his dad was still there, this time accompanied by a policeman.

His head was still foggy, and he had no perception of time. As far as Phil knew, he could have been lying in that hospital bed for weeks.

'What day is it?' he asked.

'It's Sunday, Phil,' his dad said. They'd gone camping on the Friday night, Phil remembered. It had only happened two days before. 'How are you feeling?' his dad asked.

Phil let out a brittle, jagged sounding laugh. 'Wonderful.'

He looked up at the copper standing over the bed. It was Sergeant Stephen Grace, well known long time resident and top cop in the bustling metropolis of Ballantrae. He was a big man, solidly built, with short cropped iron grey hair and a fearsome craggy face that made you think of Clint Eastwood when he's pissed off. He had kind eyes though at that moment, and wore a sympathetic expression. Then a nasty realisation hit Phil like a light slap in the face, softened only by the potent cocktail of antibiotics, tranquillizers and painkillers in his system. He'd killed Sam. Was he about to be arrested for murder?

Sergeant Grace seemed to understand his concern though. 'Just want to let you know, Phil, that there's nothing to worry about. Your friend Dean has told us everything that happened. He's signed a full confession. There'll be no charges pressed against you for the killings. As for the drugs we found at the campsite, we'll need to speak to you about that in time. I know you've been through hell, but it's my job just to ask you a few questions later, alright?'

Phil just nodded. *Fine, deal with it later then.*

The big copper awkwardly gave him a pat on the shoulder, nodded to his dad, and retreated from the room.

After a while, Phil slept again, and dreamed of a bright light. There was strength in that light, a way out of the darkness, but there was also madness, and the potential to destroy.

*

A few days later, when the administered drugs had lessened to a degree where Phil could hold up his end of a conversation

100

without nodding off, Sergeant Grace came back, and Phil told him everything he could remember.

Almost everything anyway. He didn't tell him about Cairnsey's severed head talking. Told himself that that hadn't happened, and did his damndest to not even think about it.

Grace listened patiently to it all, never rushing or interrupting, and when Phil was finished, the big copper said he was satisfied with Phil's version of events, and then he filled in the gaping gaps in Phil's memory. Stephen Grace was a lot more blunt about this than his dad had been, for which Phil was grateful. Horrified, but grateful.

After Phil had called his dad from Bennane Head that night, Grace began, his father had phoned the police from his mobile and then jumped in the car. They'd arrived to find Phil unconscious in the tent, lying in a pool of blood.

They'd also found Griff dismembering Sam's body partially eaten body with a machete.

Griff had then attacked the horrified constables, killing one of them before the other cop and Kyle Densmore had managed to overpower and knock him out cold.

'Big Ally, my constable, told me the boy moved so fast he couldn't believe it,' Grace informed Phil, shaking his head. 'Like it was impossible, the way he was just *on* them in a second.'

Phil listened while Grace explained that he'd lost so much blood that his heart had actually stopped for almost a full minute before the paramedics had been able to revive him. Then he'd had to have emergency surgery to save his arm, which apparently he almost lost due to a particularly virulent infection, the severity of which the doctors had never seen before.

They found five bodies in total, Grace told him. Sam they found at the campsite. The remains of Cairnsey, John McCabe, Eddie Jannets and Warren 'Bunny' Kerr were discovered by police with sniffer dogs inside the caves beneath Bennane

Head. That piece of information threw Phil completely. He'd no memory of encountering the trio of junkies that night. Grace went on to say how under interrogation, Griff had calmly related the events of the evening in great detail, confessing to the murders of Constable Sean Hogan and John McCabe, who accompanied by Jannets and Kerr, had attacked the four of them in the cave. Cairnsey, Jannets, McCabe and Kerr had all died in the ensuing violence, Grace said.

Griff, who was now a resident in a high security psychiatric ward in Glasgow, had taken full responsibility, relieving Phil of any involvement, other than as a victim. He'd told the cops that Phil killing Sam was purely self defence, and that he and Sam had chased him through the woods, fully intending to murder and eat their friend the second they found him. With Griff's signed confession, Grace told him, the case was closed. The official verdict was that as a result of a huge overdose of powerful lysergic acid diethylamide, Griff, Sam and Cairnsey had become disassociated with reality and murdered Jannets and his cronies in a deranged hallucinatory state before turning on each other. Just the tragic result of some bad trips gone very, very wrong.

'What about the guy that left the trips? Ozay?' Phil asked. 'If he's selling shit that can do that to people …'

'We checked it out,' Grace said, 'but there's no record of any dealers going by that name, fake or otherwise. We spoke to your dealer Barnsey as well, but he swears blind he's never heard of anyone called Ozay.'

'He's lying,' Phil insisted. 'We all heard him talking and laughing on the phone with Cairnsey after this Ozay guy never showed up.'

'Well that's the thing, Phil,' Grace said. 'We checked your friend's mobile. Barnsey's as well. There's no record of that call on either phone.'

2

It was huge news for a while, how three promising young students fresh out of high school and about to sit their final exams had gone on a murderous spree in a small town in Scotland, killing three local drug addicts, one of their own number and a policeman. SAWNEY BEANE CANNIBAL MURDERS IN AYRSHIRE – 6 DEAD, the headlines screamed with ghoulish glee. MUTILATED REMAINS FOUND IN CAVE OF LEGENDARY KILLER BEANE, and so on. The media wanted to speak to Phil of course, but he never entertained them, and soon something horrible happened somewhere else, and there were new terrible stories to chase. The whole mess died down pretty quickly, and life, as it inevitably does, went on.

Except for Phil.

When he left the hospital, he didn't leave the house for almost two months. Most of that time he spent in his room with a lot of lights on, day and night. He cried a lot, and wet the bed a couple of times, regressed to the mental state of a child, terrified of an open wardrobe in the night. Certain that a hungry skittering something would come sniggering out of the dark and take him.

The first few weeks were the worst. He refused to sleep because of the nightmares, and took a lot of speed just to keep himself awake, but found that amphetamines made him *too* alert. He couldn't stop thinking, and lived in a constant state of paranoia. Anywhere he went in the house, the lights had to be on. And when he did fall asleep out of sheer nervous and physical exhaustion, he'd have fevered dreams that were like postcards from hell. Most of the dreams were centred around the cave at Bennane Head, and though there were countless horrific variations, there was always a recognisable dark shadow that capered and shifted, never in full view but glimpsed only peripherally. Always, this presence, this entity, would be on the edge of the nightmare, never actively partaking but overseeing the bloody mayhem that ensued in Phil's mind every night for dark uncounted weeks.

In between the bouts of nightmares and waking paranoia however, he would occasionally have the dream of the strange light that he'd first experienced in the hospital. Always there was the same reassuring, yet dangerous feeling of power that seemed to come off this disembodied, whispering glow like waves on an oscilloscope. Though he didn't understand it, it gave Phil a little island of peace when all around him was a typhoon-battered ocean of darkness where unspeakable things swam.

Then in August, three months after it had all happened, he got a letter from Griff. The letter was short, only a few sentences.

Alright mate,

How's life going back home? Did you pass the exams ok? Guess I won't be going to uni as planned though, eh? Haha!

I'd like to see you, Phil. I know you must be pretty wound up about what happened, but maybe if you come and see me, I can shed a little light.

Come soon, bud.

Griff.

He knew he had to go.

The whole thing just didn't make sense. They'd taken acid plenty of times in similar circumstances; camping out in the woods or in a field outside of town, so it wasn't like Griff, Sam and Cairnsey had been new to the experience and had lost their minds. Phil remembered Sam and Griff chasing him through the forest that night. They'd been focused and single-minded in their hunt, and he knew anyone who's ever had a strong dose of acid will tell you it's near impossible to concentrate on anything for more than a minute or so once the trips kick in. Point was, it was hard for Phil to believe his friends had simply wigged out and suddenly turned to eating raw human flesh as the result of a bad trip.

He figured Griff, completely nuts as he now apparently was, might have some answers. Back at Bennane Head, when they'd fought at the campsite, he'd told Phil he wasn't tripping, yet he remembered in the caves, before he passed out, how the three of them had been falling about laughing, going on about the candle flame looking like a dancer and how weird the surface of the cave wall had felt. *That* was classic trippy behaviour. There were too many questions Phil didn't know the answers to, and he needed closure before he could move on with his life, such as it now was.

Another thing was, he missed Griff.

Strange as it was, seeing as he'd tried to kill him, but mates are mates, and since that night when Phil's world had turned upside down, he'd been without the boys he'd grown up with. The boys he'd shared so much with and who'd helped to shape the person he was, just as Phil had with them. He needed a connection to the life he'd known before Bennane Head, and besides, he felt bad that he'd been too fucked up to go and visit Griff already. Mates are mates.

3

A few days later, Phil found himself at the highly secure private mental hospital on the outskirts of Glasgow which was Griff's new home. He was checked in at reception, had his picture taken and was given a plastic visitor's badge with his photograph on it which he clipped to his shirt. A pretty female nurse came and collected him from the foyer, then led him through a baffling maze of clean, antiseptic smelling beige-coloured corridors and down a few flights of stairs to a small visiting room where his friend was waiting for him.

Griff looked pretty much the same. His hair was a bit longer, he'd lost a bit of weight, and there seemed to be a new firmness around his jaw. Other than that he was just Dean Griffiths, heir to the Earldom of Ayrshire and all round clever clogs. Phil's pal.

Griff was dressed in plain white pyjamas, and could have been a regular hospital patient except for the heavy duty glass partition that ran the width of the small room, separating him and Phil, and the fact that he was securely strapped into a wheeled restraint chair. Thick plastic belts in metal housings ran across his forehead, shoulders, lap, wrists and ankles, binding him tightly to the heavily padded seat. Despite the impressive array of restraints, a hulking orderly stood against the wall behind Griff, keeping a close eye on him. For some reason, the big guy looked extremely nervous.

'I got your letter,' Phil said as he sat down.

'Good show,' Griff responded jovially from his side of the safety partition. 'Normally, I wouldn't be allowed visitors, but some of the guys in here are alright, especially when my dad slips them a few extra grand. This one here,' he said, rolling his eyes backward in the direction of the orderly who stood guard, 'he's a bit of a prick though. Aren't you, ya big fanny?'

The orderly flinched, but didn't respond.

'How's your arm?' Griff asked.

'Better now. I've got a peach of a scar.'

This was surreal. It was like nothing had happened, Phil thought. They were just two mates, shooting the breeze.

'So what's your plan then? You still going to uni?' Griff asked.

Phil shook his head.

'I don't know. Things are a bit different now, Griff.'

He smiled, revealing teeth that looked too big for his mouth.

'Mate, you've no idea. None whatsoever, my man.'

'Enlighten me then, Griff,' Phil said, leaning forward. 'What the fuck happened down there in the caves? Is your head just screwed up now? Or is that a daft question? Here you are, locked up in a nuthouse for the rest of your days. You tried to kill me, ya dick!'

Griff just grinned. His teeth were *definitely* too big.

'But you're still alive, aren't you?' he said quietly. 'Depending on your point of view, this is either a good thing or a bad thing.'

'How could me being alive be a bad thing?' Phil asked.

'Because this isn't over until you, and a fuckload of other people, are dead,' he replied.

The hairs stirred up on Phil's arms and the back of his neck as Griff continued staring at him and grinning, obviously intentionally displaying his unnaturally large teeth. He began to draw in long breaths through his nose. Phil shuddered, remembering that night when he'd been hiding beneath the uprooted tree in the woods with Griff outside, naked and covered in blood. Hunting him. Sampling the night air with those long inhalations like a perfumer analysing a fine cologne.

'Ah, there it is,' he whispered. 'Even through this glass. Have you just shat yourself, Phil? Because I can smell how fucking scared you are.'

'You're not Hannibal Lecter, Griff, so give it a fuckin' rest,' Phil said, trying to inject a dismissive tone into his voice, even though his skin was crawling and he was thinking that Griff was *very much* like Hannibal Lecter, what with the multiple restraints and penchant for consuming human flesh. 'What happened in the caves?' he asked again, trying to take control of the conversation, such as it was.

For the first time, Griff's grin faded and he looked at Phil seriously.

'We *changed*, Phil,' he said.

*

'*Cairnsey stop it! It's the fuckin' trips, man,*' a voice shouted.

On the beach outside the entrance to the caves, Eddie Jannets, Bunny Kerr and John McCabe hesitated. More cries and sounds of a struggle could be heard from within the dark opening in the cliff face.

'*Get a grip, mate. These trips are fuckin' with our heads big time. We need to get Phil up and get out of here, alright?*' the voice yelled.

Jannets smiled ghoulishly. 'Perfect. They're all fucked,' he said, drawing the machete from his jacket.

The shouts from inside the caves quickly turned into strange cries that increased in pitch till they were shrill, horrible screams that made Bunny take a step back, his nutsack shrivelling.

108

'What the fuck's goin' on in there?' he asked nervously.

'Who gives a shit?' Jannets hissed. 'This'll be easy. Let's go.' And he strode forward into the darkness.

Bunny and McCabe exchanged a doubtful look and remained where they were.

'Get your fuckin' arses in here or I'll be takin' this steel to you cunts as well,' Jannets' voice came out of the tunnel, menacing and full of bloody promise.

They followed him inside the cave tunnel, Bunny trying to blank out the terrible wails that were emanating from somewhere deeper in the darkness ahead.

The scene that greeted them in the candlelit chamber at the end of the tunnel froze them in confusion. One guy was lying motionless on the floor, looking like he was asleep, but the other three were rolling around on the ground, clutching their faces and stomachs and screaming those horrible screams, and among them Bunny recognised Cairns, the one Jannets had come for.

'What the fuck …' Bunny gasped, and abruptly, the screams stopped as if someone had lifted the needle from a record.

For a moment, there was complete stillness as the three guys on the floor regarded the newcomers with a strange expression, then Jannets let out a roar and rushed at Cairns, the machete held high. Cairns grinned and charged towards him, seemingly eager for the fight. It all happened so fast, Bunny couldn't even move at first.

Cairns seemed to fucking *fly* off the floor, and at the same time, another one of the younger guys sprang at McCabe, who was standing just in front of Bunny.

He saw Cairns grab the hand that Jannets held the machete with, and somehow twist his arm in a movement so fast it barely registered, but there was an audible *snap* as the wrist gave way, and the machete clattered to the stone floor. Even as Jannets drew in breath to scream, Cairns had the machete in his own hand, and in a blur of motion, swept it across his throat …

*

'You should have seen it, Phil,' Griff said. 'It was as if Cairnsey just *unzipped* that cunt's neck. Like he was opening a beanbag … it was beautiful. They were *there* for Cairnsey as well. Guess Jannets wanted some payback for the kicking Cairnsey gave him and brought McCabe and Kerr along with him. Funny how it all turned out.'

Phil could only sit there in shocked, rapt silence as Griff gleefully described the slaughter in vivid detail.

*

Bunny stood frozen in horrified shock as Cairns hacked again at Jannets even as he was falling to the ground, the machete biting deep into his neck, the blood just fucking *hosing* out of him. McCabe was on the ground with the other guy who'd jumped at him, struggling in a tangle of limbs and flailing fists. The third guy was still crouched on the ground, close to the unconscious boy lying on the floor, watching with a weird expression like he wasn't sure what to do.

Then Cairns abandoned his attack on Jannets, who was now without question dead, and joined the melee on the floor, grabbing McCabe's head and pulling back, then unbelievably, sinking his teeth into his neck while the other guy was gouging at his eyes, thumbs plunging knuckle deep. McCabe let out a piercing shriek of pain and terror, which finally broke Bunny's paralysis. A weird, warbling scream rising from his throat, Bunny Kerr ran over to Jannets' lifeless body and pulled the machete from his neck, then turned back to where Cairns and his mate were now tearing at McCabe's stomach with their teeth as he kicked and squealed in panic.

Bunny brought the machete down hard, burying the blade in the back of Cairns' head.

*

'So you see, I told you the truth,' Griff said. 'I *didn't* kill Cairnsey. Bunny Kerr did. I was busy trying to kill McCabe. That's when Sam finally left you. He was still protecting you while all this was going on. But there was so much blood, mate. So *much*. And that's when *he* finally got hungry.'

*

As Bunny struggled to free the machete blade from Cairns' head, the other guy attacking McCabe was now sitting on his chest, smashing his head against the ground. The dull knocking noise of McCabe's cracking skull on the stone was sickening. Bunny gave up trying to free the weapon from Cairns' split cranium, and kicked out desperately at McCabe's attacker, catching the boy on the cheek and knocking him off to the side. Then there was a growl from behind him, and Bunny only managed to half turn around before he felt a terrible ripping pain in his side. He managed to turn all the way around, and the third guy, who'd been crouched in the corner by the one who was apparently sleeping, now stood in front of him, smiling. Bunny screamed as his attacker twisted the knife in his ribs then savagely pushed it sideways, opening up his belly from the side just above his left hip, slicing through to his navel. The guy withdrew the knife and stepped back, a thoughtful, appreciative look on his face, like he was admiring a painting or a sunset.

111

Bunny looked down and saw his intestines bulge out from the dark opening in his gut. A warm flood of blood poured down his lower body, pooling around his feet. His legs gave out under him, and he sank to the ground, a low moan escaping his lips. His head rolled limply to the side. He saw the guy who'd been smashing McCabe's head on the ground now had his head buried in his mate's stomach cavity. The grunting, tearing, chewing sounds reminded Bunny of a nature programme showing a lion at a kill.

The last thing he saw was the blade of a knife rushing at his eye.

There was pain he hadn't imagined possible, then he felt no more.

*

'After Sam put the blade into Kerr's eye,' Griff said, 'we dragged the four bodies back into the other chamber and hacked them up with Jannets' machete. Then we started chowing down. After a while, we heard you back in the killing floor and chased you through the woods, but you already know that part, right? After you knocked me out back at the campsite, which I must say, I'm a bit miffed about, I woke up, found Sam dead, and thought that you were too from all the blood you were lying in.'

'I got to work on Sam with the machete so I wouldn't have to carry his body in one piece back down to the caves – you've no idea how heavy a dead body is, Phil – then the cops showed up as I was taking a sneaky wee nibble.' He let out a chuckle at this point. 'That cop I killed didn't know what hit him. I was on him before they knew what was happening. Split his head down the middle like I was chopping wood, mate. Then the other one brained me with his baton and I was out for the count. And now ... here we are.'

He shifted slightly in his restraint chair, as much as the

112

tightly fastened straps would allow, and went on. 'See, what you have to understand here is that I'm not the same anymore, Phil,' he said. 'I'm still me, but I'm barely human these days. If I see meat, I'll eat it if I can, and I'm not talking about spare ribs or sirloins. There's a doctor in here with a couple of fingers missing because he was careless. But I'm not crazy, and this isn't because of the trips. Have you noticed my teeth, Phil?' he asked. "Course you have. The doctors here can't explain that. They also can't explain why all the fuckin' antipsychotics they've been pumping into me aren't working. They keep trying though, bless them. They've tried Clozapine, Risperidone, Olanzapine, about ten other kinds, and a bunch of other un-trialled shit that's not even legal yet. They keep increasing the doses as well. Anyone else on the planet would be a drooling zombie with the amount of drugs they've injected me with, but me? Not so much as a yawn, and they're totally freaking out! It's funny watching their faces when I suggest another type of drug. I'll be telling them "Bring on the Bifeprunox!" or "Gimme a billion cc's of Vabicaserin, stat!" It's a gas fucking with them.' He chuckled to himself again, evidently enjoying himself immensely. 'They can't explain why there wasn't a trace of LSD in my system when they tested me either,' he continued, then gave Phil an expectant look like he was waiting for a reaction to a punchline.

'But the three of you were tripping out your box,' Phil said, not understanding. 'I *watched* yous take those trips.'

'Don't be fucking dense, Phil,' Griff said. 'You never heard of a placebo? None of this has anything to do with acid. It was all about us, the time and the place.'

Phil was aware his mouth was moving, opening and closing like a fish, trying and failing to find words. What the hell was Griff talking about?

'Of course, they won't *tell* anyone any of this stuff,' his friend went on blithely before Phil could ask one of the many questions popping up in his brain. 'My old man, prick that he is, is pumping serious amounts of dough into the pockets of the guys that run this place, but aside from that, they're fucking embarrassed! Can you believe it? All those years spent in medical school, and they're completely clueless when it comes to yours truly. I'm a medical marvel, dude.' Griff laughed again. Phil noticed the orderly standing watch was visibly trembling, looking at Griff with terrified eyes.

'The best bit though,' Griff said, dropping his voice to a conspiratorial whisper, 'is still to come. Very soon, they'll come to my room to try out some new drug … and I'll be offski. Gone. Vanished into thin air.'

'Is that right?' Phil asked, trying again to put a condescending tone of sarcasm into his voice, but failing badly. The words squeaked out, and he knew he sounded every bit as scared as he really was. As outlandish as Griff's claim of impending escape was, Phil believed him.

'You're damn skippy that's right, mate,' Griff said with complete self assurance. 'I'm coming home, and I'm going to treat the place like an all you can eat buffet. I'm going to kill and eat the *fuck* out of a whole lot of people, including you. Then it'll be over. Only then.'

Phil was momentarily stuck. How do you respond to *that?*

'Why?' was all he could manage.

He just laughed.

'Unpaid debts, Phil. Us, the time and the place. It wasn't random.'

'Not random?' Phil said, baffled.

'It was *meant* to be us, mate. Things got a little screwed up with Jannets, Bunny Kerr and John McCabe turning up like they did, but it was *meant* to be us. You'll see that in time. Or maybe you won't. Maybe I'll find you and rip your throat out with my teeth before you even get the faintest idea of what's going on.'

Phil could only sit there shaking his head, at a complete loss. Griff was still smiling, purposefully showing off those big white overgrown teeth.

All the better to eat you with, my dear, Phil thought, and immediately wished he hadn't.

They sat in silence for a moment, just staring at each other through the thick partition glass. Then his smile faded, and Griff started slowly gnashing his too-large teeth together in very deliberate, evenly spaced intervals. The hard, sharp noise of it was very loud coming through the small speaker on Phil's side of the glass, and he couldn't help but flinch at each bite.

Snap

Snap

Snap

Snap

He realised Griff was doing it in time with the ticking of the clock on the wall behind him. He was counting off seconds.

Then his eyes changed. Like two expanding ink stains, his pupils abruptly spread outward in widening fluid circles, covering the irises and the whites until Griff's eyes were dead black, shark-like orbs.

Snap

Snap

Snap

Snap went his teeth.

With an inarticulate noise of shock, Phil bolted up from his seat and backed away from the glass, gasping for air in big panicky gulps.

What he'd just witnessed was impossible.

He turned and put his hand on the door handle, badly frightened and wanting to be as far away as possible from this thing that his friend had somehow become.

'Thanks for coming, Phil,' Griff softly called out behind him. 'And say hello to your brother for me.'

As he left the visiting room, Phil heard Griff start to rhythmically gnash his jaws together again, biting off the seconds.

Until what, he didn't want to know.

Snap

Snap

Snap

Snap

4

Phil strode through the reception area towards the exit, nerves jangling, itching to be away from the place, and a voice called out behind him. He turned and saw a tall, well groomed man in a white medical smock walking towards him, nervous anxiety written all over his face.

'Mr Densmore,' he said extending a manicured hand. 'I'm Steve Hetherington, the doctor in charge of your friend's case.'

Phil just stared at him. The doctor withdrew his hand awkwardly when he didn't reciprocate the gesture.

'I understand you may be a little confused by your friend's behaviour,' Hetherington said. 'He's a very sick young man, and we're doing all we can to help him.'

'His teeth,' Phil said numbly. 'His eyes …'

'Side effects of the medication he's on,' Hetherington said brusquely. 'The drugs can sometimes cause receding of the gums, making it appear that his teeth are somewhat oversized, and it's not uncommon for the pigmentation of the irises to appear altered. Again, these are merely side effects of …'

'You're a lying bastard,' Phil said simply. 'How much is Des Griffiths paying you to keep all this wrapped up? I know what I saw, and I've known Dean Griffiths for years. Don't tell me …'

'I can assure you that that is *not* the case,' Hetherington blustered, too quickly, 'and frankly, I'm offended that you would accuse me of negligence and bribe taking. These are serious allegations, Mr Densmore.'

He was trying to come off as indignant and intimidating, but the naked lie in his eyes was as visible as the black hunger in Griff's had been.

'He says he's going to escape soon,' Phil said, more to himself than the officious doctor.

Hetherington shook his head. 'I can guarantee you that that is impossible, Mr Densmore. He is being kept under twenty-four-hour surveillance and the security here is ...'

'Good luck, doctor,' Phil said, and left.

*

On the long return journey back down the coast, for which Phil had to take two buses and two trains, he couldn't get the sound of Griff's clashing jaws, or the image of his dead, black eyes, out of his head. He tried to tell himself he'd imagined it; that it was just post traumatic stress, and that Hetherington had been telling the truth about side effects of the medication. These internal arguments weren't very convincing, however, and had the ring of desperation to them.

When he got home some hours later, Phil went straight upstairs to him room and called their former drug dealer.

He'd only met Barnsey on the occasions when he'd come to drop off some gear at Cairnsey's house. Mostly Phil tried to steer clear of the guy. He was a dodgy cunt, as Sam had been fond of saying. He needed to speak to him now though. Barnsey answered on the second ring.

'Barnsey. It's Phil Densmore here. Cairnsey's pal?'
'Phil,' he said. 'Don't know if I should be talking to you. The fucking pigs pulled me a while back asking questions.'

'Don't worry about that,' Phil reassured him. 'You didn't get done did you?'

'Naw, man, but that's not the fucking point. Point is one

of you gave him my name. What the fuck's that all about? I didn't even know what the fuck they were talking about when they spoke to me.'

'How'd you mean?' Phil asked him, getting confused. 'They wanted to know about Ozay. That's why I'm phoning you. Who the fuck is this guy?'

'Listen Phil,' Barnsey said. 'I don't know who you're getting your gear off these days, but it must be good. Like I told the pigs, I don't know any cunt called Ozay.'

'Barnsey, you don't have to be paranoid,' Phil said. 'No one's listening in on this call if that's what you're worried about. Come on now. Who is this guy?'

'Jesus, I'm no paranoid. I'm telling you, I don't know anyone called Ozay. Never even heard the fucking name.'

Phil started to get scared at that point. Barnsey sounded like he was being serious.

'For fuck's sake, Barnsey, you spoke to Cairnsey about him that night he phoned you from Bennane Head, remember? About how this Ozay left a note on the back of the bench instead of turning up to meet us?'

'Aye, that's the same shit the pigs said to me when they showed up, and I told them like I'm telling you now, Phil; I've not got the faintest fucking idea what you're talking about. I never even spoke to Cairnsey that night. Probably the only time I've ever told the pigs the truth in my life.'

'But ... but I heard you on the phone ... that laugh of yours. We could all hear it coming out of Cairnsey's mobile.'

'Look, Phil. I'm goin' to tell you one last time. I don't know what the fuck you're on about. Cairnsey never called me that night and I've never heard of any cunt called Ozay. I'm sorry about what happened to your mates but get a fuckin' grip, eh?'

'Barnsey, please. This isn't being recorded. The cops aren't

interested in you. They've closed the case. You've got to tell me who this guy is. There's some seriously weird shit going on ...'
Barnsey let out a long exasperated sigh, like he was dealing with a particularly slow witted child.

'Phil, I don't think it *is* being recorded. Here, how's this. I've supplied you and your mates with various illegal drugs over the last three years or so, and I keep at least four ounces of cannabis as well as quantities of cocaine, speed and heroin in my house at all times. I've also got a handgun under my bed. That convince you, Phil? Would I say that shit if I thought this was a set up? Once more. I don't know what the fuck you're talkin' about. Last time I spoke to Cairnsey was when I dropped off that soft black a couple of days before you all finished school. Jesus, check the calls from his mobile for that night if you don't believe me.' With that, Barnsey hung up. Something icy dropped into Phil's guts. Griff had said the same thing about checking Cairnsey's phone. Barnsey didn't know what he was talking about. The cold feeling in his gut seemed to spread outwards, creeping through his veins like expanding ice and setting his skin crawling.

Phil's mobile rang, except not with his usual ringtone, and he felt the blood drain from his face as the softly plucked opening bars of *Hard Time Killing Floor Blues* issued from his phone. He hadn't heard the haunting blues ballad since the night in the caves. Phil looked at the phone's screen to see who was on the line, but it was a private number. With a less than steady finger, he pressed the green button to accept the call.

'Hello?'

'He didn't know what you were talking about, did he?' a familiar voice asked. Griff.

'Who didn't know?' Phil asked, trying to sound calm although every nerve in his body was screaming panic.

Griff laughed down the line at him. A mocking, disdainful snigger.

'Barnsey,' he said. 'He said he didn't speak to Cairnsey that night, didn't he?'

'How did you know …'

'I know lots of things, Phil. More than you could imagine.'

'What …' Phil's throat closed up and he could say no more. Griff's voice had started to change halfway through the sentence. It'd became rougher, more guttural. Phil started to get the distinct feeling this wasn't Griff at all. Although the fear that gripped him was icy cold, sweat ran from his temples and down his cheeks.

'Call me back,' the Griff impersonator said, the voice now not much more than a loathsome wet sounding rumble. The line went dead.

Calling that voice back was the last thing Phil wanted to do, but he'd the feeling that things weren't really in his control anymore and had taken on a malevolent life of their own. Phil was merely along for the ride.

His hands had been less than steady before. Now they were flat out shaking, and he had trouble scrolling through his mobile's phonebook to find the number of the hospital where they were holding Griff.

A pleasant sounding woman answered the phone.

'Hello, I need to speak to a patient there. Dean Griffiths.'

'Are you a relative or a friend?' she asked cautiously.

'A friend. I was up visiting him this morning. My name's Phillip Densmore.'

'Please hold, Mr Densmore.'

After a few minutes, a man's voice broke into *The Four Seasons* hold music.

'Mr Densmore? This is Steve Hetherington, your friend's doctor?'

The guy who'd spoken to Phil as he'd left the hospital earlier. The well manicured lying bastard.

'Griff, I mean Dean just called me,' Phil stuttered. 'He asked me to call him back. Can I speak to him please? It's very important.'

The doctor was silent for a few seconds, then said 'Mr Densmore, I'm afraid that's quite impossible.'

'Listen you prick,' Phil said, his patience officially run dry. 'I need to speak to my friend right now, and I don't give a fuck about your security procedures. It's just a simple phone call.'

'No, Mr Densmore, you don't understand,' the doctor said. 'It's impossible that your friend just called you. I'm afraid I have some bad news.'

Right away, he knew.

When Phil didn't reply, Hetherington went on. 'I'm very sorry to have to be the one to tell you this, but Dean Griffiths was found dead in his room this afternoon, not long after your visit. I'm terribly sorry …'

Phil ended the call. The phone dropped from his numb fingers onto the floor.

5

Niall McDowell sat in Steve Hetherington's office. He was still shaking.

The good doctor sat across the wide neatly ordered desk from him, a patient, understanding expression on his smarmy face, a pen in his hand and a writing pad before him.

'Thanks for seeing me, Niall,' Doctor Hetherington said with a friendly smile. 'I just want to say that you don't have anything to worry about. This interview is just standard procedure in the event of a patient's passing.'

Niall nodded, looking down at the desk and not meeting the doctor's gaze.

'You began your shift today at seven am, is that correct?' Hetherington began.

'Yes.'

'And you were assigned to room forty-eight for the duration of your shift?'

'Aye. It was my turn in the Blair Suite.'

'Excuse me? The Blair Suite?'

'That's what we'd been calling room forty-eight, the other orderlies and me. We didn't like working that room. We were scared.'

'I'm afraid I don't understand.'

'Oh, I think you do, doctor.'

'Niall, I must ask you to speak plainly. This is a very serious situation as I'm sure you are aware. Why do you and the other orderlies refer to room forty-eight as the Blair Suite?'

'After Linda Blair.'

'Who?'

'You've never seen *The Exorcist*?'

'Niall, please. We are here to discuss the tragic death of one of our patients. I really don't think this is the time for guessing games and film trivia. It's most inappropriate.'

'Aye, you're right it's inappropriate. Everything about that boy was fuckin' inappropriate.'

'There's no call for foul language, Niall. I understand you're upset about the death of a patient who was under your care …'

'I'm not upset about his death, doctor. I'm fucking glad he's dead. I might just be able to get some sleep for the first time in three months now.'

'Niall, I must warn you that you are treading on dangerous ground here.'

'I don't know, doctor. Seems to me the ground just got a whole lot *less* dangerous. I'm sure Doctor McLellan would agree. You know? The guy who lost two fingers when he was in that room?'

'Doctor McLellan has already signed a waiver freeing this facility of any responsibility for that incident.'

'I'm sure he did. What's a missing digit or two when you've a nice juicy pay off in your back pocket?'

'Niall, can we please get back on course here? I am trying to make this as easy as possible. You were present during the patient's visit this morning, yes?'

'Aye.'

'Did you notice anything unusual about the patient's behaviour during the course of his visit? I fail to see what is so amusing, Niall.'

'I'm sorry for laughing but that's just brilliant. Unusual? Are you fucking kidding me?'

'Niall …'

'Jesus Christ, you were that boy's doctor. You were in charge of his case and you're asking me if there was anything unusual about him?'

'Dean Griffiths was very ill.'

'Tremendous! "Very ill". That's your prognosis, is it? I've worked here for seven years, Doctor Hetherington, and I've seen my share of "very ill" people. Plenty of them. That lad was many things, but ill wasn't one of them. How about fucking *possessed*?'

'Niall, really …'

'If all that was wrong with that boy was a medical condition, why is that all those anti psychotics didn't so much as make him blink? You'd have been better injecting him with holy water. That lad didn't need a doctor, he needed a priest.'

'Niall, please calm down …'

'DON'T TELL ME TO FUCKING CALM DOWN, YOU SMUG CUNT!'

'Niall, may I remind you that you are an employee here, and as such …'

'You can consider me an ex-employee if you like, doctor. I think maybe it's time for a career change. I've been thinking of trying my hand at freelance journalism, know what I mean? I've got a whopper of a story to tell.'

'Mr McDowell, may I remind you that breaching patient confidentiality is a criminal offence? Not to mention the fact that the patient's father would be most displeased. You *are* aware of who Desdemona Griffiths is, aren't you?'

The implication, and the slight tilt of Hetherington's head

and the raising of his eyebrows made Niall pause, and made his righteous bravado falter. Yes, he knew who Desdemona Griffiths was. Since his boy was admitted to the unit, he'd heard plenty about the man, and a lot of what he'd heard hadn't been good. Some of it had been downright scary, in fact. High level corruption. Links to organised crime. According to one of two carefully whispered rumours, crossing Desdemona Griffiths could see you either fired, or disappeared. One of the porters had likened the guy to Keyser Söze, the shadowy criminal mastermind from *The Usual Suspects*. 'Yes,' Niall said warily. 'I know who he is.'

'Very good,' Hetherington said with a curt nod. 'Now that we have that clear, please continue.'

Continuing down his current path now seemed like a very bad idea, and Niall decided to do some quick backtracking with his attitude. 'Doctor, I'm sorry,' he said, suddenly very nervous. 'It's been a really strange morning, and I apologise if I've spoken out of turn. I promise I won't say anything to anyone.'

'That's okay, Niall. As I said, I understand you're upset. This can be a most trying profession.'

'And you won't say anything to Mr Griffiths about what I just said?'

'Of course not, Niall. This conversation is strictly confidential. As is information regarding our patients. Do you know what *I* mean?'

'Yes.'

'Very good. I'm glad we understand each other. Now let's start again. Just tell me what happened after the patient's visit.'

'I took the patient back to his room. He was calm, not as aggressive as he usually was whenever one of the staff came close to him. He wasn't trying to bite or break his restraints. I left him in his room still strapped in the restraint chair and went to the monitoring room.'

'You say he was still secured in the restraint chair when you left him?'

'Yes …'

'Please go on.'

'I went back to the monitoring room and I could see the patient on the screen, still in the chair. He was quiet and relaxed. He was just sitting there, not moving and stayed that way for about half an hour. Then there was some interference on the video feed and I saw him smile, then he started talking.'

'He was addressing you through the camera in his room? I understand he would often taunt the staff.'

'No, he wasn't talking to me this time.'

'I see. He was talking to himself?'

'No.'

'I'm sorry, then who was he talking to?'

'It was like there was someone else in the room with him.'

'There was another member of staff in room forty-eight?'

'No. The camera covers the entire room. There was no one else there.'

'Interesting. He'd never displayed that kind of behaviour before. Can you remember what the patient said?'

'Yes.'

'And what did he say?'

'He said 'It's good to see you at last.' Like he'd been expecting someone.'

'I see. And then what happened?'

'Doctor, my job here … I've got a family …'

'It's alright, Niall. Like I said, this is strictly between us and your job is quite safe. What happened next?'

'The straps on the chair …'

'Yes?'

'They … undid themselves.'

'Excuse me?'

'The restraints came loose.'

'Niall, you know that's impossible. Those chairs are manufactured to the highest standards and every one is checked daily for faults.'

'I know, doctor. I checked the restraints myself at the start of my shift, same as I always do. It wasn't a fault with the chair.'

'Then how do you explain how the straps came undone? Niall, I sincerely hope you're not covering up for someone who went into room forty-eight without authorisation. That *could* mean your job. Those restraints did not come off by themselves. Come now, who went into the room? It could only have been you or another member of staff.'

'I swear on my kid's lives, Doctor Hetherington, I'm not covering up anything. The straps on his chair unfastened themselves like there was someone I couldn't see doing it. I know that sounds crazy but …'

'Niall, I think I've heard enough …'

'No, please, doctor. You have to listen to me. There was something in the room with him. He *spoke* to it.'

'It?'

'Yes, fucking *it*! The boy thanked it for freeing him, then started talking about how he was going to go home and "kill them all."'

'Niall …'

'He got up from the chair, said "let's go", but then he stopped smiling. He said "I can do it alone", then he just started screaming, and his hair ...'

'What about his hair?'

'It all bunched up, like whatever was in the room with him grabbed his hair and lifted him off the ground by it ...'

'Niall, please ...'

'*Watch the fucking tape if you don't believe me!* It's clear as day. That boy was floating three feet clear off the floor, kicking his legs and screaming, then the blood started pishing from his nose, his ears, his mouth, even his eyes. It was like it was squeezing his brain ...'

'Like I said, Niall, he was very sick. I admit I've never seen a psychosis like his, but whatever was wrong with Dean Griffiths caused some sort of catastrophic and fatal internal cranial haemorrhaging. I know it would have been extremely distressing to witness, but you'd been under a lot of strain caring for a particularly disturbed patient. It's not unusual for psychiatric staff to see things that appear to be unnatural.'

'It threw him across the room ...'

'Niall, please, get a hold of yourself. There's no need for tears.'

6

When Phil was a child, about five or six years old, he was, as many children are, afraid of dark places in the midnight bedroom. His recent experiences had brought that fear back to him, and had made him think that maybe we're all a bit smarter about what's real and what's not before our minds are shackled by the reason and intellect of adulthood. Didn't they say that kids and animals have a better awareness and sensitivity of the supernatural?

Ever since that moment in the cave when Cairnsey's severed head had rolled over all bug-eyed and chatty, until the moment Doctor Hetherington informed him of Griff's passing, Phil'd been trying like fuck to rationalise, rationalise. He'd tried to convince himself that that lovely little scene in the cave, and seeing Griff's overgrown teeth and black eyes had simply been the products of post traumatic stress and emotional turmoil. But that just wasn't washing anymore. Denial can be a bitch, but it can also be sanity's saviour.

As his mobile thumped softly onto the carpet of his bedroom, Phil slumped down on his bed, slack jawed and wide eyes shining. At that very moment, he was as close to losing it as he'd been so far. He could actually feel the inside of his head closing in, and an overwhelming tiredness took hold of him in a great soothing flow which he swore he could feel from the very tips of his toes to his prickling, crawling scalp. It seemed like the easiest thing in the world to just let go and forget all these senseless, tiresome problems, to just slip slide away into a warm, safe place far back in the psyche. So that's what he did.

The world went away for a time.

*

When he opened his eyes, Phil was standing on a beach.

It was dusk, and gentle waves rolled lazily up the smooth sand. The evening air was warm and carried the scent of saltwater and wood smoke. Looking across the water, he could see the last sliver of the sun hovering an inch above the hills on the horizon, yet as he looked, that blazing blood red slice of light remained suspended in the sky and didn't sink out of view behind the dark silhouette of the land. Though the turgid waves continued to slide up the shingle and recede back in the eternal dance of the tide, there was no sound. Not even that of his own breath or the blood running in his veins. This was the *un*sound of the frozen void of deep space.

Phil looked left and right. The beach stretched away in a straight line to infinity on either side, without a bay or even the slightest deviation of the land to be seen.

He turned around and there it was.

The cave.

The shadowy opening in the cliff face was right where he knew it would be. Above the high rock façade, which seemed to stretch hundreds of feet into the air, the forest stood in a brooding hush, as if in anticipation of some unknowable and terrible event.

There was not the smallest acceleration of his unheard heartbeat, nor a trickle of nervous perspiration travelling Phil's brow. His palms were dry and his mouth moist. He felt a previously unknown state of calm, like the deepest sleep and sweetest dream. There was no fear, though this surreal experience would under normal circumstances have thrown him back into the arms of panic which he had come to know and fear all too well.

Despite the odd calm, Phil felt strangely ... *crowded* in some way, like he was somehow sharing his skin, mind and soul with other unknowable entities that were the source of his serenity. It was the light he'd dreamed of before. It was peace.

But there was danger here. He knew it the same way he'd known the mouth of the cave would be there when he turned around.

Something stalked in the gloom of the forest above the high cliffs.

There was still the absolute absence of sound, and Phil saw nothing, yet knew some unknown horror roamed those dark regions where no light fell between the trees. He knew it as a shadowy, tremulous vibration in his mind and in the strange awareness of the peculiar others which now seemed to co-exist within his flesh.

The cave beckoned.

Phil walked forward without hesitation.

7

In the living room, Kyle Densmore was in an armchair reading when he heard the soft thump from upstairs.

Phil had come back from visiting Griff a short while beforehand, and had gone straight to his room without a word. Kyle had resisted the urge to go after him, deciding to give the boy a bit of space. God knew he'd been through hell, and visiting his friend who had come so close to killing him would have been tough.

Phil seemed to be getting better these days, though. The kid was a lot tougher than he knew, Kyle reflected, and he'd had to be, and not only during the past few months when his world had been turned on its head. Ever since he'd been born, it'd seemed Phil had had something to overcome. He'd been premature, spending the first few weeks of his life in an incubator and it had been touch and go for a while. Then there was the constant, menacing presence of his brother, culminating in the incident with the golf club, his extended stay in the hospital recovering, and the near break up of his parents' marriage after Kyle had done what he did upon finding Phil, bleeding, burned and twisted from James' administrations with the nine iron and cigarette.

Kyle Densmore was a practical man, level headed and easy going. But on that day when he'd ran upstairs at the sound of Phil's screams and found James standing over the bloody and unconscious ten year old, nine iron raised for another swing, something had not snapped, but fucking *shattered* inside him.

Kyle Densmore had never hit a man in his life, and especially abhorred the idea of using violence against children, but in James, he saw no child. Saw no son. He saw only hate, and that hate fuelled his own rage.

In the aftermath, with Phil lying in a hospital bed, hooked

up to machines, swathed in bandages and plaster and James gone, his anger was spent and he felt only a terrible hollow ache in his chest, although he could not regret what he had done. Knew he would never regret it because he had saved Phil's life. And if he lost one son so the other could live, then so be it.

Rebecca, his wife, had a hard time coping with that horrifying, violent day, and for a while had sought solace milligram by milligram in little brown bottles. This and Phil's lengthy rehabilitation period had put a tremendous strain on the marriage and things had gotten shaky. Hell, had damn near *collapsed* under all the bad feeling, Valium, sleepless nights and crying.

And though time heals, Kyle thought, it also erodes and leaves scars. Phil could tell you a lot about that.

Kyle and Rebecca had met in Oban where they'd both lived at the time. They'd moved to Ballantrae when Rebecca, already pregnant with their first child, had been offered the job of librarian at the local high school. The proposed salary was far above the normal going rate, and Kyle, a sales liaison for IBM, worked mainly from home. The young couple had moved south to the sleepy coastal village, recently married and excited about striking out in their new lives.

After the incident with James, Rebecca had been worn down by depression and had lost something over the years. She was never purposefully cold, but she had never regained the joy she took from life, which was what had attracted Kyle to her when they'd first met. Something had gone from her eyes, and she carried a faint but constant mantle of melancholy that seemed to weigh down her previously quick and easy smile. Although there was still love between them, Kyle realised that things were never the same after that day. You couldn't suppress maternal instinct.

Rebecca had succumbed to cancer a few years later, finally expiring when Phil was only ten years old. It had happened swiftly and without any prior warning. She was diagnosed after a doctor's visit where she had complained of stomach pain. Four months later, she was gone. Just like that. Rebecca had never smoked a day in her life, and went jogging twice a week, but such factors were trivialities to an uncaring God, Kyle thought bitterly. Once a man strong in his faith, he had turned his back on the church.

In the dark days that followed, depression had set in, and Kyle, who had never been much of a drinker, developed a dangerous taste for single malt. His grief tore at him and even though he knew he had a ten year old son to care for, a boy that he loved dearly, the whisky blunted the sharp teeth of his sorrow.

It was not until a particularly black day a month after Rebecca's funeral that he woke up, but it'd been a close thing.

That morning, after his son had gone to school, Kyle had locked himself in the house with a bottle of Glenmorangie and started drinking. He'd come around some hours later to find himself sitting on the kitchen floor. The whisky bottle lying discarded beside him on the linoleum was empty, his face was wet with tears and he clutched a fistful of his late wife's sleeping pills in one hand and a photograph of Rebecca in the other.

Through his own wretched sobs, he could hear his son's small scared voice calling for him through the letterbox. If he hadn't heard that sound, Kyle Densmore doubted that he'd have seen another day. His son had pulled him back from the brink and they had been fiercely protective of each other ever since.

As he read, Kyle's head jerked up at a strange sound emanating from the upper floor of the house. There was a peculiar *hiss-snapping* noise, which was followed by a weird change of pressure in the air, like hitting an air pocket while flying. This strange atmospheric shift caused the fine hairs on his arms to writhe and a shiver to pass down his spine in a not unpleasant manner.

Kyle Densmore put his book aside and got up from his

chair, heading up the stairs to Phil's room.

He knocked on the bedroom door, but there was no answer. The door was unlocked, and he entered.

Phil wasn't there. The bedroom was empty.

8

Phil entered that dark stony passage into the caves, and although the sense of some nearby malevolent hunger persisted, there was still no fear in his heart. The feeling of another presence in his mind was like a glowing shield which he gave himself to unquestioningly and with complete trust. Still there was not a whisper of sound, and the tunnel walls were lit by the familiar warm glow of candlelight.

Phil could see the chaotic, scrawled graffiti that decorated the sides of the tunnel. The characters and lettering of the tags and mentions seemed to move and slither across the moist walls like snakes, changing their position on the rock. They flowed apart then together, morphing, swirling liquidly around the cave walls before rearranging and forming themselves into crudely drawn facial features.

A raggedly drawn gaping mouth formed, above which a creased nose and slitted eyes appeared. The bizarre portrait, although crudely rendered, was a perfect likeness of Sam. He was screaming. Another face fashioned itself on the wall, and there was Cairnsey's anguished features, like Sam, wailing in tortured stillness. A third well-known face drew itself from jumbled spray painted characters, and there was Griff, the good looks that had caused a flutter in the hearts of many of the girls in school twisted and distorted in pain.

Phil stood there for a second, still unafraid, but feeling a deep melancholy and sense of loss. Somehow he knew that his friends were trapped here, walled up prisoners in the dank and lonely darkness.

Phil felt a single tear escape his eye and slide down his cheek, curving into the corner of his lips. He could taste the salt. His heart ached for his lost friends, and though he'd mourned them already since the incident in this cave, this was a different kind of sadness. In the strange half dreaming state, Phil instinctively knew that they'd not transitioned fully into the arms of death. They haunted this place, yearning for a freedom they were not to have, and Phil could feel their anguish like a splinter in his own heart.

He turned away from the faces of his friends imprisoned in the stone, walked towards the orange glow at the end of the passage, and once again stood at the entrance to the killing floor.

Pools of newly spilled blood decorated the hard rock. Arterial sprays and fans of dark dripping crimson dashed the walls, and wide claret drag marks streaked across the cave floor. The blood was fresh, the hard iron smell and taste of it thick in the air. Phil could see the wavering tongues of candlelight reflected in the pools of tacky wetness.

And there was Cairnsey's severed head again, staring at him from the mouth of the secondary tunnel. His eyes looked sad, and seemed to fill with tears as he looked at Phil with an expression of deep sorrow.

Phil walked over and crouched down before Cairnsey's head, tears spilling down his cheeks.

'I miss you, mate,' Phil said to his friend's severed head. 'I don't know what I'm supposed to do. Everything's so fucked up, and all you guys are gone.'

There was still the void like silence in the air. His mouth didn't move, but Phil heard Cairnsey's familiar voice in his mind.

We're not gone, Phil. We're still here ... and in here. *Me, Griff and Sam. You'll see. You should go now. It's not safe ... It's coming ...*

'What? What's coming, Cairnsey?' Phil asked, pleading.

Go now. You can't be here like this ... or you won't leave.

'I don't understand! Help me, Cairnsey!'

Get the fuck out, Phil. Now!

And then he could feel it. A dark, menacing presence, getting stronger by the second. Phil turned and sprinted from the chamber, bolted through the tunnel and burst out onto the beach, just as perfect sonic stillness in the air broke. It started as a deep rumble, felt as a low vibration in the bones, then slowly rising in pitch and volume to a rushing, howling scream like a fanged hurricane.

*

Phil woke up, sprawled face down in wet sand.

He was on his feet in an instant, alert and taut as an over-wound guitar string. Recent experience had taught him that when you wake up and find yourself in a strange situation, you'd best be ready to move, but it was more than that. He felt an alien, somehow positive *current* buzzing in his bones, so faint it was only noticeable if he deliberately *tried* to feel it, yet it was there on the edge of consciousness. Like the subtlest Ecstasy you ever had.

It occurred to Phil that he wasn't as scared as he should've been under the circumstances. After all, he'd been standing in his bedroom just mere seconds ago, and had apparently involuntarily teleported, inexplicably finding himself on the beach at Bennane Head, a stone's throw away from the dark entrance to the caves.

He spat sand from his mouth and looked around rapidly, taking in the surrounding terrain with a sweeping glance, but seeing nothing threatening. The beach was his alone. The sun was just bidding its final farewell for the day as it sank behind the horizon in the west, and the incoming tide lapped lazily at the shore. The sea's soft music and the plaintive cry of a lone gull were the only sounds to be heard.

Although there was no evident danger to be seen, there was a definite and unsettling air of disquiet on the lonely stretch of sand. In Phil's curiously hypersensitive state, he could sense something discordant and unnatural in the air, and the cold feeling it conjured was strongest when he looked toward the murky cave entrance in the cliff in front of him.

Phil stood there for a moment, clenching and unclenching his fists, all too aware of the rapidly failing daylight. He really didn't want to be on the beach when night claimed dominion, but the only way off the sands was the rugged path that led up the cliffs to the road above, and the bottom of that path lay a mere six feet away from the black maw-like opening in the rock, the very spot from which the sinister aura of wrongness emanated. Summoning all the balls he could muster, Phil took a deep breath and walked briskly forwards, trying not to think about what he was doing.

With every step however, his courage quailed. The buzzing confidence he'd felt seemed to recede within his body until it was a cold hard ball, hiding as if afraid in the pit of his stomach. He forced himself on.

Ten feet away from the cave, sweat had broken out on his forehead, and he could actually feel his knees wobbling, bringing to mind a ludicrous image of Shaggy from the old *Scooby Doo* cartoons. Again, he willed myself forward.

Five feet away from the path, and the sense of hungry malevolence in the air reached a nauseating crescendo. The black opening in the rock wall to Phil's right seemed to writhe, seemed to want to pull him in. He was in no doubt that there was something very old and indescribably evil in there, and was a fraction of a second away from blind panic as he angled himself slightly to the left and stepped onto the path, the cave opening now at his back, just close enough for something to reach out with horrible speed …

On the very verge of losing his nerve and breaking into a wild run, Phil only just managed to keep his pace steady. The dry, sandy path underfoot was uneven and treacherous, and the last thing he wanted was to slip and take a tumble back down to the beach. Halfway up the trail, and the fear drew back a little. With every step away from the cave, the little bright light in Phil's gut began to grow again. His confidence returned, and finally he crested the path, finding himself standing next to the bench where the mystifying Ozay had left the note containing the trips. *Eat, drink and make merry* he'd written. And eaten they had.

He stopped for a second, winded somewhat by the brisk ascent and the after-effects of barely controlled panic. He drew deep breaths and tried to gather his scrambled thoughts.

Get a grip, get a grip. It's all right now ...

Phil stepped out onto the road, and with a terrible crushing suddenness, the sense of some predatory threat bloomed in his chest again like a rancid black flower, and the good and bright awareness within him immediately shrank back as he felt something rushing up the rock face behind him. Phil spun back towards the cliff edge.

He tried to tell himself he really wasn't seeing the ... thing ... that clambered over the edge of the cliff.

It was barely a shape at all. It had no tangible physical form, and was more of a curious bending of dark semi-opaque light that seemed to scuttle back and forth in the air along the cliff top. The feeling of hate, of hunger, and of diabolical need coming from the shape-shifting spectre was such that Phil felt his spirit wither before it. He froze, instantly turned to stone by the crashing wave of rot and despair that polluted the atmosphere around the entity. The very force of the thing's corrupt presence swept Phil up and spirited him away on black wings, and in the awareness of something unknowably ancient and foul, his muscles failed, and he stood there, still and lifeless as a statue in the middle of the road.

That was when the transit van came belting around the tight blind bend, and was upon him, in a heartbeat so close that Phil could see the grime on the radiator grille and notice that the driver had a large, ready to pop zit on his right cheek. He saw the almost comical 'o' of surprise the driver's mouth made as he came round the bend doing forty in his grubby van, only to find someone standing stock still in the middle of the road.

Phil felt the heat from the engine on his body and knew he was dead.

He flinched ... and found himself standing on the other side of the road as the van swept harmlessly by, ruffling his clothing in its slipstream.

For a second or two Phil just stood there, trying to digest what had just happened. He was untouched. Sergeant Grace's words to him in the hospital surfaced in Phil's memory. He remembered that scared look in his eyes.

Big Ally, my constable, told me the boy moved so fast they couldn't believe it. Like it was impossible, the way he was just on them in a second.

He recalled his own encounter with Griff at the campsite. The way he'd moved. That unnatural burst of speed ...

It wasn't as if he had no idea of how he'd apparently moved a distance of approximately seven feet in a microsecond. He knew fine well.

He'd dodged the van, when he *should* have been a crimson smear on the road and bloody chunks of meat on the grimy radiator.

9

Kyle Densmore, standing mystified in his son's empty bedroom, flinched at the sound of breaking glass from downstairs.

'Phil?' he called out, briskly descending the stairs again to the ground floor. 'You in the house?'

More noise from downstairs. The tinkling of glass. A hard thump. Coming from the direction of the kitchen. The rear patio door.

His heart pounding, Kyle ran the length of the entrance hall and pushed open the door to the kitchen. The patio door lay open, a gaping jagged hole in the glass, frosted fragments littering the floor. Kyle stared in shock at the mess, still taking in the scene as a voice spoke up right behind him.

'Alright, dad.'

Kyle spun around and had time to register a gaunt unshaven face with mad eyes beneath a black woollen beanie hat, then the brick the intruder had in his hand slammed into the side of Kyle's head, spilling him to the floor among the glass fragments.

His first born son stood over his inert body, expressionless.

James Densmore calmly set the brick on the kitchen counter, went to the cupboard under the stairs and found his dad's golf clubs just where they'd always been kept. He selected the nine iron then went back into the kitchen. He closed the patio door and drew the curtain across, then turned back to his father, lying semi-conscious on the floor.

'It's been a while, dad,' he said as he stepped forward, hefting the golf club.

10

Phil arrived home at around ten pm that evening. The walk back to town from Bennane Head had taken a few hours, but unsurprisingly, he didn't feel tired. His nerves were still buzzing with adrenaline after the events of earlier in the day and he was anxious to get home. It had occurred to him that if his dad had gone upstairs looking for him, he would find his room empty and would probably freak out, and as Phil didn't have his mobile, which he'd dropped on his bedroom floor some hours previously, moments before finding himself inexplicably lying on sand several miles away, he'd been unable to call home.

His dad's car was parked in front of their semi-detached house, but the windows were dark, which was odd, as Kyle Densmore usually stayed up till at least midnight before retiring for bed.

As he approached the front gate, a feeling of foreboding settled on Phil's shoulders, almost seeming to weigh him down. The new sensitivity he'd picked up kicked in, and he could sense an aura of anticipation in the air. The very atmosphere seemed electrically charged somehow, like before a violent thunderstorm.

Suddenly afraid, he quickly went to the front door and tried the handle. The door was locked. Phil checked his pockets for his keys, but he'd woken up on the beach also without his jacket where he usually kept them. The strange involuntary teleportation that had left him stranded on the sands at Bennane Head was becoming more inconvenient by the minute.

He quickly jogged around the side of the house to the back garden, intending to get the spare key his dad kept under the windowsill of his small garden shed, but then noticed the jagged hole in the patio door.

Phil stopped in his tracks. Someone was moving about in the kitchen. He could hear the crunch and skitter of glass fragments on the laminate floor.

The kitchen light came on, and through the window, the interior of the room was thrown into stark clarity as Phil stood in the darkened back garden. He could see someone in a dark woollen hat and jacket, their back turned to him. Too narrow in the shoulders to be his dad.

From where he was standing, Phil could also make out splashes of red on the white walls. A bloody smeared handprint on the kitchen door like a clumsy kid's finger painting.

He froze.

Regardless of how much blood letting he'd witnessed in the past few months, that one crimson hand print on the pristine white kitchen door horrified Phil in a new and unexpected way.

Without any effort on his part, the world suddenly sped up.

Phil found himself at the patio door, before he even realised he'd started moving. Then he was in the kitchen. The stranger in black turned towards him as he burst in. Without conscious thought, Phil's right arm shot out and caught the intruder in the throat. A hard, perfectly placed jab to the Adam's apple, fingers on one side, thumb on the other.

The tall stranger gasped, took a few steps back and collapsed on the floor, making strangled gagging sounds.

Phil scanned the kitchen. No one else there. Through the kitchen door to the hallway. His dad lying on the floor. Blood. Not coating the walls as he'd feared, but still too much. To his dad's side. He was still breathing. Alive, thank Christ. He managed to speak.

'It's James.'

A flashback to Griff's last words at the psycho ward.

Say hello to your brother for me.

Then Phil had his dad in his arms, and was sprinting up the stairs with him in his arms, like he weighed no more than a toddler, though Kyle Densmore was actually forty-five years old, and weighed sixteen stone, and Phil was a lanky teenager.

In his dad's room, Phil lay him down on the bed. He cried out.

Then the world slowed down to normal speed again.

His dad's eyes were open and alert, though he had a deep cut above his right eye and a sheet of blood decorated that side of his face. There was more blood on his chin and teeth. His left arm seemed to be lying a strange way.

'Can you talk, dad?' Phil asked. 'Are you okay?' A stupid question.

'It's James,' he gasped, grimacing in pain. 'Where is he?'

'In the kitchen. Back in a sec.'

Going back down the stairs, cautiously now, Phil tried to gather his thoughts. A lot had happened in the sixty or so seconds he'd been in the house. He tried to prepare myself for coming face to face with his long lost brother, but it was too much at that moment. He tried to not think at all, and to just trust whatever instinct he had.

Phil pushed open the kitchen door to find James just getting to his feet. James lifted his head at Phil's entrance, and for a moment, the brothers locked eyes. Neither moved for a few seconds.

The last time Phil had looked into those eyes, they'd been black and expressionless, coldly observant while Phil was being briskly tenderised by a Titleist nine iron. Eight years ago. Phil expected hate in his brother's expression. Strangely, he saw instead a bewildered terror.

The same golf club was now lying on the kitchen floor. James started to move towards it, but before he got two steps, Phil was on top of him. A brutal short, stomping kick to the inside of his big brother's right knee, destroying the ligaments holding the bones together. James' leg bent sideways in a horribly unnatural way. He screamed once then fell to the floor again, writhing in agony.

Phil picked up the golf club.

'What the fuck are you doing here?' he said, trying to keep the tremor from his voice.

'Ma fuckin' knee!' James wailed. 'Ya wee prick, you've fucked ma …'

The club came down hard and fast, connecting with James' left kneecap with a savagely satisfying crunch that Phil felt all the way along the shaft of the club and up his forearm. James screamed again, then began to whimper pitifully.

'I'm not asking you again, Jim. What are you doing here?'

He started to sob. His brother was broken. His face had hardened since the last time Phil had seen it. His lips were dry and cracked, and a large scar that looked like a knife wound scrawled across his left cheek. Heavy, dark blue half circles underscored his limpid eyes, which seemed to float uncertainly in his pale, scraggly bearded face.

'I don't know,' James blubbed, snot running from his nose onto his upper lip. 'I had to come. He *made* me.'

Confused, Phil asked 'What're you talking about? Who made you?'

Amazingly, Jim tried to get to his feet again, but his knees were both obliterated and he collapsed back on the floor with a wail.

'Jesus, ma legs! I can't walk. I need to walk, Phil! He's got to be dead. *Is he fuckin' dead?*' James demanded. 'You don't know what he'll do to me if he's not dead. I saw it. Under her coat!'

Phil hesitated, trying to unravel his brother's incoherent terrified babbling. A horrible idea crept into his thoughts.

'Who fuckin' made you come here?' He knew what James was going to say next. He was going to say Griff. Griff had made him come.

The pain cleared from James' eyes for second, only to be replaced with absolute naked fear.

'Someone phoned me this morning. It was mad. Some mad shit, I didn't know if it was real or not. Thought maybe I'd had a nightmare. Phil, I didnae have any choice. He *hurt* me. Fuckin' hurt me over the *phone*. And there was some fuckin' mental shit in the street later when I tried to stop … a wean. That wean's *face* ...' Jim's sobs dissolved into a keening wail of pure anguish. His fists pounded against his head, as if he meant to beat out some horrific, unwanted memory.

'Who phoned you?' Phil asked again. His cold certainty that his brother was going to name Griff as the caller proved to be off the mark, however.

'He said his name was Ozay,' James said.

11

The day that Jim Densmore heard from Ozay started much like any other.

He got up in the late afternoon, that is to say, he *awoke* at two pm. The afternoon sun found a gap in the grey clouds that seemed to perpetually crown the east end of Glasgow, and shone through the undressed living room window of the one bedroom flat he inhabited. He didn't immediately leap from the bare mattress on the floor and start the day with a merry whistle, but rather lazed for a further twenty minutes, one arm thrown over his eyes to block out the sun's glare and trying to think of a good reason to leave the meagre haven of his thin duvet.

He wasn't particularly hungry, so food was one reason to be crossed off the list. He didn't need to piss or have a shite, so no cause there. He wasn't currently employed, there was nothing on TV in the mid afternoon, and he'd no pressing social engagements to attend.

He figured it was safe to say the day could remain unseized for a while yet.

Just as he was considering having a wank to pass the time, the phone rang.

Jim frowned in annoyance. The flat was fucking freezing and the last thing he wanted to do was leave the relative heat of the cheap blanket to have a conversation. He wasn't expecting any phone calls. *Fuck it*, he thought. *They'll hang up eventually.*

The phone kept ringing. Ten times. Twenty. It seemed to be getting louder.

His headache, born of last night's Buckfast session, was ironically another reason to stay in bed, but the need to stop the phone's painful shrieking, which made him wince with every ring, drove him naked from the covers. Cursing, he struggled up from the mattress on the floor, yelping in pain as a splinter of wood from the bare floorboards stabbed into his big toe.

'*Fuckin' pain in the arse cunto bastard ...*' he muttered in fury as he limped to the deafening phone. He angrily snatched the handset off the wall.

'Who the fuck's this?' he demanded.

There was a weird noise on the other end of the line. No one spoke; there was just a constant static that strangely sounded like a vast crowd heard from a distance. Echoing across the unusual background hiss were short bursts of another sound, like someone harshly whispering in a guttural language. The eerie soft noise made Jim's flesh crawl for some reason. There was something about it that was just ... wrong, yet somehow familiar. A very primal and basic part of his mind seemed to recognise the discordant soundscape coming over the line. That part of his consciousness had been expecting this call in a way that Jim's normal thinking could never envisage.

'Hello, Jim,' a voice broke in. Spoken softly, with a strange accent. A guy. 'You need to kill your dad.'

That got Jim's attention.

He went cold in an instant. As if triggered by the sound of the caller's voice, the memories which lived in his daily thoughts played themselves over for the billionth time. The hate. The sheer loathing and contempt he felt for his old man. The day he left home was with him always. He'd been leaving home every day for the past eight years, bloodied and exiled. He remembered it with clarity. He'd just been fucking around with his wee brother, giving him a bit of a fright with the lit fag, and then the golf club. Alright, maybe he'd gone a bit overboard, but he'd had a hangover, and the wee cunt was being a pain in the arse. Suddenly his old man had appeared, and had kicked the living shit out of him, then threw him out the house. He remembered how his dad had physically thrown him onto the front lawn, then taken out his wallet, withdrew a wad of bills and thrown them in his face.

Take that and go. I don't want you here any more.

Jim had lurched back and forth in the small front lawn, seizing up the paper currency and shoving it into his pockets, all the while screaming blood flecked obscenities and curses at his dad, and thinking about how much smack the money could buy.

He'd never seen his family again after that day. One of the screws had pulled him aside one day in the rec room while he was in Barlinnie, and told him that his mum had died. Cancer, he'd said. Jim, who took the news as if he'd been told a stranger had suffered a bee sting, had shrugged and gone back to his game of pool.

But yes, Jim fantasized about killing his dad quite a bit.

Ever since then, every single face that Jim had ever punched, kicked, stuck the head on or slashed had been his father's. Eight years of hateful revenge fantasies, lived out in violence done to others. Even the women he mugged, fucked up as it was, had his father's face, contorted in fear as he held his knife to their throats while going through their pockets for valuables. The shop clerk in that carry out shop he'd held up had had his dad's face. Then the butt of the sawn off shotgun had turned it into pulp. The cunt he stabbed when he was doing time in the 'Linne, the screw that had fucked with him. All of them. His father's hated face.

Strangely though, this time the memories didn't bring with them the usual blind frustrated rage. Instead he felt a peculiar numbness begin to steal over his skin in an almost pleasant tingle.

'Who's this?' he asked into the phone's mouthpiece, slightly detached. His eyelids suddenly felt quite heavy.

'You can call me Ozay, Jim.'

The caller's soft voice seemed to cast a lulling spell on him. He felt like he was almost floating. A weird weightlessness washed over him in waves, numbing his thoughts of everything else. He could no longer feel the pain of the splinter in his toe, nor the cold air on his skin. There was only this voice. This purring, seductive voice. The eerie hiss in the background was still there, as were the short staccato blasts of that other sound. It all combined to lull Jim into a subtle trance. It was like a very, *very* good hit of scag.

'I don't know anyone called Ozay,' he murmured. 'That's a funny name.'

'No, you don't know me, Jim. But I *am* funny. I'm so funny I could have you screaming in seconds. You need to kill your dad.'

Deeper he slipped into the spell the caller cast upon him. His jaw hung stupidly open and a long string of saliva spilled from Jim's lower lip as his eyes glazed over, swinging there and running down his bare chest.

'That's a fine idea,' Jim agreed cordially. A tiny fragment of his mind that was still his own began screaming that this was wrong, all wrong. It was ignored.

'Yessssss,' the caller hissed. 'All wrong, Jim. Wrong that he fucked you over. Wrong that the bastard turned you away, made you just another junkie in the street. Do you know he laughs about what he did to you when he's playing golf with his friends?'

A single tear rolled down Jim's cheek, tracing a salty path through the beard stubble and joining the warm drool on his chest. His bladder let go and warm urine spilled down his thigh, puddling on the floor at his feet. He didn't notice.

'Who ... who are you?' he whimpered like a lost child, suddenly a little frightened. 'What's happening?'

Though Jim's veiled senses couldn't perceive it, the spartanly furnished room grew suddenly gloomier, as if the sun had slipped behind a thunderhead, and the background hiss on the phone seemed to shrink back as if afraid. The voice on the other end of the line changed slightly. Became rougher. The thing spoke again.

'You know who I am, Jim. I'm the *black*. I'm the thing you pretend you don't see from the corner of your eye at night.' The last word was a hoarse, drawn out rasp. *Niiiiiight.*

The pleasant sensation that held him entranced quickly melted away to be replaced with a deep hollow despair, so intense Jim swayed on his feet from its impact. His heart rate accelerated, and a layer of sweat broke out all over his body. An unbidden picture abruptly bloomed in his reeling mind. A surreal image of a barren desert landscape stretching infinitely under a black sky. Hundreds, thousands of bloody scalps littered the ground like some macabre vegetation. Shadowy creatures like huge crows, but with long, bony arms and glowing eyes sat on barbed wire fencing that stretched away to a sick yellow horizon. A tall slim figure in a crimson red cowl stood facing him. A thing with an animal's face. All teeth, black eyes and stretched parchment skin. Jim began to weep.

'I don't like this,' he blubbered, sinking to his knees, blind to all else but the mental vision of eternal desolation which he couldn't shut his eyes to.

The voice sniggered back at him.

'Your kind never does,' it said.

The hellish picture in his mind changed to a black skinned hand with too many fingers and knuckles, squeezing what looked like brain. A brutal, crushing pain suddenly exploded through his head, knocking Jim to the floor. He shrieked in agony, dropping the handset of the phone, but still the voice went on inside his head, changing in pitch to a high yammering chant which was almost deafening.

... rip it out ... grind it up ... cut cut cut ... crush them ... burn twist bite ... bite ... never coming home ... head on a pole ... crack your spine and eat your soul ...

Jim clawed at his head, trying in vain to tear out the thing that was driving him to the brink of madness. His eyes bulged from their sockets in terror as he writhed there, naked and rolling in his own piss on the cold, bare floor with the sound of an asylum ripping at him, dominating his very being.

... Kill the cunt ... little pig ... little fucking junkie nothing ... claws at your window ... teeth at your door ...

And he could hear it. A loud scraping noise coming from the door in the hall accompanied by a *tap-tap-tapping* at the living room window. He felt the presence of something drawing near. A monster.

'I'll do it,' he moaned. 'I'll do it, Jesus, please, I'll do it, just stop ...'

In an instant, the insane cacophony in his head ceased, leaving only a high pitched whine. Nothing at the door or window. Nothing seeking entry. The bare room that he called home brightened again. Gasping for breath, Jim crawled to the handset lying on the floorboards, a rivulet of blood running from his nose.

'I'll do it,' he whispered into the handset.

And the line went dead.

*

The next hour or so was a blur to Jim Densmore.

He vaguely recalled frantically crashing around the flat after the phone call had ended, all bug eyed and shaking, trying to calm down enough to dress himself and leave. It was all he could do to avoid panicking completely and running screaming and naked into the street, and this would have been the case if it hadn't been for the small part of his mind that had somehow been expecting this day for years. That fragment of his consciousness had allowed him to keep it together long enough to hastily put some clothes on and get out of the flat.

He hurriedly made his way into the city centre on foot, heading in the direction of Buchanan bus station while constantly looking back over his shoulder. He stayed in the daylight, shying away from gloomy places between buildings where shadows lay. His insides were still shaking, and his mind kept going back to the phone call and what his apparent course of action now was.

It was nuts, he told himself. *Just a nightmare. Must've been a nightmare.* But his feet kept moving him towards the bus station, as if he was no longer fully in control. Jim made a conscious effort to halt himself and succeeded in slowing his determined pace until he managed to come to a stop. He stood there in the middle of the pavement, eyes closed and trying to control his breathing as other pedestrians gave him strange looks and wide berths. The muscles in his legs still trembled, itching to be flexed in movement, and his feet shuffled restlessly on the concrete, shifting his weight from one to the other like he was in dire need of a pish. The shaking in his thighs and calves seemed to spread upward into his torso and out along his arms till he stood there, shuddering like a hopeless alky in the grip of the DTs. No matter how hard he gritted his teeth, his breathing continued to come fast and shallow till he started to feel dizzy from hyperventilation. A rising panic started to fill him from the belly upward.

Got to move, got to move, got to move ...

Just as he was on the point of breaking, he felt something tugging at his jacket sleeve. He opened his eyes and looked down.

A child stood before him, maybe eight years old. A small girl with long, unkempt blonde hair and huge pale blue eyes, her translucent skin smudged with dirt. She was dressed in a ragged knee length grey woollen overcoat, buttoned to her throat. Her feet were bare.

''Scuse me mister. I'm lost. I can't find my mammy,' the urchin appealed to him.

Jim just stood there voiceless, staring at the kid, the panic within him continuing to rise.

'Can you help me find her? I keep asking people but they can't hear me. Nobody'll talk to me,' she said.

'How come no one can hear you?' Jim heard himself ask. He wasn't aware that he had spoken, thought it impossible. He was a fraction of a second from losing his grip on immobility and breaking into a mad dash.

'They don't hear me,' whimpered the little blonde girl. 'They don't see me.'

Jim started to edge around the child, unable to stand still any longer. The need in him to move was irresistible. He began slowly backing away from her. She followed him.

'Please, mister,' she implored, starting to cry. 'I'm scared. You see me don't you? You can hear me?' Tears started to spill down her pale cheeks, cutting streaks through the imbedded grime.

Jim continued retreating, unable to take his eyes from the strange blonde waif. He nodded.

'Aye, I can see you,' he babbled, 'but I cannae help you, I've got to go. I'm in a hurry.'

The child continued to come towards him, her arms outstretched, reaching for him. Jim cringed away as if she had offered him a tarantula.

'Where are you going to? Can I come with you? Please, mister. No one sees me.' The child blinked, and when she opened her eyes again there were only black orbs like polished eight balls in her optical sockets. She kept coming, and spoke again in a whisper that Jim heard even above the noise of the traffic that passed him by on the busy main road.

'No one sees me, because I'm D. E. A. D.'

Jim's ballsack shrivelled and his arse nearly collapsed as the kid spelled out the word, speaking with all the emotion of a headstone, then started to unbutton her raggedy overcoat. She was still crying softly.

Jim didn't want to see what was under that grimy garment. He tried to close his eyes again, but couldn't. She unfastened the second button.

'They burned me, Jim,' she said. And kept coming.

Still Jim backed away from the blank-eyed child, his mind reeling in terror and his hands held out in front of him as if to placate a dangerous animal. He was vaguely aware of stumbling as he stepped backwards off a kerb.

The little blonde haired girl undid a third button as her face began to blister. Flames suddenly appeared from nowhere and swept across her small body. Jim could smell her burning.

'They burned us all. *Curse* Labhrainne and his blood,' she snarled, her small face contorting abruptly from pitiful weeping into a flaming rictus of hate.

Jim's scream joined the blare of a car horn in a discordant harmony.

'In the *Devil's* name, Densmore,' the blazing kid shrieked at him as she loosened the last coat button and spread the fiery rags.

For the tiniest slice of a second, Jim caught sight of what was below the little girl's coat ... but the world suddenly turned upside down, mercifully sparing him further exposure to the terrible sight, and he found himself observing the grey clouds overhead. Insanely, he thought, *looks like rain,* then there was an impact which spun him again, his vision turning into a confused blur of colours, he bounced off something else and went skidding across the tarmac.

'For *fuck's* sake!' Mark Wickman yelled at the skinny guy lying the gutter. 'You want to watch where the fuck you're goin' ya bam?'

The guy struggled to his feet, and looked around. 'Where'd she go?' he asked.

'Whit?' Mark asked. 'Mate, you just walked backwards into the main road and got hit by my motor.'

'The wee lassie. She was on fire,' the guy murmured, looking around as if unsure where he was.

Jesus, Mark thought. *Another fuckin' space cadet.* Seemed like the city had more of them every day. This guy was obviously off his tits on something. He had that wasted, pale look particular to junkies about him, and his eyes were rolling about in their sockets, but seemed to be amazingly unhurt. Probably fucked on smack and hadn't felt a thing. Fuckin' lucky though. He'd clipped the guy on the hip and the daft cunt had just *backflipped* out of view and bounced off the roof of his taxi. Watching with astonished shock in his wing mirror, Mark had seen the guy landing on the bonnet of a car parked at the side of the road and sliding off the front of the stationary vehicle into the gutter. Now he was just standing there as if he'd merely tripped on his shoelace. Still though, he couldn't just leave him here. He should at least drive him to the A and E at the Royal Infirmary. Losing his license over a hit and run was the last thing he needed.

'Are you alright, pal?' he asked the guy, who was still looking around as if searching for someone. ''Mon I'll take you over the hospital.'

The junky ignored the offer. 'There was somethin' under her coat,' he said softly, and then shivered. 'Where'd she go? She was right *there*,' he insisted, pointing at a spot on the pavement. He pushed past Mark and wandered off, looking around in bewilderment, seemingly in full use of his faculties. His physical faculties anyway. Then he broke into a run and sprinted away, heading in the direction of the bus station.

With no one else standing around having witnessed the accident, Mark shrugged and got back in the taxi with a sad shake of his head.

They said that God looked after drunkards and children, or something like that. The stoned pedestrian who'd performed some impromptu urban gymnastics using his taxi as a piece of apparatus was, he guessed, a drunkard of sorts. After all, sober folk don't walk backwards off the pavement into traffic and see things that aren't there.

A wee lassie on fire, that's what the guy had said. Mark Wickman had seen some weird stuff the first time he'd done acid, watching Led Zeppelin at Knebworth all those years ago, but not a wee lassie on fire. There was certainly no one there now, nor had there been. Children ablaze in a public street usually attract some attention, and Mark had seen no such thing.

*

Later, as Jim sat huddled low in the back row of the bus winding its way south down the west coast of Scotland, he tried to piece together how he'd ended up on the Intercity coach. Everything after being hit by that motor was a blank, and he had no recollection of being in the bus station or buying a ticket. It occurred to him he didn't have any money, so how the fuck had he even got *on* the bus? There was also blood on his t-shirt and more encrusted under his fingernails. Not his own. He was unmarked, apart from a taste of blood in his mouth which he put down to having sustained when the taxi had hit him.

Last thing he remembered was tearing off down the street, now *certain* that he would do as the strange and terrifying caller had bid him that afternoon.

He was on his way to murder his father.

What he had seen beneath the flaming overcoat of the blond haired waif in the street had convinced him of that. Any doubts he'd had were gone. There was no alternative. There never had been.

Jesus Christ, that thing knew my name, he thought in terror, and started to weep quietly, drawing up his legs and rolling into a ball there on the back seat of the southbound coach.

*

Some hours later, the body of an elderly man was found in a toilet cubicle in Buchanan Street bus station. The only thing stolen from the victim was the Intercity ticket to Stranraer that a cashier remembered selling the elderly gentleman when she was later interviewed by the police. The old man's throat had been ripped out. Apparently by someone's teeth.

Police were looking for anyone who may have seen a thin and unshaven young male, described as wearing a black jacket and woollen hat, acting in a strange manner. The suspect had been seen in the area and had also been witnessed following the seventy-year-old man into the toilets.

12

When Jim finished talking, he was very pale. For him, that meant he had the complexion of a sheet of tracing paper.

'Stay where you are,' Phil said to him, and turned to go upstairs to check on his dad.

'He's got to be *dead*, Phil,' Jim shouted after him, stark desperation in his voice. 'You don't fuckin' get it do ye? The cunt's got to be *dead*!' His voice cracked on the last word, degenerating into pitiful sobbing.

Phil ran upstairs, his mind whirling, praying Jim's grim wish was not a reality, and burst into his father's bedroom, suddenly certain that he would nevertheless find him as dead as Jim hoped. His dad lay on the bed, alive, but grimacing in pain and gasping. More blood, frothy with tiny air bubbles, coated his lips and chin and his skin was cold and clammy to the touch.

'Where's Jim?' he asked, his breath hitching and causing him to cough a fine crimson mist.

'He's downstairs, dad. Don't worry, he's not going anywhere. Don't try to speak. I'm phoning an ambulance.'

Phil reached for the phone on his bedside table, and hesitated. Something wasn't right. The air seemed cold, and a nervous tickle in the pit of his gut warned him that something was amiss. Dismissing it for the moment due to his dad's worsening condition, Phil snatched up the handset to call for help and punched in three nines.

The emergency operator picked up promptly, and calmly asked which service he required.

'Ambulance,' Phil said, trying to ignore the tickle in his stomach that was rapidly growing into an itch.

'Please hold,' the operator said.

The line rang a few times and was picked up again.

'Ambulance service,' an accented voice, male, prompted. 'Who's in pain?'

The odd question threw Phil for a second, and he frowned in confusion.

'Erm … my dad's been attacked. He needs help fast.'

'Is there blood?' the dispatch agent asked with a strange, almost lustful quality, like how a pervert might sound making an obscene phone call and asking about a woman's underwear.

'What? Eh, yeah, he's got a bad cut on his head and there's blood around his mouth. He's coughing up blood as well. Please, he needs help quickly.'

Amazingly, the voice on the other end of the line chuckled softly and sighed. 'Calm down, sir. Everything's going to be okay. Does the blood have little bubbles in it? Does your dad scream in *pain?*'

The itching in his gut now became intolerable, and the air in the bedroom dropped another few degrees as the warped ambulance dispatcher chuckled again.

'What the fuck?' Phil muttered.

'Sounds like he has broken ribs,' the voice went on with horrible, gleeful enjoyment. 'One or more of the bones has punctured your father's lung and the little bubbles are caused by air escaping from the ruptured sac. Broken ribs are one of the most painful things the human body can experience, and when the sharp points of a splintered bone rupture the lung it feels like you're being stabbed. Each time he coughs, it happens again. Another delicious little prick. If he doesn't die of blood loss, the lung injury will cause him to eventually *drown* in his own blood as the sac fills up. He's *fucked.*'

Phil started to shake with a combined fear and rage, each emotion vying for domination.

'Who the fuck are you?' he whispered into the phone. Beside him on the bed, his dad coughed again and gave a low cry of pain.

'Oh, Jesus, Phil, it hurts,' he moaned in misery.

The voice on the line gave a sharp bark of laughter.

'Phil, I'm the *dark*. Eat, drink and make merry.'

Ozay, for Phil was in no doubt that was who he was talking to, laughed again, then a scathing, shrieking scream erupted from the headset before the line went dead. Phil dropped the phone on the floor, staring at it in shock as the terrible scream continued, not from the handset, but from downstairs. From the kitchen.

He leapt to my feet and was halfway across the room before the door slammed shut with such force the surrounding wooden frame cracked. Phil desperately tried to pull the door open again, but it wouldn't budge. Wouldn't even give a millimetre despite his frantic efforts.

On the bed, his father coughed and cried out again, flecking his shirt with blood. More this time. He was losing consciousness.

He was dying.

13

Jim Densmore dragged his body across the kitchen floor, cutting his fingers on broken glass from the smashed patio door. His legs were a sea of agony. Every intolerable inch he gained across the blood-splattered tiles sent a bolt of pain sweeping through his entire lower body as he desperately clawed himself toward the counter, his eyes fixed on the wooden block which held an array of kitchen knives.

He had to finish the job. Had to make sure his bastard father was dead. The pain he currently felt was a mere itch compared to what he knew awaited him should he fail. The vision revealed to him beneath the burning grey coat of the little blonde girl in the street that afternoon, though it had been only a split second before the taxi had struck him, was branded on his very soul, and he was helpless to disobey Ozay's command. He would drag his shattered knees across a mile of jagged rocks to slit his father's throat if that's what it took. There was no option.

Ignoring the fiery torture in his legs, he made it to the base of the kitchen cabinets and painfully pulled himself into a sitting position, groaning in agony as he twisted round so he sat with his back against the fitting. The golf club was lying on the floor where Phil had dropped it before running upstairs, and Jim reached out and grasped the rubberised grip. Craning his head round so he could see his target, he swept the club along the top of the work surface, knocking the kitchen block to the floor at his side. He eagerly groped for the large carving knife, but as his fingers closed on the plastic handle, he became aware of a sudden chill in the air.

He glimpsed movement out of the corner of his eye and turned his head in the direction of the open patio door leading to the shadowy back garden. A large but indistinct shape was materialising out of the gloom, revealing itself slowly as it moved across the back lawn in the direction of the house. Jim froze still, his fist gripping the butcher knife's handle and the pain in his legs forgotten as a sense of horrible expectancy clutched him.

It crept out of the darkness slowly, savouring Jim's grey-faced terror and the look of dismayed recognition, then it crossed the threshold into the house, fully revealed in the bright kitchen, it towered over him, grinning.

Jim couldn't scream for a second. His throat seized up, and he just sat there, saucer eyed and drooling. He couldn't even breathe as sheer fright froze his lungs, and his already tenuous hold on sanity finally snapped before the terrible alien spectacle standing over him.

With his last conscious thought, he raised the butcher knife in front of him and turned the blade not in the direction of the unearthly thing facing him, but towards his own throat, intending to spare himself the awful fate the thing before him heralded. But he was denied even this small mercy.

There was a blur of movement as the thing lashed out with a sinewy clawed appendage, and the butcher knife, still clutched in Jim's severed hands, dropped between his legs.

And because his broken mind now realised what was about to happen, he finally screamed with such force his vocal cords tore in his throat.

The thing before James Densmore started ripping into him.

14

The dreadful screaming from downstairs went on for some time, unnervingly loud and panic pitched, evocative of torture-chamber imagery. Trying to block the terrible desperate shrieks from his mind, Phil continued to struggle fruitlessly with the bedroom door, which still wouldn't give an inch. It was as if there was no door there at all, and he was tugging in vain at a handled section of wall for all the good his frantic efforts yielded.

On the bed, his dad croaked his name. Leaving the immovable door, Phil went to the bed and gently sat down on the mattress beside him, a hollow despair squeezing his chest as he saw that his father's condition was rapidly worsening. Kyle was very pale now, his breath shallow and fast. His eyes seemed to have shrunk back into his skull, where they glittered feverishly. 'Leave it, son,' he said. Although the terrible shrieks from downstairs continued unabated and his dad was talking in a near inaudible voice, Phil could hear him clearly. 'That door's not going to open any time soon.' His hand groped for Phil's, and Phil took it, fighting back frustrated tears of grief, powerless to change what was happening before his eyes. His dad was fading fast, and the one responsible was screaming in apparent brutalised agony downstairs. James's cries were gradually becoming weaker, and though Phil hated him for what he'd done, he couldn't help but feel a measure of pity, and he hoped his brother would be silent sooner rather than later.

Kyle's eyes were closed now, and he'd stopped breathing. Phil shook him gently.

'Dad, stay with me,' he said softly, his voice breaking.

His eyes fluttered open once again, and he looked at Phil seriously. 'You've got to go now,' he said, his voice stronger than a minute ago. 'It's almost finished with James and it'll be coming after you next. Go. *Now*.'

'I'm staying with you, dad,' Phil told him. Incredibly, his father's face twisted in sudden anger and he pushed Phil away. His strength was sufficient to send him sprawling on the bedroom floor, where he looked up at his dad in shock

'Don't be such a fuckin' wee lassie,' Kyle spat. 'Don't you see you're the last one? Get out of here *now*. That thing's on the stairs.'

Phil could only sit there on the carpet, his mind a total blank. How could he know that? There was no noise of anything approaching. How had he suddenly find the strength to push Phil away like that, when seconds before he could barely breathe?

With a scream of his own, Phil's dad sat up and pushed himself to his feet. A thick stream of blood vomited from his mouth with the effort, and he staggered against the wall. He turned to his son, and their eyes met. 'I love you, Phil,' he said.

Before Phil could move, his father pushed himself from the wall, tore open the bedroom door, and ran down the upstairs hall in the direction of the stairs, bellowing in rage.

Phil called out after him, getting to his feet to give chase. He rushed down the hall and turned the corner to see his dad throw himself at a huge dark shape ascending the staircase. The light in the upper landing wasn't on, but the downstairs light backlit the figure coming up the steps, giving Phil a split second glimpse at a walking nightmare. This was the shadowy creature he'd last glimpsed at Bennane Head that afternoon. That thing that had seemed formless and insubstantial when viewed in daylight, but was now all too solidly corporeal, coming up my staircase in the near darkness. Past his dad's lunging form, Phil saw for a second a writhing mass of oddly jointed skeletal limbs that spread out like giant spider legs, barbed hooks and stretched leathery parchment, patches of matted hair surrounding several glowing yellowish points of light. The very air around this entity seemed tainted with a charged, malignant energy which he could feel as an almost unbearable pressure in his skull. Before Phil could see any more, the light bulb in the downstairs hall exploded with a sharp *pop*.

The lights went out, and from the sudden perfect blackness, there came the sound of Phil's father colliding with the hellish intruder. Almost simultaneously, Phil felt something slash at the air millimetres in front of his face, then there was a series of crashes, thumps, low snarls and rattling reptilian screams as his dad and the thing that had almost taken Phil's face off careened down the steps to the downstairs hall. Phil yelled after him, and sightlessly felt for the banister, starting down the stairs towards the struggle at the bottom.

'*Get out, Phil!*' his dad screamed. '*Don't you come down here!*'

Phil could hear jaws snapping and blows landing on flesh, his dad's enraged roars, a sibilant hissing sound, mingled with that hideous sniggering laugh. There was a sudden, loud *thud* as something hit the floor with a force that Phil felt through his trainers, and he heard a picture fall from the wall to his left. Insanely, he remembered his mother buying the cheap ceramic souvenir plate, adorned with a hand painted grinning donkey in Blackpool on a family holiday years ago. The brutal impact was followed by a scream of agony from his father, there was a loud tearing noise like ripping denim, then a horrible wet gurgling. Finally, the ghastly noises ended with a terrible liquid *crunch* that had a cold finality to it.

Phil froze then, hearing that last sound. He wished he had the nerve to utter a fearsome battle cry and charge headlong into the blackness before him as his dad had done, but that last grisly *crunch* undid him. His legs folded, and he pitched forward, toppling head first down the stairs. He no longer cared. With his dad dead, everyone he'd ever loved was now gone, and as he sailed blindly to his doom, he was actually glad it was over. His forehead struck the corner of a step. He felt the carpet leave a friction burn as his inert body slid bumpily down the remaining stairs, and he felt the beast in the black reaching out to receive him, could sense its gloating triumph.

He just prayed it would be quick. It wasn't.

PART III

Let death seize upon them, and let them go down quick into hell,
for wickedness is in their dwellings, and among them.

Psalm 55:15

King James Bible

1

HIGHLY CONFIDENTIAL – EYES ONLY

<u>Evidence File #23423KUJ</u>

Emergency call routed to Ballantrae Police Station

Recorded 04:48, 12th August 2011

Participants: WPC Annie Grainger; Mrs Helen Paton (caller)

Transcript begins

AG: Ballantrae Police Office, what is your emergency?

HP: Oh Jesus please … you have to help me … please come …

AG: Okay please try to calm down. Where are you? What's your name?

HP: Okay, okay, my name is … Helen Paton. I'm … I'm working in the petrol station just outside Ballantrae … Please … there's something outside …

AG: Okay, Helen, I've got a car on the way. Just take a deep breath and tell me what's happening.

HP: I don't know … I don't know … I was just cashing up the till … getting ready to … to finish my shift and … and I saw something at the service window … It was … It was … (*sobbing*)

AG: It's okay, Helen, you're safe. The officers

171

will be there any second. Is someone trying to rob the petrol station?

HP: No ... it ... it ... wasn't a person ...

AG: What do you mean it wasn't a person, Helen?

HP: *(sobbing)* I don't know ... Jesus Christ ... I don't know ... I don't know what it was ...

AG: It's okay, Helen, just stay on the line with ...

HP: Oh fuck it's back ... it's back at the window ... oh ... oh no ... no ... no God ...

AG: Just stay calm, Helen, you're safe inside the station.

HP: Oh my god ... it's not real ... it's not real ... please Jesus ... *(screams) (background: breaking glass, unidentified sounds, screaming)*

AG: Helen? Helen, tell me what's happening. Come on, Helen ...

(background: unidentified sounds, extended screaming)

AG: Helen? Helen are you there? Talk to me ... *(background: screaming)*

(call terminates)

Transcript ends.

2

Phil slid off the last step of the staircase, coming to a clumsy rest in thick warm liquid, the smell and taste of hard iron in his throat. He knew the feel of blood well by now, was familiar with the tack and temperature of it.

He heard the slow, rasping breath of the thing standing over him, could feel the sick pressure its presence seemed to generate in his head. He sensed its triumph and loathing, and a great wave of tiredness and apathy overcame him, and as he sensed the creature reaching for him out of the black, Phil welcomed his imminent demise, waiting to feel the puncturing pressure of claws in his flesh ...

But then he felt himself slipping away as he'd done earlier that afternoon. He tried desperately to fight it, unwilling to go on with this nightmare, wishing only for a quick death, but it was useless. There was a rushing sensation, experienced more as a mental shift than an actual kinetic movement, then there was wind in his hair. Despite his resistance, Phil burst free of the physical world, and then he was gone, hearing the monster's frustrated scream receding in the distance.

Time went away for a while, and like before, Phil, in a semi-disconnected sort of way, experienced a feeling of protection and peace, the awareness of a benign presence or presences, and in their glow, he understood that his previous desire for merciful oblivion hadn't been his own, but was the malignant influence of the monstrosity that had staked a claim in his world. For an unknowable passage of time, he floated in blissful nothingness, grateful for the brief respite from the horror movie his life had become.

Then he abruptly found himself sitting on the hillside overlooking the high school.

It was still dark, and there was a small camp fire burning to his left. He was in the same place he, Sam, Cairnsey and

Griff had spent so many good times over the years, knocking back beers, smoking joints and having drunken singalongs. How many times had they sat there on crisp autumn nights, pointing out satellites and shooting stars? How many times had Griff put on his science head on those occasions and explained the physics of the cosmos to them in that easy, drawling voice of his? Phil remembered Griff telling the rest of them how most of the stars they could see were actually suns that had died and grown cold long ago, and weren't even really there. The vastness of space just meant that they could still see their brightness travelling light-years through the darkness, even though that brightness no longer truly existed. That had been a head fuck, that one.

'Dude, remember that night last summer when we were up here?' Sam asked him. 'Cairnsey'd seen that documentary about Indian fakirs and we decided to have a bash at firewalking?'

Phil laughed at the memory. There was nothing strange about Sam suddenly sitting there with him. It seemed so natural.

'That was funny as fuck,' Phil said, smiling. 'Your trainers went up in a blue light and you were running about in circles screaming while the rest of us were rolling about laughing at you. It was tremendous.'

'Aye, uncaring bastards.'

They sat in comfortable, companionable silence for a moment.

'Sorry about your dad, Phil. He was a good guy,' Sam said.

Phil nodded. 'He saved me again tonight,' he replied. 'That freaky motherfucker would've taken my face off if he hadn't tackled it on the stairs. That's twice he's saved my life, and what did I do tonight when he needed *me*? Fuckin' shat it. Fell down the stairs like a fanny.'

'He was already gone, mate,' Sam said, shaking his head.

'You couldn't have done anything but get yourself ripped up for arse paper, and you know it.'

Phil nodded reluctantly. He knew it was true, but he also knew that guilt doesn't just vanish in the face of logic.

'Sam, that thing in the house …' he paused. 'Was it Griff?'

'Griff's gone, Phil. You saw him in the cave earlier.'

'And you?'

He smiled and gave Phil a look. 'What do you think, ya daft bastard? I'm sitting here talking to you, aren't I?'

'But this isn't real, Sammy. This is a dream.'

He shrugged in that uniquely Sam way that said *do I look like someone who cares?* 'Remember what Griff said about the stars?' he said.

Phil guessed that made some sort of sense, albeit in a really fucked up way.

They sat quietly for a moment. The sun was slowly rising away in the east, painting the dawn sky in a mellow mixture of streaky orange and early morning blue. A few stars were still out, hanging around like revellers reluctant to go home after an all night party thrown by the fading moon, which had just about crashed out.

'So what happens next then?' Phil asked his dead friend.

Sam looked at him sadly.

'Carnage, I'm afraid,' he said simply. 'Have you figured out what's going on yet?'

Phil shook his head. 'I went and saw Griff yesterday,' he said. 'He's fucked up big time. His teeth, and his eyes … He told me what happened down in the caves back in May, and then said he was going to get out and kill a bunch of folks, me included. He knew James was coming home as well.'

Sam didn't say anything.

'Barnsey never spoke to Cairnsey that night,' Phil added.

'I know.'

'So who the fuck was that on the phone, then?'

'Ozay.'

'And who exactly is Ozay?'

'A daemon,' Sam said, as if Phil had asked how many sides a square has.

'Right.' That also made sense, he supposed. It was a stupid question really. 'So that was Ozay back at my place?'

'No, dude. That big bastard just works for him.'

Interesting. Phil thought about that for a moment. The sun was up now, and he could feel a light breeze on his skin. Sam put his hand on Phil's shoulder.

'Time to go I'm afraid, dude. You're starting to wake up,' he said, getting to his feet. 'I'll catch you later.'

Phil nodded sadly. He didn't want the peaceful interlude to end, and knew that upon waking, he'd be plunged right back into the middle of a nightmare.

'One more question, Sam,' he said. 'How come you're out here? Cairnsey said you guys were stuck in the caves.'

Sam nodded slowly.

'We *are* stuck in the caves, Phil. Griff too now. But like Cairnsey said, we're in there and out *here,*' he said, motioning at the surroundings. He moved closer and gently placed a hand on Phil's chest above his heart. It felt warm and real. 'And we're in *here*. I don't know much more than you about what's going on, mate. It's bad where we are. Dark. We don't see much. Only thing I can tell you is that it's going to get bloody around here today. Just keep your eyes open, your chin up, and try not to be a little bitch about it, alright?'

176

Phil smiled. Even as a ghost, Sam was a cheeky bastard.

'Keep moving Phil,' he said. 'Get away from here and just keep on moving. See you later, mate.'

And with that he was gone.

Phil felt a deep sense of loneliness as he found himself alone again, but in this strange dreamlike version of reality, there was no real sorrow.

He lay back on the grass and closed his eyes.

3

Morning dew seeping through the back of his t-shirt woke Phil.

He sat up, not surprised to find himself still sitting on the hillside. The fire was out, but he could feel heat radiating from the small circle of stones in which it'd been built. A thin wisp of smoke still rose from the ashes, and the grass next to him was flattened down as if someone had been sitting there.

He broke down then.

All the fear and grief, it all just came pouring out in long ragged sobs and a river of salty bitter tears. He wept for his father, for Sam, Cairnsey, Griff, himself, even James. It was for all the madness and death, and for the thought of what he knew was still to come.

Carnage, Sam had said.

So he just lay there for a while, letting out the hurt. He wasn't absorbed in trying to figure out what to do next. He just needed to get his grieving out of the way before it ate him alive. He needed the catharsis.

By the time Phil stopped, his face and sides were stretched and sore, but he felt better. As well as he could under the circumstances anyway. He forced myself up and shivered in the cold morning air, then to give himself something to do, retrieved a few dry sticks of wood and kindling from the fuel dump they'd always kept wrapped in watertight plastic bags and sheltered in the hollowed trunk of a nearby tree. The menial task of preparing a fire soothed his ragged nerves, and once he had it going, its warmth and light gave Phil a small measure of comfort. He sat there staring into the flames, welcoming the heat in his chilled bones and considering his options.

Keep moving, Phil. Get away from here and just keep on

moving.

When he'd still been alive, Sam had been the person Phil had trusted the most in the world, and even though he was now dead, he couldn't see any other course of action that made any sense. That thing back at Phil's house wanted him. His dad had said it, and he'd felt it himself. Its infernal hunger and need had been a palpable, irresistible force, and Phil understood that he was being hunted by this being, a demonic monstrosity he couldn't even begin to understand.

To try and figure the whole thing out, he needed to go into hiding. He needed to leave the area, and get as far away as possible. To do that though, he needed help as he had no means of transportation, no money, and not even so much as a change of clothes. Phil briefly considered Maria, Sam's mum, but quickly discarded the idea. Despite the fact that he'd killed her only son, she'd come to Phil's house three times a week to see him after he'd left the hospital, and she'd comforted him at my lowest ebb when she'd found him crying like a baby in the graveyard at Sam and Cairnsey's funeral. Phil couldn't ask anymore of her. She'd done enough for him since he was five years old to last several lifetimes, and had been through enough herself without him showing up at her door babbling about daemons killing his family and visits from her deceased son. Phil would leave her, and Sam's dad Alan, out of this.

Griff's parents were rarely in town, but that wasn't the reason Phil wouldn't go to them either. Unlike Sam's folks, Des and Sheena Griffiths were practically strangers despite the fact that Griff had been friends with Phil, Sam and Cairnsey for over ten years, and on the rare occasions Phil had met them, both Griff's parents had seemed cold and faintly disapproving. Although they were frequently away, and a parent-free stately home would normally be like Christmas for four teenage lads, the four friends had never had parties or even hung around at Griffiths Hall, as the massive old mansion had always had a distinctly unwelcoming feel to it, like a cold and draughty museum full of dark corners and dim-lit corridors. On the few occasions Phil had set foot in the place, he'd had a distinctively creepy vibe from the place.

That left Cairnsey's family. His mum had left before Cairnsey had learned to walk, and his dad Tony, to put it delicately, was a cunt. He worked as a mechanic at the local garage, and was a skinny little rat of a man with slightly less intelligence. He had a taste for Bell's whisky and a mean temper, which in the past he'd often take out via his fists on his two sons. When they were kids in primary school, Cairnsey would show up with bruises and black eyes every once in a while, but had never made a big deal about it. He'd refused to tell a teacher about the abuse when Phil and the others had urged him to, and he'd made them promise not to say anything either. He and his elder brother Grant would sort it out themselves, he'd say. And sure enough, when Cairnsey had been about eleven years old, the bruises and black eyes had stopped appearing, right about the same time that Tony Cairns spent a few days in hospital, recovering from a serious beating he claimed he'd received at the hands of four guys who'd jumped him coming home from the pub one night. His own sons' swollen knuckles told a different story about who had given Tony Cairn's his overdue bleaching, however. As they grew older, Cairnsey had barely even mentioned his old man, as if the prick was an unwanted but unfortunately permanent roommate with whom he and Grant were forced to live. There was none of that common brotherhood rivalry between Grant and Cairnsey, because they'd grown up in a house with a common enemy in the shape of their abusive drunk of a father.

Grant was currently in his second year at Strathclyde University where he was studying civil engineering, and he'd sometimes hang out with the boys on occasion, although he also had his own circle of friends.

All things considered, if Phil was going to seek help from any quarter, it would be from Grant. He'd always stuck up for them in school when older kids had given the boys hassle, even if it meant he'd take a beating in their stead, as had happened once when he'd intervened to stop Eddie Jannets kicking the shit out of Sam. Grant had balls, but he was no fighter, and he'd ended up with a broken nose for his trouble. Sam had got away though, and from that day, he'd looked at Grant with a measure of hero worship.

Phil threw another couple of pieces of wood onto the campfire, mulling over this idea further, and decided that when it came right down to it, as loathe as he was to involve anyone else in this inexplicable and deadly situation, he'd no one else to turn to. He needed to get out of town, and Cairnsey's big brother was his best chance of being able to do so.

Grant shared a flat in Glasgow with a couple of other students during term time, but he'd moved back to town for the summer to work with Sam's dad at the local engineering firm in a placement position that came through his university course. It was a Wednesday morning, and the offices of Anderson Engineering opened at nine am. Checking his watch, Phil saw it was still shy of five am, meaning he'd need to call Grant at home. He still didn't have his mobile however, so would need to call from a payphone. He patted his pockets in the hope of finding a few coins, and his hand came away flecked with flakes of dried blood.

As preoccupied and terror stricken as his thought process had become, it was only then that Phil realised with a shudder of repulsion that he was coated head to toe in gore, and he had to force himself to not think about where all the dried blood had come from. Grasping the nature of his appearance, a new and troubling thought entered his mind.

It was highly probable that a neighbour had heard the noise from his house the previous night. All the screaming, crashing and shouting wouldn't have gone unnoticed, so what if someone, probably the elderly Mrs Hook next door, had called the police, who subsequently arrived and found two mutilated bodies and Phil missing?

Phil considered how he had already been involved in one multiple murder that year for which no action had been taken against him, but that had only been because of Griff's written and signed confession. The possibility that he might now be the quarry in a manhunt came as a cold slap in the face, and walking back into town in search of a pay phone wearing blood-soaked clothes suddenly didn't seem like a good idea.

Phil was just considering this troubling thought when the far off wail of a siren floated across the still morning air. He turned to survey the town from his high vantage point, and sure enough, he could see blue lights bombing down the main street. Then he saw more lights and a second siren joined the high pitched howl of the first. Then a third sounded. Phil could now see blue lights rushing through the streets at three different areas of the small town, but they weren't all heading in the same direction.

He frowned in confusion, then flinched as a tall pillar of flame suddenly bloomed skywards in the distance away to his right. A second later, the deep roar of the explosion ripped the morning, and he saw that the petrol station on the north edge of the village had gone up in a massive fireball.

A second later, he heard a scream from closer by. It came from the block of flats which lay at the bottom of the hill he was standing on.

The town's nightmare came with the dawn that day.

4

Police Constable Ally Marshall was scared.

As the patrol car sped through the quiet early morning streets of Ballantrae, he sat with his fists clenched in his lap, listening in growing disquiet to the reports coming over the radio. Annie, the controller back at the station, was losing her cool. He could hear it in her voice, could hear the same rising fear that he himself felt rising in his throat like icy vomit. She was scared as well. And no wonder.

Ally had started the day two hours ago by standing on an upturned plug with his first step out of bed, the sensitive sole of his bare foot coming straight down on the contact prongs. The sudden, brutal blast of agony had made him collapse back onto his mattress, screaming silently and wishing for a merciful death, and the metal pins of the plug had grinned up at him from the floor in a three pronged smile, as if to say *Got you, ya daft bastard!* In a righteous fury, Ally had stupidly swung a bare footed kick at the heavy AC adaptor that had gored him, inexplicably and stupidly certain in his rage that he would send his inanimate assailant flying across the room to see it satisfyingly obliterated against the wall. That of course hadn't happened, and as he'd hopped away in his y-fronts a second later, almost weeping in misery and holding his little toe, which he was certain was broken, he'd thought the day could only get better.

He now sat in the police cruiser next to his superior, Sergeant Stephen Grace, en route to a reported disturbance at the petrol station just outside the edge of the village. When dispatching the car, Annie had advised that the caller had been in a panic, saying that something was trying to get her.

Some*thing*, not some*one*.

That wasn't the only disturbance Annie had alerted the small local police force to that early morning. She'd also dispatched his best mate and fellow constable Davie Leish to a reported break in at the Densmore residence on Glenside Road, and a few minutes after that, Annie had received yet another call. An assault reported at Fern Drive.

To say that this volume of incident was higher than usual was an understatement. Annie would perhaps have to call officers to a scene twice a month, and the single holding cell at the station held mice and an assortment of cleaning products more often than it did hardened criminals. That's why she sounded so scared.

Something very bad was happening.

'There's another one, Sarge,' Annie's panicky voice came over the radio again. 'Seventeen Field Road. Jack Daly's farm. His wife's hysterical, saying he's in pieces.' Annie's voice rose a few notes in a jagged scale on the last few words.

'Calm down Annie,' Sgt Grace replied calmly into the radio. 'Call the station in Girvan and get another car out there right away. We're a minute away from the petrol station. What's the status at our destination?'

'I don't know,' Annie's voice came back. 'The woman isn't on the line anymore. There was a scream and the line just went dead.' She sounded like she was on the verge of tears.

'Get a hold of yourself, Annie,' Grace replied sternly. 'Get back on the radio and check in with the other cars. I want know what's going on at every location. Over and out.'

The car was speeding north along the coastal road, and as they topped a small rise, Ally saw their destination come into view a quarter of a mile away. The petrol station was on their right just ahead, facing the sea and bordered on either side by fields of tall grass.

That was when it exploded, and Ally yelped in alarm as he felt the shock wave from the fierce detonation rock the car on its suspension.

'Holy mother of …' Sergeant Grace moaned in disbelief from the driver's seat. 'What the hell is this?'

The car skidded to a stop well back from the blazing building. Grace was back on the radio, shouting urgently.

'Come in, control. Annie, get the fire brigade out to the petrol station immediately, and an ambulance as well. Probable casualties.'

'Roger that, Sarge,' Annie came back, to her credit, sounding calmer now. 'Urgent fire and ambulance services to the Jet petrol station on Girvan road.'

Ally and his superior stepped out of the car and started towards the burning garage. Another explosion from the forecourt rocked the morning air as another petrol pump went up, driving the two policemen back before the blast of hot air, rank with the acrid stench of burning petroleum. His pulse racing, Ally could feel his skin tightening in the intense heat from the fire.

'Jesus, Sarge,' he muttered. 'The woman who called …'

'Check the north field,' Grace said grimly. 'See if you can find her. I'll check the south side.'

Ally ran to the north side of the station, keeping well back from the destroyed petrol station that was now nothing more than a huge bonfire. If the fields on either side had been any closer to the structure, the tall grass would also be ablaze by now, but as it was, they were set far back enough to avoid being consumed. Ally knew however, that a single stray ember could well ignite the field he was about to enter in his search for the missing attendant.

He clambered awkwardly over the short wire fence, swearing as his trousers snagged on the barbs. He stood and surveyed the chest high grass before him, listening and watching for movement. 'Hello?' he called. 'Police. Anyone here?'

He started to make his way through the field, scanning

left and right and trying not to break an ankle on the uneven ground. He glanced nervously to his right in the direction of the burning building, expecting at any moment to see the grass burst into flames.

'Police,' Ally shouted again, continuing to look around. 'Please call out if you can hear me.'

Nothing but the whoosh and crackle of the gas fed inferno.

Ally continued searching in widening circles, calling out every few seconds. Minute by minute his hopes of finding the woman alive faded.

Poor woman's probably just so much ash by now, he thought.

Aside from the noise of the burning petrol station, Ally noticed that there was a queer stillness to the morning, a strange, indefinable hush that seemed almost tangible somehow. It was a very peculiar feeling, and despite the heat from the blaze, Ally felt a chill in his bones.

There was a scream and the line just went dead.

Something was trying to get her.

Ally shuddered, and somehow knew in his heart that the station attendant would never be found. For some reason, he found himself recalling that night back in May when he and Sean Hogan had responded to the call out at Bennane Head. He remembered that grinning kid, naked and red with gore, crouched over the eviscerated, dismembered body, a bloody machete in his hand. The way the kid had moved, unnaturally fast, in the blink of an eye cleaving Sean's head down the middle ...

His radio crackled to life, making him jump.

'Ally, the grass on this side's starting to smoke,' Sergeant Grace said. 'I'm moving back to the car. The fire engines should be here in a minute.'

'Roger, Sarge. I'll keep checking this side. Over.'

'Negative. The wind's picking up. The north field'll be up in smoke as well before long. The fire boys can keep it under control when they get here, and we'll continue the search then. Meet me at the car. Over and out.'

'Roger that.'

Ally turned and started back toward the fence, still aware of the eerie sense that the morning was somehow quieter than it should be.

Birdsong.

The word leapt into his mind, and he realised that was it. This stretch of coastline was a haven for gulls, oyster catchers, cormorants, various species of duck and other seabirds and waterfowl, and the squawks, trills and chirps of the avian wildlife could usually be heard in abundance. This morning however, the coast was unnaturally absent of birdsong. Looking around, Ally noticed that neither could he *see* any birds. Not so much as a lone sparrow sitting on the fence.

He shivered again, and hurriedly made his way out of the field.

Arriving back at the patrol vehicle, he found Sergeant Grace speaking urgently into the radio once more.

'Come in, Control. Where's the fire engine? What's the status up at the Daly farm, Annie? Over.'

Just static from the other end.

'Annie, come in,' he repeated. 'Request status at seventeen Field Road. Need also immediate response from fire service. Confirm.'

Crackling silence.

Sergeant Grace threw the radio handset down in disgust.

'Where the fuck is she?' he spat.

The radio suddenly crackled to life.

'Control, this is Foxtrot Sierra seven,' an unsteady male voice said. It was Kenny Young, one of the officers who'd gone to one of the other calls that morning, the assault out at Fern Drive near the golf club. The Delaney family who lived at the address owned a large detached villa, the only building on the road. 'We're at the scene at Fern Drive. Multiple casualties. I repeat, multiple casualties. Jesus Christ, I've got four bodies here ...'

The horror in Kenny's voice was stark, and the cold feeling that'd been growing in Ally's bowels grew spindly legs and scuttled around inside him.

Grace whipped up the handset again.

'Foxtrot Sierra seven,' he barked. 'This is Sergeant Grace. What's your status, Kenny? Over.'

'Fuck me, Sarge.' Kenny gasped in a strangled voice. 'There's four dead here, sir. They've been mutilated, but ... but *worse* ... holy God, it's impossible ...'

The field on the south side of the petrol station finally caught fire. Flames sprang up from the tall grass and immediately began to spread, fanned by the breeze coming off the water on the other side of the road. There were still no fire engine sirens to be heard.

'Hold your position, Kenny, and calm down,' Grace said calmly. 'We're coming to you.'

'Please hurry, Sarge,' Kenny said, speaking in a tone that was almost a whimper. Ally thought he sounded like a badly frightened child.

He realised that Davie Leish, the other officer on duty who'd gone to the break in at the Densmore house that morning, hadn't radioed in since he'd reported that he'd spoke to the next door neighbour and was proceeding to check out the scene.

He thumbed the switch on his own radio. He was suddenly very worried for his friend.

'Come in Foxtrot Sierra five. You there, Davie?'

Sergeant Grace was starting the car up.

'*Get in, Ally!*' he bawled.

As the patrol car bombed back towards town, leaving the burning petrol station and smouldering fields behind, Ally tried again to raise Davie on his radio. No answer.

Despite Sergeant Grace's repeated efforts, Annie still wasn't picking up back at the station either.

5

'I thought I heard something last night, must've been about ten-ish,' the elderly Mrs Hook was saying. 'I'd just taken my sleeping pills. My shoulder keeps me awake at night you know, damned arthritis, and I thought I heard someone shouting, but I was already half asleep. I've taken a tumble down the stairs before when I was going to the kitchen after taking my tablets, so I didn't want to risk that again, son. Anyway, I peeked my head over the back fence this morning, Kyle's usually up and about at that time, and I saw the patio door was broken.'

Davie Leish was writing this all down in his notebook, nodding as he did so. He stood on the front doorstep of Sophie Hook's house, next door to the Densmore residence. Andy Cummings, the other PC who'd he'd been in the car with when they got the call, had already gone next door to check out the scene. Davie could see him across the low fence separating the two front gardens, looking through the living room window. There'd been no answer to his repeated knocking on the front door.

'Did you go next door to see if Mr Densmore was there?' Davie asked the old lady.

'No, son. I went back inside and tried to get him on the phone, but there was no answer. His car was still outside and he wouldn't leave the house with the door all smashed like that, so I thought it'd be best to call you. I was going to go next door after I spoke to wee Annie at the station but she told me to stay put.'

Davie nodded again, still writing furiously. 'Quite right,' he said with a smile. 'Can't have you doing our job for us can we, Mrs Hook? The Sergeant'd skin me alive.'

'Och, I've known Stephen since he was a wee laddie. Don't let him fool you. He's a big softie at heart. I mind him falling off that wee pink bike of his sister's when he was about ten and skinning his knee. Cried his wee heart out, so he did.'

Davie let out a snigger. He'd have to remember that one the next time the Sarge was giving him a roasting for playing badminton and not a *real* man's sport.

'I tried phoning Kyle again before you got here,' Mrs Hook went on, 'but I still couldn't get any answer. I wondered where his boy Phil was. He's such a nice lad. Always round here asking if I need anything from the shops, and he always takes my bins out for me on a Wednesday night.'

'Well you did the right thing phoning us, Sophie,' Davie said, putting his notebook away. 'I'm going to go next door and see what the story is. You just stay here and I'll holler if I need some backup, okay?'

'Aye, no bother, son. You just yell and I'll come running with my rolling pin.'

Davie gave her a grin in return and walked away up the garden path. She stayed in her open doorway, curiously looking on.

'Anything, Andy?' he called to PC Cummings who was still looking through the ground level bay window at the front of the house.

'Nobody's home,' his fellow officer replied, turning to Davie with a shrug. 'I'll go and check the back door.'

Davie got on the radio to the station and let Annie know they were at the scene and were about to enter the premises.

'Roger that, Sierra Foxtrot five,' Annie came back.

Davie liked the small town policing lark. Fresh out of police college at Tulliallan, twenty-six years old and full of ideals and desire, his first posting had been in the notorious Easterhouse area of Glasgow. He'd relished the challenge, firmly believing that he could change things and make a positive difference to the lives of those in the rough area. Three years later, the crime rate in his hell hole of a section had still been on the rise, however. The area was infested with violent young teams; gangs of knife-wielding kids, some not even ten years old, who constantly ran amok, slashing and stabbing each other in a bloody and pointless never-ending territorial battle. Drug addiction, assault, murder, poverty and robbery were rife in the area, and it seemed that for every junkie, waster and bladed-up ned Davie pulled off the street, another ten took their place. While trying to break up a violent pub brawl one evening, he'd been lucky to leave the bar with his life after someone glassed him in the face with a pint tumbler and several other patrons had jumped on him, stomping frenziedly on his head and body. It was a close thing, and he'd only been rescued when backup arrived in the form of several other officers who'd stormed the bar, restoring order at the end of swinging batons. Funnily enough, that incident didn't bother him so much despite his extended stay in hospital, the metal plates in his head and arms and the thirty four stitches he received. That was a part of the job he'd been prepared for. Shit, when he joined the force and was stationed in one of the roughest areas of Glasgow, knife capital of Europe, he'd fully *expected* to get glassed at some point. Instead, the clincher came not long after he went back to work, when he'd been spat on by a seven year old girl whom he'd caught shoplifting. The gob of thick green mucus smeared on the uniform he took such pride in wearing, and the torrent of foul-mouthed abuse the unruly tyke had given him, had cut him deeper than the severe beating he'd taken in the pub had. He'd handed in his transfer request later that same day. His superior, a battle-scarred veteran who'd spent over twenty years working Easterhouse and other rough estates, had recognised that Davie made a good copper, but although he was enthusiastic and well-meaning, he knew he wasn't the right sort to be policing the rough area. To work in Easterhouse and similar urban jungles, a polis had to have a bit of the nasty about him, and the kind-hearted boy just didn't have it in him. And so he called his old pal Stevie Grace, who ran a quieter division down the coast in Ayrshire. Davie would do well there.

A week later, and Davie was walking an altogether quieter beat. The town was small, with a population of under a thousand. He got to know the locals and they got to know him. He became solid mates with Ally Marshall, a young recruit who'd just joined the force, and Davie took a good deal of bemused pride in the fact that Ally looked up to him, seemingly in awe of his crime fighting exploits while stationed in the big city. Davie enjoyed telling the younger PC war stories of his previous posting. It helped him deal with the feeling that he'd failed in his first assignment and had run away.

Barring the bloody incident back in May up at Bennane Head, his tenure in the small town had been low key when compared to his time in the city. There was the odd disturbance of course, a breach of the peace here, a case of vandalism there, but since Eddie Jannets and his two mates had perished three months ago in the horrific multiple murder, lawlessness in the small town had virtually ceased to exist altogether, and the call out he'd received this morning to investigate a break in was a regular crime spree by comparison.

He caught up with Andy Cummings in the back garden of the Densmore house. Immediately, he saw the broken pane of glass in the upper right panel of the patio door. No broken glass lying on the ground outside, meaning someone had forced entry. His police training was paying off in spades, he thought wryly. Andy was a few steps in front of him as they approached the threshold, and he stopped abruptly.

'There's blood on the floor, Davie,' he said, pointing into the kitchen.

Davie moved past his colleague. Through the hole in the glass, he saw a large reddish brown stain on the kitchen tiles, and he felt his senses picking up a notch. His placement in Easterhouse had finely tuned his sense of danger, and he reached for his radio, intending to alert Annie at the station of the situation, when there was the sound of movement from inside the kitchen.

He leaned in closer to the ragged hole in the thick frosted glass, trying to locate the source of the noise. The interior was mostly in darkness as the roller blinds on the kitchen window were closed. The only meagre light came through the glass patio door, dimly illuminating part of the left wall and the small section of the floor featuring the rusty stain. Up close to the door there was a heavy, foul odour emanating from within, a smell of burnt copper and corruption that was almost overpowering. Davie gagged. It was the smell of large amounts of blood. And something else.

The soft tattoo came again, a short staccato series of light thumps from somewhere in the dark interior of the kitchen. The sudden sound made Davie's breath catch in his throat. He took the high power torch from his equipment belt and shone the beam through the hole in the glass panel, probing at the gloom. He panned the beam around the kitchen, revealing cabinets, a washing machine, a dining table. He directed the beam on the blood stain on the floor and followed it into the gloom before a row of cabinets against the wall on the right hand side of the door blocked his view. The quiet thumping sounded again, seeming to come from that unseen area.

Davie clicked off his torch and tried the door, fearing that someone lay seriously wounded out of view behind the cabinets. The door swung open as he pushed the handle down, and a gust of freezing air tainted with a powerful, sickening sweet odour wrapped itself around him. The sudden blast of cloying, rotten air made Davie gag again, this time with such force that he couldn't help himself as his stomach revolted. He vomited where he stood, splashing his boots with chunky sour bile. He stayed bent over with his hands on his knees for a second, trying to regain his composure and breathe in as little of the foul air as possible. Covering his mouth and nose with one hand, he reached inside the door and found a light switch on the wall. He flicked it on and the darkness retreated. Davie saw that in addition to the blood stain on the floor, more smudged red streaks adorned the white walls and base cabinets, and on an interior door leading out of the kitchen, a single crimson handprint was painted.

That soft thumping noise came again from down to the right. Davie stepped inside the kitchen and turned towards the sound.

Davie Leish was no stranger to bodily trauma, having seen more than his fair share of carnage while working in the city. He'd witnessed the bloody aftermath of brutal beatings and frenzied stabbings, and had seen horribly twisted bodies pulled from car wrecks on the M8, and those sights had sickened and saddened him.

This was something else, however. Davie could not even *begin* to understand the thing that lay before his eyes.

His first thought was that someone had dumped a large pile of raw meat, bones and offal on the floor at the base of the kitchen cabinets, but there were patches of what looked like hair, black fabric and denim in the twisted, shapeless mass.

Then he saw the severed human hand clutching a carving knife lying just to the side of the thing, and became aware that he was looking at the remains of a person.

With this realisation, the air vacated his lungs in a great gasping wheeze, as if he'd been sucker punched in the gut.

He could discern the rough shape of a head and limbs, all flayed bare, lying haphazardly in unnatural positions amongst the jumbled red mass. One of the protruding appendages, impossible to tell if it was an arm or a leg, twitched rapidly, beating out that hideous soft tattoo on the kitchen floor.

Thump thump thump thump.

Bones jutted out at odd angles, teeth were scattered randomly amid the insane, glistening mess and Davie could make out the shape of kidneys, a liver and sections of intestine.

It looked like the victim had somehow been turned inside out. But it was more than that.

It was like they'd been totally rearranged.

And worse, the impossible collection of body parts *moved* obscenely, expanding and contracting slightly as if it were somehow breathing, but of course that was impossible, Davie thought to himself in an icy, dislocated way.

How can you breathe when your lungs are outside your body?

But there they were. The two sacs of greyish pink matter were half buried in the pulsing pile, inflating and deflating. He could also see the heart, still attached to the central mass by thick ropy arteries. It was beating.

Witnessing this, a very strange and dangerous calm seemed to settle in Davie's mind, and suddenly he wasn't afraid. He recognised in himself that he was in deep shock, that the sight of the thing on the floor had undone him, at least temporarily.

Andy shouldn't see this, he calmly thought to himself, turning away from the inconceivable meat puppet that somehow still lived and drummed a skinned limb on the floor.

Thump thump thump thump.

Screaming inside, he walked on stiff legs out of the kitchen, but Andy wasn't there. He'd been standing behind him just a few seconds ago, but had seemingly vanished.

How odd, thought Davie, as if he'd realised he'd put his shoes on the wrong feet.

He looked around the garden, still precariously balanced on the verge of completely losing it, and trying to understand where his colleague had gone. Standing there on the garden path outside the kitchen, he tried to call out, but found with no great surprise that his throat had seized up, and only a hoarse wheeze came out. His confusion was further added to as he felt a drop of some warm liquid strike the back of his neck and run down his spine underneath his clothing.

Slowly, so very slowly, he turned around and looked up, straight into Andy's face, which was peering down at him over the edge of the roof, twelve feet above.

Andy's eyes were gone, and as the blood dripping from his empty ocular cavities fell on Davie's upturned face like warm copper raindrops, he could only stand there with a bemused half smile.

A huge hand, clawed and misshapen, reared up behind Andy's head.

Long spindly fingers with too many knuckles crawled across his dead face and probed into his vacant eye sockets. Andy's head was yanked of sight. A second later, there came a loud, wet crunching from the roof.

His tenuous strand of sanity snapped, and Davie began to laugh.

When he was found hiding in a shrubbery at the far end of the garden several hours later, he was still laughing. Occasionally he would stop and scream for a while.

6

'Urgent fire and ambulance services to the Jet petrol station on Girvan road,' Annie confirmed into the mouthpiece of her headset, trying to keep calm.

The computerised telephone system showed there were another two calls waiting. The red icons in the lower left hand corner of her screen flashed at her impatiently. Annie wanted to cry.

She rapidly clicked icons on the computer screen and a call was placed to the nearest fire station. After a moment, a small error window appeared on the screen, informing Annie that the connection had failed and to click the *details* button for more information. She found it hard to click the small icon, the mouse pointer trembling in sync with her hand.

A further dialogue box appeared once Annie had managed to select the *details* button.

THERE IS SOMETHING IN THE ROOM WITH YOU.

Annie gaped at the flat screen monitor, the words burned into her mind.

A deafening screech of sound suddenly blared from the small speaker in her ear, making Annie jolt in her seat. She snatched off the headset in panic and threw it on the desk, then just sat there, terrified, looking at the device. From the earpiece she could hear tinny screams and an animal snarling.

Someone's being eaten, Annie thought.

She'd never had the chance before to hear what someone being eaten actually *sounded* like, but right then she knew with all her heart that that was exactly what was happening on the other end of the line.

The screams just went on and on, a woman's high,

panicky shriek, growing in intensity and punctuated by that multi-pitched squealing snarl that was just *wrong* and made Annie's teeth feel like she was biting tin foil.

Unable to hear it anymore, Annie snatched the headset's connecting wire out of the console, and the hellish bedlam instantly erupted a hundred times louder from behind her, making her jump a clear foot from her chair and whirl around in terror.

Nothing there but the intercom speaker on the wall, screaming obscenely at her.

Annie clasped her hands to her ears and tried to block out the sound, but it was impossible. The awful, completely unnatural sounding noise ate at her ears, making her wince. She began to sob in little hyperventilating gasps, shaking her head and pleading for it to just *stop*. It didn't.

It's not possible, Annie kept telling herself. *It can't be coming from the intercom. That's not connected to the phone lines. It's not fucking possible ...*

The sonic assault went on and on. Rising impossibly high in pitch until Annie felt something give way inside her head as one of ear drums burst. A thin trickle of blood ran down the side of her face.

She ran across the communications room in a blind panic, heading for the door. It was locked, even though she was the only person in the building and hadn't locked the door from her side. She began to tug frantically at the handle with both hands. The thin inner membrane in her other ear also ruptured, and a second rivulet of blood ran down her. She gave up her futile attempt at escape and slid down to the floor, her back against the door, hands clasped to either side of her head and her eyes screwed shut. Pain like she'd not experienced even when giving birth to her daughter last year swept through her head as blood continued to seep from her ruined ears (*but burst ear drums don't bleed*, she though to herself) and the screaming and terrible, many-throated snarling went on and on and on ...

Then stopped.

The sudden silence made Annie flinch. There was now only a high pitched tinnitus whine in her head, accompanying the pain that throbbed in time with her rapid pulse. She opened her eyes. The communications room was still. The only movement came from her headset, which dangled from the edge of her desk, lazily swinging back and forth.

Annie got to her feet, and warily made her way back to her desk. She badly wanted to flee, but she swallowed her fear. She was responsible for the communications room and knew she had to keep in touch with the officers at the multiple crime scenes of the morning. Something very bad and very strange was happening in the village, and she couldn't abandon her post. She prayed that her husband Ross and little Amelie were still asleep at home, safe in their beds.

Making her way across the room to her desk again, the room swayed slightly as if she was walking on the deck of a boat in rough seas, and the strident ringing and ache in her ears made her feel like she'd received a heavy blow to the head. There was a slight odour of burnt plastic in the air, and Annie noticed a thin wisp of smoke rising from the intercom speaker on the wall.

The message was still on the computer screen.

THERE IS SOMETHING IN THE ROOM WITH YOU.

Just the sight of those words on the screen caused her windpipe to contract. Annie stood there, desperately trying to come up with some sort of logical explanation. *Someone hacking into the system maybe? A computer virus?*

She picked up the headset from her desk and plugged it back into the console, intending to call the Sarge to let him know about some sort of screw up with the communication system.

Something wrapped itself around her ankles under the desk.

Annie had time to gasp once and look down. She caught sight of what looked like several black tendrils wound around her lower legs.

Even before she could scream, her feet were savagely pulled out from under her and she went down with sufficient force to knock her breath out. The back of her head rapped sharply off the floor and before she blacked out, she got a second's glimpse of the thing which dragged her into the leg space under the desk.

Unconsciousness spared her the awareness of where she went and what it did to her.

She was never seen again.

7

The scream coming from the flats at the bottom of the hill abruptly stopped dead. The way the high ululating sound cut off so suddenly was far more frightening than the noise itself.

The block of flats lay at the foot of the hill on which Phil was standing, about a hundred metres downhill, and the morning air was so still that the sounds that followed carried with easy and terrible clarity up the hill to his position.

An escalating series of yells, screams and sounds of desperate struggle from the flats filled the air, and Phil could only stand there, rooted to the spot and numbly transfixed by what he was hearing. There was a gunshot, a second, then no more. Terrible bangs and crashes accompanied the cacophony of panic, as if the building itself and not just the occupants were being torn apart.

There was also the sound he feared the most; the sibilant hissing and sniggering of the thing that had taken his dad the previous night, and he could feel that nauseating, sick pressure in his head again.

Phil was close enough to the flats to see a woman in a nightdress desperately trying to open a window on the third floor. He could even make out the look of naked horror on her face before she was abruptly jerked out of sight. A second later, the window where she'd been standing exploded outwards, and amid the glittering rain of shattered glass, there sailed a headless dismembered torso. The body fell to the unforgiving concrete below, and Phil heard the flat, brutal impact from where he stood.

Then more windows in the building simultaneously burst open, vomiting forth a bloody hail of mutilated bodies. The air outside the building was suddenly full of falling glass and torn corpses.

Phil ran, the sickening music of tinkling glass and impacting torsos following on his heels.

8

The Harvester stands in a blood soaked room. In minutes, it has turned what was a human habitation into an abattoir.

The feeding has been good here. Over a score of souls in one delicious red sweep. With those already taken, it needs only a handful more before its quota is complete.

Labhrainne's blood still runs though, and the Harvester cannot return to its own plane of existence until it runs no more.

Even after the frenzied slaughter of the humans in this small tenement, its infernal thirst and rage burn. In other areas of the village, it simultaneously gathers more souls through physical embodiments that are extensions of itself. It experiences the carnage at each kill, sings to the slaughter and continues bloodily and relentlessly on, tearing and feeding, twisting and perverting at random locations like a hungry and unstoppable tornado until its work is complete. The harvesting of souls is the very essence of its existence. It knows, nor cares, for any vocation other than to hunt and kill.

It hesitates before moving on to its next killing ground, sensing there is a presence close by. One with energy akin to its own, yet somehow different.

Its atoms immediately collapse into nothingness, and its essence rises upwards, passing like vapour through the roof of the ransacked building that's walls run red with blood, and it scans the outside terrain.

There. Moving away at speed across the top of the hill.

Labhrainne's blood. Its prize quarry.

There will be extra satisfaction in snuffing out this one, the blood is strong, and it has already escaped once, somehow slipping out of the Harvester's grasp even as it lay helpless in the cruor and maimed flesh of its father.

It will not escape again.

The Harvester follows.

Phil had no destination in mind as he ran from the hill overlooking the block of flats. The presence of the predatory entity thick and foul in his head, feeling its bottomless hate and hunger, he simply needed to move, and quickly.

He found himself flying across the fields at a supernatural rate, the bracken and gorse bushes speeding past him in a blur as he hurdled fences and dykes with ease, sure-footed and never faltering on the uneven ground. He felt elemental, at one with the wind and the land, and a great sense of excitement swamped Phil's mind, pure and dangerous. He again experienced the peculiar sensation of sharing his body with something that was at the same time part of him, and yet independent. The thrilling light surged through him as he ran, and he realised he was screaming in half-demented ecstasy as he bombed across the landscape, accelerating further still, and feeling utterly indestructible. He realised that the corrupt feeling of pressure in his head had gone, and sensing that he was in no longer in immediate danger, Phil made a conscious effort to slow himself. As he came to a reluctant standstill, he found himself standing in the middle of a fairway on the golf course located just past the south end of the town.

The hill where he'd been standing before was about two miles north of this point, and figuring that he'd ran for about twenty seconds, Phil was stunned to realise that this meant he'd been moving at around three hundred and sixty miles per hour.

The thought was just there, already formed in his mind, and Phil frowned in confusion. Maths had never been his strong point. Griff though, had had that uncanny ability to figure numerical problems out in his head …

Phil turned in a circle, trying to figure out his next move, and saw that the big detached villa belonging to the Delaney family was close by. He could see the rear side of the house across the road which ran down the south side of the golf course to his left. Phil knew their son Jamie from school, and although they never socialised, he was friendly enough with the guy having played with him in the school football team. A fucking fantastic left mid player, and there'd been rumours that Jamie had been watched by talent scouts from Kilmarnock and even Rangers. Phil also knew his sister Susie, who was in the year below him and whom he'd once winched at a school disco. A tall, pretty blonde lass with hazel eyes and a wicked tongue.

He made his way toward the house, thinking he could maybe explain his gory appearance by saying he'd been in an accident, then use their phone to call Grant and maybe even borrow a change of clothes. It was at best a half-arsed plan, but the best Phil could come up with at the time.

10

Sergeant Stephen Grace glanced across at Ally Marshall, sitting rigidly in the passenger seat of the speeding police car. Until now, the lad had done a decent job of hiding his fear, but it was plain as day on his face now. The young constable tried the radio for the tenth time since they'd sped away from the burning petrol station, the nervous tension evident in the tremor of his voice.

'Foxtrot Sierra Six to Control. Come in, Annie.'

Static.

He tried again.

'Come in Foxtrot Sierra Seven. What's happening at the Delaney place, Kenny?'

More static. They'd heard no more from Kenny since his last transmission, when he'd been babbling about mutilated corpses.

Ally threw the handset down with a frustrated curse.

'Keep your head, son,' Grace advised. 'I don't know what's going on, but you need to stay calm. What's your primary duty?'

'My what? Sarge, I don't …'

'*Your fuckin' primary duty!*' Grace roared. 'What's the first and foremost duty of a police officer? What did they teach you at Tulliallan?'

'The preservation of human life, sir,' Ally responded automatically. 'The first duty of a police officer is the preservation of human life.'

'Good. Now sort yourself out, son. You won't save any cunt's life if you're not calm.'

Grace's own training officer had used this same method on him when he'd been a new recruit, a week out of training and faced with a running battle between Hearts and Hibs fans after an Edinburgh derby game. Grace had been petrified, the sight and sounds of the hundred or so men brutally punching, kicking and slashing at each other in ferocious, unrestrained hand-to-hand combat had temporarily unmanned the young recruit, and he'd frozen, unable to move in the face of the mass pavement dance. His training officer had grabbed him roughly by the collar and screamed in his face, *What's your primary duty?* and that had done the trick. PC Stephen Grace had managed to collect himself, and had waded into the fight in a seemingly impossible attempt to restore order. He'd come away from it with a fractured cheekbone, a concussion and a shallow but painful stab wound to the leg, but he'd done his job. Now it was time for Ally Marshall to do the same.

To be fair to the lad though, this situation was different to a mob of football casuals knocking fuck out of each other. Very different.

Stephen Grace had over thirty years of police experience on his young charge, but the real reason he was keeping his calm better than Ally Marshall was that in the back of his mind, way down deep in his sub-conscious, he'd actually been expecting something like this to happen sooner or later. For a long time, he'd felt that there was something wrong with the village of Ballantrae, as if the town were built on a sleeping volcano.

He could count on one hand the amount of people who'd lived in the village for more than twenty years, himself included, and that incident in the summer with those kids up at Bennane Head had awoken memories in him that had started to fade from his thoughts.

What had made that senseless carnage even more chilling to him, as if it wasn't bad enough already, was that one of the boys involved was from the same family that had been mixed up in the other bloody business that had occurred decades before.

Young Dean Griffiths even bore a remarkable resemblance to his late grandfather.

Grace's troubled thoughts were interrupted by Ally Marshall trying the radio again.

'Control, come in. This is Foxtrot Sierra Six.'

Grace gripped the steering wheel more tightly and wrung the leather cover between his large calloused fists. His own training, forty years distant, hadn't covered what the procedure was in the event of losing contact with your controller *and* all other cars and officers on shift. He doubted Ally's more modern instruction had prepared him for dealing with such an eventuality either.

'Davie, are you there? This is Foxtrot Sierra Six calling Foxtrot Sierra Five. Control, come back. Kenny? Annie? *Does anybody copy?*' Ally's voice had taken on a frantic pleading tone as he desperately sought a response from the mocking empty static.

'Give it a rest, Ally,' Grace said. 'We're here.'

The car topped the rise in the road that ran parallel to the eighth fairway of the golf course, and the Delaney residence came into view. Kenny Young's patrol car was parked outside, the driver's side front door lying open. Grace eased off the accelerator, braking to a halt just behind the other vehicle.

Ally was already scrambling out the passenger side door and Grace clumsily followed him, his arthritic hip sending a twinge of pain through his lower body as he exited the car. Ally was moving hastily towards the broad one storey villa.

'Wait, Ally,' Grace called after him. He knew from experience that it was essential to check your surroundings before rushing into a potentially hazardous situation.

The house showed no signs of life. The green painted

wooden gate that gave access to the path running down the left side of the villa to the back garden was open, and swayed back and forth lazily in the faint morning breeze. Its unoiled hinges made a high pitched squeal with each movement. It was the only sound to be heard.

'Kenny? You there?' Grace called loudly, breaking the eerie silence.

There was no answer.

Grace became aware of an odour on the air. The sweet, subtle stench of something rotten. From the grimace on Ally's face, he knew the young constable had detected it as well.

He walked around the empty police car, searching for some sign of the missing constable. There was no sign of a struggle. No blood spots or any damage to the vehicle that he could see.

'Sarge, look at this,' Ally said.

Grace turned around, seeing the younger man crouched down, examining the ground closely. The driveway leading up to the front of the Delaneys' house wasn't paved with tarmac, but instead covered with small, rounded pale stones, the kind that made that homely *crunch* sound beneath foot and tyre. Ally was on his haunches, pointing to an area of the drive where the pebbly covering seemed to have been disturbed.

There were a series of short parallel furrows dragged through the small stones, around an inch apart, exposing the dirt underneath, as if someone had dragged a small-headed rake along the ground. Grace walked past Ally, noting that the marks ran in the direction of the front door of the villa, which was lying open. The narrow furrows were only about a metre long before they ended. There followed an unmarked area of the ground for a further ten metres or so before the small driveway stones showed further signs of disturbance. This time, Grace could make out a wider, single indentation some four metres in length and a half metre across, as if a wide piece of heavy tubing had been dragged along the ground. This larger marking ran all the way to the front door.

Grace squatted down to examine the indentation more closely, and detected a faint but noxious odour that stung his nostrils and was separate from the other sweetly rotten stench that he now could tell was coming from inside the house. The small stones of the driveway here also seemed to glisten somewhat in the morning light, and Grace reached down and ran his fingertips across the pebbles. They came away slicked in a viscous transparent liquid like semi-opaque snot. His fingers immediately began to tingle and he quickly wiped them on his trouser leg.

He looked up to inform Ally of this strange find.

But the young policeman was gone.

11

Phil was just approaching the rear garden of the Delaney place when he heard the sound of a car approaching the front of the house. The crunching noise the tyres made on the stones made him freeze for a moment. Phil remembered that Jamie's dad had made him help pave the driveway with those little white stones the previous year, and he remember Jamie moaning loudly at football training about his back being buggered from the forced labour.

The sound of the engine cut off, and Phil heard car doors opening and closing. There was the crunching of footsteps on the driveway, and then a voice, which he recognised as that of Sergeant Stephen Grace, called out for someone named Kenny, who Phil assumed to be Kenny Young, one of the other cops who worked in the area. Wanting to avoid the attentions of the police, he threw myself to the ground, hiding in the long grass of the scrub land between the rough of the golf course and the Delaneys' back garden. He lay there in frustrated indecision, wondering if it might be better to just go and announce his presence to the big Sergeant. He knew Phil quite well, and had treated him kindly after what had happened earlier that year, but part of him still insisted that it would be a foolish move. As he crouched in the reeds, unsure of his next move, a faint but familiar tingling sensation in the pit of Phil's gut warned him that he was not alone. That nauseating pressure began to build again in his skull. He frantically looked around, seeing nothing, but he could feel the diseased presence of that other malevolent entity getting closer.

The pressure in his head suddenly increased rapidly, and Phil clutched the sides of his head, wincing in pain. It seemed to be coming from right on top of him, but still there was nothing to be seen. The sick swelling sensation grew even heavier, and with a low agonised moan, he fell back in the grass. Facing upwards, through eyes half shut in agony, he could now see a faint shimmer in the air above him.

It floated there for a second, a formless patch of nothingness in the air that shimmered like a heat haze, only it didn't give off pleasant waves of summer warmth, but waves of a bleak winter chill that made Phil feel black and decayed inside.

It descended slowly, and he sensed it was taking a twisted joy in his distress, savouring it. It came closer, closer, until he could have reached up and touched the thing had it had physical substance. The shimmer began to take on a dark colouration and form twisting, roiling tendrils that whipped through the air like thin smoky tentacles.

Phil lay there on the grass, helpless and paralyzed once again in terror as one of those vaporous appendages morphed into a very solid looking curved claw with a wickedly serrated underside. This obscene talon, a metre long, midnight black and imprinted with sickly red striations, hovered above Phil's prone body, twitching in anticipation. He heard a guttural chuckling in his head, hideous with an unmistakable note of victory.

Phil Densmore closed his eyes and waited to die as the disembodied claw slowly pushed down on his left shoulder. A horrible numbness and deep, deep cold spread in him as the manifestation of the thing pierced his flesh and pinned him to the ground beneath his thrashing body.

12

The Harvester floats above its helpless, writhing quarry and enjoys this moment of power.

It feels the fear pouring off Labhrainne's blood in waves and drinks it in, taking sustenance from the human's terror. At these close quarters, the Harvester senses with new depth the strange otherness of this particular insect. Beneath the aura of fear and despair, there is a spark of energy that is somehow like its own, a unique spiritual signature that only those that walk on both sides of the veil possess. Something that should not be present in a mere mortal.

Interesting.

The Harvester senses other humans nearby. It visited this particular location earlier this same morning in one of its many manifestations, and had fed upon the souls of a family of four and one other, what the humans called a 'policeman'. A peacekeeper in the realm of the living. It took particular pleasure in the devouring of those who fought to preserve order in any dimension of existence, and the Harvester had already tasted the souls of another three of their kind this very bloody and glorious of mornings. Born of chaos, it exults in the destruction of those who seek to maintain order.

While it holds the strange defenceless human beneath it, impaled through the shoulder, it seeks out the nearby others and finds that they too are 'policemen'. The Harvester is a creature ruled by sensation, and can ill resist the alluring pleasure that slaughtering a further brace of peacekeepers will bring.

With a single thought, the Harvester splits its consciousness. Part of it remains observing the peculiar struggling worm pinned beneath it, while another piece of its being returns to the hunt, eager to drink of the souls of more 'policemen'.

13

There hadn't been a sound.

Grace had turned his back to Ally Marshall for only a couple of seconds, and he'd vanished as if into thin air.

A very real fear now gripped Stephen Grace, and he drew the baton from his equipment belt. This didn't make him feel any safer in the slightest.

'Ally?' he called.

No answer. He hadn't, in truth, expected one.

He very slowly moved back towards the two patrol cars on the driveway, noting the *crunch, crunch, crunch* his boots made on those little polished pebbles underfoot. Unless Ally had leapt, from a standing position to the edge of the wide driveway, and landed on the grass verge, a good three metres away on either side from where he'd been standing, all in complete silence, there was no way he could conceivably have moved from his spot without Grace hearing him.

He checked both cars anyway. Both empty of course. Under them. Nothing. He checked the embankment on each side of the road leading up to the house. Nothing.

Grace once more stood by his patrol car, for the first time in almost forty years of police work, at a complete and utter loss as to what to do next. And scared shitless.

'What's your first duty?' he asked himself quietly.

The mystifying disappearance of two of his officers, and the inability to raise Annie at the station or Davie Leish and Andy Cummings at the Densmore house, were inexplicable. But he still had a duty to protect the public, and he'd come here to the Delaney place in response to an emergency call. His first duty was to protect the populace of the town.

Fortified somewhat now that he'd shaken off his indecisiveness, Grace boldly moved towards the front door of the Delaney villa again, the driveway stones *crunch, crunch, crunching* loudly under his determined strides.

A soft, fluttering noise made him look up.

Falling from the sky was an assortment of objects. The gentle flapping sound came from one of these items, which billowed out on the air, revealing itself to be a white short sleeved shirt.

All around Grace, items of clothing fell to the earth, landing on the ground around him making their own little crunches as they hit the driveway. A black boot, a police issue equipment belt, a handheld radio, a police constable's hat, another black boot, a single black sock, closely followed by another sock, this one a different colour. Finally, a pair of white y-fronts with bright red lettering proclaiming 'LOVE GOD' emblazoned over the seat landed at his feet.

Grace could only stand there, stunned by the bizarre event and looking around at the assortment of clothing and police equipment that had inexplicably fallen from the sky.

With a heavy wet *flop*, a large pale object like a deflated balloon landed in front of him, joining the collection of garments and gear strewn on the ground around him.

'What the holy fuck ...' he whispered.

A tremendous crash of rending metal and smashing glass suddenly erupted from behind Grace with shocking, brutal force, causing him to spin round in fright and fall backwards. He landed on his arse atop the strange balloon like thing that had just a second ago landed in front of him.

He became aware of a few things simultaneously. The first was that the front end of Kenny Young's patrol car was destroyed. A weird red mannequin, that had apparently also plummeted from the heavens, was draped across the ruined bonnet in a bed of dented metal and shattered windshield glass.

The second thing he realised was that the deflated balloonish object in which he'd inelegantly planted his backside was wet and warm.

He dumbly lifted a hand to his face and saw that it had turned bright red, like he'd dipped it in a can of paint without realising it. Grace quickly pushed himself to his feet, backing away from the weird bloody pile on the ground. That's when he noticed the hair on it. And the tattoo.

A stylised gecko, drawn in an Inca or Mayan style, he could never remember which. Ally Marshall had had that etched on his upper left arm last year and took great pride in showing it off round the station.

He whirled around again, once more facing the pulverised patrol car and the glistening red tailor's dummy that now adorned the smashed front end, like the world's most grotesque hood ornament.

It was breathing.

With very slow steps on very stiff legs, Stephen Grace approached the skinned human being that had fallen from the sky and written off the vehicle.

Will the insurance cover this? he thought crazily.

The eyes, shockingly white in the raw red flesh of the face (*what face?*) stared at him intently with a surprised look.

Of course he looks surprised. He doesn't have eyebrows. Or eyelids for that matter, Grace thought.

'*Saaaaaaj ... Saaaaaj ...*' Ally Marshall pleaded, his words distorted due to the lack of lips on his peeled head, one raw arm reaching out to his superior.

Grace's legs went, and he sat down for the second time that morning on the Delaneys' crunchy driveway.

Then something else dropped out of the sky and landed before him. This was *not* however human. Nor was it a pair of odd socks.

It stood a good nine feet tall. Partly skeletal, partly insectoid, partly arachnid, and wholly alien. A shifting mass of glowing orbs, fangs, claws, tattered wings and waving tentacles.

Still sat down on the driveway, Grace couldn't look at it. The very sight of the thing offended him. He could feel something wanting to give way in his head and realised it was his own sanity. He groped desperately in his psyche for something solid to cling to, something recognisable, tangible and safe, something that might save him from losing his hold on reality, which with the arrival of this impossible *thing*, had just performed a slippery, twisting backflip.

He bowed his head, averting his eyes from the ungodly monster, and found himself looking between his legs at those little furrows that had been dragged into the stones covering the driveway. He suddenly had an idea about how those marks had been made, and on the heels of this thought, realised that the application of logic was perhaps his best defence when the world went insane. It was something to hold on to. Something he knew.

'Fingers,' he said aloud. 'Someone was dragged along the ground and their fingers made those marks. I'll bet there's a fingernail in amongst the stones there somewhere. And that other big mark over by the door, where the wee stones are coated with slime, that'll have been made by some sort of tentacle, eh? That's what grabbed the poor bastard.'

The abhorrent thing before him let out a weird hissing, stuttering series of clicks and whoops that he thought sounded like mocking laughter, and Stephen Grace suddenly wasn't afraid anymore.

He was angry. Fucking raging.

'What's your first duty?' he asked himself again through gritted teeth.

He remembered that day in the backstreets of Edinburgh. How he'd momentarily been paralysed by fear, but reminded of his primary duty, had overcome it and waded into the affray, taking punishment, but protecting human lives. He remembered the exultation he'd experienced once he was in amongst the mass brawl. The heat of battle, the huge surge of adrenaline born of a potent mix of fear and wild excitement, so pure that he hadn't even felt that knife biting into his thigh.

He looked at his hand and saw he was still gripping his baton.

Pushing himself to his feet once more, he raised his eyes and faced the thing that had brought chaos and death to his town that morning.

'Fuckin' 'mon then, ya big cunt,' he snarled.

Sergeant Stephen Grace waded in.

14

Back in school, in the biology lab, there'd been a glass case mounted on the wall which displayed a collection of insects that had been pinned to a felt covered board. There'd been a small magnifying glass attached by a string to the side of the display case with which students could get a close up view of the unfortunate bugs, and Phil had always been a bit creeped out at the sight of the insects' faces when viewed at close quarters.

As he lay on the ground that morning, pinned to the ground through his own shoulder by a giant semi-corporeal claw that had materialised out of thin air, he felt real empathy for those bugs.

He was, once again, waiting to die. To all intents and purposes, dead already, just as dead as those desiccated moths and wasps in that dusty display case. He also was being scrutinised, examined just like an interesting creepy-crawly. To the thing that held him there, that's exactly what Phil was. He could hear it inside his head, through the pain.

What are you? it whispered silently.

Some sort of link had been established between them, perhaps because a part of its essence was physically impaling Phil to the ground. He could feel its contempt, its puzzlement, its gloating satisfaction at having him completely at its mercy. He was also aware of its ability to split its consciousness and physical self, and Phil understood that while it held him there, another part of it was elsewhere.

Being subjected to its thoughts in this strange way was nauseating to his very soul. Through their physical and psychic connection, it showed Phil what it did to Ally Marshall. He saw what it had done to all the others that morning. What it had done to his brother. To his dad.

What are you? It asked again inside his head.

221

It twisted the disembodied talon that pinned Phil down, bringing a fresh blast of agony searing through his body, but it wouldn't let him scream. Phil was made a slave to the demon, mind and body, and he saw things impossible to describe in any language known to man, because it was an experience not *of* this plane of existence. Its thoughts were his thoughts, its memories his memories, and though much of it was beyond human understanding, Phil understood that it was a harvester of souls. It had a quota to meet, and it was particularly interested in him, though it didn't know, or care, why. It was a mere soldier, mindlessly and unquestioningly carrying out its orders in the name of some other.

Through his agony, his mental centre of gravity tottering precariously, Phil thought he could perhaps find some answers in this thing's mind if only he had courage enough to look. As he expected to die anyway, he thought, *fuck it.*

Without thinking about how it would be accomplished, just *doing* it, Phil mentally *pushed* at the thing's invading thoughts, and felt it reel back in alarm. His mental touch was as repulsive to this being as it's was to his own. Its hold on him, both physical and mental, wavered for a second before it pushed back with mind and claw. The flare of pain was terrible, but through the fear and torment, Phil felt a slow, smouldering anger begin to build.

He pushed back with his mind again, harder and more focussed than before, eliciting a satisfying mental scream from the foul entity. He felt its fear for a moment, but when it came, the phantom's retaliation was brutal, cleaving through Phil's consciousness like a black locomotive. It delved deep into his thoughts and memories, and found the dream like encounters with Cairnsey and Sam.

Why, human? it hissed in Phil's mind. *Why do you commune with the dead? What* are *you?*

It gave another savage twist of the bony talon, keeping up both its mental and physical assault.

Through the pain, Phil's anger flared brightly again. The

sense of the strange *other* that intermittently shared his body was strong.

Fuck you! he thought-screamed back at it. *I'm Phillip Albert Densmore! I play centre midfield for Ballantrae Juniors! I support Glasgow Rangers! I love to listen to stoner rock! I loved my dad and hated my brother! Fuck you! Sam Anderson, Josh Cairns and Dean Griffiths were my best mates and they're IN HERE!*

He pictured Sam the previous night, placing his hand on his chest.

We're in here, Phil, he'd said.

Phil felt a raging heat build in his chest, emanating from where Sam had placed his hand. Without knowing what he was doing, he used his right hand to reach across his chest toward the breast pocket of his bloodstained shirt.

The thing above him suddenly sprouted another clawed appendage from its dark roiling mass. A huge scorpion-like barb, jointed like a skeletal finger and wickedly tipped, reared back above Phil's face.

Aware of its thoughts, he knew the creature now meant to kill him, its curiosity now outweighed by doubt. The wicked, bony stinger snapped down, and Phil's fingers closed around an object in his shirt pocket. With an enraged scream, he drew it out and slashed it through the air above his face, simultaneously feeling the inner fury in his chest explode in a great purging wave.

There was a brilliant, blinding white flash, and in Phil's mind, he heard the thing scream in agony.

The monstrous carapace-like stinger shattered mere millimetres from his face, as did the black talon pinning him to the earth. Both dissolved in burning grains that blew away on the air like disintegrating ash.

Phil looked and saw that his right fist, clutched tightly around the object he'd pulled from his pocket, glowed with a flashing blue and white aura, and he instinctively struck out again at the shimmering black haze that still hovered above him.

There was another great flash of pale blue light, accompanied by the pungent scent of burning ozone, and the twisting entity abruptly vanished in a puff of glowing atoms.

Phil was suddenly on his feet, aflame with an intense righteous fury.

During his mental congress with the thing, he'd been aware of it standing in front of Sergeant Grace on the Delaneys' driveway.

Before he knew he was going to do it, Phil was bursting through the undergrowth, a guttural snarl in his throat and wrath in his heart.

15

As Stephen Grace ran at the thing standing in the Delaneys' driveway, he didn't expect to live much longer, but he was determined to at least get a few good digs in at the hellish creature before he went.

In the flood of adrenaline that rushed through him, Grace's heightened senses took in every minute detail of the scene, and he experienced everything in highly defined, slow-motion clarity. Although it happened faster than the blinking of an eye, he clearly perceived the grotesque thick tendril which ended in a foot-long serrated blade, bursting from the monster's body and whipping towards him. He knew he couldn't avoid the deadly appendage, which would surely cut him in half, and he closed his eyes, not expecting to open them again. He pictured his late wife's face in his mind, wanting her smile to be the last thing he saw, and he smiled.

There was an unmistakable screech of pain from the creature, instantly followed by a hard impact across his chest. Grace was spun by the force of the blow, and he pirouetted off the side of the driveway, landing in a heap in the shallow embankment. He opened his eyes and saw the thing staggering backwards, seemingly in distress, howling and thrashing its multitude of bladed, clawed and pincered limbs in the air.

He looked down at himself and found that his clothing had been slashed neatly across his upper torso. His protective knife proof vest had also been parted as if cut with a laser. Quickly feeling inside his ripped shirt, he found a long but shallow laceration that ran diagonally from his left shoulder down to his sternum. There was some blood, but not enough to signify a mortal wound.

Looking back at the thing on the driveway above him, he saw the creature start towards him again, bellowing and hissing in rage. Somehow, the creature had been distracted at the very instant he should have been sliced in two, and had only landed a glancing blow. Grace knew he wouldn't be so lucky a second time. Knowing now the blinding speed with which the monstrous creature attacked, he understood that he was ridiculously outmatched, and his hopes of getting in a few good digs withered. He knew that its next assault would snuff him out like a bloody candle, but regardless, he wearily climbed out of the embankment and raised his baton again.

'You couldn't finish your fuckin' dinner, ya big poof,' he taunted the advancing nightmare.

Faster than he could register, another thick tentacle shot out and was wrapped with crushing force around his neck before he could draw another breath. His air was instantly cut off, and he was lifted from his feet, then slowly drawn towards the entity, thrashing in silent suffocating desperation, like a fish on a hook.

It dangled Grace a few feet above the ground, watching as his kicking legs frantically tried to find purchase in thin air. It brought him closer, and he saw a horizontal fissure suddenly tear open in the monster's bristling bony torso with a liquid snapping noise. The grotesque hole in the creature's body twisted into a mutated mouth, sprouting needle-like teeth that dripped black liquid. Fighting vainly for air and flailing uselessly with his baton at the cable-thick tentacle that gripped his neck, Grace watched as this new orifice widened and pushed out from the central mass, morphing into an elongated, wolfish snout. Small worm-like things waved obscenely inside this horrific new feature, writhing between the dripping fangs and beckoning him closer. He was now inches away from the demon. His vision seemed to come from the end of a long black tunnel that grew increasingly thin as his oxygen starved brain screamed for air that wouldn't come. The thing's shriek of victory filled his ears, and as the blackness closed over his sight, he could feel and smell the rotten carrion stink of its breath as his head was pulled into the gaping maw. Grace felt those repugnant internal worms squirm into his ears and nostrils …

There was a sudden crack-flash of noise and light that penetrated the darkness blanketing his vision. The irresistible pressure around Grace's throat was suddenly gone, and he felt himself falling, landing heavily on his back. He gratefully sucked in a big gulp of precious air and opened his eyes.

A boy stood over him. He was screaming and driving the aberrant organism back, and throwing lightning bolts from his fist like some sort of enraged god.

16

Phil burst out onto the driveway from the undergrowth at the side of the road, and in his accelerated state, took in the scene in a nanosecond.

The nightmare entity stood in all its diabolical glory in the Delaneys' driveway. It was holding Sergeant Grace in the air by a thick black tendril that was wrapped around his throat, and it was pulling him towards an obscene fanged muzzle that protruded from its body. Seeing the thing revealed in broad daylight was a visual ordeal that confounded Phil's senses. The thing, the *Harvester*, seemed to be more fluid than solid, constantly changing shape and consistency, randomly sprouting course hair where there had been bare stained bone or insect-like carapace a second before. It seemed at one moment to resemble a monstrous, upright spider, but then its contours and lines would bend and morph into something that looked more like a scaly, winged cross between an octopus and a wolf. It was all and none of these things; a formless antithesis of creation, born of another dimension where the physical laws of nature didn't exist.

Phil saw it slowly pull Sergeant Grace's head into that disgusting dripping mouth, and half mad with a demented need for retribution, he charged. Lightning flashed from the object in his hand, sending a bolt of blue and white flame sizzling into the shifting central mass of the thing's body.

It shrieked and staggered back, releasing the big copper. Phil pressed forward, stepping over Sergeant Grace and putting himself between him and the thing, continuing to punch his fist towards it, blasting flare after flare after flare of purifying lightning into it.

Giant arachnid legs, barbed stingers, tentacles and tendrils blew off the torso and disintegrated as Phil pummelled the screaming, thrashing monster with blue white fire. It continued to back away, turned, spread tattered wings and attempted to take flight, but more bolts of brilliant azure light from his fist blasted flaming holes in the stretched leathery parchment, and it crashed to the ground again where it attempted to crawl away, emitting a shrill, ululating howl of agony.

Phil pursued it mercilessly, never letting up his frenzied assault. Another bolt of lightning blew apart the disgusting maw that jutted from its body. More pulverised the entire lower half of its morphing torso, blasting a collection of scuttling scorpion-like legs to ashes. Phil was screaming obscenities, venting his hate and disgust as he tore it apart.

'*Mother (flash) fucking (flash) piece of (flash) shit (flash) cunt (flash) sick (flash) murdering (flash) bastard (flash) fucking (flash) cock (flash) sucking (flash) ugly (flash) evil (flash) bastard ...*'

At last, there was only the head left.

It was roughly the size of a large beach ball, with a sloping, apeish forehead dotted with a cluster of sickly glowing yellow orbs, now growing dim. Underneath, the lower portion of what passed for its skull was a singular row of jagged and serrated eight inch fangs, like one half of an oversized bear trap armed with grossly enlarged shark teeth.

The yellow orbs flared again briefly, and Phil heard it speak in his mind.

The quota is not complete, worm, and you have won nothing. Others will come, and slaughter will find you. You will have no peace in this world, and when your cursed soul is reaped, the void will welcome you into the arms of oblivion. For eternity, you will scream and suffer...

Phil didn't know what the fuck it was talking about, and sick of its pish, he interrupted the rambling hateful diatribe with a final massive blast of energy that blew the head apart.

The ashes blew away on the morning breeze, until there was nothing left but the smell of charred air.

17

Stephen Grace pushed himself to his feet for what felt like the thousandth time that morning, and watched as his saviour, who he now recognised as young Phil Densmore, threw a final bolt of bluish fire into the misshapen head of the shifting monstrosity, destroying it utterly.

For a moment he just stood there behind the lad who was visibly panting, his shoulders heaving in the aftermath of the incredible outpouring of power he'd wrought.

Grace's mind was a blurry whirl. The morning had started as unusual, had taken a turn for the strange, and had rapidly descended into a ditch of impossible madness. His understanding of the very nature of reality and the laws of physics had been irrevocably changed in the last few minutes, and he doubted he'd ever sleep again.

As he stood there watching the boy's breathing slowly return to normal, Grace felt the shallow laceration across his chest begin to tingle. Abruptly, there was a stabbing flare of pain that caused him to hiss between his teeth. He sank to his knees, but after a moment, the pain receded. He remained kneeling on the ground, trying to catch his breath, feeling the wound throb with a peculiar prickling sensation.

The Densmore lad turned towards him, and Grace realised for the first time that the boy looked like a walking underdone steak. He was coated in blood, most of it dried in large maroon-coloured stains that covered his clothing, but there was also fresh claret oozing from a large puncture wound in his left shoulder that looked like it had been sustained only recently.

In his hand, the boy was holding what appeared to be a playing card, and there was something about his eyes that was … very, very wrong.

The Densmore boy took a step towards him and Grace,

still on his knees, shuffled back, raising his hands in a protective gesture.

'It's alright, Sergeant. I'm okay now,' the lad said.

I don't think you are, son, Grace thought, regarding him cautiously. *Not at all.*

The look in the lad's eyes was fading, but for a brief second there ... Holy Christ.

It wasn't that his eyes had looked dead. Just the opposite in fact. They'd been very much alive. *Too* alive, somehow, and for a moment Grace had been more scared of this skinny, battered teenager than he'd been of the tentacled, shape-shifting nightmare the kid had blown apart.

Phil held out a hand to Grace, who took it after a further moment's hesitation. He was surprised by the ease with which the boy pulled him to his feet.

'Thanks for that, Phil,' he said.

The boy just nodded, not meeting his eyes.

Grace remembered his young constable Ally Marshall, and turned to the wrecked patrol car. Ally, or the horrifying flayed spectacle that Ally had become, lay draped across the crumpled and blood stained bonnet, indisputably dead.

Shaking his head sadly, Grace moved towards the front door of the Delaney house.

'Where are you going?' Phil asked behind him.

'Need to check the house, son,' Grace said, continuing forward.

He felt a hand on his shoulder.

'Don't,' the boy said. 'They're all dead. Your other guy, Kenny as well. It showed me what it did. You don't want to see.'

Grace shrugged off the hand, wincing as the movement

pulled at his chest wound, and strode forward again. 'They're my responsibility,' he muttered as he crossed the threshold.

A few minutes later, Grace staggered back out the door, pale-faced and retching.

The boy, who'd remained outside, waited for him to finish and compose himself. He said nothing, but gave Grace a sympathetic look.

Grace took a deep breath and asked, 'Is this morning connected to what happened with you and your mates in May?'

The Densmore boy nodded slightly.

Grace returned the nod and made a decision.

'You'd better come with me, Phil,' he said. 'There's some things you need to know.'

He started walking towards the functioning patrol car, and after a pause, the lad followed him.

As he sat down in the driving seat, the pain in Grace's chest went up a few notches, and he hissed again through his teeth.

'It hurts?' the boy asked, climbing into the passenger side.

'Aye, son. Hurts like a bastard.'

Grace removed the damaged protective vest, unbuttoned his shirt and examined the wound. Already the ragged lips of the wound were swollen and angry red, and a foul smelling, semi-opaque brownish liquid seeped slowly from the shallow laceration. He could feel a certain heaviness in his legs now as well. A mere infection wouldn't flare up so quickly. This looked and felt more like the effect of a bad snakebite. Grace tried to imagine what kind of toxins and venom might be delivered in the strike of a creature like the beast that had almost taken his head off, and decided he really didn't want to know. He looked across at the Densmore boy who, sensing his fear, gave a slow, sad shake of the head.

'How long?' Grace asked.

'Maybe an hour. I'm sorry.'

Grace fixed him with an even stare.

'How can you know that?'

The boy slowly and delicately tapped the side of his head in an extremely creepy way that made Grace shiver. 'I was in its mind for a few seconds, Sergeant Grace,' he said. 'A hospital won't do any good.'

Grace grunted. The closest hospital was a two hour drive away in any case. He sighed in resignation.

'Best get a move on then, eh?' he said, starting the car.

18

Phil didn't ask where they were going. It didn't seem to matter, and he figured Sergeant Grace had his own questions to ask himself right then. He knew the big polis knew he didn't have long to live, and Phil thought he took it pretty well, considering.

So they drove in silence, away from the Delaneys' villa and the horror that lay inside and out of it.

Phil's shoulder didn't hurt anymore, he noticed. Lifting aside the left half of his torn and bloody shirt, he could see there was just a pale patch of scar tissue where the thing's talon had pinned him to the ground. It looked like an old wound long healed. Why it wasn't weeping and poisoned like the unfortunate Sergeant Grace's injury, he didn't know.

What Phil did know was that the effects of his encounter with the demon went way beyond the mere physical. It was in his mind and his soul that Phil Densmore took the most punishment that morning.

He looked down at the playing card that he found spinning through the fingers of his left hand, turning over and under the digits, forward and back, forward and back with dexterous speed. Phil remembered Sam's words to Griff that sun-soaked evening in the back of Cairnsey's car as he threw that very card down, winning the game of Switch they'd been playing.

'Pick up five, just for being so shite at this game,' Phil said aloud.

Sergeant Grace looked across at him with a raised eyebrow. Phil just shook his head in response and the big copper returned his attention to the road.

Back and forward, the King of Spades spun through his fingers. It'd been Sam's party piece and they all used to think it was cool as fuck, but none of them could ever replicate the quick, fluid movement and dexterity of hand Sam possessed, no matter how much they tried.

Phil was doing it now though, just as smooth as Sam ever had, flicking that single card over and under the fingers of his left hand, forward and back again. Phil wasn't even left handed. Sam had been though. He'd had a right handed Stratocaster copy that he used to string and play upside down, just like his hero Jimi Hendrix had, but without the awesome talent. Sam had always played that beat-up guitar with a lot more volume and enthusiasm than skill.

We're in here, he'd said, placing his hand above Phil's heart. Placing the card there.

Looking out the passenger side window of the car, he realised they were on the road that lead to the residence of the dying policeman who sat beside him in the driver seat. Sergeant Grace lived in a former crofter's cottage up on the hill overlooking Ballantrae, not far from the house they'd just left.

Looking out to his left down the hill, the village lay spread out before Phil. Just a sleepy little hamlet with fields beyond the north and south ends, hemmed in by the grey Firth of Clyde on the west and the hills and forest to the east. He was amazed at how quaint and peaceful the village looked from here. It all appeared so normal. Tranquil even. A small, sleepy Scottish coastal town fit for a tourist postcard. Phil wound down his window and found the morning to be as quiet as it looked.

He knew though, that behind many doors down in the village, there were rooms painted blood red, lives destroyed and terrible carnage. The peaceful silence that hung over the village like a cosy blanket would soon be torn away once the residents that had slept through the Harvester's passing started to discover those who hadn't been so fortunate, and the village would never be the same again.

The car continued up the hill until they eventually stopped

in front of Grace's single story white-washed cottage. It was only natural, Phil guessed, to want to die in your own home.

With a wince and a hiss of indrawn breath, the Sergeant got out of the car. Phil followed him up the garden path into the house where he'd lived alone since his wife had passed away a couple of years previously. Cancer had taken Lila Grace, Phil seemed to recall.

On entering, he saw the narrow hallway was lined with pictures of Sergeant Grace, his late spouse, and younger similarly-featured people who Phil assumed to be their children and grandchildren. The usual assortment of snaps taken on holidays, birthdays and the like. All the pictures were perfectly aligned in relation to each other and set at military-precise right angles. Phil could imagine Sergeant Grace assiduously checking each one with a protractor and spirit level. There wasn't a speck of dust anywhere, and the house had a comforting smell of furniture polish, coffee and cigarette smoke that was homely rather than stale. Phil was acutely aware he could separate and distinguish all three individual smells, and could even make out an underlying whiff of boot polish.

Another new talent.

He remembered Griff stalking him through the woods that night, sniffing him out.

Phil followed Grace into his living room where the first thing he did was open up a drinks cabinet and take out a bottle of Glenmorangie eighteen-year-old single malt. He poured a healthy nip into a heavy looking cut crystal tumbler and downed it in one, then looked over at Phil briefly as he refilled his glass with a second, equally generous measure.

'It's a damned sin to just down this stuff like it was cheap tequila,' he said, 'but right now, a quick shot's what's in order, son.'

Grace poured another hefty measure into a second tumbler and held it out to Phil.

'Get this into you, Phil,' he said in a voice that indicated he would brook no protests.

Phil hadn't yet acquired a taste for the stuff, having only made the alcoholic leap from cider to lager two years before, and he'd almost thrown up when he'd taken a swallow of Whyte and Mackay that Sam and him discovered in his parents' drinks cabinet one night. This particular morning had been one of many changes, though, and he took the proffered drink, knocking it back as Grace had done and welcoming the fiery flow in his gullet that seemed to explode like sweet napalm in his belly.

Grace's living room was as neat and orderly as the hall. The fairly spartan, uncluttered domain of an ageing bachelor, yet here and there were small things that denoted a woman's touch. The collection of miniature china dolls that adorned the mantelpiece. The knitted throw that covered the back of the armchair, and the delicate and intricate hand-made doilies on the low well-polished coffee table.

Grace sat down with a heavy sigh in his armchair, resting the bottle of scotch and his glass on the coffee table, indicating that Phil should take a seat on the overstuffed couch to the side of him. Phil put his own whisky tumbler down on a doily and Grace promptly refilled it, then took a packet of Regal cigarettes from his shirt pocket and offered Phil one, which he accepted.

For a moment, they just sat in the quiet living room, smoking and sipping scotch, each absorbed with their own personal thoughts and demons. The only sound was the low *tock-tock-tock* of the grandfather clock which stood in the corner. It was a sound Phil always associated with death for some reason, and he used to get nervous when in a room in which one of those imposing timepieces always seemed to dominate. Here though, the deep regular ticking was as comforting as the single malt.

'Do me a favour, Phil,' Grace asked, breaking the silence. 'Stick some music on, would you? The stereo's in the low cabinet under the window there.'

Phil got up from the couch and opened the doors of the squat cupboard that nestled in the curve of the room's large bay window. To his surprise, he was greeted with a very nice, and no doubt expensive, Bang and Olufsen sound system and a thoroughly decent CD collection, which consisted of mainly jazz and blues, but which also included some albums by Black Sabbath, The Who, Led Zeppelin and even Nirvana. Cairnsey would have approved of the man's standards, Phil thought with a twinge of sadness.

'Anything you want to hear?' he asked.

Grace was thoughtful for a few seconds, then a slow smile grew on his craggy face and he nodded to himself.

'Robert Johnson,' he said.

Phil nodded, noting without much surprise that he had picked Cairnsey's all time favourite performer.

He inserted the CD into the opulent stereo, pressed play and went back to the couch where his cigarette was still smouldering away in an ashtray rendered in the shape of the cockerel of Portugal. A holiday souvenir that his wife had probably picked up. Somehow that cheap, tacky and chipped little ceramic ashtray was one of the saddest things Phil had ever seen.

The high quality Bang and Olufsen speakers subtly came alive with the hiss and crackle of deep blues. Red raw music, as Cairnsey would often describe it, put down *au natural* on early recording equipment back in the early years of the twentieth century. *Me and the Devil Blues* came slithering out of the high definition speakers, stark and chilling. The legendary bluesman's anguished, howling voice, as expressive as a suicide note and twice as mournful, backed by the chugging, impossible sounding guitar chords played on a battered acoustic, washed over the Sergeant and Phil as they sat in his living room, feeling the blues in a very real way. Johnson sang of the Devil knocking on his door that morning, and how he believed it was time to go.

238

Phil didn't say anything. He knew he'd still be alive at the end of that day, and he was the only person in the room who could say that. If Grace wanted to sit quietly, sipping Glenmorangie, smoking fags and listening to the man who sold his soul to the devil in exchange for unearthly musical prowess, then Phil was cool with that. After the morning they'd had, a little quiet time with some tunes, a smoke and a nice single malt or two was just dandy.

He waited till the song was done, then Sergeant Stephen Grace began to speak.

'Did you know your pal Dean's grandfather?'

'Grandpa Griff? Of course. Everyone knew the big guy,' Phil replied.

'Did your pal ever tell you about the murder that happened around here back in the eighties, and how Alex Griffiths was involved?'

This was news to Phil. He shook my head in surprise.

'I don't think even Griff knew about that,' he said. 'He was always telling stories, same as his grandpa. No way he wouldn't have told us about something like that.'

'You lads were pretty close, eh?'

Phil nodded. He'd never had any other real friends but Cairnsey, Sam and Griff, but he'd always known that the relationship between the four of them was special in some indefinable way.

Sergeant Grace continued. 'Alex Griffiths was, for a time, the chief suspect in a murder case. This was in eighty-two, just before my time working here. The case was handled by an old mate of mine, Andrew Swanney, and when he died, I took over his job, but the case, such as it was, was closed by then.'
'This is news to me,' Phil said. 'I didn't know about any of this.'

'Not many people do, son. It was all handled very quietly

at the time, and when it was over, no one talked about it at all. There were a few reasons for that, and it was partly because Alex Griffiths' money and businesses kept this town alive during the recession that was happening at the time. There would've been no sense driving him away with gossip after he was cleared, and then watching the town die. Since then, just about everyone who lived here at the time has died or moved somewhere else, so there's only one or two people still around who know about what happened.'

Sergeant Grace refilled his whisky tumbler and lit a fresh cigarette, offering Phil another, which he took. As he leaned forward with the packet of smokes, Grace gasped in pain and clutched at his chest. He sat back in his armchair breathing heavily, trying to collect himself. He eventually got his breathing back under control. 'Guess I'll not have to worry about being hauled over the coals for breaking the Data Protection Act by telling you this, Phil,' he said. Grace smiled through his pain and began his tale.

'Going from the case notes I inherited from Andy Swanney, and from what information I picked up from other coppers who worked here at the time before I arrived from Edinburgh, the office got a call one night in July of nineteen eighty-two.

'Craig Hamill was a local lad that had been fined for poaching a couple of times, and he called into the station one night saying he'd found a body out in the woods near Bennane Head. Said his dog sniffed it out and had started digging. He never did say what he was doing that far into the woods at night time, but word round town was that he was into badger baiting as well as poaching.'

'Anyway, he dragged the boy that was on duty that night away out into the forest, and right enough, they found a corpse in a shallow grave way back in the deepest part of the woods, partially decomposed.'

'Well, you can imagine this was a big thing to happen in a wee place like this, and it made the papers. The usual appeal for witnesses went out, and a few days later, a man by the name of Ray Vize called the station, saying he had some information.'

'Ray was a homeless guy who lived in Glasgow at the time, but he was originally from here. He'd owned a wee engineering outfit that took care of the local fishing fleet and such, but he hit the bottle when Alex Griffiths bought up a bunch of the local businesses, his included.'

'So he was the original owner of Anderson's?' Phil asked, referring to the engineering company now currently run by Sam's dad, but which was owned by Griff's family.

Grace nodded.

'Vize, according to talk in the village, had always claimed that Alex Griffiths swindled him in the deal for the shop, and tricked him somehow into parting with the place for a pittance. His wife left him and he ended up in Glasgow, living between a hostel and a park bench in Glasgow Green, tanning any drink he could get his hands on. By the time he called the station saying he had information about the murder, he'd been homeless in Glasgow for three years and was a hopeless jakey.'

'Anyway, he calls in and says he'd seen the victim, who was a seventeen-year-old lassie from Dundee. A missing runaway named Lisa McKeown. She'd been identified through dental records and her picture was in the paper with the story.'

'Vize said that he's seen her in a nasty wee pub near the Barras in Glasgow where he would sometimes get a drink if he had a couple of pounds in his pocket. It was that sort of place that sold cheap bevvy, didn't ask questions, and was popular with the tramps and strays that hung about that area of the town. According to him, he'd seen the lassie speaking to someone who he recognised, and the two of them had left the pub together. It was Alex Griffiths, he said.'

'And Alex didn't recognise this Ray Vize while he was in the pub?' Phil asked.

Grace shook his head.

'By this time remember, Vize had been living on the streets for a few years. If Griffiths had seen him, he'd have thought he was just another manky tramp with a beard and long hair. He'd have looked nothing like the man Griffiths had known back in Ballantrae.'

'Anyway, when Andy Swanney found out that this Vize guy was naming the town's financial saviour as a murder suspect, he got nervous. Alexander Griffiths, the Earl of Ayrshire, had bought up most of the town's businesses during the recession, pumped in a shit load of cash and made them more profitable, and now Andy had to go and question him about a murder, all on the say so of a homeless bevy merchant that was known to hold a grudge against him.'

'Griffiths was brought in of course, but he had an alibi. Said he'd been in Edinburgh on business the night Ray Vize claimed to have seen him in Glasgow. They checked the alibi, naturally, and a lad working in the bar of the hotel where Griffiths said he'd been staying confirmed he'd spent the whole evening there, from the start of the boy's shift at six pm, till the bar closed at midnight. What's more, Griffiths even had his receipt from the hotel. As alibi's go, it was tighter than a duck's arse.'

'So Vize was just talking shite to make trouble for Griff's grandpa after all?' Phil asked.

'Well, more than that as it turned out. That's what Griffiths claimed as well of course; that Vize was bitter about how his life had gone, and blamed him for it. From the transcriptions of Vize's first official interview though, he categorically stated that he *didn't* blame Griffiths for the way he'd ended up. He still maintained that he'd been conned in the business deal, but he was big enough to admit it was his own fault that he'd hit the bottle and lost his wife and home.'

'As it turned out Ray Vize was arrested and charged with the murder a week later.'

'*Vize* was the killer?'

Grace shrugged.

'That's the way it went. Someone else, a ticket seller working at Glasgow Central, came forward and was interviewed. His name was Brian Bishop, and according to him, he'd been working in the ticket booth one night when a young, blonde lassie accompanied by a scruffy looking, older man with a beard and long hair came to his window and bought two tickets to Stranraer. He said he remembered thinking it was odd that a pretty girl like that was hanging about with a guy dressed in pish-stained jeans and a jacket full of holes. Quite a pair they made, and they seemed to be an item, as the trampy-looking guy was holding the girl close, with an arm round her shoulders. But he said that the lassie had looked and sounded nervous as she bought and paid for the tickets, and that as they were walking away from his booth, he thought he might have seen, just for a second, something that could maybe have been a knife in the guy's hand, but he'd only seen it for a split second, and couldn't say for sure.'

'Going on this, of course, they hauled Vize in for questioning again and searched him. He did have a blade, which he claimed was for protection. That would have been fair enough, with Glasgow being as rough as it is, especially back in those days, and even more so for somebody sleeping rough most of the time. When they searched the hostel where he stayed on and off though, the coppers found a pair of the dead girl's bloodstained knickers. The lassie's poor mother confirmed that they had belonged to her wee Lisa.'

'Fuckin' hell,' Phil said.

'Aye,' Grace went on. 'Griffiths was off the hook, and Vize went down for life, but he didn't do much time in prison.'

'Why not?' Phil asked.

''Cause someone stabbed him to death inside Barlinnie

jail before he'd even done a month.'

At this cold information, Phil briefly thought about his brother James. He'd heard that Jim had been suspected of knifing someone during his stay at that same prison, several years later.

'Right up till the day he was murdered in his cell in the 'Linnie,' Grace continued, 'Ray Vize maintained that Griffiths had taken that wee lassie out of the bar that night and had then set him up to take the fall.'

Grace abruptly succumbed to a coughing fit at this point, his whole body wracked with great, heaving spasms. Phil poured him another slug of Glenmorangie, which he took gratefully. Fresh blood now flecked the front of his shirt. He didn't have long left.

From his tale, Phil thought the evidence against Ray Vize was pretty damning, but he sensed there was more to the story.

Grace valiantly got his breath under control again and resumed talking.

'So, Griffiths was in the clear, and according to some of the people in the village, it was made crystal that he wouldn't take kindly to any further defamation of his name. He might have been regarded as a bit of a character and a storyteller, but there was another side to Alex Griffiths. Some people, quietly of course, saw him as little more than a gangster with a title rather than as the jolly, rich local philanthropist. He was friendly to everyone, but he was definitely someone you didn't fuck around with.'

'With Ray Vize locked up, it all died down, and for a few months everything was quiet. Then out of the blue, my mate Andy Swanney, the station Sergeant here at the time, turned up dead. They found him in his wee cottage down by the shore, just round the back of where the post office is now. There was a typed suicide note and an empty bottle of Valium. It was all … wrong.'

'Wrong?' Phil asked.

'I was in the same year as Andy in school here in Ballantrae before we both went to the police college. We were good mates, just like you were with your pals. Really close, you know what I mean? Well, Andy's suicide note said that he'd been in love with a woman in Ayr that owned and worked in a brothel, but who he didn't name. It said he was heartbroken because she had refused to see him anymore after he confided in her that he was on the force. Not only that, but she'd also threatened to send an anonymous letter to headquarters letting them know that not only was one of their Sergeants a regular customer in an Ayrshire whorehouse, but he was also a heavy user of illegal substances.'

'Andy's note confessed to it all, and ended with how he couldn't handle the shame of losing his job. It was all bullshit. I hadn't seen him in ten years, but I *knew* Andy, and that wasn't him.'

'Jesus,' Phil said. 'I'm sorry.' He was actually thinking that as convinced as Grace was that his friend hadn't been the sort to indulge in hooker and coke orgies, he apparently hadn't seen this Andy Swanney in ten years. A person can change a lot in a decade.

He also reckoned that a policeman faced with the prospect of being publicly scandalized, losing their job and doing time inside might see a suicide note and a bottle of Valium as a tempting way out.

'I know what you're thinking, Phil. That it makes sense that a head polis might take the easy road faced with that situation? That's very true. If he'd been found guilty of solicitation and drug charges, he'd have been sent down, and I'm sure you realise how unpopular coppers are in the jail. Thing is though, there was something that only I knew about Andy Swanney. He was gay.'

Grace let that sink in for a second before going on.

'He first told me back when we were still in school, and

by that point we'd already been mates for years. He never tried anything with me, but I'd always wondered why he didn't seem to be chasing the local lassies as much as the rest of the boys our age did. Like I said though, we were close, and it didn't bother me. It was his business what he did and who he did it with and it didn't change the fact that we were best pals.'

'We kept in contact over the years through letters and the occasional phone call when I was through in Edinburgh, and we'd meet up now and again for weekends where we'd knock about with the other lads we'd been mates with as kids, but I was the only person he ever told about his preferences. He kept it a secret, and he had to, otherwise he'd never have got on to the force. Things weren't as liberal back then as they are now. That's how I know the suicide note was faked. For fuck's sake, Andy even had a secret boyfriend that he told me about in his last letter to me before he died!' Grace laughed, but his amusement dissolved into another racking coughing fit that lasted longer than the previous attack. When he finished, there was blood on his chin.

'The note was faked,' he went on. 'I knew it, and not just because of what I knew about Andy. The thing had been typed, but in ten years of writing to me, not one of his letters had ever been done on a typewriter. And the suicide note wasn't signed either. It just didn't add up.'

'Wasn't there some sort of investigation?' Phil asked. 'Surely a copper's suicide would be looked at closely by the guys he worked with, especially if they thought something was dodgy.'

Grace shook his head.

'The boys at the station here were cut out of it. They loved Andy to bits, as he was the best guy you could ever meet, and a top notch Sergeant. They'd have moved heaven and earth to get to the bottom of it, but the official word was that as he was the ranking officer in town, an impartial team from another station in Ayr would look into his suicide, so as not to cloud the investigation with any emotion the local police may have felt.'

'Fucking bullshit if you ask me though. In all my years as a copper, I've known a few who've topped themselves, and I never heard of any rule that says the investigation has to be carried out by someone from another division.'

'When I heard he'd died, I'd already been looking for a new beat for a while as I'd been in Edinburgh for so long and wanted a change of scenery, so I applied for his job. I got it, and the first thing I did when I got back here was speak to the Ayr headquarters, requesting the case files on his suicide. I was told to forget about it and to let the man rest in peace. I kept at them though, and was eventually told, in not so many words, that to keep asking wouldn't be good for my career.'

Phil tried to make sense of what Grace was telling him. This was a lot of information to be taking in.

'Hold on,' he said. 'If the suicide was faked, then you obviously think someone killed him. Why? I don't see what it's got to do with the murder either. The case was closed and Alex Griffiths was innocent, right?'

'That was something I could never figure out,' Grace said. 'Not completely anyway. Andy had no enemies. Everyone in town knew and liked him. There was no reason for anyone to kill him and fake his suicide. He had no family, obviously no wife or kids, and only a couple of close friends. Nothing was missing from his house when they found his body, so he hadn't been robbed, and no one benefited in any way from his death. There was no motive for someone to kill him. Like I said, I'd been told to forget about it by my superiors, but Andy was my mate, and I wasn't about to let it go.'

'When you're a copper, Phil' he said, 'you can get access to information that's not normally available to the general public, and I decided to make a couple of phone calls, in a non-official capacity of course, to see what I could find out. A quick call to another polis I knew in Glasgow that worked in the comms department gave me Andy's phone records, incoming and outgoing, which I wanted to check out. The last call he ever got was listed as being received the night before he died. It was from a Glasgow number that was registered to someone called Brian Bishop.'

The name had already cropped up in this story before, Phil realised. After a second, he had it. 'The ticket office guy that saw Ray Vize with the murdered lassie?' he asked.

'The very man,' Grace replied, nodding. 'At the time though, to me it was just a name and a phone number. I didn't know at that point that Bishop had been connected to the murder case. I only found that out later. Anyway, I tried calling the number, but it was a dead line.

'After that, I tried speaking to everyone that I could think of that knew Andy to see if I could find anything out, but there was nothing.'

'A few months later, I was cleaning out my desk in the station, and I found a writing pad at the back of a drawer that was full of scribbles. The sort of thing people keep beside the phone to write down names and numbers, you know? I recognised Andy's handwriting, and so I sat there behind my old mate's desk, just flicking through it, remembering him, and that's when I found the connection between Brian Bishop and the Lisa McKeown case.'

'There was a line written on a page near the middle of the notepad that read "Brian Bishop, witness re. McKeown case" and a phone number underneath. I remembered the name from when I'd checked out Andy's phone records a few months before.'

'I still had the records my mate in telecoms had given me, and sure enough, when I compared the two phone numbers, they were the same. It seemed strange to say the least that the last call Andy ever received had been from the guy who was the key witness in a high profile murder case that'd been closed for months, so I dug out the McKeown case files, spent the next three weeks going through them, did a bit of digging, and found out a couple of things.'

'Because Bishop's phone number wasn't working, I called the ticket office at Glasgow Central where he worked and ended up speaking to a guy who was a colleague that he'd been friendly with. You know what I found out, Phil?'

He'd started to get a creepy feeling about where this was going, and hazarded a guess.

'He was dead,' Phil said.

Grace chuckled and nodded in approval.

'You'd make a good polis yourself, son,' he said. 'Dead as a doornail. Apparently he'd died in a car accident a few days after he spoke to Andy Swanney, but that wasn't all I found out. He'd been diagnosed with a brain tumour and would have been dead inside a year if he hadn't died in that crash. On top of that, he'd been in a serious amount of debt to a private loan company, and guess who was the owner of that loan company?'

'Jesus ...' Phil murmured. He'd a pretty good idea.

'Not quite,' Grace replied. 'Alexander Griffiths. The Earl of Ayrshire had his fingers in a whole oven full of pies, Phil, and owned businesses all over Scotland. Not directly of course. Everything was owned by one company which was run by another firm that had ties to another organisation, but in the end, it all filtered back to him. Loan companies, engineering firms, restaurants, property and interestingly enough, hotels. You see where I'm going with this?'

'His alibi,' Phil said, that creepy feeling tightening somewhat. 'The hotel in Edinburgh.'

'Exactly. One of the many hotels that Griffiths had a vested interest in was the one he'd supposedly been in the night Ray Vize said he saw him in Glasgow. I called the hotel and asked to speak to the lad working in the bar who'd confirmed Griffiths had spent the evening there, but surprise surprise, the boy had been let go a few months previously. Oh yeah, and they didn't have any contact details for him either. Seems his record at the hotel HR office had been destroyed

249

after he was fired. I had his name and home number of course, he'd given it to the coppers who'd spoken to him, but when I called, it was a dead line. I also tried tracing him through the Edinburgh police where I still had friends, but it turned up nothing. It was as if the lad had vanished off the face of the Earth.'

'I went to my superiors again with all this and tried to get the McKeown case reopened, but they told me in no uncertain terms to drop it. Even when I pointed out that Griffiths' alibi was unreliable and the connection to Brian Bishop through the loan company, they said it was all paper thin. Coincidental and circumstantial. Not enough to reopen a closed case. That's when I knew something was rotten with the whole thing, but again, it was made clear that digging any deeper would be detrimental to my job.'

'But how is that possible?' Phil asked, sceptical that Grace's superiors would on two occasions be so reluctant to reopen cases that were so obviously flawed.

Grace gave him a sympathetic look.

'You're young, Phil, and I'm not patronising you, but you've a lot to learn about how the world works. Especially for those with money. A guy like Alexander Griffiths has a bottomless bank account, and it's frightening what money can do if you know how and where to apply it. You can buy people, even the police,' he said. 'You know how many bent coppers I've known in my time? You can own people,' he went on. 'Especially people who owe you money, like Brian Bishop did. You can get them to say things that maybe aren't true in return for you calling off the debt collectors and the broken knees and writing off their debt. You can frighten people, like maybe that guy in the hotel bar was frightened of losing his job, or maybe his thumbs, if he didn't say that Griffiths was in the hotel bar that night.'

Grace leaned forward, fixing Phil with his icy blue eyes.

'And you can kill people, Phil, like maybe Andy Swanney was killed after he spoke to Brian Bishop. Bishop had less than a year to live, and according to his friend at the ticket office, he was a timid, but genuinely good-hearted man. Suppose he felt bad about what he'd told the police about seeing Ray Vize with that girl, and decided to set things right and tell the truth when the doctors told him his number was up? Suppose that was why he called Andy Swanney? I checked the station phone records as well, and the afternoon of the day Andy died, less than twenty-four hours after he'd gotten the call from Bishop, he phoned Alexander Griffiths. Suppose he told him that he wanted to speak to him again? Suppose the Earl of Ayrshire got nervous, and used his bottomless bank account to see to it that both Andy and Brian Bishop stopped talking? A bottomless bank account can buy you all the suicide notes, Valium and car accidents in the world, Phil.'

Sergeant Grace picked up his tumbler, knocked back the last of his whisky and gently set the thick glass back on the table. The blood staining the front of his shirt was more plentiful by then, and Phil noticed he was suddenly paler than before. His voice had also become steadily weaker as he told his tale.

'There's a safe under the couch there, Phil,' he said. 'The combination's four eight four eight four eight. Open it up for me, would you?'

Phil rose from the couch and pushed it back, revealing a section of carpet that looked normal, but on closer inspection, you could see that in one area about a half metre square, the stylised floral pattern was upside down. This disguised section of fabric lifted away to reveal a floor safe with a digital lock. Phil keyed in the combination and was rewarded with a green light and a soft click. Inside were thick bundles of bank notes held together with sturdy elastic bands. He turned back to the dying man in the armchair, not understanding.

Grace's face was ghastly.

'I stayed here because I always ... I always had a feeling that there was something bad in Ballantrae,' he said. 'Now it's fucked, this town, but my first duty is the preservation of human life. This is still my town, fucked or not, and there's still people here.'

'I wish you all the best, Phil, but I've got a feeling that you're not right, son. It's in your eyes. It's all over you. I'd advise you to go somewhere that other people aren't.'

He coughed again. There was more blood. Quite a bit of it this time.

'There's ten grand there,' he said, pointing at the floor safe. 'My yacht fund. Never trusted the bank with it, the fuckers. Take it, Phil. And leave. It'll buy you some mileage.'

More hacking coughs. More blood.

'If you want answers,' he said, his voice starting to slur and halt, 'speak to Des Griffiths, but watch your back … bastard's a snake … just like his old man … something wrong with that whole family. Always has been. My grandma … used to tell me Griffiths Hall was … bad place. Haunted …'

Phil thought of the brooding, unwelcoming atmosphere he, Sam and Cairnsey had felt on the few occasions they'd been up at Griff's place, and reckoned the Sergeant's grandma had had the right of it.

The blood stain on Grace's torn shirt suddenly bloomed larger, like a bizarre rose opening its petals. His breath was coming in short gasps now, the remaining colour visibly running out of his face. He was on his way out, fading fast.

'The photo … there … mantelpiece …' he wheezed, pointing.

Phil solemnly handed him the silver-framed black and white portrait of his wife, Lila. Grace clutched it to his bloody chest with one hand. Phil knelt in front of him and took his other hand in both of his own. No one should die alone, he thought, even though it's a journey we all ultimately make solo.

Tears spilled down his cheeks.

'Thank you,' he whispered.

And Sergeant Stephen Grace was gone.

19

Desdemona Griffiths, Earl of Ayrshire, was a man constantly in complete unquestioning control of his life and everything in it.

As a light-hearted Christmas present, a woman whom he'd employed as a housemaid at Griffiths Hall, and whose name he hadn't known then and didn't know now, had once given him a ceramic mug emblazoned with bright red lettering that read 'I'm not a control freak, I'm THE control freak'. Although the sentiment was accurate enough, Desdemona had fired the scrubber on the spot, disgusted with the stupid woman's skewed perception of the line between master and serf.

Now, as he stood over his wife's throat slit body, he contemplated the blood stained bone dagger in his hand, and thought about the concept of control.

The weapon, which was carved from a human femur, was slender sharp and centuries old. Extensively filigreed, strange markings, runes, symbols and etchings bedizened the off-white blade and twisted decoratively around the handle. Although it was an exquisitely rendered object that displayed the skill and control of the craftsman who had wrought it, it wasn't an efficient weapon, uncomfortable to wield and not designed for use in battle, but deadly all the same if used with precision and control.

Control.

He lived for it.

Every singular aspect of Desdemona's life was internally screened and meticulously scrutinised for the slightest folly or inefficiency. It was the only way for a man to conduct his affairs, as far as he was concerned. To Desdemona Griffiths, the heart was merely a muscle; a dumb, insentient engine that's only purpose was to keep blood supplied to the brain, and not to be considered when making decisions and planning strategy.

The heart brought unpredictability. Irrationality. Chaos.

The mind and will brought efficiency. Order. *Control.*

The second home in which he now stood, a stunning half-mansion in the most affluent part of Glasgow's west end, was one of just many fruits his philosophy of domineering ruthless control had borne. The extensive chain of flourishing businesses, the top of the range BMW parked outside and the four other equally opulent automobiles he possessed, the beautiful, compliant, and thoroughly vacuous wife whom he'd murdered the previous night, and the will to stand motionlessly in wait over her cooling corpse since.

All of it was made possible by the application of control.

When he'd been a powerless frightened child, nightly terrorised by the otherworldly thing that had stalked his family for centuries, it was the eventual taking of control that had saved him from the fate of drooling insanity that had befallen so many of his ancestors. Ancestors who'd been irrational idiots, too cowardly to take control of their lives and carry out what was necessary in order to free themselves, and too wrapped up in what they stupidly believed to be their duty. Although he shared common genetic material with that ancient line of fools, Desdemona was a breed apart. He'd no interest in the continuation of their misguided traditions, nor in holding to their archaic beliefs, and so he had taken control in order to save himself, and to bring the long line of madness to an end.

For years he dedicated his mind, will and virtually limitless wealth to his purpose. Like a shadowy puppet master he pulled the strings of people's lives, making them dance to his tune. In the execution of his plan, he controlled the existences and fates of unwitting others, and saw himself as godlike in this regard. He'd been meticulous in his design and planning, and it was the work of many years to set in motion a chain of events that would finally pay the debt with which he had been so unfairly burdened by those blind generations who'd gone before him.

Control and mastery of his natural parental instincts had been necessary, not that he *had* any real fatherly affection for his offspring. Dean had been a highly intelligent child, and had he shown less interest in such insipid notions as friendship, kindness and humour, perhaps Desdemona would have felt more regret over his sacrifice. As it was though, for all his brilliance, his son had never shared his father's belief in the importance of control, a fact illustrated succinctly in the boy's fascination for chaos theory; a nonsense concept that was the very antithesis of control. Even if his death hadn't been necessary, the sheer wastefulness of such a sharp mind made it easy to accept.

The demise of his wife was nothing. Desdemona mourned the loss of the Persian rug that had been ruined by her arterial blood more than he did the loss of his spouse. The mindless bitch had been but a vessel, and she'd served her purpose eighteen years hence. His entire masterplan hinged on him having an heir, and Sheena had been no more to him than a hired womb. He'd only kept the idiotic cunt around as an occasionally useful ornament after Dean was born, and in the end, she'd been no more than an extra bargaining chip.

Of equally less import were the others who had to perish in the fulfilment of his plan. The bovine population of a nowhere village. They were as dumb cattle, of precisely zero worth to him other than as living currency that he would exploit in the settlement of a debt. Pounds of flesh, if you will.

It had all been a means to an end. If that end had to be achieved through the bloody obliteration of one hundred and forty four lives, including that of his own son, then so be it.

And yet, as a businessman, Des knew that random fate and unpredictable developments could derail even the most cunningly crafted and meticulously thought out endeavour. Ordinarily, through the application of logic and outside-the-box thinking, he was able to overcome unforeseeable deviations when they cropped up in his dealings, and reassert control.

But this time, despite all his planning, painstaking research, unseen influence and subtle puppeteering, everything had gone badly awry, perhaps irrevocably so. Events had spiralled wildly out of control, and Desdemona Griffiths was unsure what scared him the most; the fact that he was for the first time as an adult powerless over what happened next, or the thought of what the consequences might be of this. He would have been angry had he not been so afraid.

The mind bending terrors of his childhood had returned, and all he could do was wait to see what happened next, unable to influence events any further and completely terrified.

You have to do it, son, his father's voice echoed in his mind. *It's our family's duty. We do it in the King's name. We do it in the Devil's name.*

*

On the night of his ninth birthday, Desdemona Griffiths takes the funny white knife from his daddy's hand.

He looks up into the big man's face, then down at the little girl who's about the same age as him. She's tied up without any clothes on and lying in the hole in the ground his daddy made him dig. It's cold out here in the woods at night time. He only wants to go back home and play with his toys.

'Go on, son,' his daddy says kindly. 'It's your time to become a man.' His daddy says nine is an important number. Something about the power of three times three.

Desdemona looks up at the big man standing above him on the edge of the hole in the ground, and starts to cry.

'I don't want to do it, daddy,' he blubbers.

His daddy looks angry now, and slaps him hard across the face. Des falls down in the hole next to the little girl. He can hear her making little scared noises through the rag his daddy has stuffed in her mouth.

'Stop it right now. Stop your crying,' his daddy shouts. 'Do you want the Bogey Rogey to come and eat you up? Because he will, Desdemona, if you don't cut this wee hoor's throat.'

Some of his friends at school sometimes talk about monsters under their beds or in their wardrobes at night, and how their mummies and daddies always tell them they don't exist. That they're just nightmares, and Desdemona thinks that they're probably right.

But Desdemona's daddy doesn't tell him the Bogey Rogey isn't real, because they both know that he is. *The Bogey Rogey doesn't only come out at night either. The Bogey Rogey lives anywhere that's dark, and even in the daytime there are dark places.*

Just the other day, he'd been playing with his toy cars at the top of the stairs at home, when the hatch that covered the entrance to the loft had slowly opened, and the Bogey Rogey had smiled down at him with its big teeth and yellow eyes. Its long bony arm had reached down out of the dark and tried to grab him up, but Desdemona's legs had went all wobbly from the scare, and he'd luckily fallen down the stairs out of reach. Even as he'd fell down the stairs he could hear the Bogey Rogey chuckling up there in the loft.

Then he'd run and told his daddy that the Bogey Rogey had tried to get him. Daddy didn't tell him it was his imagination, like other daddies did. His daddy looked just as scared as he was for a second, then had shouted at him, saying not to bother him, he was busy. Then he shouted at mummy, telling her to see what the fucking wean was greeting about.

His mummy was nicer. She held his hand and hugged

*him, telling him it was okay, there was no Bogey Rogey.
She wanted to take him upstairs to show him there was no
monster in the loft. Desdemona wouldn't go with her though,
and he screamed and screamed and hit her when she tried
to pick him up. Then she'd got angry and put him down and
went to go upstairs herself and he begged her not to. He
loved his mummy and didn't want the Bogey Rogey to get
her, but she went up anyway.*

*When she came back down she asked him how he'd
opened the loft hatch, and gave him into trouble because it
was so cold up there now. She didn't believe him about the
Bogey Rogey of course, but he didn't mind so much. As long
as his mummy was safe, it was okay. It was good she didn't
believe in the Bogey Rogey.*

*His daddy did though. You could see he was scared as
he stood there in the forest, looking down at him, all angry.*

*'I swear to Christ, Desdemona, if you don't kill this wee
bitch I'll put you up the loft and lock you in, and the Bogey
Rogey'll eat you up. You want me to do that? He's very
hungry, son, and that's why you've got to do this. Just once
across the side of her throat like I showed you, and then he'll
eat her instead of you. But if you don't do it, so help me, I'll
tie you up and leave you in the loft for him, and good fucking
riddance.'*

*'No, daddy!' Desdemona screams. 'Don't give me to the
Bogey Rogey! I'll be good, I'll be good!'*

And he does what his daddy says.

The funny white knife goes all red.

*

A sudden awareness of a change in the room's atmosphere
interrupted his memories.

259

It was suddenly very cold in the room, and there was that smell of moist, rotting things and burnt meat.

The lights flickered. Went out.

And then he heard it. That awful, low chuckling laugh that sounded like a dead body turning over in a swamp.

Coming from the dark hallway behind him.

He couldn't turn around to look. He wouldn't.

It was here again. The thing passed down through generations like a genetic disease. The Bogey Rogey he'd known as a child, but that as a man, he'd come to know by another name.

Ozay was in the house.

It had come to him for the first time in almost thirty years back in May, when things had first gone so spectacularly wrong. Miraculously, he'd managed to buy some time. He'd begged and gibbered in terror, saying that all was not lost; there was still Labhrainne's blood, he said, royal blood, and he might yet darken and fulfil the blood price.

The daemon had given him a reprieve of three moons, and for those twelve weeks, Desdemona feverishly prayed that the Densmore boy would turn.

Yesterday, after three moons had waxed and waned and the debt remained unpaid, Ozay had come to him again. Once more, Desdemona had fallen to his knees, tearfully beseeching his master for mercy, promising undying loyalty and never ending service. He had somehow brokered another deal, offering up the Densmore boy's brother and father, the last males of their valuable bloodline, plus his own wife and son, all in payment for the summoning of an infernal entity that could finally see the blood price paid. A Harvester. Once again, the daemon had agreed to the terms, promising to revisit his pet on the morrow, whereupon he would either set him free, or take him away.

Now Ozay had returned to him again, and Desdemona Griffiths didn't know what was going to happen.

Heavy, slow footsteps came from behind him. The *clack, clack, clack* of approaching claws on the luxury hardwood floor.

Still he refused to turn around and face it. Face *him*. He remained rooted, staring down at his wife's body.

The footsteps came closer still.

Stopped immediately behind him.

He could hear it breathing, then that hideous, gurgling chuckle again. An icy talon gently caressed the back of his neck, almost soothingly. Marrow numbing terror gripped Desdemona, threatening to loosen his bladder and bowels, and he fought the old urge to void himself. Clenching his eyes shut and grinding his teeth, balling his fists so tight his nails brought blood from his palms, he didn't shit himself, but he couldn't stop the trembling and the cold sweat that coated his skin.

The claw on his neck stopped its sickening caress, and the thing spoke inside his mind, as was its way. Its voice was of the void, empty and cold.

Labhrainne's blood has destroyed my Harvester before it could fulfil the quota. A quota that your *spawn and the other cursed children were supposed to fulfil. Twice now you have not kept your side of our bargain, Desdemona Griffiths, Earl of Ayrshire. Thrice the deal has been broken. It is over.*

His bladder finally let go at this news, and he began to weep as piss leaked into his hand-made Italian loafers. Desdemona Griffiths fell to his knees sobbing. He felt the claw return. It drew a scratching line up the nape of his neck, then a huge leathery hand closed over his skull, holding him firmly.

'Please, master,' he moaned in total despair, already knowing it was useless. 'I did as we agreed. I brought them together. I gave you the Densmore line. I gave you my wife and son …'

Tell me, Desdemona, Ozay whispered. *Did you love your wife? Did you love your son?*

'No, my lord,' he wailed between sobs. 'I love only you. I serve only you. Please! *Please!* I have suffered in your majesty my whole life! Set me free as you promised, I beg you!'

If you did not love them, the daemon asked, *then what worth does your sacrifice hold?* The hand started to squeeze.

For the souls you have provided me, I thank you, Ozay said, *but the contract is now three times broken. As we agreed, your suffering will end, Desdemona, but only on this plane. You are mine. Now and forever.*

As the pressure on his skull increased with maddening horrific slowness, and he started to scream, Desdemona Griffiths had a very clear vision in his mind of his future. It was without time, without mercy, without any cessation of unimaginable suffering, and completely and utterly without control.

With a loud crack, his skull caved in under Ozay's grip.

As his eyes fell from their crushed sockets to dangle by the optic nerves on his cheeks, the last thing they saw was his dead wife's face.

She was smiling, and he knew she'd be waiting for him in the timeless black into which he plummeted.

20

Phil called Grant from Sergeant Grace's house. His dad Tony picked up.

'Who the fuck's this?' Tony Cairns obviously wasn't used to getting phone calls this early in the morning.

'It's Phil, Tony. Is Grant there?' he said.

'Phil who? You know what fuckin' time it is?'

'Phil Densmore. You know? Josh's pal? Sorry if I woke you up. Is Grant there?'

'Phil Densmore? Oh aye. You're the one that killed yer mate aren't ye? What the fuck d'ye want to speak to Grant for?'

Phil was too emotionally exhausted by everything that had happened in the past few hours to be stung by the arsehole's words, and Tony Cairns didn't hurt his feelings by bringing up Sam. He *was* starting to get on Phil's nerves though.

'Listen, you old cunt,' he heard himself hiss into the phone. 'Put Grant on the line right now or I'll come over there and fuckin' kill you as well, ya prick.'

The hatred Phil heard in his own words scared him a little. He was stressed, no doubt about it, but threatening to murder a cantankerous old man who was trying his patience was something else.

Thing was, Phil found that he'd meant exactly what he'd said.

Luckily, there was no need to test his resolve, as Tony must have heard something in Phil's voice that convinced him of his homicidal intent. Phil heard him stomping a foot on the floor of his bedroom where he imagined Tony lying in bed with his daily hangover. There was a click as the downstairs phone was picked up and Grant was on the line.

'Hello?'

Phil had only spoke to Grant once or twice since May. He'd called a few times to see how Phil was doing, but his head had been in such a state he hadn't been in the frame of mind for it, and the few conversations they'd had were brief.

'Grant, it's Phil. Can you meet me at the workshop, mate?'

'Aye, no bother. I'm just leaving for work the now. You alright? You sound weird.'

No shit.

'I'm alright, mate,' Phil lied. 'I'll see you in five minutes.'

'No bother. See you soon.'

'Grant? Can you grab me a change of clothes? I need jeans, a t-shirt and a jacket.' He'd cleaned his face and hands as well as he could in Sergeant Grace's bathroom, but Phil's clothes were still covered in his dad's blood. He'd considered searching for something that fit him in Grace's wardrobe, but the big cop had been almost twice his size. 'And go straight to the offices, Grant,' Phil said. 'You'll probably see some weird shit on your way but don't stop, alright? Just meet me there and I'll explain everything.'

'Eh? What's going on, Phil? I thought I heard sirens earlier on but I was still half asleep.'

'I'll tell you about it at the workshop. Please mate, you've got to trust me. Just go straight there and don't stop for anything. *Anything*. And one more thing, can you bring Josh's phone with you? See you in five.'

Phil hung up before Grant could ask any more questions, hoping he'd do as he'd said. Grant was a good guy, loyal and dependable, but Phil wasn't sure he'd be able to handle the sights he suspected he might encounter on the way over if he stopped for a close look. Grant had always been the kind of guy who wouldn't hesitate to help someone in need, and Phil wanted to spare him from what might happen if he acted on his good nature.

He found a sturdy rucksack in a hallway cupboard, stuffed in the ten grand Grace had given him before he'd died, and left the house, heading for the office of Anderson Engineering.

Grant had already arrived before Phil when he got there, and he could tell from Grant's face and nervous demeanour that he had indeed seen some weird shit on the drive over.

He paced back and forth by his car outside the workshop and office gates, his face pale and haunted, and he kept looking over his shoulders every few seconds. He was obviously badly scared. He saw Phil approaching and started towards him, but stopped halfway as he clocked his blood splattered appearance.

'Jesus, Phil, what happened to you, man?' he blurted. 'Are you okay?'

'It's fine, mate. Not my blood.' That probably wasn't the best thing to say, Phil thought, as Grant backed off a few steps.

'It's alright, Grant. I'm not going to hurt you. My dad's dead. It's his blood. Please, I need your help.'

Grant still didn't look convinced.

'On the way over here …' he stammered, 'I saw blood in the streets … there's people walking around like fuckin' zombies, a couple of houses on fire … and this, this red *thing*. Jesus, I thought it was a body … but it couldn't have been … the shape of it … something *bad's* happened.'

'I know, mate,' Phil said. He'd seen them himself as he'd made his way to the workshop from Sergeant Grace's place. The people who'd lived through the morning, and had found what the shape shifting demon had left behind. There'd been folk sitting in shock on the pavement and stumbling around in the street, staring into space, weeping, screaming. And bodies. There'd been a lot of bodies, the vast majority of them unnaturally twisted and mutilated.

'Let's go in the office. I'll explain everything,' Phil said.

Grant nodded, and they went inside, Grant locking the outside gates and door to the office behind them as they went. Once inside, he handed Phil a duffel bag containing the change of clothes he'd asked for, and Cairnsey's phone. Phil excused himself for a minute and went to the small office toilet where he stripped out of his bloodied shirt and jeans and cleaned himself up as well as he could with cold water, sanitation gel and paper towels. He recognised the replacement clothes Grant had brought as things that had belonged to Cairnsey. A black Led Zeppelin t-shirt, worn jeans and his battered brown leather jacket. It felt right wearing his clothes.

Phil studied the phone for a minute, debating whether or not to do what he'd thought he should.

Was there any point in checking the call register?

Fuck it, he thought. *Why not?* Things couldn't really get any more messed up.

He pressed the power button and waited for the phone to start up. Once the irritatingly cheery Nokia jingle and start up animation had finished, the screen displayed a photograph Sam's mum had taken with the phone. The four of them in shorts and t-shirts, reclining on sun loungers in Sam's back garden, grinning like fools and toasting the camera phone with bottles of Budweiser. It'd been Sam's birthday. The youngest member of their little tribe, he'd been the last of them to turn eighteen. The photo had been taken on a sunny Saturday evening a week before they'd finished school. Just a week before they'd gone to Bennane Head.

Seeing that digital image just a few hours ago would have set Phil weeping, but by now he was all cried out, and he just

266

smiled.

It was good. It was alright.

Putting the fond memory aside he pressed the green button, bringing up the dialled numbers register.

He remembered the phone call clearly; Cairnsey calling Barnsey just after seven pm to ask what the deal was with the cryptic note they'd found pinned to the bench where they'd been supposed to meet Ozay. Barnsey's annoying donkey laugh braying out the phone so loud it'd seemed like he was doing it on purpose.

The call wasn't there, of course. The last entry on the dialled numbers list was a call to Phil, made at six forty-five, fifteen minutes before they'd been meant to meet Ozay. Phil also remembered *that* phone call. Cairnsey had called to let him know he and Griff were on their way in his car to pick him up.

According to Cairnsey's mobile, the call to Barnsey at just after seven pm had never happened.

Barnsey'd been telling the truth. Cairnsey hadn't spoken to him that night. Hadn't spoken to *him*, but to someone else who'd reassured them it was okay to take the trips contained in the sheet of paper. Phil knew then that if he were to check the phone records from his house the previous night, there'd be no listing for the call to nine-nine-nine he'd made as his dad had lay dying, his ribs smashed and his perforated lungs slowly deflating like blood-filled balloons. Likewise, there'd be no record of the call his brother had said he'd received when he'd been violently prompted to commit patricide, and if Phil had been able to check his own mobile, he knew he wouldn't see any record of the call he'd received after speaking to Barnsey, when he'd had that brief conversation with something pretending to be Griff.

Because calls made by and answered by daemons wouldn't really exist in the human version of reality, would they?

Phil quickly turned the phone off again, shoved it into Cairnsey's jacket pocket and left the toilet.

Grant was sitting at one of the cluttered desks in the office, a bottle of Aberlour single malt and a glass containing a healthy shot in front of him. It seemed everyone Phil met that morning liked a drink. Understandable under the circumstances.

He offered Phil a glass, which he declined, and then Phil sat at the desk opposite Grant and just started talking. He'd said he'd explain everything, but that'd probably been the wrong choice of words. Phil told him everything he knew, and everything that had happened, but he couldn't *explain* much of it.

It all came out in a great torrent of words. The night at Bennane Head, the three months of paranoia, nightmares and fear that came after, his meeting with Griff in the psych ward and all the madness that had followed immediately after. His spontaneous teleportations, the incredible bursts of speed, the other new physical and mental talents he'd seemed to somehow inherit from his dead friends, the monstrous shapeshifting being that had decimated the village, an abridged version of Sergeant Grace's story.

Phil told it all.

By the time he'd finished, Grant was finishing his third glass of whisky, and was about to top it up when he seemed to think better of it, and put the bottle aside on the desk.

He leaned back in his office chair and let out a shaky breath.

'Jesus Christ, Phil,' was all he said. There was no hint in his voice that he didn't believe what Phil had told him, as insane as it all was. There was no sceptical look of disbelief in his eyes either. Only a naked look of fear.

'Before I left the house,' he said, 'my dad told me you'd threatened to kill him. And the way you look. I mean, you look the same, but … you're not the *same* anymore, Phil.'

The only thing Phil had held back from telling Grant was the feeling that somehow, he wasn't entirely safe to be around anymore, and he'd sensed that the way Grant had taken a few steps back when Phil had shown up at the workshop had less to do with his bloodied clothes than some indefinably dangerous aura that he now gave off.

Phil nodded. He was ashamed at the way he'd spoken to Tony Cairns, even if he was a cunt. The harsh words had seemed to leap from his throat before he'd even thought them.

'I'm sorry, Grant,' he said. 'Ever since I woke up in the hospital, and especially since that thing touched me, had me pinned through the shoulder … I don't know, man. It's like there's something deep down in me that wasn't there before. Something bad. I swear to you though, mate, I'm not here to hurt you. I'd never do anything to you, and I'm sorry about what I said to your dad.'

Grant abruptly gave a short bark of laughter.

'Fuck's sake, don't worry about *that*, Phil. Many's the time the same thought's crossed my mind. Old prick. I'm not worried about him, I'm worried about *you*.'

He hesitated for a moment before continuing, giving Phil a strange look and squinting through half-closed eyes as if straining to see something faint.

'It's like … you're surrounded by something that for some reason I can't really see. I can't describe it, Phil, but it's like … death.' He nodded slightly, as if confirming something to himself. 'I know that sounds fucking weird, Phil, and I don't know where I'm getting it from, but that's *exactly* what it is. You've got death all over you, man.'

Sergeant Grace had said pretty much the same thing, right before he'd died.

Phil and Grant just sat there in silence for a few moments.

'So what happens now?' Grant asked.

'I need to leave,' Phil said. 'Just go, and keep moving. Away from people. I don't want anyone else to get hurt because of me. I need to go and see Griff's dad first though.'

Grant nodded, then snatched up his car keys.

'Let's get going then,' he said. 'Sooner the better. This town's going to be swarming with police pretty soon I'd imagine. It'd probably be best if you weren't here when they arrive.'

Phil nodded and got to his feet. As he started towards the office door, he stopped dead.

For a second there, just as Grant had stood up to leave, his face had been covered in blood, then it'd suddenly been gone again.

'Hold on, Grant,' he said. 'You stay here.'

'What?'

'I should go alone.'

'No way, Phil. If Des Griffiths had something to do with what happened to Josh ...'

Phil shook my head.

'Please, Grant. Just stay. I think something bad might happen if you come with me.'

'I trust you, Phil,' he said. 'I know you wouldn't do anything to me. I'm coming with you. It's my motor anyway, so you've not got a choice.'

He turned back towards the door and made to leave.

Without thinking, Phil snatched up the whisky bottle from the desk.

Swung it at the back of Grant's head.

The split second before the impact seemed to last an hour. Phil meant to just knock him out. Just hit him hard enough to put him to sleep without hurting him too badly. As the bottle swung at Grant's skull though, an urge to put all his strength into the blow suddenly bloomed up in Phil's chest, and for a horrifying moment, he absolutely meant to cave Grant's head in. He saw it in his mind. Grant lying motionless on the floor while Phil stood over him, swinging the thickened bottom of the glass bottle into his pulped cranium again and again and again …

With a huge effort of will, Phil only just managed to pull the blow at the very last instant, twisting his wrist, turning what would have been a full force and probably lethal strike into a glancing blow.

It was enough. Grant dropped like a sack of spuds and lay crumpled on the floor of the office. Phil checked his pulse, found it strong and regular, and then put him into the recovery position, noting as he was doing it that he'd never had any first aid training. Griff had though, of course.

'I'm sorry mate,' he said to Grant's prostate form on the floor, snatching up his car keys.

He didn't know what would've happened, but the brief vision he'd had of Grant's face coated in blood had all the grim solidity of a tombstone. If he'd stayed with Phil, he'd have died. Maybe not by Phil's hand, maybe a car crash on the road to Glasgow, but Phil knew that being in his presence would have been a death sentence to Cairnsey's brother.

As he left the office and started towards Grant's car, it occurred to him that he'd never had any driving lessons either. Cairnsey had though, and sure enough, sitting behind the wheel felt completely natural, and Phil instinctively knew what he was doing without thinking about it. He pulled smoothly away from the offices of Anderson Engineering and pointed the car out of Ballantrae.

He never went back.

21

As he passed Bennane Head just a few miles outside the village, Phil got a sense that he wasn't alone in the car. So much so that he checked the rear view mirror, half expecting to see someone sitting in the back seat. There was no one there, but the feeling persisted until he was past the cliff tops. On a hunch, he turned on the car radio, and there was Mick Jagger again, and he was most definitely free to do what he wanted, any old time.

Phil smiled, and knew that the graffiti down in the caves was just graffiti again, not the twisted portraits of his tortured and imprisoned friends.

As Grant had predicted, Phil passed a few police cars, ambulances, fire engines and what looked like a military vehicle on the road north, all speeding south down the coast towards Ballantrae with sirens wailing. He had a few bad moments thinking someone might pull him over. No-one did though.

The rest of the drive to Glasgow was uneventful, and he arrived a few hours later in the early afternoon. It didn't surprise him that although he'd never been there, he knew instinctively where Griff's dad's west end residence was.

The three storey sandstone half-mansion sat well back from the street in a quiet leafy cul-de-sac off Great Western Road. Desdemona Griffiths' sleek black BMW M3 was parked in the wide driveway to the left hand side.

The building boasted a large and immaculately maintained lawn to the front, through which a stone path the same reddish colour as the mansion's façade led to the imposing front entrance which was flanked on either side by massive ground floor bay windows.

As soon as he pulled up outside, Phil knew something was wrong. The building had a feel about it of not being used; a palpable air of desertion which he could sense even sitting in Grant's car outside. The BMW parked in the driveway said otherwise though.

Getting out of the car, the sense of abandonment got stronger as Phil walked up the path to the wide front door, which he found was unlocked. Stepping into the wide, luxuriously decorated hallway, a rush of cold air carrying the now all too familiar scent of blood washed over him, making him shudder where he stood.

Despite the filtered light coming from outside through the stained glass window above the front door, the hallway seemed unnaturally dark and foreboding. The big house was crypt still. Not so much as a ticking clock could be heard. Knowing he would get no answer, Phil nevertheless called out a greeting.

'Mr Griffiths? Are you home?'

Nothing.

A search of the downstairs rooms proved fruitless. The lounge, dining room, massive kitchen, conservatory and downstairs bathroom were all beautifully upholstered with the finest furnishings and appliances, but completely silent and lifeless as a vacuum. The pervading scent of blood was strongest in the hallway, and as he ascended the wide, polished walnut stairs, the smell of human waste was added to the increasingly pungent bouquet.

Phil found the two bodies in the study.

One was Griff's mother, Sheena. In death, her normally beautiful, porcelain smooth skin had taken on a waxy pallor. Her eyes were open, and she seemed to be smiling slightly. The front of her expensive white dress was covered in dried blood which had apparently originated from the precise laceration on the side of her throat at the location of the jugular vein. Despite her apparently violent demise though, she'd still had the easier death of the duo of corpses.

The second cadaver was a man dressed in a black suit.

He lay on his stomach, arms straight by his sides. Where his head should have been, there was just a pulped pile of crushed bone, brain, hair and tattered skin. A few teeth, roots still attached, were scattered around the hideous remains. One eyeball seemed to curiously peer at Phil out of the red mess that was all that was left of Desdemona Griffith's head.

By now, Phil was almost used to this type of carnage, but somehow, this terrible tableau seemed different to what he'd witnessed before. The wound in Griff's mum's throat was mundane compared to the horrific sights he'd seen recently. As tame as it comparatively was though, it sickened Phil in a different way. He looked up and noticed the odd looking pale knife that lay beside Griff's dad's body. Stepping closer, he could see that the handle and blade were constructed from one singular piece rather than separate parts, and the whole object had been intricately carved and decorated. For some reason, where the blade was unmarred by Sheena Griffiths' blood, the off-white, almost yellowish colour drew Phil's attention, and he forgot momentarily about the two dead bodies with which he shared the study.

Bending down for a closer look, he could better make out the fine detail that had gone into the filigreed patterns and the twisting, vine like forms that had been carved around the dagger's handle. It was a singularly beautiful object, obviously the work of a master craftsman.

He had to hold it.

At that moment, it suddenly seemed the most important thing in the world to have that exquisitely fashioned dagger in Phil's grasp. Nothing else mattered. Not the corpses of Griff's parents, not the evil that had destroyed his home, family and friends, not the fact that he'd been … altered in some indefinable and frightening way.

All that mattered was that dagger.

Phil suddenly knew in his heart that it was made of bone.

That excited him.

Kicking aside the pile of offal that used to be Desdemona Griffith's head, Phil bent down and took hold of the object that filled him with a terrible, craven need.

Once again, the world went away for a while, and he saw.

He saw it all, and Phillip Densmore finally understood.

PART IV

Thou shalt not suffer a witch to live.

Exodus 22:18

King James Bible

It is not normal for a king to attend the birth of his child.

This child however, is special.

Conceived during forced ritual intercourse with an imprisoned peasant woman, this child, whom he names Labhrainne James Densmore, will be the king's protégé in the dark arts.

The dungeon beneath the castle rings with the woman's screams as the child is born in a rush of blood. The infant's lusty cries join that of his mother's for a second before the king steps forward, an ornately carved bone dagger in his hand, and with a flick of his wrist ends the mother's wailing in a gout of crimson that splatters the stone walls of the cell, then he uses the bone wrought weapon to sever the umbilical cord.

The squalling child is anointed in his mother's blood and sacred rites are chanted by the king and the other assembled devotees of the coven, pledging the newborn to the same dark deity whom they serve.

Later that night, a dark winter's evening in the year of our lord fifteen ninety-seven, the king retires to his chambers high in Edinburgh castle to continue work on his latest book; a delightful, secretly ironic piece of literature condemning the very practices to which he clandestinely devotes himself.

King James the Sixth entitles the book *Daemonologie.*

*

The child is raised in seclusion in the castle, hidden away in secret from all but his tutors and his royal father, who makes frequent visits to monitor his progress.

The boy is daily instructed in the lore of the dark arts, mysticism, witchcraft and black worship. The women, themselves brought to the castle dungeons under charges of consorting with the Devil, are used as teaching tools. Blank flesh canvases upon which the boy can hone his growing skills in torture, ritual abuse and blood sacrifice.

Twenty-three years pass, during which time the boy's father is instrumental in the publishing of the holy bible which bears his name. The king, publicly pious and regarded by his subjects and the church itself as a great champion of Christianity, finds this most amusing, and takes delight in instructing and directing the scholars responsible for writing the text. He knows this will be the definitive version, to be used throughout the coming centuries, and the thought of his corrupting influence on the supposed word of God brings him a lasting satisfaction.

In spring of the year of our lord sixteen twenty, the boy, now a man, is given the title Earl and Sheriff of Ayr, and is sent under royal instructions to take charge of the Southern Coven and continue the tradition of ritual sacrifice in which he has been well trained throughout his youth. The sacred sacrificial dagger goes with him, along with the blessing and complete protection of the king.

*

Labhrainne James Densmore quickly establishes himself in the flat southern lands of Scotland, feared and respected by commoners and the gentry alike as a ruthless lawman. Free from all consequence under the protection of the king, he is free to indulge his bloodlust, and this makes him a figure of awe to the acolytes who worship him with unwavering adulation and devotion. They say he is blessed and favoured by their lord Satan for the frequency and volume of his sacrifices, which are tenfold what the black priests had been offering before his arrival.

Men and women are apprehended almost daily for the slightest of petty crimes or under false accusation of witchcraft, fear of which is rife throughout the land. Those taken are never seen again, for the Earl and Sheriff of Ayr does not believe in public trial and punishment.

But even with frequent 'lawful' arrests to quench Labhrainne's thirst for blood, his dark appetites, nurtured in the dungeons of Edinburgh castle throughout his young life, demand further satiety.

Men and women begin to vanish without trace. Then the children begin to disappear.

The populace of south-western Scotland begins to grow afraid. Mothers hold their children close, and no one ventures out after sunset for fear of whatever devilry stalks the night.

Still the disappearances continue, until the vanishings all across the province of Ayrshire are a nightly occurrence. The locals demand justice, and look to their protector, the noble Earl of Ayrshire, Sheriff Densmore, to rid them of this evil. He cheerfully answers their call for justice.

Many are accused, arrested and publicly punished most severely before baying crowds. It pleases him to be the bringer of this fear which has inspired such madness and bloodlust among the peasants.

Still though, there is no cessation to the disappearances.

Mass hysteria and suspicion grips the region. Vigilantism is widespread, turning neighbour on neighbour in the search for the monster, and whole families perish in blood feuds sparked by the rampant climate of hostility and paranoia.

And still the vanishings continue.

Meanwhile, the depths of Densmore Hall, seat of the Earl and Sheriff of Ayr, are awash in blood. The bone dagger drinks deep in the bodies of the disappeared each evening. The great furnace which burns in the mansion's bowels runs night and day, constantly fed by a seemingly never-ending supply of fleshy, dismembered fuel.

The commoners who live in the vicinity of the Earl's sprawling residence notice the smell of roasting pork that pervades the air around his great hall of late. Labhrainne Densmore finds it amusing to spread the word that he keeps a large pig farm on the extensive grounds of the house, and more amusing still to distribute generous servings of 'pork' to the poor, which they accept with delight, praising the good Sheriff's generosity and kindness of spirit. They are oblivious to the torture and slaughter that nightly plays out in the hall's depths, and which often keeps their bellies full in these hard, fearful, times.

Eventually, word of the widespread disappearances reaches the king, who fears that his bastard son and protégé has lost control and is slaughtering his subjects merely to satisfy his own depraved needs, and not in the Devil's name, as he was taught.

The king sends word to his bastard. The decimation of the populace must be brought to an end as it is attracting much attention. A specially assembled troop of soldiers, led by a man by the name of Captain Hugh Cairns, arrives in Ayrshire to assist the Sheriff in bringing those responsible to justice.

Captain Cairns, also a follower of the dark religion, also carries a message straight from the king's mouth. Labhrainne's royal father knows the truth of the disappearances, and orders his son to quell his appetites. He is to find a suitable scapegoat to take responsibility for the vanishings, apprehend them, then return to Edinburgh immediately with captives in tow.

*

The small coastal settlement just a few miles north of the village of Ballantrae has been there for years.

The inhabitants of Bennane have ever made their peaceful

way in the world by living off the surrounding forest, fishing the Firth of Clyde, and trading with other nearby settlements. They are a small community, numbering forty-eight souls in all, and though they have no elected officials, they recognise the man who founded the colony, Alexander Beane, as their leader.

Beane's wife Agnes, a woman of singular beauty and grace, is skilled in the arts of natural herbal remedies. She possesses a deep knowledge of the medicinal use of roots, plants and compounds and is a well-respected healer and midwife, sought out by people from all across the region who come to her seeking cures and advice for a variety of ailments, which she provides gladly and for no return of coin nor favour. This morning, she has discovered she is with child again, and intends to tell her husband that evening over supper. Though he loves their eight-year-old daughter Marie intensely, Agnes knows Alexander has always wanted a son, as is natural amongst men, and she hopes to provide him with what he desires. She is a woman loved by many, not least by her adoring husband, who cherishes her with an uncommon ferocity.

Not all however, look upon Agnes Beane with favour. In the nearby village of Ballantrae, the religiously pious members of the Kirk regard her with a degree of suspicion. How can it be that a woman who is never seen in church and who shuns the women's circle in Ballantrae is blessed with such uncommon beauty, a fine God-fearing husband, an equally comely child and widespread love and renown? Her talents and knowledge of the application of natural cures are also known to the church elders, and it is not long before their jealousy and suspicion breed whispers of witchcraft and of bargains struck with the Deil. The church elders of Ballantrae feel it is their godly duty to report any word of heathenry in their midst to their lord protector, the good Sheriff Densmore.

It is all the reason Labhrainne Densmore needs.

On the day the soldiers come, the peaceful existence of

the settlement of Bennane is brutally shattered.

They come on galloping horses, armed with slashing swords and booming muskets. The settlement's inhabitants have never known violence, have never had to deal with any sort of attack, and are quickly beaten into submission with rifle butts, fists, cudgels and boot heels. They are rounded up in the centre of the settlement, battered, bloodied and terrified.

Sheriff Densmore pronounces them all under arrest, names them the perpetrators of the recent plague of evil that has pervaded the land, and judges them guilty of consorting with devils and of committing uncounted heinous crimes against God.

Alexander Beane steps forward and speaks out, calling out to the good sheriff and pleading his people's innocence of any crime.

Densmore does not speak. At a nonchalant flick of the Sheriff's wrist, Captain Cairns trots forward on his armoured horse and casually smashes the butt of his musket into Beane's temple. He drops like a stone. His wife Agnes screams and rushes to her husband's aid, and is quickly seized by two soldiers. She struggles, and a mailed fist crashes into her face. Still Agnes fights against her captors, cursing and spitting like a furie. She manages to wrench an arm free and rake one soldier's face with her nails, drawing blood. The soldier screams and reels away clutching at his cheek. Captain Cairns dismounts slowly, walks forward, and slams his fist into Agnes' belly. She falls to the ground to lay aside her senseless husband, her unborn child already dead inside her.

One of the soldiers who had been restraining Agnes has taken notice of her fine features and shapely body. As she writhes gasping on the ground, her homespun shift ridden up around her thighs, the soldier's tongue wets his lips in lust. He tells his captain that he's never fucked a witch before. Several of his comrades claim the same.

Densmore gives his consent, and orders that the witch be taken to the caves beneath the cliff to receive immediate justice. Agnes is dragged away by her hair, screaming and kicking all the way down the path that descends the cliff face to the beach and into the dark network of tunnels beneath Bennane Head. The villagers use the caves only as a communal latrine that the river cleanses with the coming of each high tide.

Densmore watches from atop his horse, smiling slightly in approval.

Cairns leads ten of his men in carrying out the Sheriff's command in the caves, and afterwards finishes the violated, beaten and bloodied woman with a dagger to the throat. Her corpse is left among the shit to be washed out to sea with the tide.

The village is put to the torch. The livestock are slaughtered and the people of the settlement, wailing in bewildered horror, are fettered together in a marching column, wrist to ankle. Men, women and children, babes in arms included.

Alexander Beane, their unofficial lord and protector, is dragged senseless behind a horse from the burning village.

*

The road to Edinburgh is long and hard.

The captives, chained together like wayward cattle, walk, stumble and crawl for two full days without food and only the barest minimum amount of murky water to keep them alive. Their ragged exile is harried along by the mounted soldiers. Hard, cruel men are they. Beatings and rapes among the prisoners of the Earl and Sheriff of Ayr are common on the road, and not all the villagers make it to the city. Several of the old and sick, a couple of the women, and more than one infant perish on the forced march to the kingdom's capital. They are the lucky ones.

The dungeons of Edinburgh castle are far worse.

Overseen by a grotesque giant of a man known only by the innocuous name of Anderson, the dark depths of the seat of King James is a waking nightmare for any unlucky soul who should find their future in its dank embrace. The surviving villagers of Bennane are cast into this black hell, half-starved and screaming. In the past two days, all have lost their home, their freedom, and their very humanity. Several have lost kin.

Captain Hugh Cairns comes on the first night of their incarceration and seeks out Alexander Beane, finding him chained to the wall along with his fellow captives. Cairns squats in front of the battered village leader, and solemnly describes in detail how he murdered his wife Agnes after he and ten of his men had repeatedly raped her. There is a deadness to Cairns' voice and eyes. When his baiting elicits no response from Beane, who keeps his eyes downcast and refuses to react, Cairns eventually gives up and leaves. He has other business in the dungeon.

Cairns has noticed of late how sloppy some of his men's martial skills have become, and he desires that they be more efficient with their weapons. To this end, ten of the captives are led from the dungeons into a courtyard and bound tightly to thick, tall stakes driven into the ground. They are used for weapons practice.

Later, Cairns returns to the dungeons and again squats in front of Alexander Beane, this time recounting how those in the courtyard had died, twitching and rent from spear, axe, sword and arrow wounds. Cairns does not seem to take any joy in these strange confessions, remaining as animated as a rock as he describes his butchery. Indeed, there seems to be a terrible sadness in his eyes, yet somehow at the same time, not so much as a glimmer of anything that could be called humanity.

The head jailer Anderson also pays a visit to Beane that first night in the dungeons. He has taken a twisted, predatory interest in Alexander Beane's daughter Marie. A skinny, ethereally beautiful blond-haired waif with huge eyes of the palest blue, which she inherited from her mother. On that first night in the dungeons, Anderson comes to the crowded cells and drags her away from her frantic father, who this time struggles with all his might against the unyielding iron chains. Little Marie is carried away to Anderson's private quarters, and her father is forced to listen to her screams as they echo about the cold stone walls the dungeon.

Now come the Questioners, led by a tall gaunt man by the name of Lachlan Griffiths. He is not long returned from Rome, where for the past eight years he has studied the methods of witch finding. He is also the king's most trusted advisor, mentor and tutor in the ways of witchcraft.

Every day, coldly overseen by the skeletal Griffiths, each of the captives are subjected to the talented hands of his torturers. No exceptions. On Griffith's order, the children are the first to be interrogated. Torn away from their screaming parent's arms, they are taken and put to the question. Some do not return.

They all confess eventually.

It is only a matter of time before the instruments of the interrogators loosen their tongues, often literally. The tools of torture are wielded with extraordinary skill. Some white hot, others cold, hard and very, very sharp.

All the sinners have to do to make the pain stop, Griffiths whispers to them, is confess.

And they confess.

Oh, how they confess.

They confess to entering pacts with daemons, of bringing plagues, misfortune and sorrow to the God-fearing small folk of the land. They confess of their abilities to turn themselves into animals, of having familiars and of partaking in wanton, lustful nights of deviant sexual revelry in the company of devils. They confess it all. Yes, they are the perpetrators of the deathly scourge that has plagued the south west coast of late. They confess to abducting, murdering and devouring countless lost travellers. Men, women and children, all taken and eaten indiscriminately. Hundreds, maybe thousands, all assailed on the road atop the cliffs at Bennane and dragged into the labyrinth of caves below to be butchered and consumed.

They confess it all, just to make the strange, hard men with the dead eyes stop.

One among the torn and brutalised remains of the village population refuses to confess, however, regardless of what they do to him. They burn, cut, gouge, twist and stretch him, yet still he does not confess.

He *will* not confess, because Alexander Beane is consumed with hate. An uncommonly strong hate that few ever truly experience. A hatred so all-consuming that the brands, blades, ropes and spikes are to no avail. The kind of hateful wrath strong, bright and violent enough to attract a certain kind of attention.

To some, hate is sustenance, and wrath is currency.

And so for three full turns of the moon, in the depths of Edinburgh castle's dungeons, the systematic torture and rape of the small folk of Bennane continues unabated, and their leader's white hot hatred grows stronger and more potent still with the passing of each agonising day.

By the time the guards march them to the courtyard for the public trial, fewer than half of the original population remain among the living.

The trial itself is a mere formality. Beane and the others are kept in squat cages in full public view, pelted by the baying crowd with rotting vegetables and effluent while the court, presided over by Sheriff Densmore, passes its judgement. Through their own confession, they are found guilty of practicing witchcraft and of the abduction, murder and cannibalisation of the unknown scores of innocents who have gone missing from the south west coastal area that year.

They are sentenced to death, by way of purification by fire.

As the verdict is read out, Beane, caged along with the pitiful remains of his village, holds his daughter close. The child has not spoken a word since the first night Anderson took her, and her eyes, once so full of light and life are empty, vapid pale blue pools of disconnected despair. Heartbroken for his child, Beane tries to take solace in the fact that their suffering will soon be over, and death will release them of their torment.

Yet through his sorrow and yearning for an end, the hate within him burns stronger and hotter than ever, and a terrible thirst for retribution outweighs his despair.

As the pyres are prepared, an unseen entity slinks among the jeering crowd. A presence that takes delight and nourishment from all the hate, fear and prejudice so prevalent in the air this day. The negative energy that pours from the yelling mob, and from Alexander Beane in particular, is like a beacon to this thing, which is known by some humans knowledgeable in the ways of daemons as Ozay. A creature of chaos, an agent of the Great Black, it thrives on Beane's hate and senses opportunity.

The sentence passed, the doomed villagers of Bennane Head are dragged, wailing in terror, from their cages. They know the fiery death that awaits them, and some cling in desperation to the bars of their iron pens. Captain Hugh Cairns orders that their grasping hands be struck from their arms in order to hasten proceedings, and they are dragged to the pyres, hacked ragged stumps bleeding on the ground.

When they come for Alexander Beane and his daughter, four guards are required to wrest the mute, limp child from her screaming father's arms. He struggles valiantly, in an enraged frenzy of hate, and only a fierce blow from a sword pommel to the back of his head which knocks him senseless is enough to end his brief but futile struggle.

And as the blackness takes him, the creature Ozay moves in, and begins whispering.

Do you hate, son of man? Does your soul not burn with hatred?

The voice, purring and seductive, comes slithering into Alexander's subconscious like a black snake. All around him is darkness. He cannot see, hear, smell, touch nor taste, yet this voice he can sense in his mind, and he finds he can answer.

Who are you?

A friend, Alexander. These men, these hateful, cowardly men have killed, tortured and debased you and your people. Your wife, raped and left to die in shit, deep in the caves, with your unborn son already dead in her belly, snuffed out of existence, insignificant as a candle flame in a tempest. Your daughter. How Anderson violated her sweet innocence! These men have taken it all from you, and yet they name you *murderers, eaters of men and heretics. In the name of their god, they judge you, and now your people will burn for your crimes.*

I am innocent. My wife, my children, my village are all innocent.

You need not tell me this, Alexander Beane. I know you are a good man. The guilty are those that accuse you. This is known to me. The good Sheriff and Earl of Ayrshire Labhrainne Densmore and his acolytes are the ones who have wrought so much blood from the land this past year. They sacrifice in the name of a myth they call Satan, who is no more real than the God they falsely profess to worship. Densmore knows you are innocent. He knows you have done nothing, yet still you and yours are riven and burned at his command. 'Tis not right.

But why? Why did Densmore come to our *village? Why*

would he choose us? We have harmed no one.

You were betrayed, good Alexander. Look to the people of Ballantrae for your accusers, my friend. With jealousy and suspicion, it was they who sent the good Sheriff to your hearth.

I will kill them all. I swear it. Every single one who had a hand in this. From the grave if need be, I will take my due, paid in their blood.

No. You will burn and you will die, my friend. Nothing can change this. But there is a way. Tell me, good Alexander, what would you give for vengeance? What would you give to see those who have wronged you suffer as you have suffered?

Anything. Everything.

Speak true now, son of man. I seek no earthly possession that you, nor even a king, could offer. My price is that which is eternal and everlasting. Do you know of what I speak?

My soul? You wish my soul? So be it. Take it. It is yours. I have no more need of it.

And your daughter's. And those of what remains of your people. You are a good man, Alexander, but you are tainted by hate, and your soul alone will not pay for your vengeance. As her father, it is your right to offer your daughter up to me. As the first among your people, their souls are likewise under your protection. The spirits of you and your people will soon be wasted and lost to the void, but give them over to me and three of those who have wronged you will suffer and die for every one of your people that have perished. Your village numbered forty and eight. I swear to you that one hundred forty and four of those who that have done this to you will pay, and pay so dearly as to make your own torment seem a pleasure. This is the way of things, Alexander. What is reaped is always sown threefold.

You think me a fool, daemon? I know whence you come, and I will not condemn my daughter nor my people, to Hell. I care not what you offer in return. Take my soul, do as you will with it, but my little Marie's suffering ends this day, and she will have peace.

You speak of what men call Hell, Alexander? Hell is a fancy and nothing more. It is a fiction invented by the very caste of men who now burn you and your daughter alive. And why? It is no more than a tool used to control you with fear. There is no hell, good Alexander, other than that which men create for themselves. Nor is there any such fallacy as heaven, that fool's paradise to which they promise your soul will fly should you bend the knee to these hypocrites. Your soul, and your daughter's, are nothing more than wisps of energy that scatter to eternity when your flesh expires. But to me and my kind, your soul, your light, is useful and need not be wasted. Fear not the fires that the liars call Hell, my friend, for you are already there. Hell is what is happening to you and your villagers as we speak. Even now, as your body sleeps, the pyres are lit, with you upon one. Your daughter is bound atop another. Parlay with me and your suffering will end, and those who have done this to you will pay dearly. Name me four men, and their suffering will be legendary, and the people of Ballantrae will likewise feel the wrath of your vengeance, for they are the ones who brought this hell upon you. Decide quickly, son of man. As we dicker here, little Marie's golden hair is aflame, and the fires lick at your flesh. I may be what you call daemon, Alexander Beane, but I do not lie.

At that instant, Alexander Beane regains consciousness. The black silence is violently torn away and he finds himself engulfed in flame, bound to a stake atop a woodpile. The pain is monumental, colossal and all-consuming. His flesh blisters, bursts and runs like tallow from his bones. Around him are other pyres which hold the last of his people, and his daughter. They are all as torches, screaming hideously.

He agrees to the terms.

The searing agony of the fire is gone in an instant, as if it never was, although his body burns still and he yet clings to life. The voice of Ozay returns to him.

We have an accord, Alexander Beane. While you still can, give voice and name me your four.

Alexander Beane looks out from his pyre across the people gathered to watch him and his people roast. Before his eyes explode in their sockets from the terrible heat, he seeks out and in turn roars the names of his four chosen.

Griffiths.

Anderson.

Cairns.

Densmore.

The voice speaks again.

It is done. When next the sun rises, you shall have your vengeance. Griffiths, Anderson, Densmore and Cairns name you man-eater, and so man-eaters they shall be, for what is sown in sin is always reaped. While they lie asleep this night, I will give them hunger such as they have never known, my friend, and they will visit slaughter on the folk of Ballantrae until three lay dead for every one of your people.

His body cloaked in flame and reeking greasy smoke, Alexander Beane laughs until he can laugh no more.

Ironically, the only one who did not confess to the Questioners was the one who, at the end, *was* guilty of consorting with daemons.

*

When the burning is over, and Alexander Beane and the remains of his village are reduced to ashes, the crowd is dispersed. Justice has been done.

Lord of the Questioners, Lachlan Griffiths, receives word to attend the king immediately, and makes his way to the throne room, oblivious of the unseen entity which now follows his every step.

Upon his arrival, King James dismisses all present in the room, servants and nobles alike. When only His Highness and Griffiths remain, James begins to speak.

The Earl and Sheriff of Ayr, his bastard son Labhrainne, has lost control, and risks much, he says. The King James edition of the Holy Bible has been in use throughout the entire realm for almost a decade, and should the truth of this matter at Bennane ever be known, the entire kingdom, the church and even Christianity itself, could be thrown into chaos.

James commands that Griffiths dispose of the troublesome youth whose appetites have put his very rule in jeopardy. Likewise, Anderson the jailer, Captain Hugh Cairns and his men, and Labhrainne's acolytes in the south are also to be silenced. All who know the truth of the matter must take the secret to their graves.

The king promises much in return for this favour. Lachlan Griffiths will take Densmore's place. The rank of Earl and Sheriff of Ayrshire, and the role of high priest of the New Southern Coven, will be his. Once the madman is dead, Griffiths is to take up his new post immediately, and remain there in his family's new seat in Ballantrae. Part of his role there will be to ensure the story of the Beane clan is kept alive. No one must ever know the truth, or the whole monarchy could crumble. The coven must also be kept quietly alive, and King James charges the Griffiths family to serve their religion always, and under his protection, to make but a single human sacrifice each year.

In the King's name.

In the Devil's name.

Later that night, Lachlan Griffiths carries out the king's command.

Labhrainne is visiting the dungeons to satisfy his

bloodlust on some poor unfortunate, and Lachlan comes to him under the pretence of joining him in the ritual sacrifice of the young girl. When James' mad bastard, naked and splattered with gore, passes the sacrificial dagger to Griffiths so he may take his turn rending the flesh of their victim, the head of the Questioners instead plunges the bone dagger into Labhrainne's throat.

In that same night, Griffiths, accompanied by his personal guards, goes to the homes of Anderson and Cairns. Both men are dragged from their hovels, presented with a signed royal decree and accused of treason before being executed on the spot with a single musket ball to the heart. Their bodies are left in the street for their screaming families to deal with. An hour later, Griffiths and an entire company of his men force their way into the barracks of Cairns' soldiers. They are also briefly shown the royal command, then quickly and efficiently executed on charges of treason.

Lachlan Griffiths rides south the following day, accompanied by his followers, and promptly summons the acolytes of the Southern Coven to the newly named Griffiths Hall. On arrival, each one is put to the sword and then burned. As the last of Densmore's Satanists dies, so does the truth. The only ones left alive who know that the people of Bennane were innocent are the king and his new Earl of Ayrshire, the high priest of the New Southern Coven, Lachlan Griffiths.

And so it is that the deal made between the creature Ozay and Alexander Beane is broken for the first time, but bound by the infernal pact, the essence of the unpaid debt lingers on like a slow cancer in the only one of the four named men who yet lives, and the hex festers like an infected wound through the ages, unfulfilled for centuries through a simple twist of fate.

For ever after, the Earl of Ayrshire is a marked man, each generation haunted by the daemon Ozay, who is bound to the family by Alexander Beane's unpaid due. Many of the earls through the centuries die in strange, unnatural ways. Heart attacks are rife in the Griffiths blood, it seems, as is madness. The family believe that the manifestation of the spirit that plagues them is a dark blessing, proof of their connection and servitude to their king and to their lord Satan, and so they bear this terrible burden, in their twisted reasoning seeing it as the price they must pay for their privileged position both on Earth and in the beyond.

The house of Griffiths continues to carry out its task as charged by King James, and each year, a single innocent quietly falls under the exquisitely carved bone dagger, murdered in the Devil's name. That they are never brought to justice for the annual killings is seen as further evidence of the esteem in which they are surely held by their dark master.

The family likewise continues in its other sworn duty; to maintain the legend of the terrible clan of cannibals who once dwelt beneath Bennane Head, snatching unwary travellers from the road above and feasting on their flesh. For centuries the myth is repeated, embellished and twisted until it passes into the very realms of folklore and becomes a story to scare children with, part of the country's subculture.

And so it goes through the passing of uncounted summers until almost four hundred years after it all began, when everything changes.

*

Desdemona Griffiths, son and heir of Alexander Griffiths, Earl of Ayrshire, has been haunted all his life by the malignant presence he calls the Bogey Rogey. Keeping with the age-old family tradition, his father has drilled into him since childhood their sworn duty; to continue to make sacrifice annually in the Devil's name, and to keep the legend of Sawney Beane alive.

At the age of nine Desdemona makes his first kill, when

under the supervision of his father he opens the throat of a girl his own age while kneeling in a shallow grave deep in the dark heart of the forest outside Ballantrae. For the next nine years, he assists his father in the yearly sacrifice, personally performing the blood letting ritual himself every second year.

Although he develops a taste for the kill and keeps up the pretence of being a loyal follower of his father's twisted religion and the family tradition, Desdemona secretly cares nothing for either, and seeks only an end to his torment, for as he has grown, the manifestations have become worse and more frequent, but such frequency does nothing to dilute the terror that seizes him when the Bogey Rogey comes calling. Instead, the shadowy nightmare that plagues him night and day becomes *more* terrifying, more *real*. He fears that his mind is starting to unravel, and is afraid that he will go the way of his grandfather, who was committed to an asylum before he saw fifty years, raving and insane.

His father's blind reasoning that the haunting is some sort of unholy blessing and a due they must pay is lunacy, and Desdemona decides that he must take control of his fate and finally bring the madness to an end.

He reads anything and everything he can find relating to demonology. The library in Griffiths Hall has a vast collection of literature dealing with this subject, amassed by his ancestors over hundreds of years. Most of what he reads is superstitious hokum, full of half-baked Christian and Satanic theories and dogma, but one book, which bears no title and cites no author, is different. Two hundred years old and written in German, in which he is fluent, it deals with the subject from a non-religious perspective. It instead describes daemons as highly intelligent trans-dimensional entities with their own complex hierarchy and sets of rules, as malevolent and conscious beings that exist only to feed on negative energy and to trade in the life force that men know as souls.

He reads the fascinating book over and over, until he is

able to quote it from memory. Despite his new knowledge, the visitations continue and lose none of their power to terrify him. He knows that he must end it soon, or he will surely lose his mind.

In the year of our lord nineteen eighty two, his father is brought in for police questioning regarding the murder of the seventeen year old girl whose remains have been found in the woods. A girl that Desdemona had in fact killed. It had been his turn that year. Her name had been Lisa, he recalls.

Money changes hands, pressure is applied where it needs to be applied, a few threats and promises are made and before long, some worthless drunk known to bear a grudge against Alexander Griffiths is arrested for the crime, freeing Desdemona's father from suspicion. It had been close however, Desdemona frets. The family have been carrying out the annual killing for centuries, and never once had suspicion fallen upon them. He knows the family can no longer continue on this bloody path, heedless of the prospect of incarceration. Sooner or later, their luck would run out, and he is aware they are being watched closely by a certain policeman going by the name of Grace.

For the past couple of years, Desdemona has been forming an idea in his mind, and believes he may finally be able to bring his torment, which has by now reached near unbearable levels, to an end. He will not be able to carry out his plan, however, should he find himself in a jail cell.

On the eve of his eighteenth birthday, the Earldom of Ayrshire and all its obligations pass to Desdemona Griffiths, and his father presents him with the sacrificial dagger that has spilled the lifeblood of scores of victims through the ages. Desdemona swears a blood oath to continue the family traditions, the lie falling easily from his lips. His father, in a rare show of affection embraces him tightly and tells him he is proud of him.

He retires to his bedroom and waits, scared almost witless about what he must do.

In the lonely witching hours after midnight, it begins with a familiar scratching in the wall behind the bed where Desdemona sleeps.

He feels the drop in temperature that always heralds the arrival of the entity. And the smell, that noxious, rotten aroma as of something dead left in the sun for too long. Absolute terror grips him. Although he has prepared himself as well as he can for this moment, he is helpless in the face of the horror that these manifestations conjure in his breast.

He watches the wall above his bed bulge and distort, much in the same way that Phillip Densmore would witness in a strange dream many years later. The bedroom wall takes on the elasticity of soft rubber, and long bony fingers, hooked at the tips, push through and reach for him, stretching the plaster impossibly. The nausea-inducing smell grows stronger, cloying in Desdemona's terror-tightened throat. The frigid air plummets further in temperature, and he can see his rapid, fearful breath crystallise before his eyes.

Control, he tells himself through his fear. *You must have control.*

'I … I wish to make a deal,' he stammers.

The daemon laughs. A liquid cackling sound that has no place on Earth.

'Please,' Desdemona begs. 'I am the Lord and Earl of Ayrshire, but a mere worm before you, and I seek an accord.'

The terrible laughter intensifies. The wall over his bed bulges further. Cracks begin to appear in the plaster. It is breaking through.

Desdemona prostrates himself in supplication, face down on the floor. He is by this point a trembling, panicked wreck, but he manages to croak out a further entreaty.

'Master, I beseech you. I will do anything, whatever you command. I will give anything. I only wish an end to my torment. I know not why you haunt my family, but I seek to bargain with you. An insect in your magnificence I may be, yet I know something about the workings of your great and terrible kind. I know you trade in souls …'

There is a loud crack and crumbling sound as the plaster finally gives way. The very oxygen seems to be sucked out of the room as the entity manifests itself physically. Desdemona struggles to breathe, yet keeps his face pressed into the carpet, unable to raise his gaze to the monster he knows now stands over him.

You know nothing, human.

The voice, the sound of a wailing multitude heard from a great distance, echoes in his head. Unable to control his body, his bladder and bowels void themselves at the sound of the daemon's words. *My kind are beyond the limits of human imagination,* it says.

'Yes, yes. Forgive me, my lord,' Desdemona whimpers. 'Your glory is not for such as I to comprehend. I only wish to serve you. To give you all that I have in worship …'

The thing known as Ozay senses opportunity here, a chance to put right an unsettled debt centuries old. The boy has now taken on the mantle of his father, and as such has ancient and natural rights over the souls of others. He could prove to be profitable.

It makes a decision, and with a thought, rearranges its atoms into another form. Something that will not drive the boy instantly insane to behold.

Rise, Desdemona, it says.

Desdemona forces himself shakily to his feet, raises his eyes slowly, and finds a man standing before him. He is unremarkable. Just a normal looking male of average height and weight wearing non-descript clothing. He has plain brown hair of average length, and a thoroughly forgettable face neither handsome nor ugly. He has the appearance of someone you would barely notice, such is their ordinariness.

Until Desdemona looks closer and sees the faint shimmer outlining the body that speaks of the glammer which is the plain-looking man's form. And the eyes. Desdemona realises the eyes are dead black orbs. As the eyes gaze back at him out of that prefectly normal face, Desdemona experiences a peculiar *draining* feeling, as of something being leached from his body. He quickly drops his gaze again and the sickening emptying feeling fades.

My kind do not favour unpaid debts, Desdemona Griffiths, it says, still speaking in his mind. *If you wish to be free of my attentions, the original pact must be paid in full.*

'How can I do this, Master?' Desdemona asks in stupefied awe, still averting his eyes. 'If you will but name your bounty, it will be done.'

And so Ozay and Desdemona Griffiths make a deal.

In return for an end to his haunting, the heir to the Earl of Ayrshire swears to use his family's wealth and influence to once again bring together the four bloodlines of Cairns, Anderson, Densmore and Griffiths. Only then can the curse be carried out as was originally intended, and the debt can be finally paid. Desdemona is well aware that lifting this hex from his head will mean sacrificing his own child in the future, not to mention the death of a hundred-and-forty-four people, but he reckons it is a price worth paying.

And so it is that he devotes his life, time and money to tracking down the far scattered remnants of the four families and bringing them together again. Months are spent in libraries and public records offices, poring over archives and genealogy records, and an immodest fortune is invested in private investigators, bribes and a thousand other expenses borne of his enterprise.

He locates the descendant of Labhrainne Densmore first, a man going by the name of Kyle Densmore, a sales rep for IBM who lives in Aberdeen. Through one of his many investigators, Desdemona learns that the man is recently married to a woman named Rebecca and they have a child on the way. Within weeks, man and pregnant wife have relocated to Ballantrae after Rebecca receives out of the blue the offer of an unusually well-paid job as librarian at the local high school. Their first son James is born later that year.

The Anderson line is next to be found. Alan Anderson, a twenty-three-year-old engineer, works for a firm in Greenock, and has recently become engaged to his long-time girlfriend Maria. The Griffiths family own an engineering business in Ballantrae, and soon, Alan Anderson is the new manager. Desdemona makes a generous contribution to their wedding fund and sets them up with a nice house, one of many he owns and which he sells them for a very reasonable price.

The Cairns family seems to fall into Desdemona's lap. While on a business trip to Glasgow, his car hits a deep pothole and he finds himself in a grotty garage in want of a replacement wheel. While angrily leafing though a tattered magazine in the dingy nicotine-stained waiting room, fuming about the inconvenience, he hears one of the troglodytes who works in the stinking garage refer to another by the name 'Cairnsey'. The recognition of the name grabs Desdemona's attention, and an hour later he is buying a pint of lager in a cramped smoke-filled bar for Anthony Cairns, a weasel-faced man with a sour disposition and an obviously addictive thirst for alcohol. Desdemona asks many questions of the man, who is at first suspicious of the well-dressed businessman's interest, accusing Desdemona of being a 'fuckin' queerhawk'. A few more lagers and whiskies loosen the man's tongue, though, and Desdemona is furnished with answers to his questions about where his family is from and what he knows about his ancestors. It turns out that Cairns is not the type to be interested in family trees and 'all that pish', but Desdemona has a strange feeling about this bipedal rat of a man. He excuses himself and makes a quick phone call to a government employee who owes him a favour and who has access to more genealogical information than Cairns is able to supply. He is amazed when it is confirmed that the borderline alcoholic is the direct descendant of Captain Hugh Cairns.

Returning to the table, Desdemona buys a few more drinks, then offers Cairns a job running a garage he owns down the coast. The job offer comes with a lucrative salary well above what he is currently earning and Cairns immediately accepts, drunkenly toasting their arrangement and proclaiming that Desdemona is 'a good cunt after all'.

Cairns, who is inconveniently single, is in Ballantrae two days later, where it is soon seen to that he meets a dim-witted local girl named Karen Smart, who ironically is anything but. A few thousand pounds in her cheaply-made purse is enough to convince the simple-minded girl that she would look just *great* on the arm of the new mechanic in the village, a young man from the big city no less. She is pregnant less than a month later and their son Grant comes along later that year.

In the year of our Lord nineteen ninety-three, it all comes together, and Desdemona Griffiths' masterplan finally bears fruit.

His wife Sheena, whom he has already been married to for seven years, finally gets her act together and fulfils her only task of bearing him a brat, whom she names Dean. Desdemona doesn't give a running fuck what the kid is called.

That same year, the Cairns and Densmore families each welcome a second son to their home, and the Andersons, who Desdemona had been starting to worry about, are also blessed with the child they have been trying to conceive for so long.

And so it is that the four accursed bloodlines of Griffiths, Densmore, Cairns and Anderson are brought together again by Desdemona's insidious influence. Four male children born in the same year and living in Ballantrae, which they will then decimate when all four come of age, just as was meant to happen long centuries in the past.

It's so perfect it seems like it's meant to be.

PART V

They shall be burnt with hunger, and devoured with burning heat, and with bitter destruction: I will also send the teeth of beasts upon them, with the poison of serpents of the dust.

Deuteronomy 32:24

King James Bible

9th September 2011

My earliest childhood memory is of a family holiday to America when I was about three years old. Me, my mum, dad and James, who would only have been about eight at the time, spent three weeks in a rented log cabin in the Adirondack Mountains in upstate New York, miles from anywhere. We spent the days wandering in the deep woods, fishing and canoeing on the nearby lake and having picnics. It's the only time I can recall when our whole family had been really happy. James had begun having 'problems' when he'd turned nine, unsurprisingly. The same age Desdemona Griffiths had been when he made his first kill, I now knew. The power of three times three and all that …

When I came to after grabbing that carved bone dagger, the first thing I became aware of was the scent of the forest and the sound of birdsong.

I opened my eyes and found myself sitting on a rough bench made of cut logs, gazing across a large lake surrounded by tall pine trees. The sun was high in the azure blue sky, and there was just the faintest of breezes on the pleasantly warm and incredibly fresh air. There was a dirt path leading down to the water from the bench where I sat, a small jetty jutting into the lake's glassy mirrored surface and the wooden boathouse where the canoes were stored. I turned my head to the left, and there was the log cabin. Just as I remembered it from some fourteen years previously. The great spread of moose antlers above the door which had fascinated me as a child was still there, as was the chopping block and woodpile where my dad had enjoyed hewing great chunks of pine for the massive open fireplace inside. The only thing different from my memory of the place was an air of abandonment. The bench on which I sat was weathered and rotting in a few spots, in need of replacement. Likewise, the jetty, boathouse and the cabin itself had a dilapidated look. A few planks of wood were missing from the jetty's walkway and the paint was peeling on the boathouse walls. I knew that no one had been here in a long time.

As before, I felt no alarm at finding myself suddenly teleported to another location, this time thousands of miles across an entire ocean from my point of origin in Glasgow. Again, I felt the presence of that benign other that assured me I was safe.

I leaned forward and ran my fingers through the long grass. Real.

'We thought this would be a cool place for you to lay low for a while, dude,' a familiar voice said behind me. 'There's a lot of people looking for you back home and we figured it'd be best if you weren't around.'

'Cheers, Griff,' I replied without turning. 'Nice choice. So, is it over now?'

'Pretty much. The deal's broken three times. Game's a bogey.'

'And you boys?'

'We're good. Don't worry about us. Thanks, Phil. You did fuckin' brilliant.'

'Don't mention it,' I said.

Griff came round the back of the bench and sat down beside me. He looked just the same as he always had. When he smiled, I saw his teeth and his eyes were again completely normal. We looked over the lake in silence for a few moments, enjoying the peaceful scene.

'So your old man was a bit of a bastard, eh?' I said to him.

'No shit,' Griff replied. 'Never did get on with the guy, but I never thought he was a complete sociopath. Sorry about … well, you know … at the campsite that night, and in the nuthouse …'

'De nada, amigo,' I said, clapping him on the shoulder.

'You weren't quite yourself. Drugs are bad, m'kay?'

We laughed, and once again I wondered at how good and normal things were in this dreamland version of the waking world. Despite the horror of everything I'd gone through and everything I now knew, it felt completely natural to bounce the conversation back and forth between us, making light of horrible, horrible things.

'One thing I need to tell you though, dude,' Griff said, 'Keep an eye out. It's not just the cops that are looking for you, know what I mean? Ozay can't go near you now because his deal got fucked up three times. That's just the way it works. There's plenty more like him though, and they know about you, because you're different now. They'll come looking for you. Nothing personal, it's just what they do, you know?'

I just nodded. It made sense in a very messed up way.

'It's not all bad though, mate,' Griff said to me. 'You know what's out there now, all the bad things, but you can't spell *slaughter* without *laughter*. Always remember that. You can't have one without the other.'

'Equals and opposites. Yin and Yang. Duality, right?' I asked.

He nodded. 'You're not as dumb as you look, mate. Black and white, cowboys and Indians, salt and pepper. There's good guys and wanks, and the good guys look out for each other.'

That was good to know. It did beg a troubling question however.

'Are you sure I'm one of the good guys, Griff?' I asked, thinking about what I'd said to Tony Cairns on the phone and of how close I'd come to pulverising Grant's head with that whisky bottle.

Griff hesitated.

305

'Shades of grey. Nothing's every *totally* black and white, Phil,' he said, somewhat evasively. 'You understand what's happened to you?'

I thought I did.

When Griff used to tell us stories, he'd often say how every legend has a kernel of truth in it somewhere. I thought about what the stories say bites from vampires, zombies and werewolves did to their victims, and I thought about how I'd almost lost my arm due to the infection from the bite Griff had given me when we fought at the campsite that night. They'd told me that my heart had stopped, and that I'd been revived, brought back from the dead. It seemed clear to me now that I just hadn't come back all the way, or maybe that I'd brought something back *with* me.

I thought about being pinned through the shoulder by that disembodied talon like a bug in a display case, and about sharing my mind with the Harvester.

I guess when you have contact with the other side and manage to walk away, you carry some of it inside you, like bits of shrapnel embedded deep in your flesh.

'Aye,' I said. 'I've got an idea.'

Griff nodded. 'You'll need to try and keep a lid on that side of it, mate,' he said. 'It could go either way.'

I sat there on the bench, digesting all this.

'So what do I do now, Griff?' I asked after a moment.

'I don't know, dude. Go canoeing?' he suggested.

I laughed.

He got up from the bench and stretched, as if he had physical muscles that needed stretching. 'Time for me to make like a tree, dude,' he said. 'We'll be keeping an eye on you.'

'Cheers, Griff. Much appreciated.'

'Remember what I said though, Phil,' he said. 'Keep a lid on it. Keep it tight and together as best as you can. You're going to need to be strong, but there's some stuff in the cabin in case it gets too much, alright? I'll see you around.'

And he was gone.

I just sat there for a while after that, looking out across the lake, not really thinking about much.

After a bit, I heard something moving in the forest behind me, rustling through the bushes.

Instantly, I was on my feet. I turned and looked into the shady depths of the woods, ready for some new abomination to come rushing at me out of the underbrush.

It was just a dog. A medium-sized mongrel that came casually sauntering out of the murk, its haphazardly patterned brown and black coat matted and tangled. It came right over to me and sat on its haunches, looking up at me expectantly with bright eyes and a silly doggy grin, tongue lolling from one side of its jaws, dripping drool.

I bent down and scratched the mutt behind the ears, finding a worn brown leather collar with a metal name tag attached. I read it, and smiled.

'Hi, Sam,' I said.

*

After everything inexplicable that had happened to me in the past few months, it didn't seem so outlandish to find that the boys had sorted the place out for me, even if they *were* dead and had somehow done so from beyond the grave, like some weird crossover of *Most Haunted* and *Sixty Minute Makeover.*

The interior of the cabin was long unused and there was

dust and cobwebs aplenty, but the large walk-in pantry in the kitchen area was well stocked with tinned food, bottled water and dog food, and there was an iron wood-burning stove, fuelled and good to go. In the huge open fireplace, a big pile of thick wedges of pine and kindling had been laid, and a large iron basket by the side was full of chopped logs. I could still smell the sap, as if the fireplace had been prepared and stocked only minutes before I walked in.

In a room just off the main sitting area, there was an old double bed and mattress under a dust sheet, and a wardrobe which contained sheets, blankets, pillows and even a few changes of clothes. From this bedroom, another door led to a small en-suite bathroom featuring a working toilet and shower. They even left a towel and several bog rolls for me. There's a storage shed built onto the side of the cabin, and in there I discovered a large chest freezer and a beat-up but functioning pickup truck, the keys in the ignition. The cabin has plumbing and working lights, and yet there's no evidence of power lines connecting it to the grid and there's no generator either.

Inexplicable, but when compared to recent events, not that weird.

Back in the main room under a large dust sheet, I found the writing desk and this typewriter. The typewriter looks like an antique, a big old heavy thing made of metal, but it works perfectly, and I found that the ribbon was fresh. When I pressed a few keys, the softly distinctive *clack-clack-clack* noise had a very definite *rightness* to it, and I knew straight away I was meant to put all this down on paper. I remembered Cairnsey once talking about how he had kept a journal since he was seven years old, and how it had helped him deal with all the bad shit that was going on in his life with his dad. Writing is therapy, he used to say as we grew up. I guess he figured I could use some therapy now.

The desk itself is a plainly constructed, grungy bit of furniture, worn and battered, and has seen some years itself going by the look of it, but it's heavy and solid and looks like it could last for another thousand. Opening the several drawers, the interiors of which I noticed had been lined with metal to make them fireproof, I found several reams of blank paper, spare typewriter ribbons, an old half-used candle and a large box of kitchen matches.

Griff had said there was also some stuff in the cabin in case it got too much, and I found these items in the bottom drawer to the right of the desk's leg space. Several bottles of Diazepam, and a loaded .45 calibre handgun. These items gave me a chill, but like the typewriter and desk, they had a certain rightness to them. A belonging.

After I'd finished checking out my new home, I simply stood for a moment in the centre of the main room, watching as Sam wandered around the cabin sniffing, exploring everything with his nose. After a second, I lit a fire and then sat down at the desk, took out a ream of paper from one of the drawers, loaded up the typewriter and just started hammering away at the keys.

*

Well, that's it. It was a week ago I found myself here and started this account, and now that I've finished and we're up to date, I'm not really sure what to do with myself.

I know there's more to come. Griff's warnings and the fact that there's a loaded gun and enough jellies to drop a herd of rhinos in one of the desk drawers makes that clear.

I guess I'm not done writing yet.

5th October 2011

Decided to go into town today to see if I could find a few books to read and stock up on some supplies. I won't be going back.

When I found myself here in mountains, I still had the backpack with the ten grand Sergeant Grace gave me, and on the way into town I thought the fact that it's in sterling and not dollars would be a problem. Amesville's a small place, maybe a little bigger than Ballantrae, but I found a post office which kept a stock of a few foreign currencies and the old guy behind the counter changed some notes over for me. I tried to strike up a conversation as I hadn't spoken to anyone but Sam in weeks, and I thought he'd be intrigued about my accent and maybe ask about where I was from, but he just took the two hundred pounds I gave him, did a quick calculation and handed me back a wad of dollars without so much as saying a word.

He looked scared, as if he thought I was going to violently rob the place.

It was the same at the general store. The girl at the checkout actually gasped and backed away a few steps when I walked up to her till pushing my trolley. As she passed my items through the barcode reader she kept her eyes downcast, as if afraid to look at me. By the time she'd added up my purchases and mumbled the total, she was almost hyperventilating and I got the feeling she was a second away from abandoning her station and bolting from the store in terror.

Walking back to the truck, people on the street gave me wide berths or crossed the street altogether to keep a safe distance from me, as if I were wearing a painted sign round my neck declaring me to be a plague carrier. In a car that was stopped at a traffic light, there was a young woman behind the wheel and a toddler in the baby seat in the back. As I passed, the kid took one look at me through the window and started screaming hysterically. The woman saw me, visibly flinched, and put her foot down. She ran the red light in her haste to put distance between me and her child, and her car came very close to colliding with a lumber truck that was passing through the intersection.

I found myself getting angry at the townspeople's unprovoked reaction to me, and realised I was grinding my teeth and muttering curses under my breath. A strong urge to lash out at someone was building up inside me, and I had to stop there in the middle of the sidewalk, my arms loaded with grocery sacks, and take a series of deep breaths to get myself under control.

It's like Grant told me. I've got death all over me, and people can see it.

10th October 2011

Took a pill for the first time today.

Since my visit to town, I'd felt my nerves getting more frayed day by day, but I'd been resisting reaching for the desk drawer for a Diazepam. Had to do it today though.

At first I was just waking up in a bad mood. Thought maybe it was just plain boredom and frustration brought on by sitting about with nothing to do, but today I caught myself pacing back and forth in the cabin, grinding the shit out my teeth and seriously pissed off for no reason, then I started kicking at the walls.

The Valium helped calm me down a little, but I don't want to get dependant on them. There's been enough jelly heads in my family.

19th October 2011

I'm getting worse.

Pacing and kicking at the walls again today, also throwing punches at nothing and cursing out loud, almost shouting. My blood feels like it's heating up somehow, although the air temperature's started to drop as winter approaches.

Decided to go outside and chop some wood, thinking I could burn off some of the causeless rage. I grabbed the axe from the storage shed and went out to the woodpile in the yard and just started swinging. It helped a little, and I've now got more cut wedges of pine than I can fit in the iron holder by the fireplace, but I still had to reach for the desk drawer again.

Up to three pills a day now.

23rd Octopber 2011

Seven pills today. Hardly make a dent

Took a kitchen knife to the cabin wall earlier. Kicking it just wasnt doing it anymore.

Stabbing fuck out of itt felt great.

I wished it was more than wood I was stabbing.

Been thinking about the gun. Is it for me? Isit for others?

Sam wont come near me

?

The pills are almost gone now. Lost count of hoq many I've had today but it doesnt matter. barely working anymore. The anger just wont quit. Dontknow what the day or the date is. Starting to lose track of time. Losing track of ME.

Found myself sittting behind the wheel of the truck earlier. the GUN and the AXE weer on the seat next to me.

Didnt know how I got there.

Sams gone.

?

Finished the pillz.

Came too sat in the truckk with the GUN and the AXE agaim. Drivven a few miles doen the road thiss time asif hedding to town.

I need too ddo something before I KILLSOMECUNT. SOFUCKINGHUNGRRRYLOSINGITHELPMEPLEASEI REALLYREALLYWANTKILL SOMECUNTCUNTCUNT C U N T T T T T T T T T T T T T T T T T T J K K D F K I U G H I D U S F G H K I S D T R J G H S E R K U G H K S DTGHUHKGHUKGT HJIO;TRHJO;RHIOJ

Winter 2011

I'm feeling a lot better.

I don't remember leaving the cabin. It was like I abruptly woke up from a broken nightmarish sleep and there I was, flying through the woods with that supernatural speed, dodging between trees, leaping over small semi-frozen rivers, hurdling deadfalls and crashing through snow drifts and bushes, swifter and more agile than any forest animal, and snarling deep in my throat. Oh yeah, and I was naked.

When I saw the deer, I instantly knew what I needed. It ran from me of course, but I was faster. Much faster.

I'd torn it up pretty badly by the time the black rage that'd been consuming me finally abated. I found myself sitting in the bloodstained snow with its red steaming carcass strewn all around me. I'd eaten a fair portion of the big antlered buck, and I could still taste its hot gamey blood and raw flesh in my mouth. It was very *very* good.

For the first time in what must be weeks however, I was clear-minded and calm. The obsessive urge to maim and kill something, anything, everything, was gone.

I was pretty disturbed about what I'd done, but when I thought about what the alternative had almost been, bolting through the snowy forest in the buff, chasing down a deer on foot and ripping it to pieces with my bare hands and teeth was, by comparison, perfectly acceptable behaviour in the grand scheme of things.

It occurred to me that even so, I probably should've been more freaked out about what I'd just done, but I just didn't feel it. Part of the new me I guess.

It was close, but I think I'll be okay for a while now. Sam's back and he's not afraid to be around me anymore, and that's good. Keepin' a lid on it, boys.

Winter 2011

I took Sam out for his walk this morning and there was a very deep, unnatural silence in the woods. I'd noticed that the forest had been getting steadily quieter over the past few weeks, but I put it down to the onset of deep winter. Now though, the only sounds to be heard are the wind blowing through the pines, the creak of slowly swaying trees, the soft crack of contracting bark and the occasional soft *flump* of collected snow falling from boughs.

Of animal sounds though, there's not so much as a single twitter of birdsong.

I've found myself going into the forest a little less regularly these days. I don't know if it's the fact that winter continues to tighten its grasp on the mountains and it's fucking freezing, but walking in the woods isn't as enjoyable as it was when I first found myself here. The chill in the air seems to be somehow more than just the onset of winter, and the shadows between the trees seem … threatening. Sam doesn't like the forest much now, either. He keeps close to my side, whereas before he'd always bolt happily away and disappear in the underbrush to chase rabbits. He's also started staying close to the cabin when I let him out to do his business, and seems reluctant to stray too far.

Don't know the date or even the month for sure. I'd previously been keeping a note of the date using the calendar on Cairnsey's phone, but the batteries are long dead. It's been weeks since I killed the deer, and I've not had any more reoccurrences of the black fits of rage, which is just as well. There are no deer in the woods anymore. The unnatural silence tells me there's nothing alive in the woods now but me and Sam.

I think something is on its way.

Winter 2011 (2 days later)

I was right.

I let Sam out for the toilet about an hour ago before going to bed, and was standing at the cabin door, keeping an eye on him. He's been increasingly reluctant to leave the cabin the past few days, and refuses to go outside altogether unless I'm standing guard.

He quickly went over to his spot by the wood pile and cocked a leg, but stopped suddenly in mid-piss to whirl around and face the opposite direction. He was looking into the shadows between the trees that encroach on the left side of the cabin, and growling low down in his throat. It's clear tonight, and the moon's huge and bright and fat, giving a good amount of light as it reflects off the snow, so from where I stood I could clearly see the raised hackles all along Sam's back. I called him back inside, but he wouldn't come. He just stood there, snarling at the deep shadows that the moon's light couldn't penetrate.

He abruptly let loose a rapid series of loud aggressive barks and took a few steps forward, baring his teeth. I left the cabin threshold then and went to him, meaning to take him back inside, and starting to get a very bad feeling, but as I reached for his collar he bolted off into the murk between the trees.

Without thinking, I gave chase, blindly running into the forest after him. I could hear him barking ferociously somewhere ahead, and ran towards the sound, frantically calling his name as I ploughed through the knee deep snow, stumbling through the thick undergrowth and tripping over hidden roots.

Sam's barks suddenly changed to a frightening series of savage yowling snarls, and I knew he'd come into violent contact with whatever had been spooking him. I kept going, crashing faster through the snow-shrouded bushes towards the sounds of the struggle emanating from somewhere in the dark forest ahead. I heard Sam let out a loud yelp of pain, and then silence slammed down as if a door had been closed.

I froze in mid step. The way Sam's cry had been cut off awoke a familiar fear in me, and I was suddenly back on that hill in Ballantrae, hearing from the block of flats that first woman's scream that had been so abruptly silenced. Shivering, lost and afraid, I could only stand there, surrounded by the night forest, knee-deep in snow with my breath coming in laboured gasps that froze in the air before my face. I called out for Sam. My quavering voice was muted by the cold white blanket of snow, and came out with a flat, dead quality. Not much moonlight penetrated the thick grove of pines where I was standing, and my field of visibility was a matter of inches.

Something hit me from the side.

I fell back in the snow with a yelp of fright. I couldn't see anything, but my mind conjured some very bad ideas about the unseen monstrosity that had attacked me. I desperately tried to scramble to my feet and flee, but I felt it grab my ankle. I screamed and fell forward in the snow, then instinctively kicked out behind me with my other foot and heard an unmistakeably canine whine of pain. I turned over onto my back and was extremely relieved to discover it was just Sam.

I reached out and took hold of him. He flinched and yelped at my touch, but I soothed him with soft words and gentle strokes. He licked my face, whining in anxiety.

I stood and turned in a circle, trying to get my bearings. Logic dictated that to get back to the cabin, I need only follow my footprints back through the snow, but as I started in that direction, Sam grabbed the cuff of my jeans and pulled me back. His intent was clear.

Not that way.

I crouched in front of him again, stroking his head. 'Okay, boy,' I said. 'Show me. Take us home.'

And he did, taking a roundabout route through the trees that eventually led us back to the cabin. During that return trip, I had a palpable sense that we were being watched, and several times Sam stopped, sniffed the air and changed direction, leading us away from some unseen threat that I thought I could sometimes hear whispering and scuttling among the trees. It could have been the wind, but I don't think so.

When we got back inside the cabin I closed and bolted the door, then stooped to examine Sam. He had a series of thin bloody scratches along one side of his face and a few tufts of hair missing from his coat. His physical injuries aren't serious, but we got back over an hour ago, and he's still shaking.

They've found me.

Winter 2011 (the next day)

Didn't sleep after last evening's incident. Just lay awake all night, jumping at every creak and groan from inside the cabin and out. With sleep evading me, I tried to think of what to do, and it came down to the basic option of fight or flight. I came to the conclusion that it's a miracle I'm still alive after everything that's happened, and thought it best not to push my luck. I decided that in the morning I'd load up the truck, take Sam and leave. I'd no real destination in mind, but figured anywhere was better than here.

As soon as the sun was up, I went out to the truck to start loading it up and found all four tyres had been slashed repeatedly at some time during the night. Clawed.

I'm going nowhere.

(later)

Sam's seemed increasingly nervous all day, pacing around the cabin as if on patrol. I got up to see if he wanted to go out earlier, but he immediately placed himself between me and the door, growling at me in warning. Point taken. I didn't want to open the door anyway. The sun's gone down now, and the dark's like a solid presence pressing at the windows, as if it wants to get in.

I took the playing card out a few minutes ago, the King of Spades, hoping to sense some sort of power like before, but there was nothing. It's just a card now, so I took the handgun from the desk drawer.

The .45's not for whatever's outside in the woods. I know it wouldn't do any good. The gun's for me. What you might call my exit strategy.

If it turns out that I can't fight whatever is out there, and it doesn't look like I can, then I'll be glad to have the gun at hand. When the time comes for this to end, it'll be *me* that ends it. It may be a petty victory, but fuck it. Pettiness I can die with. They won't have me.

I ask myself if I really have the balls to do it, and then I think of the things I've seen. What their kind leave behind after a kill. And then I know.

Pressing the barrel of the gun to the roof of my mouth and pulling that trigger, applying the necessary four pounds pull weight required to fire a .45 calibre handgun, well, nothing could be easier. Nothing at all.

It'll be over then.

The gun's fully loaded, but I only need two bullets. They won't have Sam either.

Fuck.

Something just ran across the roof outside. Sam's started growling and there's that sick feeling of pressure in my head.

It won't be long now.

They're coming.

(later)

There's something laughing out there in the woods. Sounds like more than one. More things running across the roof, tapping and scratching on the walls outside, looking for a way in.

Every once in a while, like now, I'll hear a high scraping squeal on a window pane that cuts through the chorus of mad cackles and the knocks and gnawing at the walls, and if I look round quickly, I'm sure that for a split second, I can see something out there grinning in at me.

Sam's now running back and forth between the windows in a frenzy, snarling and barking at the darkness outside.

They're playing with me. Drawing it out. They feed on fear, and I must be providing a feast, because I'm fucking shitting myself.

Sam, Griff, Cairnsey, I could really use your help. Please.

Jesus. The lights have started to flicker.

(later)

This will be my last entry.

They're inside the cabin.

When the lights started to fail, I managed to claw open the desk drawer and grabbed the old half-used dinner candle I knew was in there. Before I could light it, though, the lights went out completely, and I heard the window by the door breaking. Cold air rushed in and I sensed something coming at me out of the total blackness as I tried to touch a kitchen match to the candle wick. Sam had been sitting at my feet, mewling in distress, but at the moment the lights went out and the window smashed, he charged fearlessly into the dark, barking and snarling, going for the thing that was rushing us.

I heard Sam growling and snapping, a hideous screech, then a screaming yelp of canine agony that was almost human, then nothing.

He gave me just enough time to light the candle. In the dim pool of meagre illumination it cast on the floor, I saw a slowly spreading pool of blood expanding across the floorboards, black in the candlelight, and I wept for poor, brave Sam.

He saved my life, because I think it's only the flickering light from the candle that's keeping them back.

They're all over the cabin. I can hear them right now as I type this, on the floor, the walls, on the ceiling and among the rafters above me. They're sliding and slithering, whispering and chittering in the blackness beyond the small pool of light from the candle, and there's not much of the candle left. Maybe three inches. My watch tells me it's half past midnight. It'll be hours before the sun rises again, and the candle won't last till then. When it's gone, they'll rush me.

My only option is to try and make it across the room to the fireplace. There's plenty of kindling and logs stacked up there. If I can get a fire going, maybe the light from the flames will hold them back till dawn. I'm afraid to even touch the candle in case it goes out though. The wind's blowing through the broken window, and I'm afraid the slightest draft will extinguish the already weak flame.

If it doesn't work, I've still got the gun.

They won't fucking have me.

EPILOGUE

Article from the *New York Times*

December 19th 2011

MYSTERY SURROUNDS UPSTATE FOREST FIRE

Authorities have been left baffled by the circumstances surrounding a large forest fire that raged through an extensive area of the Adirondack State Park last week.

The blaze, which investigators believe began at an abandoned cabin on the shore of Lake Simona, devastated an area of some five square miles before co-ordinated teams of park rangers and fire crews were able to contain it. Strangely, no identifiable remains, animal or human, have been recovered from the ashes by search and rescue teams.

Kevin Dougliehill, a volunteer fire fighter and resident of nearby Amesville said,

'It's very strange. Normally fires like this will kill large amounts of the local wildlife, but we've not uncovered so much as a single bone. It's as if there were no animals here in the first place, and that's just not possible. It's obviously great that we've found no human remains either, but the whole thing is just plain weird.'

When asked how the fire could have started, Fire Chief Connor McKnight stated, 'Most likely arson, but there were some reports received of an unusual localised lightning storm in the vicinity of Lake Simona around the estimated time the blaze began. This was witnessed by a party of climbers on Debar Mountain five miles away, who had a good view down the valley from their position. It's common for forest fires to be sparked in this way.'

When asked in what way the lightning storm was said to be unusual, Chief McKnight replied that aside from the rarity of such storms this late in the year, the group of climbers claimed that the lightning appeared to come from the ground rather than the sky, and manifested itself in a series of small but intense bursts of bluish light. It is thought among investigators that the phenomenon known as 'ball lightning' is a possible explanation for this.

In a further strange twist, unconfirmed reports have also surfaced that among the ashes of the cabin where the inferno is thought to have originated, a bizarre manuscript was found in a steel fireproof drawer which survived the blaze. It has also been rumoured that several pages of the supposed manuscript are recently dated, suggesting the possibility that someone *was* inhabiting the cabin which was originally thought to be abandoned. When asked to elaborate on this aspect of the story, Fire Chief McKnight refused to comment, saying only, 'If that were the case, we'd also have found some trace of whoever wrote it. As you already know, we've found nothing.'

Davina Andrews

Some other books from Ringwood Publishing

All titles are available from the Ringwood website and
from usual outlets.
Also available in Kindle, Kobo and Nook.
www.ringwoodpublishing.com

Ringwood Publishing, 24 Duncan Avenue, Glasgow
G14 9HN

mail@ringwoodpublishing.com

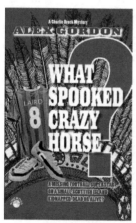

What Spooked Crazy Horse?

Alex Gordon

Derek 'Crazy Horse' Laird is hot property:
one of the highest-paid footballers on the
planet, with a right foot coveted by Europe's
greatest clubs and what the pundits call 'a
good head on his shoulders'. So everyone is
flummoxed when Crazy Horse skips training,
flees his adoptive country and heads back
to his homeland, incognito.

Caught up in the tale is sports-journalist-
turned-detective Charlie Brock. Before long,
and unawares, both men are ensconsed among the boozy, windswept
eccentrics who inhabit the Isle of Cumbrae. It is late November, the Firth
of Clyde is growing peevish and a small army of international police and
ill-intentioned hacks are about to descend on the island, scenting scandal.

The locals, however, remain oblivious. All Wee Effie, Vodka Joe and
Dr Hickory Dickory have on their minds is sex, booze and ferry tolls. A
hilarious, affectionate and rollicking mystery about two worlds colliding,
What Spooked Crazy Horse? is the sequel to *Who Shot Wild Bill?*

ISBN: 978-1-901514-34-6   £9.99

A Man's Game
Alan Ness

On a Saturday afternoon in central Scotland, both Davie Thomson and Stuart Robertson have scored goals for their respective football clubs: Cowden United FC and Glasgow Athletic. Once team-mates in the Athletic title-winning side of 1997, their subsequent fortunes could not have been more different. Whilst Robertson had gone from strength to strength, winning titles and the love of the Scottish public, Thomson had slipped out of the team and down the leagues, with alcohol and a weight problem contributing to his fall. Whilst scanning the results, James Donnelly, reporter for the Daily Standard connected the two and remembered the tragic events which would forever link them and their team-mates from that ill-fated side.

ISBN: 978-1-901514-27-8   £9.99

Between Two Bridges
Brian McHugh

New York, 1933. Prohibition is coming to an end, but not everyone is celebrating. A few astute businessmen realise that by legally importing liquor before the Volstead Act is repealed, they can net themselves a small fortune. Charlie McKenna, an Irishman who spent time in Glasgow during the Great War, is sent to complete the deal with Denholm Distillers.

Glasgow, Present Day. Still reeling from the murder of their pal, three friends are knocked off-course by the resurfacing of a battered diary. It soon leads them back into their investigation of Julie's grandfather, Charlie McKenna. More troubling tales of war, gold and gangsters begin to surface. The sequel to Brian McHugh's *Torn Edges*, *Between Two Bridges* is a fast-paced adventure with a well-researched historical setting.

ISBN: 978-1-901514-35-3   £9.99

The Activist

Alec Connon

When Thomas Durand embarks on a cycling trip around Britain with two fellow students, his life changes forever. A chance encounter inspires Thomas to leave home and drop out of university. As he roams, his eyes are opened to the harm inflicted by humans on the natural world. Driven by an increasingly passionate interest in marine conservation, what begins as a typical gap-year turns into a decade's worth of activism on the open ocean. Here the stakes are highest of all: Thomas enlists with Sea Shepherd, a controversial organisation dedicated to the protection of marine life. It is a commitment that will soon place his life in danger.

The story follows Thomas, from his first tentative steps into the life of an activist in Vancouver, to his battles with a Japanese whaling fleet in the Southern Ocean. An ecological thriller, *The Activist* will shock and inspire anyone with an interest in marine life, conservation and the splendour of the natural world. Without preaching, it is also a clear-eyed demonstration of why this cause is worth fighting for.

"Alec Connon's extraordinary adventures into the world of the whale epitomise the vast disconnect between the human and natural world. In this heartfelt novel, he explores the outer edges of the world which we have dominated, and the price it has had to pay for that domination. In picaresque episodes which are by turns funny, tragic and deeply moving, Connon addresses, in a highly personal and evocative manner, the ways by which we might make amends for what we have done."

Phillip Hoare, Samuel Johnson Prize winner and author of *The Sea Inside*

ISBN: 978-1-901514-25-4   £9.99